COME, MY BELOVED

By Pearl S. Buck

"Come, my beloved, let us go forth into
the field; let us lodge in the villages."
—*The Song of Solomon*

Come, My Beloved

by *Pearl S. Buck*

THE JOHN DAY COMPANY
NEW YORK

Part I

I

THE desk at the Grand Hotel in Bombay was crowded with incoming guests. A ship had arrived in harbor that morning and the big lobby was noisy with many tongues, the chief of which was English. It was the English, it was clear to see, who got the first attention. Even a maharajah, encircled by his entourage, was sitting in jealous impatience in one of the big reed chairs. His brilliant headdress, his glittering costume and the fluttering many-colored garments of his entourage made his group look foreign, though this was India. The English, calm and patient, were unconscious of the jealousy of anyone and they stared straight ahead as they stood in line.

Among them was an American, a tall heavily built man of middle age, dressed in a dark grey business suit and a black felt hat. He gazed about him with interested curiosity, as calm in his way as the English, but not afraid to show his enjoyment of the scene. Only America bred men so assured, so naive and so humorous. He surveyed even the Englishmen with eyes amused and tolerant, and he did not hesitate to hold his place in the line, in spite of English pressure, secret but unmistakable, to shove him aside. His broad shoulders retaliated by being immovable as slowly he approached the desk. Once he turned to speak to the tall slender young man behind him, obviously his son. They had the same bold profile, though the son had dark eyes instead of grey and smooth dark hair instead of a red-grey shock. His face was smooth, too, olive skinned, but the father had a close-cut beard and mustache, grizzled red, and his eyes were deepset under fierce eyebrows of the same hue.

3

"Hold hard, son," he said.

"I will," his son replied.

The English clerk at the desk threw them a shrewd look as the father wrote his name in the register, David Hardworth MacArd and Son.

"You're from America, sir?"

"Yes," MacArd said. "New York."

He looked thoughtfully at his name for a second and then with a strong stroke he crossed off "and Son" and turning again he said half humorously,

"I guess it is time for you to stop being 'and Son.'"

"I don't mind, Father," his son said in a mild voice.

"No, no," MacArd said, with a touch of insistence, "I remember very well your mother not liking to be merely 'and Wife.'"

His son smiled and without reply he wrote down his own name, David MacArd. His handwriting was youthful and flowing in contrast to his father's angular thick letters.

"We have your rooms reserved, sir," the clerk said. "You wanted them for a week, I believe. And we have made your train reservations for Poona. It is a fairly short journey. I am glad you have come to us in the best season. There's no mail. Are those your bags? They will follow you at once to your rooms."

"I expect no mail," MacArd said, "and they are our bags."

The pile was not formidable, his own English leather bags were worn, but he had bought David new pigskin ones. Leila's bags of alligator skin, mounted with silver, were certainly not suitable for a young man. Besides, he had ordered them put away with all the rest of her things when she died three months ago.

Only three months! He turned to his son with the faint tightening of the muscles of his face which meant that it would not do to think about her. "Shall we go upstairs now or have dinner—tiffin, I suppose I'll have to call it here."

"I'd like to change," David said. "It's hotter than I thought it would be."

The clerk, busy with another guest, overheard him.

"Keep a topcoat handy, sir," he advised. "Bombay is hot at

4

midday and very cool at night in this season. Delightful, really, once one gets used to keeping a topcoat about."

"Thank you," David said.

They turned, father and son, toward the wide marble stairs, and mounted them side by side. Their rooms were on the first floor and down a marble corridor wider than the stairs. Ahead of them the two Indian bellboys who were carrying their bags stopped at a door which stood open to reveal an inner jalousied half door that was locked. On the floor and leaning against the wall a Muslim man sat half asleep, his head on his arms folded on his knees and his fez askew. One of the bellboys kicked him gently.

"Awake, your master is here!"

The Muslim sprang to his feet, vividly awake, his emaciated body quivering with eagerness.

"Sahib sir!" he cried. "I know you, sir! I am waiting this long time. I have my cards, sir, my letters, I am waiting to serve Sahib and Son. Grand Hotel recommends me, please!"

The bellboys were already in the rooms but the Muslim had interposed himself skillfully so that the two Americans could not enter. His hands were full of cards and dirty envelopes which he had drawn from within the bosom of his white cotton garment.

"Let me pass," MacArd said abruptly. He pushed the man aside, or rather the man seemed to melt away at his touch, and he went in. David threw the man a half smile of apology as he followed and instantly with renewed zeal the Muslim urged himself upon them, standing upon the threshold and holding open with his left hand the jalousied door, while he extended the right one, filled with the envelopes and cards.

"Please, Sahib and Son!" he cried in his high urgent voice. "Without bearer you can do nothing. You will be cheated everywhere by Hindus. As for me, I know them. With me at your side, none will dare to come near. I am Wahdi."

"The guidebook did say we'd have to have a bearer, Father," David said.

"Allow me to think of one thing at a time," his father replied. "I must pay off these fellows."

5

"The head boy," David suggested. "The guidebook said that, too."

"Me, please, Sahib," the head boy said. "I give to both."

MacArd took out a note from his wallet. "Be sure you do."

The man made the Hindu gesture of thanks. "Americans always give kindly," he murmured. "And I, Sahib, will tell you something. This man, Wahdi, is good, though he is Muslim. You may trust him. He will not cheat you if you are also kind to him."

He put his hands together again, the note fluttering between the third and fourth fingers of his right hand, and thus he went away, the other boy following.

"Well," MacArd said, fingering his beard. "I suppose we do have to have someone. It might as well be this fellow. I can always fire him if he turns out badly."

"I rather like his looks," David said.

To the son Wahdi addressed himself, still trembling with anxiety. "I am very good, little Sahib. It is true that some bearers cheat, but never I."

"Your English is good," David remarked.

"I studied in Christian school many years."

MacArd, who had been opening one of his bags, turned at this. "Are you a Christian?" he demanded with sudden interest.

Wahdi was abashed. He looked from one face to the other and decided to laugh.

"It is too difficult for me, Sahib," he declared. "Christianity is good, but I have no time. I have my parents to support, also my wife and eleven children. When I am old and can work no more, I will be Christian."

David laughed. "He's honest, Father."

MacArd grunted and returned to his unpacking.

"Then I am your bearer, Sahib?" Wahdi pleaded.

"Oh, I guess so," MacArd grunted, not lifting his head.

"Thank you, thank you, Sahib and Son," Wahdi was in an ecstasy of gratitude. "I will do everything—you will see. Sahib, let me—I unpack. I will do all. Please now take tiffin. I will finish."

Without knowing how it happened they found themselves outside the huge room in the marble corridor again and on their way to the dining room. Behind them Wahdi was bustling about the rooms, opening the vast teak wardrobes, one after another, and deciding where his masters' garments should hang.

"So and so and so," he was humming like a zealous bee.

"I can see we have a manager," David said. "I didn't even get to change my clothes."

"Ha!" MacArd said. He had already forgotten Wahdi, and with his pocket guidebook in his hand he was studying a map as he walked. Between him and the map came a sudden memory of his dead wife's face as she had looked on their last trip together. Wait, it was in London, and he had taken out a map then as now, and had begun to plan the hours ahead, but aloud and to her.

"Oh dear," she had sighed, pouting her pretty mouth, "I must have some time for doing nothing, you monster!"

He had been amused.

"How can one do nothing?" he had demanded. "Something but not nothing you are compelled to do by the very nature of time. There is no such thing as nothing."

"Oh, but there is," she had insisted, and he could see her lovely wilful face, the eyes so dark under the dark soft hair.

Well, she was right. There could be a nothing, and it was death, her death. He was tortured day and night by the need to believe that somehow and somewhere she still lived. While she had lived he had not needed faith but now he must find it again as once he had found it in his father's manse. His father had been a country preacher, a simple powerful man, who had turned evangelist after he had come home from the war. In MacArd's childhood faith was as plain as poverty, as simple as bread, as inevitable as birth and death. He had grown impatient in his adolescence, for his father was a severe man, and he had struck off for himself after a quarrel, and early in the struggle for what he had decided was success, he had lost what his father called religion. He was already a successful young businessman when he married Leila Gilchrist, the daughter of his senior partner, and with her he began to go to church again on Sunday, a very different church from the country church where

7

his father preached of heaven and hell and the immortality of the soul.

The night after Leila's funeral, in his sleepless need to know that she lived though her beloved body lay where he had seen it placed that day in the earth, he had called up Paul Barton, the rector.

"Barton," he had said hoarsely over the telephone. "It's MacArd."

"Yes, Mr. MacArd. What can I do for you?"

"Can you assure me that my wife is really still alive somewhere?"

"I believe that she is, sir."

"Have you proof?"

"I have faith."

"Why don't I have it? I'm a member of your church."

"A very generous one," Dr. Barton had said in his rich pulpit voice.

"Then why can't I believe she is alive?"

"You must simply affirm that you believe," the minister replied. "Affirm it and faith will follow."

Well, he had affirmed it over and over again. Leila could not be dead. Still, he was a practical man and there was the matter of the body. No one could deny decay. So what would she look like as a spirit and would it be the same? He wanted everything to be the same. Either Leila existed or she did not, and his willing her alive had nothing to do with the facts, as far as he could see. He had not thought of his father and mother for years, for they had died before he and Leila were married, but now he almost wished his fierce old father was alive again. His father had always seemed to know what he believed and why.

He put the map away and they went downstairs, he and his son, in silence. The boy was always silent these days, missing his mother, doubtless, though he never mentioned her.

"Let's go out right after we eat," he said abruptly.

"Very well, Father," David said.

The lobby was almost empty now. Only the maharajah remained, surrounded by his bright flock, while his business manager, a Eurasian, argued at the desk with the clerk.

They went into the vast dining room and sat down at a table by

8

the window and an Indian servant in a white uniform and a red sash appeared at once. Over their heads an immense punkah moved to and fro, and stirred the idle air.

The sun burned in a blue white sky as they stepped out of the hotel. MacArd had bought sun helmets in London for them both and David had fetched them from upstairs after their meal but nothing protected their faces from the upward glare of the streets, crowded though they were with people in every variety of costume and color. No white people were to be seen except an occasional carriage of English ladies going out to make their noon calls, a strange custom which had its sense, as the guidebook had told them, only because everyone later in the day went to the parks and the clubhouses to enjoy the coolness before night fell.

"Can you tell one native from another?" MacArd inquired of his son, to make talk. One of his most difficult tasks now was this burden of conversation. While Leila had been alive they had not known that it was she who kept communication constant among the three of them. Her laughing comment on all they saw and did had provided the articulate meaning of their life together. Now without her translation of life into words there were times when MacArd felt his son almost a stranger, or would have except that David, trying to be friendly, answered his slightest effort.

"I suppose you know what every one of them is," David replied.

His father's persevering study of the small library of books on India which they had brought along had moved him at times to secret shame and so to mild teasing. But he could not fix his mind on reading. His mother's death had left him in apathy.

"That's a Pathan, I'll guess," MacArd announced, nodding in the direction of a handsome aging man, his dark skin set off by a snow-white cotton garment, his head wrapped in a small turban. "That one," he went on, "is Marathi." The Marathi wore loose white trousers and a coatlike tunic, and his turban, entwined with a golden cord, spread wide over some sort of hidden shape.

"We see only men," David said idly. "I suppose the women are in purdah or something."

9

Nevertheless at this moment they saw a group of Marathi women emerging from a doorway, wrapped in vivid saris and wearing jewels in their left nostrils, a strange and pretty sight. The Marathi man shielded them and herded them into a carriage and they drove toward the crowded native city.

Toward this city MacArd now abruptly turned, away from the sea and the pleasant parkways of the English. It was hot and he summoned a small vehicle, a gherry, drawn by a brisk white bullock.

"We can postpone Malabar Point," he said to David. "I'd like to see where the people live."

They sat in silence in the rocking uncomfortable vehicle, facing each other upon hard wooden seats, and the parks and the wide streets gave way to narrow alleys, the handsome English buildings to small two-story houses of brick or stone, whose carved and painted fronts made them look like toys. The hot air steamed with scents and reeks, pepper and acid mingled with the bland fragrance of flowers and fruits. People crowded the streets, walking, standing, leaning against the walls, or lying on the pavement, curled in sleep. They were dark, and yet not all of the same darkness. Sometimes a child had a creamy skin, sometimes a young boy's cheek was almost white. Faces turned to gaze at them with eyes large and liquid and soft, except occasionally those deep set in the hawklike head of a Pathan or a Sikh. They saw no white man in the mingling crowds of Hindus, Muslims, Malays, Parsees wearing tall hats of horsehair, Afghans, Chinese, Japanese, Tibetans and even black men from the southern coasts. The colors were vivid and random, a pink turban and a green scarf, a purple robe and a tunic of crimson velvet and gold, orange and scarlet mingled with blue and yellow and rose, and now in the native city, the common women came and went, draped in bright and graceful saris. Their brown faces were decorated with necklaces, earrings and tiny jewels in the nostrils and their bare arms and ankles tinkled with bracelets and anklets. To the Americans, they were a pageant to look at and to pass.

The cross streets were narrow even for the gherry, but the driver, muttering something over his shoulder, drove the bullock toward a row of shops, jewelers and dealers in precious stones, and then as though this were the ultimate destination, he stopped and motioned that they were to descend.

"Well," MacArd said with a faint smile all but lost in his beard. "He seems to know what he wants us to do."

"We may as well obey," David replied.

They got out and the driver tucked his head into his dirty cotton robe and prepared to sleep.

The shops, or bazaars, whatever one chose to call them, were crowded with people examining jewels and ornaments, arguing and exclaiming and comparing. A few women turned their backs as they saw the white men but the beggars swarmed around them. Jewels were in rich display, rubies and pink Indian pearls, amethysts and diamonds, turquoise and Chinese jade set in elaborate gold, decorations for women's necks and wrists and ankles, or to set in the turban of a man. Seeing the Americans, the shopkeepers called to them from every side. MacArd hesitated, struck suddenly by a pang at the heart. There was no one now for whom he cared to buy jewels. Had Leila been with him, as once they had planned she would be, for she had a curiosity about the East, and especially India, fostered, perhaps, by missionaries who came to her church, why then he would have delighted to buy for her the necklace of pearls, the emeralds set in a heavy bracelet of yellow gold. Indian emeralds were the most beautiful in the world, and how well her dark hair and eyes would have set off that vivid green, and how dearly he would have enjoyed her wearing them at home, sitting at the far end of his vast table. He would have boasted to his guests, "Yes, we bought Leila's emeralds in India, in the Street of Jewels. There are thousands of shops, six thousand, they told us, and we thought these the finest gems we saw."

Leila was dead. That he must repeat to himself. He looked at David, standing quietly beside him, gazing not at the jewels but at the people.

"Shall we go?" he asked.

"Whenever you say," David replied.

They climbed back into the vehicle to the disappointment of

jewelers and beggars alike, and prodding the driver awake with his cane, MacArd pointed him back again to the English city, to the wide streets, the great houses of green and grey stone. There Mac-Ard dismissed the wretched conveyance and they got into the horse-drawn streetcar for Malabar Point.

"An American named Kittredge built this streetcar system," he informed his son, making conversation again.

"Did he?" David murmured.

They were passing the Cathedral and near it stood the statue of Lord Cornwallis, the Governor-General of India after England lost the American colonies, a statue raised, the guidebook said, by funds from the merchants of Bombay.

"Cornwallis," MacArd said briefly, nodding at the haughty figure. David looked and did not reply.

North of the bay stood the Towers of Silence. They had been told at the hotel that surely they must see the Towers, "A very interesting sight," the clerk had informed them with condescension.

"Are you tired?" MacArd asked in sudden anxiety. His son's cheeks were pale.

"I feel odd," David said with some effort. "I feel smothered. It's only the heat, I think."

"We'll get off and go back to the hotel," MacArd said firmly. Again they descended, and catching a car returning from Malabar Point, they were within the half hour back in their rooms. Wahdi, asleep at the door, leaped to his feet. MacArd ignored him.

"You are not ill?" he insisted, gazing anxiously at his son.

"Oh no," David protested. "Perhaps, again, it's the ship. I seem to feel the sea still rising and falling. I will lie down."

"I fetch you tea, Sahib." Wahdi, hovering about them, increased the oppression of the atmosphere.

"Fetch it then," MacArd commanded. "And David, take a cool sponge. It will refresh you."

"Thanks, Father," David said. "Don't bother. I'll drink the tea and be better."

He longed to shut the door between the rooms but he did not wish to wound his father. He had never before been alone with his father for days and weeks. There had always been his mother between them, and now she was no more. He must learn to live without feeling oppressed by this powerful personality. He smiled at his father and then taking courage he shut the door between them.

In his bathroom MacArd poured water over himself in the fashion that the guidebook had suggested to them. He stood on the sloping stone floor and with the metal dipper he dipped up water from a large porcelain jar and poured it over his head and shoulders. It was refreshing, he had to admit, feeling the rills of water running down his white body, the dead white of the red-haired, so much less beautiful than Leila's lovely cream color. That abundant joy was his no more. He strove to be stern with himself, to repress the vitality of his vigorous frame. He must shape all his time now to other ends, undertake new work, busy himself—but with what? While she lived, his life was full every hour of the day and night, and now, suddenly it all had come to an end and so quickly that still he could scarcely believe it. Her heart, which none had suspected, had in the night, a night like any other, simply ceased to beat, without reason, without will, a mystery except that in her pretty, wilful way she never went to doctors. Not since David's birth and the painful operation after it, which had made it evident that there would be no more children, never after those weeks in the hospital had she been willing to have a doctor. She treated herself in secret ways and he knew it only because he found bottles of medicine sometimes on her table. Then, terrified, he demanded to know if she suffered pain or felt ill and she never would tell him. She had laughed at him and had showed him her lovely round arms and had bade him look at the color of her cheeks.

"Do I look like an invalid?" she had demanded.

What could he say but the truth that she looked like health itself? Afterwards the bright eyes and the quick vivid color, were, the doctor said, the very signs of death.

MacArd gave a groaning sigh as he remembered, and then wrapping his linen bathrobe about him, he sat down in a deep wicker chair in his bedroom. Immediately the weight of his loneliness, his

13

distance from home, the knowledge that even though he returned to his house it would be empty for him, overcame him, and he closed his eyes and leaned back his head. He had not for years really prayed to God, although it was his nightly habit, because it had been Leila's, to kneel at his bedside for a few minutes. Sometimes he had prayed during those minutes, but usually it had been sheer pretense, the wish not to hurt his wife, who had the habit of devoutness natural to her generation and his. Since her death he had put aside pretense, but suddenly now here in this distant room in India, prayer burst articulate from his frantic heart.

"Oh God, show me what to do with my life and my money that in the end I may rejoin my beloved wife in heaven!"

He did not doubt for one moment that Leila was in heaven, if there were such a place, for she had been a tender woman of such goodness and purity that she had already been an angel on earth. That she was ever petty or that she had ever made him impatient seemed impossible to him, and he thought now of such moments as entirely his own fault, although he had not always recognized it so when she was alive. She had sometimes complained against him because, she said, he was only interested in making money. It was true. His life had been absorbed in establishing the vast network of his interests. He had founded his fortune in railroads, and he was still the president of that, his oldest corporation, but railroads, as half a dozen men in his country knew, were merely arteries for trade, and now, with the nineteenth century in its last decade, the young and hungry country in which he had grown up yearned for more railroads and more trade. To pursue his golden way had been his business, but it had been his excitement and achievement, too. It had been fun as well as glory, and he did not care how much of his money Leila gave away. He liked to see his wife's name heading a charity, "Mrs. David Hardworth MacArd, five thousand dollars."

What did Leila want him to do now?

He held his eyes tightly shut, surprised at the cry from within himself and even a little frightened. Were there secrets that he did not know? He was a practical man, he had no time to read books, although he used to enjoy listening to Leila tell him about the books she read, and since her death he had opened some of them, seeking to recover the sound of her voice and the vision of her tender face. But without her the pages were dead. Where then could he find out about her now?

"Oh, Leila, honey," he muttered, teeth clenched, "can't you break through to me somehow?"

He sat rigid and listening, and he heard unrecognized sounds rising from the streets, high wailing voices speaking unknown tongues, voices as mournful as a dirge, mingled with the sharp cry of the beggars. His loneliness became agony and something as near terror as he could feel lent energy to his soul, searching for lost love. Certain words that had haunted his childhood in the country manse sprang alive in his memory, and he heard his father's big voice declaiming scriptures from the pulpit.

"It is easier for a camel to pass through The Eye Of The Needle than it is for a rich man to enter The Kingdom of Heaven."

Why, this was a monstrous thing to remember, for he was a very rich man, and it was not like Leila to remind him of it, but maybe she was doing it because it was the only way she could do it, through his memory. He used to hear those words when he was a small boy, bitterly poor with his family, and none of them had ever seen a rich man and he used to wonder what a rich man did and what he had to eat and to wear, and when he was a rebellious adolescent, he wanted to be a rich man because that was the kind of man his father had hated, a man who could never go to heaven. So maybe this was Leila's way of telling him that those old words were true and if he wanted to get to heaven where she was he had to do something good now with his money.

He was distracted here by the door opening slowly, inch by inch and he saw Wahdi, smiling at him. He came in on tiptoe, bearing a tea tray, and from his right hand hung an immense basket of white flowers.

"From Govmint, Sahib," Wahdi said proudly. "A chit, Sahib, telling all." He set the tray on the table, put down the basket and took from his bosom a large square envelope and gave it to MacArd. Then he stepped back and stood proudly while he waited.

MacArd tore open the heavy paper and drew forth a single sheet embossed with the insignia of the English crown. There was nothing formal, however, in the handwritten message, signed by the Governor-General himself.

Dear Mr. MacArd,
We shall be delighted if you care to have tiffin with us privately either Tuesday or Thursday without other guests, and shall quite understand if you don't. I have given instructions that you are to see what you like in the city and that reservations are to be made on whatever railroad you choose to travel. We understand the tragic circumstances of your visit and shall await your inclination.

Yours, etc.

MacArd was not deceived. He was not a conceited man, but he was proud. He was invited to the Governor-General's mansion because he was rich, and wealth was his pedestal.

The incident restored MacArd to himself. He had been shaken, but he must wait. He must think things over, he told himself. Meanwhile here was this invitation.

He pondered it while Wahdi waited majestically, sharing the glory of a master who received flowers from Malabar Point. MacArd's Scotch blood, inherited two hundred years ago from Scottish ancestors who did not wish to be vassals of Englishmen, tempted him to toy with the idea of refusing the invitation. Courteously as it was worded, it was nevertheless a summons. His prudence conquered. Some time or other he might want to do business in India. It seemed unlikely, but it was within the imagination that railroads might make some day a network around the world, connecting with vast steamship companies. It was an age of expansion. He went to the teakwood desk and wrote a brief note of acceptance. Wahdi received it as an honor and bestowed it upon the waiting messenger outside the door with the air of one conferring gifts.

"We have given the Indian people an extraordinary freedom," the Governor-General was saying. "In the old days they wouldn't have

16

thought of criticizing Government. Now, however, British tradition has taken the young Indian intellectuals by storm. We've taught them English and they have read our English newspapers and have learned our ways. They read our vigorous and independent editorials, not understanding that in England criticism does not mean disloyalty, and so they criticize us and are disloyal. It began in the time of my predecessor, but it crystallized at the first meeting of the Indian National Congress some few years ago. I hope it may not lead to final rebellion. Lord Lytton felt it very wrong and he passed an Act for controlling the native press, but it was repealed four years later. We English are incurably conscientious and Indians are not used to that."

A turbaned manservant in a bright scarlet tunic, white trousers and gold belt waited at his elbow and he helped himself to curry and rice, a pheasant curry delicately seasoned for the English palate.

"Who are the leaders?" MacArd inquired.

There were only the four of them at the long table, and although he faced David, his host and hostess were so distant that he repressed an inclination to raise his voice.

"The young intellectuals, the leftists, as remote from the peasants and the small town and country people as you and I are," the Governor-General declared.

"Will they be able to persuade the peasants to follow their lead?" MacArd inquired. He disliked curry and took only a little of the dish which the gorgeously garbed Indian servant now held at his left.

"If we keep on educating the Indians in English schools there's no telling what will become of the Empire," the Governor-General said frankly. He went on, his disarming smile belying his words and the stiffness of his tall thin frame encased in a white linen suit. "We destroy ourselves, we English. We can't be proper tyrants. We insist upon our conscience and it makes tyranny impossible."

David listened, his dark eyes calm. MacArd was proud of his son, sitting there at the vast table at ease, yet with suitable deference in

17

the presence of his elders and of dignity. The Marquess was looking at him, too, and he saw her rather cold blue eyes soften.

"My two sons are in England," she said suddenly to David. "The elder is only sixteen. They left India when they were five and eight. We kept Ronald later than usual so that Bertie could go with him. I haven't seen them now for three years."

"You are going home again in May, my dear," her husband reminded her.

"I only hope they still remember me, as I am, I mean, and not as a sort of maternal figure," she said.

"It's one of the many prices of Empire," he remarked.

"Ah, but the women pay for it," she said rather sharply.

MacArd turned to the Governor. "I guess you, too, have missed your sons, though."

"Yes, certainly," the Governor-General replied, "yet I yield to my wife. It's quite true that she misses them more than I do, and also that I have rewards that she has not. English women have a difficult time of it in India, I'm afraid."

The long elaborate meal drew to its close, and they rose, the Governor-General saying that since his wife was the only woman, they would not linger at table while she sat alone in the drawing room, and so they left the dining room with her.

The palace at Malabar Point was a series of bungalows, the many rooms were large and cool, and the doors opened upon deep verandas shaded by great trees and flowering vines. MacArd had been in the White House, summoned to Washington by the President before he set out for India, but this palace was far more magnificent and nothing was more magnificent than the Governor-General's own bodyguard. The tall Sikhs, their faces dark under huge and intricate turbans, were splendidly handsome above their scarlet uniforms. MacArd had seen them at the gatehouse, where they stood with their long spears, watchful and waiting. They had none of the servile humility of the crowds on the streets. They were soldiers of Empire, and rejoiced in what they were.

He was compelled to acknowledge, as they reached the blue and gold drawing room, that the Englishman and his wife were worthy enough of their position. Titled in their own right, both tall and equally blond, they carried themselves with a simple and powerful dignity which he could not but admire, and could not but acknowledge, too, was not to be found in his own country. Only men and women who had lived for generations above competition could maintain such serene confidence in what they were. In his own country all were subject to competition. He himself had fought and struggled to reach his present height, and it would be impossible for him to pretend either to dignity or serenity. Such dignity as he had was the result of sheer physical mass, his six feet three now the more imposing because he was no longer the slight fellow he had been when he was young, although he had kept his figure well enough. He wore his London suit of tropical pongee with sufficient ease, and David was handsome in white linen. He saw the Marquess look at his son again and again and at last she forgot her remoteness and motioned to him with a wave of her long narrow jeweled hand to come and sit on the sofa beside her, which David did, without appearing absurd. His mother's sense of humor, that dark sparkling laughter which MacArd had so loved to see in his wife's eyes, had kept their son from self-consciousness or conceit.

"Never forget that your grandfather was a country preacher," Leila used to tell the boy, "but a very good one because he was your father's father," she had always added, dimpling.

"Tell me what you have chosen for your career," the Marquess was saying to David in a sweet coaxing voice.

"I don't know yet, ma'am," David said. "I have just finished college."

"College?" she repeated.

"Harvard."

"Is it the same as Oxford and Cambridge?"

"I think so."

She smiled at him with a distant tenderness. "And so you have no inclination?"

"Not yet, ma'am," David acknowledged. "Perhaps this journey with my father will reveal something."

"He can always come into my offices," MacArd said.

19

"Oh, but you won't make him?" she asked almost pleadingly.

"Certainly not," MacArd replied. "He needn't do anything, so far as I am concerned, although I think he'll want to make some sort of place for himself.

"No interests?" she asked, looking at David again.

"Too many," he said frankly.

She refrained from more questions, her delicate reserve descended upon her again, but she rose and went to the rosewood piano and brought two large gold framed photographs.

"These are my sons," she said.

David took the photographs, one and then the other, and looked into two thin serious faces. The photographs were finely colored and both boys were blond, blue-eyed and pink-cheeked.

"Look at those cheeks," their mother murmured. "They couldn't have had them here in India."

"Oh, it's quite impossible to keep English children here," the Governor-General said.

His rather sharp voice served some sort of notice upon his lady and she said no more. She put the photographs quietly down on the couch beside her and motioned to a resplendent man servant to fill her small gilt cup again with coffee.

The Governor-General was talking now, explaining to MacArd the difficulties of his position, and indeed of all Englishmen in India.

"The Indians educated in English schools simply do not know the history of their own country," he declared. "They fancy that all was peace and joy here before the British took over. As a matter of fact, the whole country was embroiled in tyranny and disunity and the common people were at the mercy of every local bully. Yet if any sensible elder Indian mentions this fact he is at once attacked on the grounds of toadying to Empire. They are determined to hate us."

David spoke unexpectedly. "My mother would have said that they should be Christianized."

The Governor-General was frankly surprised. "Quite the contrary," he said coldly. "An Indian is infinitely worse when he becomes a Christian. When he forsakes his own gods he usually ends by being a scoundrel. Never trust an Indian when he says he's a

Christian—it's become an axiom. Besides, only the lowest castes will change their religion."

MacArd interrupted. He felt in some way that Leila was belittled by what the Governor had said. "My wife was a truly religious woman. If there were more like her in the world, we'd all be better for it, I guess."

Nothing could be said to this and nothing was said. The Governor-General could be silent with ease, and the Marquess looked thoughtful. She said, after a moment, "Christianity is so different, isn't it, in different people."

MacArd got to his feet. He felt his skin hot, his hair bristle, and he restrained his impulse to defend his wife's religion. He did not want to talk about her and he was surprised that David had mentioned her. He said to his host, "I think we ought to get on our way. My son and I want to visit the Towers of Silence. We hear it is one of the sights."

The Governor-General rose promptly. "You should see it, by all means. Have you got your permission?"

"Is it needed?" MacArd asked.

"You must get permission from the Parsee Secretary to the Parsee Panchayat. Wait—I'll send a man and get it for you. It will be waiting for you at the Towers."

"Thank you," MacArd said.

They made their farewells, he touched the lady's hand quickly, withdrawing his own at once. Since Leila died he had found it unpleasant to touch a woman's hand, even so coldly. But with a sudden compulsive movement, the Marquess took David's hand in both her own. "Thank you," she said, "thank you for reminding me of my boys."

The Towers of Silence stood upon the top of a high hill. No roofs could be seen as they approached, for the encircling wall was high, but as they drew near, the gate of the outer temple opened, and a priest, grave and dignified in his robes, stood to receive them.

They came down from the carriage and the priest addressed them in English.

21

"We have received the message from Government House, Mr. MacArd, and we are happy to receive you and your son here in our sacred temples of the dead. Will you rest a while before going on?"

"Thanks, no," MacArd said. "We will proceed, if you please."

David looked into the tall palm trees inside the gate. Dark and sullen shapes roosted among the fronds.

"What are those?" he demanded.

"They are the vultures," the Parsee said tranquilly. "They are very well trained. They do not come down unless the time is suitable. Even when the corpse is ready, they will not come down until the bearers are gone and they are alone with the dead. Some of the vultures are very old and they teach the young ones."

David knew the process well enough, he had read of it, but MacArd saw his face whiten.

"Want to go on?" he asked.

"Of course," David said briefly.

The priest described the services as he led them, moving before them with a singular grace and stillness. "The funeral services are performed at the home of the dead. The body is then put into a hearse, not in a coffin as with you of the West, but simply laid there as upon a bed, and covered with beautiful robes and shawls. In great solemnity, our priests lead the way hither and after them come the male members of the family and the friends. The dead is brought first to the outer gates, where the priests take charge. They place the dead in that temple, which you see yonder, sirs, but where I cannot lead you, for it is open only to members of our faith. I can tell you that it is very simple, and that the sacred fire burns there eternally."

"Why not burn the body?" David asked in a low voice.

The priest looked shocked. "Fire is pure," he declared. "It must not be polluted by the bodies of the dead. Water is also pure, and neither should the earth be polluted for it is the source of food and strength."

As though this could not be contradicted, he did not speak while he led them along the path through the beautiful and utterly silent grounds where not a bird sang or any sound penetrated from the

22

city below. There were five towers, and into one of them the priest led them, and then he spoke again.

"It is not usual to come into one of the towers, but you are guests of the Governor-General and I will go beyond what is usual."

The tower was roofless, the walls about forty feet high, spotlessly clean with whitewash. The gate to this tower was high and they had to climb steps to reach it. At the gate they stood, for the priest forbade them to enter. "You can see what it is," he said. "You need not to enter, if you please."

What they saw was a series of paths, running like the spokes of a wheel to a depressed pit at the bottom. Between the paths were rows of small compartments for the dead.

"For the men, the women, the children," the priest explained.

"There are most for the children and then for the women," David said.

"Most children must die," the priest said calmly, "and more women than men, as is their fate."

They gazed about the place, and as though their presence were a portent, vultures rose from the trees and, moving their heavy wings, they flew slowly over the tower.

"Into these compartments the dead are placed," the priest intoned. "First, they are taken into the anteroom and the vestments and coverings are taken away, these are purified and returned to the family. Then the corpse, naked as it was born, is laid into its roofless cell and the bearers withdraw. It is now that the vultures do their sacred work. They descend and strip away the flesh, and the bones are left clean. No human comes near. Then the elements do their work. The sun shines down and bleaches the bones and the rain falls and washes them clean until they are pure and white. When the cell is needed for yet another of the dead, the attendant priests, the Nasr Salars, enter with gloves and tongs and take up the bones and cast them into the central pit, where they turn to dust. All the water that falls into this tower and into each of the other towers is gathered by drains and runs down into the pit, which is perforated so that the water carries away the dust of the dead. Below are charcoal filters through which the water must pass and then it flows into a great conduit and so to the bay and from thence to the eternal sea."

"Does the pit never fill?" David asked in a voice infused with horror.

"Never," the priest replied. "In hundreds of years it has never filled. The elements do their work well."

MacArd was stricken in silence, troubled and moved at the same time, revolted and impressed. The priest continued to speak in the same reverent voice.

"It is our faith that before God all men are equal, and here there is no difference between the rich and the poor. All the cells are alike and all the dead alike are given over to the sun and the rain and the sea. All alike find the same rest."

"But to have no grave from which to arise!" David exclaimed.

"Nevertheless we do believe in the resurrection of the dead," the priest declared. "It is our faith that our bodies will rise again from the elements, glorified by a new life which as yet we cannot comprehend."

For MacArd the scene changed, the horror disappeared, and he grasped at the immortal faith. "You believe that, too!" he exclaimed.

"All those who are truly religious believe in the eternity of the soul," the priest replied.

"That's very important," MacArd cried.

David was surprised at the sudden excitement in his voice and still more surprised when at the gate MacArd put into the priest's hand a roll of rupees.

"It's been interesting," MacArd said. "It's been very interesting. I'll never forget this."

The compartment on the train to Poona was large and Wahdi had provided comforts. He had rented bedding from the hotel and had filled a high wicker basket with tinned foods, enough for a journey many times longer than the one to Poona. The windows were closed against the dust, but ventilators were open in the ceilings and dust drifted in as fine and dry as powder. David lay on a couch of quilts spread upon one of the wide benches, sleeping. He

24

wore only his underdrawers, but the smooth skin of his youthful body was damp with sweat.

MacArd glanced at him now and again, recognizing in his son with love and pain the grace of Leila, his mother. His own heavy frame had none of this shapely slenderness, this delicacy of ankle and wrist. Yet David was not feminine. His shoulders were broad and his hips were narrow, and his height MacArd himself had bestowed. But the boy's face was not at all his, and the dark coloring was contrast enough when they were seen together, so that strangers remarked upon it. He was glad that David could sleep for there was little enough to see from the dusty windows, plains as barren as winter, though it was already so hot that one could scarcely endure the windy heat. Upon the plains the earthen villages were pitilessly bare under the blazing sun. The villages were scarcely more clear upon the landscape than molehills heaped up, and out of them crawled the most dreary creatures he could imagine upon the earth. Yet they were human, though they seemed scarcely different from the pitiful skeleton shapes of the cattle which roamed restlessly over the barren ground, searching for food that did not exist. Men and women and cattle alike were waiting for the rains, still months away. A few days of rain, Wahdi explained, and these dry barrens would spring into instant green. The seed was there, waiting for the life-giving water.

"There is always life," Wahdi declared.

MacArd recalled the words now as he sat staring out of the window. Wahdi was a Muslim and so the Muslims must believe in it, too. It was a queer thing if he, a Christian, as he supposed he was, should find in a heathen country the faith to believe that Leila still lived. Yet these were very ancient people and they had been religious for a long time and maybe they knew more about such things than fellows like Barton did. He ruminated awhile, and feelings of warm pity stirred about his heart. It was too bad that people so religious, so good, should live half-starved, their land as bare as a desert under a summer sun and all for the want of water and railroads and trade, which was what had made Americans comfortable and rich.

He slapped a fly from his cheek. In spite of the spraying that

25

Wahdi had performed before they left Bombay, there were flies inside the closed car. Flies crawled through the solid wood, he was ready to swear. They were starving, too, and ravenous, teasing any object in repose, if this racking shaking travel could leave anything in repose. The railroads were a disgrace. Something ought to be done about India. The people had no chance. The English were a curious lot, so proud when there wasn't much to be proud about. A few Americans now, young fellows, trained to develop the people themselves, could accomplish a lot in a few years. Only how would they get in here? The only Americans were a few missionaries. Well, maybe missionaries—

He forgot the flies and the dust and fell into one of those intense reveries which Leila used to call his darkness before dawn, his pre-creative mood. He was feeling about for the big idea. It would not come down out of the sky or alone. It grew as a twister grows out of a tornado, drawing winds and earth into its shape until it rises to the force of explosion. Then perfectly clearly he saw his big idea.

Why shouldn't he make his own missionaries and send them to India?

At Poona Wahdi settled them in a good hotel, but MacArd was restless, and he set out to see the city at once, though the afternoon was late. David did not come with him. He had met in London at Claridge's a young Indian, Darya Sapru, and this young man had invited David to his home if he came to Poona, and there David decided to go. Meanwhile MacArd wandered about the streets at his usual swift pace, startling the people who fell back before him, fearful of his size and good garments. The big idea was with him now day and night and everything he saw was subject to it and became part of it. Here in Poona he found two rivers joining to wind themselves like sluggish serpents among the houses. Behind the city the hills rose to a high tableland and upon one of those hills, his guidebook told him, was an ancient aqueduct, built long ago by a Marathi family. Its source was in a well. Water there was close to the surface of the earth. It would be easy to send it over the whole

26

region, and the land need not lie barren until the monsoons brought rain.

He went back to the hotel at nightfall, and his idea was beginning to grow like a tree. It stretched down roots and sent out branches. He would train his young men and send them here to do his work. There must be a place to train them, a great school, an institution endowed—why not in the name of his beloved wife? That would be an immortality in itself, the Leila MacArd Memorial—

He opened the door of their rooms and found his son waiting and excited by his own afternoon.

"It was a wonderful house, Father," he exclaimed, "the most extraordinary gardens along the river. I've never seen such a place—marble floors in all the main rooms and a huge separate dining room connected with the house by a long passageway, lovely in itself. There's another huge room—open, too, the sides all carved in wood—where Darya says the family really lives. The drawing room had the handsomest ceiling I've ever seen, all done by Poona artists."

MacArd said absently, "A contrast to the rest of India, I should say."

His son looked at him with a peculiar humor in his mild dark eyes, but he did not notice it. The conversation died, nor was it resumed for the next few days while they came and went.

Poona was more easily traveled than Bombay, a large city divided into parts like wards, and spotted by the usual monuments and bridges erected by rich Indians. By the fifth day MacArd was ready to go beyond into the surrounding countryside. He was thinking furiously now about water, and how it alone might change the face of India. He saw a country threaded by silver canals, a network of irrigation, independent of rains or even of rivers. Let them use the Mutha and the Mula rivers here in Poona and the Ganges itself in the northeast for electric power, but irrigation canals, the water drawn deep from the earth, alone could provide the steady life-giving stream to the plains.

Yet who could do it except the Indians themselves? The resigna-

27

tion of the poor and the selfishness of the rich must be blasted by new force. The merchants, the wealthy princes, were willing enough to make vast buildings and public monuments, but they did nothing to relieve the poverty of the hopeless peasants. What they needed was a new religion, a practical religion, that built irrigation systems and railroads as well as churches. He would send a new kind of Christian here, a man who worked while he preached.

On that fifth day he made his decision, and it came from a peasant, a Hindu, naked except for the white turban about his head and the scrap of white cotton about his loins, a thin dried man of about fifty, but one could never tell the ages of men and women here, and probably he was only twenty or twenty-five. The man was a potter, such a potter as any Indian village may have and MacArd was walking with only Wahdi, for David was again with Darya. He came upon the potter as he crouched upon the dusty floor of the earth, running with his foot his potter's wheel while his narrow graceful hands, the fingers supple and swift, shaped a mass of whirling clay. He had looked up to smile fearfully at MacArd, a foreigner and a white man, and to Wahdi he made his excuse that at this moment he dared not rise to give proper greeting, lest the vessel be spoiled.

"Tell him I want to see what he is making," MacArd ordered, and Wahdi translated with the distaste he always showed when he spoke to a Hindu.

The vessel was finished in a few minutes, a common bowl of clay made from the dry dust of the fields mingled with a little precious water, and the potter set it to dry in the burning sun.

"Ask him if he will take time to show me the village and the fields," MacArd said to Wahdi. "Tell him I will pay him."

This in turn was translated, the man nodded, his face lit with a bright good humor, and stepping carefully ahead of MacArd he led him about the small collection of mud huts from which men stood and stared and in which the women hid. The children ran everywhere naked and grey with the dust.

But it was in the fields that MacArd saw the strange sight which persuaded him, like a vision, to the determination which was there-

28

after to shape his life. The potter was some twenty feet ahead of him upon the narrow path between the fields when suddenly a serpent lay across the path, a cobra, as MacArd instantly recognized. He had not seen one before, except in the pictures of the guidebook, but there could be no mistaking the raised and hideous head flattening and spreading out with fright and rage. Wahdi leaped away but MacArd cried out. "Let me get him!"

He raised his cane, a heavy malacca stick tipped with metal.

The potter shook his head and would not let him pass. He had stopped only a few feet from the cobra and now he stood motionless. He raised his hands and placed them palm to palm, touching his forehead with the tips of his fingers. The cobra swayed back and forth in ever diminishing waves of motion, his sickening head resumed its natural shape and while the potter waited in the attitude of prayer, the cobra gradually subsided, uncoiled its stubborn length, and crawled away.

The potter waited until it had disappeared into a wide crack in the field and then he turned to MacArd. Wahdi was creeping back again, seeing safety, and the potter spoke to him.

"He tells, Sahib," Wahdi said in some scorn, "he tells that the snake is a god. It is sin to kill a god."

MacArd was repelled to the soul. This, then, was why poisonous snakes abounded in the vile soil, and this was why they could not be destroyed!

He turned abruptly from the potter. "I will go back to Poona now," he said to Wahdi. "Pay this man something."

All the way back to Poona he kept seeing the flattened devilish head of the snake, and between him and it the slender graceful figure of the potter, a good man as even he could see, but one who did not dare to kill the snake, the curse, the menace even to his own life, because of his religion.

MacArd strode into his hotel bedroom and forbade Wahdi to come in.

"I want to rest," he told Wahdi. "Go away, amuse yourself, eat a meal, anything you wish."

"Yes, Sahib," Wahdi said. He was used now to this harsh American who was foolishly liberal with his money. He went away complacent over his own superior common sense and MacArd sat down in a wicker chair. David was not back and he was alone in the room.

Religion! Was that religion, being willing to wait for a snake to strike, passive and waiting, no protest, no self-defense? No wonder the people sat upon the barren land, waiting for the rains.

He struck his big clenched fist on the bamboo arm of the chair. He would put an end to it.

The vision rose before his eyes. The dry land would grow green, the hungry would be fed, the poor would be rich. And he would go to heaven, at last.

II

He entered his own house with a firm step a few weeks later, and he gave his hat and stick and his gloves and overcoat to Enderby, the butler.

"Well, Enderby," he said in his usual brusque greeting.

"Mr. MacArd, sir," Enderby replied, bowing his head slightly. "I hope you had a good trip."

"Excellent," MacArd said. He turned to David, waiting just behind him. "Well, son?"

"Yes, Father?" David said. He understood his father well, he knew that the grizzled head held high and the blue eyes fierce with resolution simply meant that there was to be no mention of his mother. The house was empty in spite of its warmth and the many flowers arranged in the magnificence of the vistas. He felt very tenderly toward his father.

"What are your plans?" MacArd asked.

"I have none, Father," David said in his equable voice. "I think I shall just go to my rooms and take my time, unless there is something you want me to do."

"Not at present," his father replied. "If you have nothing on your mind, I shall go on to my office and be home for dinner tonight."

"Yes, Father," David said again.

It was still early, they had breakfasted on the ship, and there was nothing he wished for so much as to be alone for reflection and meditation. Above all, he needed relief from his father, that dominating and oppressive presence which he knew was also powerfully loving. He had shared its weight with his mother all the years of his

31

life, she had taught him to value his father and yet to know that he was unchangeable, and David could bear the knowledge while he had her with him, her gaiety, her humor, her life-giving vitality. The talent she had for absorbing herself in him and in his father, quite separately and yet always keeping the three of them together, had made the atmosphere of this immense house. Now that she was gone he was resolved to maintain it so far as he could do so alone, for her sake, and yet he had a quiet independence, his father's thought filtered through the gentle blood of his mother, and he was determined also to find the life he wanted for himself and to live it.

"Will you have your luncheon served in your own sitting room, sir?" Enderby was asking, in a slightly raised tone.

"I'm sorry! Yes, if you please, Enderby, I shall spend the day there, I think, until my father comes home. I want to put my photographs away myself. I brought back a lot of them from India."

"Very well, sir," said Enderby, for whom India did not exist.

He went away and David mounted the wide marble stairs. There was an elevator at the end of the hall, but he liked the steps. His mother had descended them often while he stood at the bottom, his face uplifted to watch her come down, beautifully dressed, perhaps for the theater or a dinner party. When he was small he had raced down to be ahead of her so that he could see her descend, her train trailing behind her, and her arms and bosom bare except for her jewels.

His rooms were on the second floor, in the east wing, and a wide carpeted corridor led to the door. The house was completely quiet, and this was strange to him, for when his mother had been alive it seemed full of pleasant sounds, music somewhere, the piano or her lovely voice, an almost brilliant voice, or if not such music yet the house had been full of the sounds of living, her friends, the bark and whines of her pet dogs.

He entered the outer door to the rooms he knew so well and there they were before him, the doors open between, his bedroom and dressing room and bath, and here where he stood in his sitting room, and beyond it his study and library combined. The colors were crimson and cream; his mother had chosen them for him while he was

32

in college, and the rooms looked fresh and yet familiar. He sat down in his favorite chair, and leaning back he closed his eyes.

India had made a profound impression upon him or perhaps it was not India but Darya. He had not been able to explain to his father how he felt about Darya. He had been drawn to the slender young Indian when he met him in London but there had been no time to talk with him. Darya was reserved then, he had seemed even cynical, at least dangerously humorous, his dark eyes quick and haunted, as though he saw everything and told nothing. He had wished that Darya was taking the same ship to Bombay for then he could have satisfied his curiosity about a man who attracted him so much and yet who seemed beyond the reach of understanding, but Darya had passage on a French ship a few days later and did not seem inclined to change. "I never travel on English ships," he had said briefly. Yet he had no rancor toward the English there in Claridge's, where he had the best suite of rooms.

All the days they were in Bombay and when he was alone in Agra, wherever they stopped until they reached Poona, David had kept thinking of Darya. He had written to him before they left Bombay, reminding him of their agreement to see each other and Darya had replied courteously that he was at home, that he hoped that David would spend at least an afternoon with him.

That afternoon was, in a way he could not explain, the first comfort, the first assuaging, since his mother's death. Until then he had simply followed his father, trying to be pleasant, as his mother would have said, but he had not been able to think at all, even about what he was seeing. He guessed that his numbness had made his father anxious, and that perhaps his father had felt him a burden, too. But Darya had lifted his heart or stirred his mind, he could not yet tell which, though Darya had said very little actually that he could remember. There was no entertainment beyond some cakes and honeyed milk, brought in by servants. None of the family appeared. They had simply wandered about the beautiful house and the flowering gardens, and Darya had pointed out one thing and another, the ivory carving set in a stone wall, the marble lattices brought from an ancient palace. It was not exhibited in pride or

33

vanity, for many handsome objects Darya had ignored. He showed David the particular things that he loved, sharing with him the reason for his pleasure in them. The lotus, blooming in the vast central pool in the garden, their rose pink petals open under the sun, had moved Darya one day to suggest that they sit down on a marble bench and look at them.

"When the sun begins to sink," he had said, "you will see the petals quiver and if you are patient, you can watch them close. You cannot actually see them move, you understand, but while you wait they close over the golden centers."

And while they had sat in that garden of beauty where they seemed to be completely alone, although Darya told him that his two brothers and their wives and children lived here also, and that his married sister was visiting his parents with her children, Darya asked him a question which would have seemed strange except that they were in India and an Indian asked it.

"David, what is your religion?" This was the question Darya had asked.

He asked it as one might ask about an ancestor, a nationality or race, or a destination.

David had hesitated for an instant. "I suppose I am a Christian," he said at last. "At least I am a member of a church."

"Of Christianity I know nothing," Darya said almost indifferently. He stooped and plucked a small purple flower that grew between the marble stones of the terrace encircling the pool. He wore his Hindu dress, and this made him less a stranger, David reflected, than he had been in the London hotel, dressed as an Englishman. There was an air of informality about the white silk robes that left Darya's arms and legs bare, and he wore sandals instead of leather shoes.

"I know too little, myself," David said honestly. "But my mother believed in God and in prayer. She taught me to believe, I suppose."

Darya interrupted him. In London he had spoken like an Englishman, but here, though he used English perfectly, he spoke as an Indian, dulling the consonants and rounding the vowels.

"Your religion is not a part of your life?"

34

"In a way it is," David said. He wanted to be wholly honest with Darya. He yearned for friendship, a peculiar friendship where they could speak to each other from the heart, because they were strangers to each other. He could not so speak to those whom he had always known, who knew his family and especially his father. To Darya the name MacArd seemed to mean nothing and he took wealth for granted. It was doubtful, David reflected, that all his father's fortune could match the riches that Darya would inherit.

"How?" Darya persisted. "Tell me more, David, for I wish to know you, and to know a man's religion is the best way to know him."

David said, somewhat astonished, "I am afraid that it is not true of me—or of most of us. Perhaps we mean different things by religion."

"Explain yourself," Darya commanded with an imperious air. He had a handsome head, smoothly waved dark hair cut short about his oval beautiful face. His large brown eyes, very dark, were fixed on David's face, and it was impossible to resist their magnetic power.

"With us," David said diffidently, "religion is or should be expressed in practical works. It would be impossible, for us, I think, to endure or allow such poverty as you have here in your country, Darya. We would try to do something about it and that would be part of our religion."

"What else?" Darya demanded again, his gaze not wavering.

"What else? Well, I suppose the church, its worship and so on."

"But what of the soul?" Darya pressed. "What of the mind, the heart, the communion with God?"

"It is individual," David said.

"You," Darya said relentlessly, "what is it to you?"

"Not very much, I am afraid," David acknowledged. "I have gone to church with my parents, I take communion, the bread and wine, you know. I used as a child to pray, I do not do so now. Since my mother died, I have thought about such things more than before, but I do not know how to begin to pray again. I cannot pray as a child and I do not know how to pray as a man. Indeed, I am not con-

35

vinced of the reality of prayer, though certainly I believe in God, or I cannot say I do not. I have no explanation, otherwise, for the universe."

"All this is not religion," Darya had said thoughtfully.

It was true that one could see the lotus closing. David noticed at this moment when Darya spoke that the heavy flowers were lifting their petals slowly from the water, their movement imperceptible, yet positive, as the sun sank down behind the walls of the garden.

"Then what is religion?" he asked and turning his head he looked full into Darya's wonderful face, so living and lighted a face, so young, so confident.

"I cannot tell you," Darya said. "You cannot see it and yet it is everywhere. Shall you go to Benares?"

"I don't know," David had answered. "My father is somewhat unpredictable since my mother's death. We are not yet accustomed to being alone."

"You must not say she is dead," Darya said. "I read of it in the newspapers in London and that is why I was friendly with you at once when we met. But she is not dead, she is born again."

"We also are told that the dead live," David said.

"Ah, but I mean really alive," Darya said with enthusiasm, "and you need not grieve for her. You may even meet her and you should be watchful."

"You spoke of Benares," David reminded him. He did not care to think of his mother living again in an unknown shape which he could not recognize, and he supposed that was what Darya meant.

"Ah yes," Darya said, "it was only to say that there you could realize what religion is. Oh, it is a filthy city, you know, but you must remember that it is as old as Egypt, already great when Rome was founded, and that all India hopes to go there, Buddhist and Brahmin alike, to die beside the Ganges. I doubt a western city could be clean if for thousands of years millions of people had gone there to die. It is a repulsive city, I acknowledge it, it is full of beggars and fakirs, but it is also full of pilgrims and it is full of people who most earnestly seek God and with every breath and every act, so that all their life is religion. It is a place where rich men build palaces, where there are wide streets and costly clothes, this silk of my tunic was made there, and Benares is famous for its tapestries of silver and gold. In the old and narrow streets there are beggars and mangy dogs and naked children and unkempt women and peddlers of cheap stuffs and lazy sacred cows and bulls, and lepers—all the dregs of India, if you like, and yet people are driven there by the need for God. Unless you can understand—but how can you? Promise me not to go to Benares, David. I wish you to understand India, and it is there that you will or will not, and I feel your understanding is necessary to me."

"I promise not to go without you," David said.

The evening air, the massive lotus flowers closing their petals over their hearts, the heavy fragrance that flowed from them in the dusk, the magic silent garden spread about David an atmosphere which he had never breathed before. He had never felt so close to any human being as he now did to Darya, not even to his mother, for Darya was a man and young, his own age, and life was before them both, a different life for each, in what different worlds he well knew, and yet their need was the same.

He had longed then to be able to speak profoundly to Darya of Christianity, but he could not. He did not know enough, all that he had learned had been from others and he had nothing of his own to give. And Darya, perhaps, was feeling the same way, longing to give him, an American, the richness he believed was in Hinduism.

"Our religion," Darya said suddenly, "does not spring from one source. Into it many religions have poured their streams, it is great enough to comprehend all and yet it has distilled something unique and individual. Some day I shall be able to explain it to you, but not yet."

They rose, for the dusk was suddenly chill.

"The lotus flowers have closed, just as you said they would, and it is a sight that I have never seen," David said.

"You will see it often," Darya said. "You will come back again and again to India."

"And you will come to America," David replied with young warmth. "When you do, you must always stay with me."

"When I come, if I do," Darya said, "I will stay with you, and meanwhile we will sometimes write to each other."

It was a promise. They walked side by side through the garden and he felt his hand taken by Darya's hand, not closely or even warmly but delicately, kindly, as a token and only of friendship. It would have been a strange act in an American and even repulsive, but somehow it was not so here. He had often seen young Indians walking hand in hand and the act was one of brotherhood. This young Indian accepted him as a brother, and he had never had a brother. His heart stirred but he did not know what to say, and at the gate he still did not know what to say. While the gateman waited, the gate opened, he turned to Darya and put his other hand over their interlocked hands.

"I shall never forget you," he said.

"Nor I you," Darya said.

They had planned to meet again but there had been no other meeting and no visit to Benares. Instead his father has decided abruptly to leave India. Long ago his mother had told him never to interfere when such moments came.

"Your father is a sort of genius and you and I are not. We must be humble about it, Davie."

That was what she used to say, and so he had learned to be quiet in the house, not to ask questions, not even to insist on saying good-night when he went to bed and good-by in the morning when his father went to the office—not for a while, at least, until his father's fearful energy was fulfilled in some new explosion of creation. Thus the MacArd railroads had drawn into their iron grasp vast industries of oil and steel, coal and ore mines, ships and bridges, and these in time produced immense industrial plants and business buildings.

Was it over? He wondered where his father's powerful imagination would lead him now. He sighed, helpless before the dynamo, and then he drew from the bookshelf near his chair a small leatherbound book. It was the New Testament his mother had kept on her table. When he left her for the last time, she was lying dead upon her bed. He had not been allowed to stay. Strangers tiptoed in and

38

waited for him to be gone so that they could begin their work. He had turned away, distracted, and at that moment he saw the little book and took it and alone in his room he had tried to read it and could not and so had thrust it into this shelf.

Now he could take it again, no longer fresh from her hand, and yet her touch was upon it and upon him. He let the pages fall open and his eyes fell upon a passage she had marked. She was given to marking lines in books and especially here. "Except a man be born again, he cannot see the Kingdom of God."

He read the words slowly. Rebirth, the words that Darya had used, but what did they mean, not in India, but here and now, for him?

MacArd was back in his office. Here he was used to being without Leila, and he plunged into the affairs which had accumulated during his absence, the large affairs which no one but himself could settle. He had trained his men to bring to him nothing except the crucial and the fundamental, and MacArd men knew better than to bring a problem to him unsolved. He expected them to present their problems with their own solutions for his approval or disapproval.

"I pay a man to solve problems, not to bring them to me," was his favorite retort.

Everywhere through the immense MacArd Building one came upon placards whereon was printed a sentence in capital letters, EVERY PROBLEM HAS A SOLUTION—FIND IT and MacArd men were hired and fired upon the basis of whether they took the slogan seriously. He allowed no ribaldry, no mockery, not even mild joking about it. A young man had once been making merry with a parody and MacArd had come stalking in to dismiss him as he stood.

"There is a time to laugh and a time not to laugh," he had thundered.

He knew his Bible and he was fond of speaking in Biblical language. He liked to think, and sometimes to say that he had been blessed with gold and possessions; with thousands of acres of land in the west, wherein sat mines of iron and silver; with networks of

39

steel in railroads; with merchant ships upon all the oceans of the globe; with vaults in many banks, hiding their treasure of stocks and bonds in a score of vast interlocking industries. The numbers of men who served MacArd were thousands, men whose faces he never saw, men who spent their lives in mines under the earth, who drove his great engines, who manned his machines in factories, who captained his ships, and busied themselves upon the intricate matters of accounting and accumulating the figures which presented to him daily exactly what he was worth. He spent his days in this big office overlooking the harbor and the Statue of Liberty, a room as big as a house, furnished in velvet carpets and hangings and great mahogany tables and chairs, and his desk was his fortress.

While his wife lived, she had made his sole alternative to this life. When he came home at night she was there, a figure of sweet gayety and mild ironic humor, a woman who loved him and who was never afraid of him. He knew she was not afraid, and it was good for him to know that there was one person who did not walk softly before him, and before whom indeed he must not assume even his rightful air of conquest. For he had never wholly conquered her, she had remained her wilful independent self, taking refuge in wilfulness and refusing logic if she chose emotion.

"But why—" how many of his sentences to her had begun thus while they talked.

She never allowed him to go on. "Oh why, why, and I don't care why, that's why!" Thus she had chanted until at last after years of stubborn persistence he had given up and then somehow when he had given up and she knew that he had, their relationship became sweeter and deeper than ever, and he had fallen in love with her again. He was a man passionate and faithful, a righteous man, secretly romantic at the core, and she knew it. She held him by the heart.

There were times now, since he came home from India, when he starved for her, when, in the midst of his day's work, absorbed as he was with the space and the speed of all he did, he stopped for a moment, for ten minutes or for an hour, to battle with desperate loneliness. While she was alive he could forget her all day, but now

40

that she was dead her spirit came dancing into this room where actually she had been but a few times while she was alive.

"I dislike that castle of yours," she had said. "You sit there like a king on a throne. King David, King David, but I am not your subject, just the same!"

He could almost hear her laugh. This morning near midday, here in his office he could have sworn that he heard the echo of her laughter, and he lifted his head sharply. He was alone, studying the pages of a proposal for the purchase of new mines in South America, and he heard in the silence of the great room her distant laughter. She was not here, of course, not even the presence of her spirit was here, yet who could tell? He had always rejected the dreamful wishing of men who sought mediums and tried to raise the spirits of their dead, and yet he believed at last that somewhere she lived, cut off from him by an impenetrable wall. Who knew the thickness of the wall?

Since that day in the hotel in Bombay when he had been reminded, or had reminded himself, he was not prepared to say which, but at any rate, when inexplicably he had remembered the words concerning the narrow Judean gate called The Eye of the Needle, through which a camel could hardly pass, as hardly as the rich man could pass into the Kingdom of Heaven, since that day he had not once felt near to Leila. He had tried to imagine what she might want him to do, but she was afar off, and he had rushed away abruptly from India without finishing the journey. Now here in the midst of his day's work, he felt her near again.

He sat tense, his fists clenched upon the desk, concentrating upon the thought that she might actually be nearer than he knew, and sweat burst from his skin. He all but saw her, he felt her presence surely for an instant. Then he could not persuade himself that it was anything beyond the longing of his own heart and he turned cold, his sweat chilled, and he collapsed and bent his head upon his folded arms. In the depths of his disappointment he felt impelled to prayer.

"God," he groaned aloud, "God, show me what she means. What is it I am meant to do?"

41

He waited in the silence and no voice spoke, until he heard his own voice lifted up, continuing, or so it seemed, in prayer.

"Thou knowest that all I have is Thine."

These were the words he stammered, they came from within him, they spoke themselves, as though someone else spoke through his lips, someone voiceless using his voice.

It was a strange experience quickly over, he was himself again almost immediately and yet he felt changed. He was bewildered, he was almost sure that more than his imagination had been here, yet he would have been ashamed to confess it, and had the door opened and one of his employees come in he would have been more brusque than usual. Had Leila somehow managed, not quite to break through the wall, but still to touch his memory again and so impel him to the words he had just spoken? Did she want him to know that if they were to be united beyond the wall there were things that he must do which he had not yet done, a consecration of his wealth which he never made? There was the chance. He was a practical man, but like all incredibly successful men who made their own miracles, he had regions past belief, imaginations which were possible realities. Much that had once been only imagination had indeed become real, and so why not anything?

"All that I have is Thine—"

The echoes lingered, and after an instant he struck the bell on the desk harshly. A middle-aged man came in, his secretary. He had never taken to the fad of having a woman in his office, he did not think women should be in business, certainly he did not want a strange woman near him now.

"Thomas, see if Dr. Barton is at home and ask him if he will lunch with me today at one o'clock?"

"Yes, sir," the man replied.

He went away and returned in a few minutes, noticing no difference in the grizzled figure at the desk. "Dr. Barton will be delighted, Mr. MacArd. Shall I give orders for the small dining room?"

"Yes," MacArd said. When he was alone he had a tray brought him from the kitchen suite on the top floor. When he had a business conference he ordered luncheon in the paneled dining room, but there was also a small glass-enclosed room on the roof, from where one could look out over the river and see the ocean far beyond. Only a most intimate associate ever lunched with him there, and sometimes Leila had come to dine with him on days when he could not leave the office at night. Together they had eaten and drunk, and then for a few minutes, before he went back to his desk and she went home, he always turned off the lights so that she could see the dazzling city spread before her.

"All yours, my sweet, my queen," he used to say. "Yours, if you want it, to play with or to weave in a necklace or in your hair."

He had not used the room since she died. Now, when Thomas was gone, he threw down his pen and whirled his desk chair to face the wide window at his back. There gazing over the roof tops into the mild blue sky he reflected upon what it might cost him to acknowledge the full meaning of the words that an hour ago had been torn from his own lips.

Dr. Barton listened respectfully to this richest man in his congregation. He was not a coward and had he felt it his duty he could have spoken plainly even to the great MacArd. Fortunately it was not likely that such would ever be his duty. MacArd was a man rigidly respectable, without grace, perhaps, but good, and if there were rumors of his ruthlessness in business, Dr. Barton supposed that a certain amount of that harsh quality was necessary for success. Caesar had qualities which did not belong to Christ, but which nevertheless were entirely suitable to Caesar.

"It is a stupendous idea, Mr. MacArd," Dr. Barton said with profound feeling.

He had enjoyed the luncheon, the dishes were prepared with perfection, and he had tried to check his appetite. MacArd ate with careless speed, accustomed doubtless to such food, but it was a feast even for a minister as well placed as Dr. Barton. He knew that gluttony was the vice into which many men like himself fell, and he struggled continually against it. A fat man of God, a voluptuous

43

priest, was repulsive if not actually sinful, and he did not deceive himself. Gluttony was also a sensual vice.

"You like it?" MacArd demanded. "You see the need?"

"It is an idea worthy of your managerial genius," Dr. Barton replied.

"It is the fruit of my trip to India," MacArd replied. "The Indians need a decent religion, a creed that will make men of them instead of supine animals. Practical Christianity is the answer, Barton, a vital, missionary creed that will destroy their idols, clean out their vile temples, and give them energy. I say India, but I mean the world. I want to establish a center of virile Christian training from which men will go out into all the world, preaching a gospel of faith and works. I shall make it a memorial to my beloved wife. I want it called the Leila MacArd School of Theology. I want the standards to be the highest and the men to be of the best. I want you to help me find the right place for it and then choose the best men in the country for the faculty. When a man says he is a graduate of MacArd, it must mean that he is a man of natural technical ability trained to the highest degree to spread the gospel of Christianity."

A waiter came in noiselessly to remove the plates and the butler served the dessert, a creamy ice and small cakes and hot coffee. MacArd pushed his dish away.

"Bring me apple pie and cheese," he ordered.

"Yes, sir," the butler replied, and taking the dish away he was back again with a quarter of apple pie, while the waiter presented a tray of various cheeses.

MacArd pointed to a sharp Norwegian cheese and talked on rapidly while the waiter served him.

"First the place," he proclaimed, "then architects to design the finest possible buildings."

Dr. Barton was overcome. "Do you have any financial figure in mind, Mr. MacArd?"

"I am not thinking in figures," MacArd replied. "I am thinking only of achievement."

44

"Admirable," Dr. Barton murmured. "It is quite possible that the world will be changed as a result of what you do."

He ate his cream ice thoughtfully and nibbled a cake. He hoped that he was not thinking of himself, he earnestly strove not to do so, but it was quite possible that Mr. MacArd would offer him the position as the first President of the MacArd School of Theology. It was of course to be a memorial to Mrs. MacArd, but inevitably it would be known as the MacArd School. She would have been the first to recognize that necessity. He remembered her as a slender tall woman, always gracious, and disturbing only because one was not quite sure whether she was about to laugh. Sometimes when he was preaching with the utmost sincerity he had chanced to look down upon her in the MacArd pew, the central front pew, and he met her eyes fixed upon him and he had caught in them the brightness of laughter. He had learned not to look at her in church.

MacArd tapped the tablecloth with his large fingers. Bunches of red hair shone between the knuckles.

"Well," he said briskly. "I guess that's all, Barton. You have your job cut out for you. You can have any help you need here at the office, leg men and so on."

"Thank you," Dr. Barton said. "I prefer to do some preliminary reconnoitering myself, if you don't mind. We don't want to duplicate existing institutions."

"There doesn't exist such an institution as I plan," MacArd said heartily. "It is something unique, something great, a center of missionary force. MacArd men must know it is their duty to go into all the world, not settle down in some comfortable pulpit here at home."

Dr. Barton tried to be humorous. "I trust you are not speaking of me."

"Of course not," MacArd replied. "Our churches have to be supplied. Besides, you are not a young man. It is the young who must undertake the sort of thing I have in mind."

Dr. Barton was relieved. He rose, conscious of an atmosphere thickening with impatience.

"I shall let you hear from me in a very few days, Mr. MacArd,"

45

he said. He rose, a pleasantly rotund figure, and shook hands warmly with his chief parishioner and went away.

Summer crept over the city in a mist of heat. Great houses along the Avenue were closed and the families went away to Bar Harbor, to Newport and the coasts of New England. In other years David had gone with his mother to a quiet beach in Maine that faced the south because of the curving bay. This year as a matter of course he stayed on in the city, breakfasting each morning with his father and he was there at night to dine with him when he came home. He knew that his father worried about him intermittently between bouts of work, and he endeavored freshly every day to be cheerful and sympathetic, ready to listen to whatever his father chose to tell him. It did not occur to him to share his own thoughts or feelings, not only because he had never done so, but because there was nothing, he would have said, to share. He was not unhappy, the loneliness for his mother had settled into a dreamy melancholy and he spent his days in a continuing peace which he knew was only an interval. Some time soon he must make up his mind about what he wanted to be. One thing he knew, that he would not go into his father's offices, but this was not expected of him. So much his mother had done for him during the years she had made it quite plain that David was not like his father and must not be expected to follow in those immense footsteps.

"David will do something quite different from you, King David," she had said. The name his mother used for his father suited him and yet she had taught the son to perceive that however autocratic his father might be there was always the core of romance in him. "It's romance that makes your father want to conquer the world," his mother had once told him. "Long ago I tried to make him stop, we had enough money, more than we could ever spend, and then I saw that it wasn't more money he wanted but greater dreams. Each dream leads to another as it becomes reality. The world is his theater and he is playwright, designer, producer, director, and star actor."

She had laughed that day and then was suddenly grave. "And

46

never forget, David, that he is really a king, a man among men. Your father could never do a small or petty deed. Oh, he can be cruel in a big way, but I've always known that if he saw the human beings he was cruel to, he would stop everything to rescue them, even from himself. The trouble is he doesn't see them unless someone shows them to him. That is my business. Only I don't always find them."

She had made it her business to keep his father human and sometimes in the long quiet days David wondered if now it were his business, too, to keep his father aware of men, the average men, the little men, above whom he towered so high that he seldom stooped to see them. Yet he had seen them clearly enough in India, not individually, perhaps, but the mass of them, swarming in misery upon the starving earth, and he had been angry at their misery.

"What are you doing with yourself, David?" his father asked abruptly one morning at breakfast.

"Nothing at all for a few months," David replied. "I hope by then I shall know what I want to do. Something, of course."

"Want to go to Maine?" his father demanded.

"No, thank you," David said. "I had rather be here with you."

MacArd did not answer this. The words gave him comfort, his son's presence made this still a home, but he must not grow to lean on the boy. He had said nothing of his big plan, and now he felt moved to share it. David might think it absurd, one never knew what the young felt, and there was a good deal of atheism in the colleges. He had never asked David anything about his religious beliefs. He said,

"You might like to help Dr. Barton in a job I have just put up to him."

"What is that?" David asked half idly. He liked the family minister, though without profound feeling. He was an adherent, like the family doctor or dentist, better than Enderby, of course, but he had not liked the sermon Dr. Barton had preached at his mother's funeral. Barton did not understand his mother or appreciate her depth and charm.

"I am planning a great memorial to your mother's memory," Mac-

Ard said. "It is to be a school of theology, a comprehensive institution dedicated to a practical missionary purpose. Barton is looking for suitable sites and we shall engage the best architects. I told him that he could have men from my office if he wanted them, but it occurs to me now that you might enjoy helping him yourself. Perhaps enjoy is not the word. I mean, it might interest you, give you some comfort, to help him. Then you and I could work together, too. I shall appreciate that."

David was too surprised to speak. A theological seminary with a missionary purpose? He was not at all sure that his mother would have chosen such a memorial. But then she would have chosen no memorial at all. She had a gay humility, she disparaged her own gifts merrily and constantly, she rejected the monumental as pompous. Yet he knew her well enough to know, too, that if his father had wished to present her even with a monument, she would have accepted it with tender charm. "How fascinating!" He could hear her say the words again, as he had once heard her say them when his father had given her a preposterous showy necklace of square diamonds from his South African mines.

"Why a school of theology, Father?" he asked.

MacArd undertook earnestly the task of explaining himself to his son.

"It came to me after India. I saw the enormous contrast between the English and the Indian, or between ourselves and those wretched natives, for that matter. There must be some reason why the western world has risen in wealth and power. Call it the favor of God, if you like to use religious terms, which may be as true as any other. But the fact is that the people over there are oppressed by the weight of an evil and superstitious religion, whereas our religion has made us free men. We have overthrown our tyrants, we have been inspired by our faith. Surely men are not so different that what inspires and strengthens some cannot also and likewise strengthen and inspire others. If this is true, and I believe it to be so, then it is my Christian duty to share with the whole world what I myself have, and I am sure your mother would have agreed with me, if she had been with us in India. This is the logical conclusion. The only way

48

to put a big idea into big action is to train plenty of men to carry it out. I propose to do it at the MacArd School of Theology."

"I see," David said. He had listened attentively, his quick mind, accustomed to his father's concise speech, seizing and enriching every word. He had expected to be repelled but he was not. In spite of the unconscious arrogance of his father's voice and bearing, the words themselves had not conveyed arrogance. His father did not, then, despise those dark and hopeless people clinging to their barren land. On the contrary, he implied that had they inspiration like his own there was no reason why they should not have all that he had.

"I'd like to think about what you have told me," he said. "It is interesting. I can see that it might be important."

"It is very important," his father said with emphasis. "I intend to make MacArd Memorial the greatest center in the world for a practical progressive Christianity that will improve the world."

He got up. There was no need for answer. It was time for him to be downtown.

"Good-by, son," he said in his heartiest manner. "Think it over and come with me if you can. It would mean a lot to me."

David said nothing but he gave his mother's smile and MacArd saw the smile and felt the old pang at his heart. So much Leila had left him when she died, and yet it would never be enough, because she had taken herself away. He must so live and so conduct himself that the hope of meeting her again in some eternity might be realized, if such hope was a possibility, as he now believed it was. Indeed, he must believe it was. He tried to return his son's smile, raised his hand in silent gesture and went away.

David poured himself a second cup of coffee. His mother had made it a family habit that they be left alone at this meal, and Enderby did not intrude after he had brought in bacon, eggs, rolls and toast and coffee. Unless someone pressed the bell he would not return until he was sure that no one remained at the table, and David sat drinking his coffee and gazing reflectively into the formal garden upon which the French windows opened. Flowers were

49

blooming in neat beds and at the far end a figure of Italian marble, a slender girl pouring water into a pool from a jar on her shoulder, made a focus for his eyes. His mother had been fond of the figure, a symbol, she had once said to him while they sat together at this table, of life-giving water, flowing from a deathless source. Once when they had been driving through the mountains north of the city they had come upon a vast overflowing lake, one of the reservoirs which supplied the city water, and she had pointed it out to him saying, "The water in our fountain comes from here, and it is the gathered waters of all these hills and valleys, pouring together."

He remembered the way she had looked that summer's day in her duster and veil, her face vivid, her eyes dark and alive, and he felt again the symbolism of her words. Was there indeed an eternal source for man's life, a primal cause, a true reason for the little span of years? He had passed through his first phase of grief, the vivid moment of return had passed and his melancholy now was expressed in vague and thoughtful questions to which he could find no answer. He was lonely and he had begun to long for the companionship of others who were like himself as he now was, and not as he used to be in college. It was impossible to return to the childishness of sports and games and routined lessons. He must penetrate far more deeply into learning, but where and how should he begin? He turned over in his mind the plan his father had put before him. For a moment it seemed preposterous and he doubted his father understood fully what he himself had conceived. A school for religion could grow far beyond the confines of expressed theology. If a body of young and inquiring minds gathered into such a center, who knew what together they might discover? He allowed his imagination to play about the school, developing a place very different from that which his father planned, a place fulfilling a deeper concept, providing an energy not yet in motion, establishing a channel between man and God, such as had never yet been found, discovering if indeed God did exist. When he faced his primary question he could almost heard his mother cry out to him across the space between. She, who had never read theology or cared to hear the reasoning of logicians, accepted the being of God as the simplest explanation of created form and beauty. From whence had come the earth and its flowering if not from Someone?

"It is so much easier to believe than to doubt," she had said to him.

He finished his coffee and went to the telephone and called Dr. Barton.

"This is David MacArd, Dr. Barton."

"Oh yes, David, what can I do for you?"

"My father has just told me of his great idea. He suggests that I might be useful to you."

"Yes, indeed," the ministerial voice was professionally cheerful. "I have just been looking at some sites. That's the first thing, isn't it? The place is important, the repose, the proper isolation and yet not too remote from railroad stations. The practical combined with the spiritual, eh, David? Come along to my study, my dear boy. You'll find me in a fog of confusion. I shall be glad of your listening ear."

"Very well, I'll be there soon."

He hung up and then climbed the wide stairs slowly. The house was as still as a tomb and on a sunny morning like this he was glad to be out of it.

The air in Dr. Barton's office was warm and slightly fragrant, as though a fire had been lit, sprinkled with incense and allowed to go out again. The dying smell of old leather-bound books and the mildly acid taint of printer's ink mingled with the scent of an immense bowl of roses on a table under the window.

"My wife's contribution to the day's work," Dr. Barton said when he saw David's eyes straying again and again to the roses.

"They make me think of my mother," he said.

"Ah, we miss her," Dr. Barton replied, with emotion that just escaped being unctuous. "But it doesn't do to think of the past, dear boy."

"She doesn't belong to the past," David said.

51

"Ah no, of course not," Dr. Barton agreed quickly. "Shall we proceed, David? I don't want to hurry you, if you feel you would like to talk a while of your dear mother—"

"No, it was only the roses." He drew his chair to the desk and took up the sheets of paper that Dr. Barton had put down.

"You will see," the minister said, "that I have nothing conclusive. A fine tract of land lies over here northwest of the city. It can be had for ten thousand dollars. There are good building sites on it. What would you say to running up there today and seeing it for yourself? Then you could corroborate what I am planning to tell your father on Friday at noon, when he has kindly invited me to come and have luncheon with him again, a report of progress, so to speak. It is a great responsibility."

"I would like to go and may I take this map?"

"By all means," Dr. Barton said. He was secretly a little glad to be rid of so grave a young man to whom nevertheless he must be cordial, since he was the son of a benefactor. Why, he wondered, had MacArd decided to offer his own son as an aide? Did he distrust, possibly, the minister's practical judgment? He took out his watch. "There is a train in just three quarters of an hour which will get you there nicely before noon. It is only an hour's run. At the station you can ask for the livery stable, it is not too far, and half an hour's drive with horse and buggy will get you to the spot. There's an old farmhouse near by. Just ask for Miller's Creek. There's a train back at five o'clock."

David took the map and studied it a moment. The dismissal was a trifle too swift.

"What do you make out of my father's plan, Dr. Barton?" he asked after a moment. He folded the map and put it into his pocket.

The minister looked surprised. "A very noble idea," he replied. "A center of the best training for young leaders of the church."

"My father emphasized to me the practical missionary aspect," David said.

"Ah yes," Dr. Barton replied in his swift smooth agreement. "Quite rightly. The church militant is a missionary one. 'Go ye into

52

all the world,' and so forth. A civilizing uplifting influence, proclaiming the gospel, teaching men the right, revealing the true faith. This is an age of expansion, and if our country can carry aloft the banner of God, we cannot fail."

David leaned back in the comfortable chair, his hands in his pockets, his eyes intense and thoughtful upon Dr. Barton's smooth-shaven, well-fed face. It would be unwise, if not useless, to argue at this point when there was not even a piece of land for the school. Later he would talk with his father. He was astute enough to divine by instinct that Dr. Barton looked upon him as a potential enemy, wanting no son between himself and the father.

He rose, "I had better move on if I am to catch that train."

Dr. Barton was still anxious. "Will you report direct to me, dear boy? I feel responsible to your father."

"Certainly," Daivd said. "I realize that I am supposed to be helping you, sir."

They shook hands and he left the close sweet air of the study and went into the outer freshness. It was one of the city's rare days, the winds blew in from the sea and cleansed the streets of smoke and mist. He headed for the station, reaching it early enough to buy a couple of sandwiches for his luncheon later on in the hills. In the train the car was almost empty at this hour of the day, and he sat by a window and gazed at fleeting tenements and dirty streets, comparing them in his mind with the crowded sidewalks in Bombay and the dusty squalor of Indian villages. Why should his father dream of sending missionaries to India and China or to any part of the foreign world when here not five miles from his own door were heathen as valid as any to be found? He knew very well the answer to this. His father would declare again, as he had often declared before, that idleness, the fruit of laziness, was the sole cause for poverty in a rich country, and he would give himself as proof. Had he not been poor, the son of a country parson, and had he not raised himself without help until today he was one of the richest men in the world? What he had done others could do in any free and Christian country.

"But could I?" David inquired of himself. He did not believe that he could, if he had been born in a filthy room level with the track. He looked into one sordid cell after another as the train rolled by and he saw dirty children, frowsy women, unshaven men, broken furniture. Had he been born there he could not have pulled himself out of it. Crushed by such fate, who would have delivered him? No one, for no one came to deliver such people.

He turned his troubled mind away from a problem he could not solve, and was grateful that the tenements gave way to scattered streets and then to the pleasant countryside. Here was something better to be seen, indeed, than the countryside of India. Instead of dry and barren fields, dust beneath the heat of a burning sun, here were green crops, trees and grass and comfortable farmhouses, barns to store harvests and place for children's play. Why should not a practical religion destroy the tenements? But he knew that his father would say that tenements could not be destroyed. If they were, others would spring up to take their place. In their separate ways Darya and his father were alike. Darya would say that tenements did not matter. They were man's fate, but man's abodes were transient, and there was no reason why a tenement could not be as suitable as a mansion, a habitation for a saint.

Nor would Darya consider the obvious retort. "But you, Darya, live in a mansion and it is easy for you to talk of a tenement as suitable. You will never live in a tenement."

And Darya would say in his laughing fashion, "Ah, but I was born in a mansion, and I live only where I was born. Had I been born in a tenement, then I would live there. It is meaningless, this difference between mansion and tenement, so long as I am one with God."

His father, David knew very well, did not dream of destroying poverty, which was the result of what he would call shiftlessness. Poverty was a very proper punishment for such behavior. His father believed that through the right religion civilization could develop which would provide opportunity for all, and then men like himself would rise as he had risen, and those who did not make use of op-

54

portunity were the surplus, the scum, useless except as they provided labor. That, in a few words, David thought grimly, was his father's gospel. God was on the side of the strong.

And perhaps his father was right, and who could say he was not? Perhaps the battle was to the strong and the race to the swift.

III

At midafternoon David left the hilltop and walked down toward the river, the Hudson, at this distance from the city a wide and placid stream. He was hot, for he had chosen to walk instead of hiring a rig, and the coolness of the morning had changed to a still white heat under the blazing sun, and the thought of a swim in the river had become a necessity. He had found the site suggested by Dr. Barton, it was a beautiful place, he agreed, a low hilltop surrounded by higher mountains, facing the distant vista of the river. Yet it was strangely remote and silent, far from human life. He had eaten his sandwiches on the grassy flat, his back against a grey rock, his feet outstretched, and he had tried to imagine buildings, people, young men and their teachers, living here. It was too much like a monastery, he decided, too different from the crowded streets of Bombay and the tenements of New York, and he began to be troubled by the whole idea of the school which was to be a memorial to his mother.

How did men learn of God? How be born again? It would be easy to absorb the message of earth and sky, and creation might seem divine at this height, but would the lessons learned in such idyllic schooldays serve when the days were over? He searched thoughtfully his own experience of religion, nothing very valid, he feared, the usual business of Sunday School and church, and then when he was at prep school and college the required chapel. He could not say that he had ever had an experience of God, although he had joined the church of his parents when he was sixteen or so because it was the right thing to do, or perhaps only the proper thing, and for normal human beings that might be the same thing. He knew that he was not a natural rebel, there had been nothing in his life against which to rebel, and he had found life good until his mother died. He lay back on the grass after he had eaten and lying with his arms under his head and his eyes closed, he thought about his mother. It was impossible to believe that she was not alive, in whatever form she might be. She had been too vivid a creature, too positive, too gay to be dead. It was easier to believe that she lived, and that from somewhere at this very moment she looked upon him and knew what he was thinking. She had always an instinct so aware of him that she had often been able to divine his thinking. People were talking a lot about mental telepathy these days, but it might be something more. Nobody knew, and perhaps faith was the easiest way when the alternative was ignorance. It was as wise to assert as to deny when there was no way of knowing anything. Even science was limited. Thus far, it could only deal with chemicals and physical forces. One had to choose.

The sun beat upon him and the wind died down and he slept for an hour and awoke thirsty and hot. Yet he was conscientious and he roamed about the hilltop before he decided that the place was good enough, beautiful if one wanted that, and that he might as well agree with Dr. Barton. The wide silvery band of the river shining through a valley between the low mountains tempted him. It could not be more than a mile or two away straight downhill, and the railroad ran near enough so that he had only to follow it southward to come to a station. He found a small path and by following it or leaving it to crash through trees, he reached a level height on a mild cliff which he had not noticed from above.

The level was that of a spacious lawn where the grass had not been clipped and in the midst of the lawn he saw a large and even splendid house. It was occupied, there were chairs on the porch behind the massive pillars which reached from the roof in the style of the Greek Renaissance in the South. Yet, despite the splendor, the house looked untended. Terraces led down to sunken gardens on either side and there the rose bushes grew too high. A solitary

57

peacock walked slowly on the edge of the upper terrace, its tail folded and dragging.

He drew near and saw that the wide front door was open, although no one was about. A magnificent site this, he thought, only a few hundred feet above the river, which made a sweeping westward curve as though to add more magnificence. Then the peacock saw him and began to screech and bridle. It stretched its small foolish head and lifted its tail and almost immediately he heard a girl's voice from the garden.

"Oh, Pilate, do be quiet!"

She stood up and David saw her, a dark pretty girl, too slender for her height. She saw him and walked toward him, a trowel in her earthy hand, and there was mud on her forehead where she had brushed aside her hair.

"Hello," she said, "what do you want?"

"I am looking for the river," David said. "I want a swim."

"Well, the path goes there." She pointed with the trowel. "You'll find some decrepit wooden steps and at the bottom of them is the river. If you don't trust the steps you'll have to slide down the cliff. It's not too steep."

"Thanks," David said and lingered. She stirred his imagination. "What a beautiful house," he said.

The girl came toward him and stood a little distance from him. "It is beautiful, isn't it?" she agreed. "It's my home. We don't live here in the winter since my father died, but we come as early as we can in the spring, my mother and I, so that I can get the flower beds into shape. Still, it's July before I get it anything like the way I want it."

He restrained his curiosity. Why had she no help? "It's a job," he said. "I shouldn't like to have to do it all myself. Haven't you any neighbors?"

"No," she said rather shortly. She was not thinking of him, that was clear, she was biting the edge of her crimson lower lip. Her mouth was very pretty, almost perfect in its bow, but it was too small. Her smooth olive skin was flawless, and her dark brown eyes were clear. Her hair was straight and she wore it pulled back tightly

58

from her face and knotted rather high from her nape. The hand that held the trowel was small, too, and just now badly scratched and very dirty.

"The place is for sale," she said abruptly.

So that was what she had been trying to say, he thought, she had been trying to decide whether she could bear to say it. He could see that she loved the house.

"I am sorry to hear that, since it is your home," he said gravely.

"Oh, it's no use!" She made the words a sudden cry and she threw down the trowel. "I know we can't keep it up. Mother tries to do the housework and I try to do the gardening, and we can't. We used to have six servants here and they were always busy."

"I can imagine that," he said, wanting to help her not to weep. "We have a place in Maine something like it. My mother is dead, and I don't think I'll ever go back there."

At this moment his own inspiration came to him. If the house was for sale, why should not his father buy it and make it the center of the school? There could not be a better site, the trees were old and handsome, the gardens ready to cultivate again, and the house had the air of life about it, in spite of its present state. It did not seem remote, it was not a piece of wilderness, it was a place where people had lived and could still live.

"Look here," he said to the girl, "this seems very brash, perhaps, but it happens that my father is looking for a place to found a theological seminary as a memorial to my mother, and it occurs to me that this might be the place—if you really must sell, that is."

The girl looked at him, her dark eyes penetrating.

"No?" he asked, half smiling.

"I am frightened," she replied. "I was almost daring God to help me, hating him, really, because I am so desperate. I know this is our last summer. My mother can't go on, and I couldn't possibly manage alone. But what does one do? I haven't been taught how to earn my living. And I was just saying, God, if you don't help me now, I'll never say another prayer, or I'll never believe in you again. Then Pilate screeched."

"I suppose many a prayer has been answered by coincidence,"

59

David said, hesitating for the right words. The girl was so intense, so vivid in her darkness. "I might say that God answered my prayer, too, that I find the place I wanted to find for my father."

His native prudence touched him at this point. The matter of price was not his concern and he must not discuss it, or seem too eager.

"Come inside," the girl said. "You'll want to see the rooms. There are twenty of them, quite large."

"I ought to introduce myself—David MacArd."

"I am Olivia Dessard." She put out an earth-soiled right hand and he clasped it for a second. "Mother will be glad to see you. We don't have guests any more."

She led the way along the brick path and up the stately steps to the wide porch beneath the pillars, and then into an immense hall which ran straight through the house and opened upon a wide terrace and the vista of the curving river. "Please wait in the drawing room," she commanded him with a gesture. "I will find my mother."

He went into a room of fading magnificence, a museum of mahogany pieces of French furniture and tapestries. It was clean, the furniture dusted, and upon the center table was a bowl of small white lilies. He sat down in a highback chair and waited. Great windows stretched from ceiling to floor, and at the end of the room a marble mantelpiece supported a group of Watteau figurines. The place was well beloved, he could see that, and the more he looked about him, the more enamored he was of his idea.

He heard footsteps but no voices, and then Olivia came, holding by the hand a small grey-haired woman with a tired imperious face. "This is my mother, Mr. MacArd."

"Mrs. Dessard," David said. He put out his hand and took a hot swollen little hand, still soapy from dishwashing, he supposed, or scrubbing of some sort.

"Olivia is so impetuous," Mrs. Dessard said in a high voice. "I hadn't time to dry my hands properly. You must excuse the dampness."

He decided to come to the point. "Your daughter has told me of your courage, Mrs. Dessard. I admire it immensely."

Mrs. Dessard sank down on a satin covered chair. "Olivia says you are interested in buying the house for a religious purpose. That would make me be very happy. I have always been religious, although our faith has been sorely tried in late years. But God works in mysterious ways and maybe this was all planned." She broke off, her eyes suddenly filled with tears, and she shook her head. "You mustn't mind me. The loss of my dear husband—" her voice broke on the words.

"Miss Dessard told me," David said gently.

Olivia interrupted. "Is your father David Hardworth MacArd? Mother asked me."

David turned to her. "Yes, he is," he said unwillingly.

"We read about your mother's death," Mrs. Dessard said. She had got the better of her tears. "We met once or twice, I think, at Mrs. Astor's parties. But we have lived very much abroad. My dear husband was French, not Catholic, however. His family was Huguenot, but they did not emigrate further than Holland, and then they went back again. Mr. Dessard had business in New York and Paris. Olivia is our only child, though we lost an infant son—"

"Mother, Mr. MacArd is not interested in our family history," Olivia said.

Mrs. Dessard bridled. "I am sure he is, Olivia. It is important to know with whom one deals and he will want to tell his father. Mr. Dessard lost his fortune in the panic, Mr. MacArd, else we would never have been left as we are now. We could live in Paris, of course, and indeed we own a small house there, inherited from Olivia's grandfather Dessard, but she loves America. She will not live in France."

"I love this house," Olivia said wilfully.

Mrs. Dessard turned to her with the impatience of old unended argument. "I know, my dear, and so do I, but what can we do?"

Olivia turned to David impetuously. "Will you let us come and visit you sometimes?"

He laughed. "Of course, but the house is still yours. My father will want to make up his own mind."

It was time to go. The two ladies, each wilful after her own fashion as he could see, must not take for granted that the house was sold. He got up and put out his hand to each in turn.

"Good-by, Mrs. Dessard, good-by, Miss Dessard."

"Oh, but you must see the rooms," Olivia cried.

He had forgotten. "Ah yes, though perhaps we could wait until my father—"

"No, now," Olivia declared, "then we will feel we cannot change our minds."

She began to walk away as she spoke, and he was compelled to follow while Mrs. Dessard looked after them.

"This is the drawing room," Olivia said, throwing open a closed door, "and here is the dining room. The other side of the house is taken by the library and behind that the ballroom. The kitchens are connected but they are in separate buildings above which are the servants' quarters."

He looked at one vast room after another.

"The man who built this house had a perfect sense of proportion," he observed.

"You notice that?" Olivia asked eagerly. "It was my father. He built the house for my mother when they were married. He thought then that they would move to America altogether and he sold his possessions in France and built this house for her and furnished it with heirlooms from his family. Mother was an orphan and she lived with her grandmother. Do you know—?" She named a famous old name of New York.

"Indeed I do," he said respectfully.

"She is the last of that family," Olivia said. "I of course am a Dessard. Now come upstairs."

The staircase was double, winding spirally from each side of the hall, seemingly unsupported and he followed her up the right side and into a circular upper hall, from whence heavy doors gave into bedrooms.

"There are eight bedrooms on this floor," she said, "and six

62

on the floor above. My father wanted a big family and he loved to have guests. You cannot imagine what this house was when I was a child. We lived here the year around, and my father had his own road built to the railroad station. It would have to be repaired, but the roadbed is still good."

She was a competent and clever girl, he could see, besides being handsome. She had a proud carriage in spite of a manner almost unsophisticated, but she was not in the least like the girls he knew in New York, the daughters of Fifth Avenue families, and the children of his mother's friends. She had perhaps been educated abroad, and yet he did not believe so. Perhaps she had simply grown up with her parents here. He could not remember her name among the debutantes of any recent years, but then he had been much away from home.

"This is my own room," she said throwing open a door. "I like it better than any place in the world."

He looked about half shyly; he had never looked into a girl's room before, and this was one strangely feminine for so strong a young girl. The color was rose, the canopied bed was draped in rosy curtains and rose and net were at the windows. The carpet was a bed of flowers.

"It is very pretty," he said.

"I love—I love—I love it," she said passionately.

"I wish you could stay here," he said.

"But I can't," she rejoined, pressing her lips together.

She shut the door abruptly. "I won't show you Mother's room—she wouldn't like it because she hasn't made her bed. She doesn't like me to make it. I make mine before I go outdoors. You see how neat my room is? I am like that."

"Beautifully neat," he agreed with a glint of laughter.

She suspected the laugher and frowned quickly. "There is no need to show you the kitchens. Everything is done well and you would not need to make changes, unless you had many people here."

"Such changes could be made later," he agreed.

They went downstairs, and Mrs. Dessard was still sitting in the

63

chair. She had gone to sleep, however, her head leaning against the cushioned back.

"Poor petite Mama," Olivia whispered. "She is always tired. Yes, we must sell this house. I see it, and I thank God you came today. It makes up my mind."

They tiptoed out of the house and he stood on the terrace overlooking the river.

"Are you religious?" Olivia asked suddenly.

"I don't know," he said honestly.

"I also do not know," she said. "Before my father died, I was not religious, but somehow his death has made me wish to be so, if I know how. That is, I feel now that I would like to believe in God, I mean, really to believe."

"I know," David said.

He turned to her and saw in her dark eyes an honest yearning. He had never met a girl like this, someone so naive and yet so adult.

"I wish we might be friends." He spoke these words with an eagerness not usual to him.

"I would like that also," she said frankly. "I have never had a friend. When Papa was alive we were always coming and going, there was no time."

They clasped hands suddenly and strongly. "I will come back," he promised and he left her standing there on the terrace gazing after him.

He reached home late and tired. "Where's my father?" he asked Enderby as the door opened.

"In the liberry, sir," Enderby answered. Reproach was heavy in his voice. "He's fit to be tied."

"I'll go to him first," David said.

So he went straight to the library and there found his father waiting in motionless anxiety. He knew very well that still terror. He had seen his father waiting like that when his mother died.

MacArd looked up grimly. "Well," he grunted. He took his handkerchief out of his pocket and wiped his forehead. "You're late."

"Terribly," David said. "I should have telephoned, but there was a train waiting when I reached the station, the last, they said, until ten o'clock. I jumped on and thought to explain when I got here."

"You had better get washed and come into the dining room," MacArd said. "The dinner must be dried up."

"You shouldn't have waited, Father."

To this MacArd did not reply. He walked away slowly. He felt weak, exhausted by fright. His quick imagination, so valuable when he was making a plan, could be a curse when it came to someone close to him, the only one close to him since Leila died. He had not imagined it possible for her to die, and since she had, the existence of his son seemed fragile. Yet he must not protect David, it would ruin him. He ought to have had a dozen children. It was impossible to substitute for one's own flesh and blood, but the sooner he got on with his project the better, it would take his mind off himself and his vulnerability.

In the dining room Enderby pulled out the heavy oak chair at the head of the table and rang for the soup to be brought in. He stood looking solemn and thinking that Mr. MacArd should not wait longer for his meal. He was not as young as he once was and the death of his wife had aged him too fast. The second man brought in the tray with the soup tureen and Enderby took up the silver ladle, and filled a plate and put it before his master. At the same moment David came into the room, his face red from quick scrubbing and his hair wet.

"I didn't take time to change, Father," he said in apology.

"Doesn't matter for once," MacArd replied gruffly. He began to eat his soup, an excellent beef broth laced with a dry sherry—very comforting. The plate was empty before he spoke again.

"Well?" he inquired.

David smiled at his father. "What have I been doing all day, I suppose? I think I've found the spot. Of course you have to see it."

"Barton said something about it," MacArd said in the same gruff voice.

David hastened on. "Yes—well, I saw the spot he meant, it's very fine, but I found another nearer the river and it seems to me even

65

better. There's already a road to the railroad station, only about two miles, I walked it and it wasn't bad. There's a house on the spot already, it's for sale, a mansion I ought to call it, twenty rooms, pillared porch, you know the sort of thing—"

"Come, come, catch your breath," MacArd commanded.

Enderby took the soup plates away and the second man brought in a fish filet and steamed potatoes. Enderby put down fresh plates and served the second course.

"Now," MacArd said, "go back and tell me exactly what you found."

David, between bites, told him, dwelling upon the magnificence of the house set upon a leveled hill above the sweeping curve of the Hudson. He described the rooms, the plenteous lands about it, space enough to build a dozen dormitories and halls, the great oak trees and maples, the view across the river for a hundred miles.

"And who did you say owns the house?" MacArd asked.

He had eaten his fish in silence and now Enderby took the plates away and the second man brought in roast beef and vegetables in covered silver dishes.

"A Mrs. Dessard and her daughter," David said. "Mrs. Dessard said she had met Mother at Mrs. Astor's house."

"Dessard—Dessard," MacArd said, reflecting. "Where have I heard that name?" But he could not remember.

"The family was originally French, though of course now they are American," David said. "Mr. Dessard failed in the panic, and then he died, and they have struggled along ever since. They have a small house in Paris but Olivia——"

MacArd frowned, "Olivia?"

"I should have said Miss Dessard," David said hastily.

MacArd ate for a while without speaking and David devoted himself to his plate. He ate slowly and fastidiously and his father ate quickly, and disliked to be kept waiting.

"I suppose," MacArd said at last, "I had better have Barton go and see the place."

"Perhaps I should have told Dr. Barton about it first," David said.

"Nonsense," MacArd retorted. "He can come over tonight."

66

Enderby took away the dinner plates, replaced them with service plates and then sent for the dessert. It was strawberry shortcake with whipped cream and he served it tenderly.

"Will you have coffee now or later, sir?" he asked MacArd.

"Later," MacArd ordered. "Serve it in the library. I shall ask Dr. Barton to join us."

"Yes, sir," Enderby murmured.

David did not speak. They ate their dessert and then MacArd got up abruptly and David followed. They had not taken coffee in the drawing room since his mother died. The doors of the room were closed, and they passed it and went on into the library. The second man had already put the tray on the table and Enderby served the coffee. MacArd took up the telephone and in a few minutes had reached Dr. Barton.

"Come along over now if you can," he suggested in so forcible a tone that it was a command.

Dr. Barton agreed, David supposed, for in a moment his father replied. "Good—we aren't waiting, but there will be a cup of hot coffee for you." He hung up.

"Did you say anything about the price of this place?" he inquired.

"No," David said, "I didn't think that was proper. You may not like the idea at all, or Dr. Barton may not."

"Dessard," MacArd murmured, "Dessard? I have heard it somewhere."

They sipped their coffee in silence. Whatever MacArd was thinking he did not tell his son, and David sat relaxed, his mind roving over the day. He felt rested and weary together, weary in body and rested in spirit from the day of sunshine and air and widespread views. He had not been in the country since they left India, and this was different country indeed. He had a comforting sense of richness and plenty, of confidence and security. It was good to be American, he was glad to be born what he was. And then he thought of Olivia and her lovely troubled face. She had such a pretty mouth, though too small, and magnificent hair. Very likely such hair would come far below her waist if she allowed it to hang. His mother's hair had been long like that, dark, too, but not coal

67

black as Olivia's was. They were not alike, except that both of them had an intrepid air, a natural daring. Olivia had no laughter, and laughter had been his mother's golden gift. Olivia had not once laughed while he was there, though it was not to be expected perhaps, when they had talked of so somber a matter as selling the house she loved.

"Dr. Barton, sir," Enderby said.

The handsome grey-haired minister came in, smiling and cordial. David sprang to his feet, but MacArd did not rise as they shook hands.

"Good of you to come on a moment's notice, Barton."

"I always come if I can when you send for me, Mr. MacArd." Enderby poured fresh coffee and MacArd turned his head.

"Leave us now, Enderby. Nobody need stay. David can let Dr. Barton out."

"Yes, sir, good night sir."

"Good night," David said because his father did not answer, and the door closed.

"Well, dear boy," Dr. Barton said cheerfully to David, "you are quite sunburned."

David smiled agreeably and looked at his father and MacArd began to talk.

"David has found an interesting place—"

David watched Dr. Barton's neatly bearded face. It was impossible to tell whether he was displeased. The light blue eyes did not flicker, the ministerial calm did not change.

"Splendid—splendid," Dr. Barton murmured now and then.

He was pleased, David decided, perhaps because if the School opened earlier, so much earlier would his place be set in it. Then he despised himself for his readiness to suspect a man perhaps innocent and when his father finished he said somewhat impatiently,

"Father, shall I write Miss Dessard that we will come next week?"

"If you wish," MacArd said, surprised. "I was going to have Barton write to the mother."

"On the contrary," the minister said gracefully, "it will make it more informal if we allow the young people to be in charge."

David changed the subject abruptly. "There are the most awful tenements on the way. One expects them in India but not here."

"Not at all," MacArd said. "That is where men like Parkhurst make such a mistake."

Dr. Barton did not speak. Parkhurst, the minister of a fashionable uptown Presbyterian church, had chosen to ruin himself by attempting to clean up New York. Other ministers observing his predicament had prudently refused to endorse his accusations.

MacArd went on, "It is impractical idealism to think that we can do away with the weaknesses in human nature which produce misery. Nothing is further from my purpose. I intend to bring to the MacArd School of Theology the finest and strongest young men we can find and fit them to go out and preach and practice a virile gospel that will attract men like themselves. I purpose to offer an opportunity to all alike, but I know perfectly well, whether this be done in our own country or in India or anywhere in the world, that only a few will respond."

"Many will be called, but few chosen," Dr. Barton murmured.

"Exactly," MacArd said, "but those are the few who count. They are the men who change the world."

David lifted his head sharply, but his father's eyes were not upon him.

A week later MacArd stood on the terrace of the Dessard house overlooking the river. He was pleased with his son's imagination. The place was beautiful, the house was sound. He liked having a great mansion at the heart of his memorial to Leila. New buildings could be grouped about it, but the center would be here in these lofty rooms.

He turned to Olivia Dessard. "I will buy the house," he said abruptly. "If your mother cares to sell some of her larger pieces of furniture, I will include those. My lawyers will visit her here or in the city, as you please. By the way, the name, Dessard—it seems to be familiar to me and yet I cannot place it. What was your father's business?"

Olivia looked into the deep-set grey eyes under the thick grizzled red eyebrows. "He owned land in the West, Mr. MacArd, much land, and he raised beef. But he was ruined because the railroad on which he depended for shipping his steers increased its rates until he could no longer ship."

MacArd remembered suddenly. A small railroad, ending in Chicago, served at its farthest reach an area in Wyoming on the eastern side of the Rockies. It was only one of the small railroads which he had absorbed into his own great central system and he had done it by lowering freight rates until competition ceased. He had then bought the small railroad cheaply. Dessard was not directly connected with him, but that was how he had heard the name. A Dessard had been one of several owners who had brought suit against his main company and they had lost. He wondered if this girl, standing here so trim in her white shirtwaist and black skirt, knew that story. If she did, she gave no sign of it and he did not make a test of her memory. A fate brought him here to Dessard's house, God's leading, if one wanted to call it that, something more at least than coincidence. He resolved to be generous to Dessard's widow and daughter, not because of obligations, for he had won the suit honestly in the courts, but merely because he liked to be generous when he could.

"I believe your mother suggested tea," he said abruptly.

"Yes, please, in the drawing room," Olivia said.

She led the way and he found Mrs. Dessard and Barton already seated and waiting for him. The girl, he noticed, left them at once, and a few seconds later he saw David walking with her away from the terrace. They were off together, then. He pondered for a moment the possible meaning in this and then decided against its distraction. He had come here to make a bargain.

"With your permission, Madam," he said to Mrs. Dessard, "I will make an appointment for my lawyers to call up yours."

"Very well, Mr. MacArd." Her slightly withered cheeks were very pink but she gave him a cup of tea with a hand that did not tremble.

He had accepted Mrs. Dessard's invitation to drink a cup of tea in the drawing room, but he could not forget that while he and Barton sat with her over the fragile china she had set out on the tea table, David was wandering away somewhere with the girl. He listened to Mrs. Dessard's random talk and to Barton's ceremonious answers and waited.

"Will you show me the path to the river?" David asked. He was confused by his own pleasure in being alone with Olivia again.

"It is easy to find," she said carelessly, but she led the way while he followed.

She was used to the path, he could see, and she guided him down, sure of foot, touching his hand now and then when he offered it to support her over a rock. She was handsomer than he remembered, but still not beautiful, he decided, so much as unusual in her looks. The severity of her white shirtwaist and the black of her skirt and the short waist-length jacket suited her black hair and white skin. He longed inexplicably to know her better, and it was easy to talk with her for she was frank and not at all shy. He had known many girls casually, girls whom he had met at birthday parties when they were children and later at dances and Christmas cotillions and college proms, pretty fluffy merry girls of whom he was wary because he was the son of his father. His mother had laughed at him often for his wariness, pretending distress lest he never present her with the delightful daughter-in-law she pretended she wanted. She made David's wife into a figure at once imaginary and real, and had done so since he was out of knickerbockers. Perhaps had she been less mocking he would have found earlier someone who could attract him.

He was not quite sure that Olivia did attract him so much as interest him. She was a grave sort of girl, unchanging, or so he imagined, who if she gave her word, would stand by it, whether or not it made her happy to do so. But today she almost smiled at him a few times and once when he made a joke she gave a quick laugh, broken off as though it surprised her. They sat down on a log and he talked about India and Darya, and she listened with so remote a look upon her face that he did not know whether she was interested.

71

"Curiously enough, it was India that gave my father the inspiration for all these plans," he said.

"How strange!" she said. "My grandfather Dessard was once in India. He went there to study Hinduism when he was young. I remember he said that India changed everybody who set foot upon her soil."

David laughed. "It didn't change my father—it merely inspired him to want to change India."

At this moment he heard his father's voice and looking up he saw that tall and grizzled figure standing at the top of the cliff shouting for him.

"David! I am ready to leave!"

"Coming!" he shouted upward. He turned to Olivia. "I must go, as you see. But may I come back alone? Then I shall stay as long as you will let me."

"Do come back," Olivia said. Her eyes were fixed upon his face, eyes black, intense, veiled with doubt and question. He smiled, but her look did not change.

IV

He did not see her again for many weeks, partly because of a strange cowardice when he remembered the last look she had given him, partly because he did not want to be present or near while his father took possession of the house.

For MacArd moved with his usual resolution and speed once his attorneys had settled upon a price and he had paid it. He summoned architects to plan three new buildings and design necessary changes in the mansion. For the present the upstairs was to be made into an apartment for the president of the seminary, Barton he supposed, since it was obvious that he wanted the job, and Barton would be obedient to his wishes. He ordered the architects to please the minister and his wife, he ordered Barton himself to call together a suitable number of men to form a Board of Trustees of whom he himself would be chairman, and he directed that the seminary open in the autumn of the next year, with suitable installation services and an imposing catalogue. He designated men from his own offices to carry out his plans, distrusting Barton's practical ability.

"You put your time in on getting the best men you can find for the faculty," he ordered. "I don't know anything about that. Pay them whatever is needed to take them away from their present jobs."

"Historical Theology," Dr. Barton murmured. "Hebrew and Greek, Systematic Theology, Classical Languages, Church History, Exegetical—"

"Yes, yes," MacArd broke in, "that's all your business. What I want is a certain kind of man, you understand, a sound pioneer type."

73

"We shall have to approach the colleges and universities for their best graduates," Dr. Barton said solemnly.

"Of course, of course," MacArd agreed, his eyes restless with impatience. "I am simply telling you what I want. If there is any difficulty about money we can arrange scholarships, though I don't see why we can't get other men in the church to contribute scholarships as their part in it."

"Or chairs of theology, for that matter," Dr. Barton said, anxious to be practical.

MacArd nodded and drummed his fingers on his desk. The interview was taking place in his office, and he was anxious to be done with it, though determined to carry through his plans without delay.

He had an overwhelming anxiety which he could not explain to so simple-minded a man as Barton, who had nothing to do with business. The production of gold this year was evidently going to be the lowest in the history of the country. His figures had arrived from Washington only this morning and they showed an incredible lag in the production of the precious metal. At this hour of the country's magnificent growth, when everything else was expanding with glorious speed, wheat pouring out of the new lands in the west, oil wells spouting fountains of eternal wealth, manufacturing soaring, the total number of miles of his railroads more than three-times what they were a quarter of a century ago, even the population rising to a new height, only gold was short, its increase far behind the demand. Gold simply could not be mined at sufficient speed to meet the need for basic money. He had long toyed with the idea of a process whereby gold could be extracted from low grade ore. Only by such a miracle could prosperity be saved and he saw the miracle like a mirage upon a desert, the glory of a new era, an era when the mountebank, William Jennings Bryan, would be defeated, when all the wild socialistic ideas of Populists and Greenbacks and the Silver Party would be deflated by plentiful gold, when the angry farmers ready to join the ranks of the long-haired Bryan would be appeased. A sound government based on gold would be the foundation for such an expansion in business as the country had never yet seen.

74

"Now, Barton," MacArd said firmly. "I shall have to ask you to get about your business so that I can get about mine. I have to make the money for you, you know."

"Be assured that I take the task as a sacred duty," the minister replied.

His back was not turned before MacArd was roaring into his office telephone, banging a great outspread hand palm down upon his desk. "Get the lawyers here, and tell them to come now!"

Through the days of his father's absorption in a business he did not explain nor David try to understand, the year moved on. There were no parties and no dances, for MacArd had decreed a full year of mourning, and David was left idle, and yet he was not discontented. He had finished college, he had not lived at home for eight years, and while he still missed his mother, there was a pleasant sense of growing freedom in the vast quiet house on Fifth Avenue. A letter from Darya had reached him in the late autumn, and he was moved to write back inviting the young Indian to come for a visit. He had broached the idea to his father today, who, absorbed and abstracted, was nevertheless willing.

"I suppose you are lonely," he said abruptly to David. The morning was grey with approaching November and the house looked somber. Even he could see that a young man alone for the day, and day after day, might find it grim, in spite of luxury and warmth.

"I am not lonely," David said, with his usual good humor. "But I would like to know Darya better."

"Well, have him come, by all means," MacArd said, and then fell into his abstraction again. There was no use in trying to explain the labyrinth of his thoughts. He was going through a creative period during which he could have explained nothing to anybody. He watched the charts of the production of gold as they were prepared for him weekly. As yet very little had happened. The necessary machinery had to be designed and produced, and there had been delay and mistakes. It would be a matter of five years, he began to fear, before gold would become plentiful enough to make the currency of the country sound. Meanwhile the National Treasury was being robbed by anyone who could produce a silver dollar and get its equivalent in gold. The gold thus got did not go into banks but was hidden under mattresses and in chimney nooks and tied up in old stockings. Gold was actually disappearing from circulation, and if this went on long enough a new panic was inevitable. Nothing could stop it. The currency was being debased to a point where it would soon begin to affect the prestige of the nation abroad.

He got up from the breakfast table where he had been grinding out these gloomy thoughts. "Yes, yes," he muttered. "Go ahead and invite the fellow. Tell him to stay the winter if he likes. You could take a trip somewhere, you two. I shan't be able to get away for I don't know how long."

"I wish I could help you," David said, troubled by the grayness of his father's face.

"Nobody can help me," MacArd said.

"It isn't money, is it, Father?" David asked.

"Not my money," MacArd retorted. "But the nation is going bankrupt unless this robbing of gold can be stopped. That long-haired fellow Bryan will be president one of these days if we aren't careful."

David was the usual young college graduate. He did not understand business, finance or politics. If he made up his mind to go with his father he would have to understand them some day, but he was not sure now that he wanted to work with his father. He longed for another life, a different world, where mind and spirit were more important than making money and shaping politics. Why was his father so terrified of William Bryan? Perhaps he would make a good president. It was all in the muddle, the puzzle, the scintillating changefulness of life ahead, and he did not want to face it yet.

"Give me a year, Father," he said with his boyish smile. "A year, and then I shall settle down and try to understand these things, and be of some use to you."

"Take as long as you like," MacArd grunted. Nothing would be solved in a year. He wiped his grizzled mustache with his napkin and left for his office.

It would be a pity, Darya thought, folding David's ardent letter, to leave Poona now just when the weather was at its best and coolest. A few months hence, in February or March, the dry heat would be suffocating and then it would be pleasant to take ship at Bombay and cross the Red Sea and the Mediterranean, saunter through Europe and England and reach America perhaps in June. He had never seen America, although he knew England well. His father was one of the Indians who admired England and who had brought up his children to be half English. Darya spoke English as well as he did his native Marathi, and he had finished at Cambridge with first honors. So that his children could be thoroughly at ease in England his father had built an English house within the compound here at Poona and had employed an English tutor, a Cambridge man, to live there with his sons. All during his youth Darya had been compelled during the week to eat lamb chops, roast beef and Yorkshire pudding, boiled cabbage and potatoes and sweet puddings for dessert. This, his father declared, would fit him for life among the best Englishmen when he went to Cambridge. Only on Sundays were he and his younger brothers allowed to join the family in the big Indian house and eat the delicious spiced Indian foods.

The years in England had passed easily and quickly, he liked English life, although he was often troubled because of the difference between English people in England and in India. In England they were kindly and they did not show airs of superiority, yet once they came to India as rulers they changed and became arrogant and proud. Even the Eurasians, who were only half white, took over these airs. Some day, his father said, it must stop, but no one knew yet how to stop it.

Darya had been attracted to David MacArd in London, and it was natural enough that there should be equality between them, but he had hesitated long before the meeting in India. Yet in Poona David had still been charming and unaffected and different from any white man that Darya had ever known. He was curious now to see the

77

young American in his own country, his own home. The singular attraction held and drew him westward, for what purpose he did not know. He was fond of his pretty Indian wife but his marriage had been arranged by his parents and he did not expect to find companionship of mind and spirit with her. Nor was it easy to find anywhere, for he was repelled by the Anglicized young Indian men, and dismayed by the softness of those who had never crossed the "black waters" to England. In his somewhat singular loneliness he saw the young American as friend and brother.

In May, for it was against his instinct to show haste in spite of his wish, he left India and many weeks later, his ship drew near to the dock in New York. It was his first visit but he had heard of the city, fabulous and new, rising high from its island base. He stood on the deck among the other passengers, ignoring their curious stares, and gazed at the buildings massed against the sky, and he wondered at the skill of the hands that had built them and fixed them there, in spite of storm and earthquake. A foreboding of future power in this white man's land crept over him. There was nothing to stop such men, and he wondered again, as he had so often before, what spirit of restlessness filled the white men of the west, driving them to greater distances, vaster wealth, more abundant power until some day they might conquer the world. As the ship edged nearer to the shore, he half wished that he had not come lest David might not be the modest and gentle young man he remembered.

But his fears were soon forgot. When he came down the gangway, dressed in his best London suit and topcoat and carrying a gold headed cane, he heard David's voice.

"Darya, how glad I am!"

It was the same David, Darya's swift Indian instinct assured him, and then he was shaking hands, both hands, his cane under his arm, and the two young men were gazing at each other with delight, not seeing the glances that were cast at them from other eyes.

"Come along, the automobile is waiting," David urged. He pulled Darya along by the arm.

"I say," Darya protested, "what about my luggage?"

"Oh, that will be attended to," David said. He was ruddy with

78

exhilaration and good spirits, the day was one of soaring wind and bright sunshine and he was proud of the city glittering under the brilliant sky.

"Come along," he cried, "luncheon is ready at home and we shall be alone. Ah, I'm glad to see you, Darya!"

Darya had never been so greeted before by a white man and he felt his heart glow in his bosom with love and excitement. A wonderful country where white men could be like this, where he was urged to come to a white man's home as though he belonged to the family!

"I can't tell you how happy I am," he stammered.

David laughed and then saw the glimmer of tears in Darya's dark eyes. "Why, dear fellow," he exclaimed, "what's the matter?"

"Nothing," Darya said. "I thought perhaps you had changed."

"I change?" David demanded. "Why should I?"

"I don't know," Darya said. But he did know. He had seen too many white men change when they saw an Indian face.

"My friend," Darya said, "you should marry." He had been in the luxurious American house for three weeks, he had seen the city, he had visited the shops and bought gifts for his mother, his young wife and the two children, his three sisters, his aunts and cousins, his father and uncles and nephews. He had gone with David to the theaters, had heard the new music and on Sundays he had even gone to church with David and his father and had listened in some amazement to Dr. Barton, whom he professed not to understand.

David smiled and then blushed faintly. "What makes you say that?"

The two young men had come to a point of intimacy where anything could be said.

"This vast house," Darya said, waving a dark and graceful hand to signify endless empty rooms. "Your father, who has only you. There is a great deal to be said for many sons. I am glad I have two already."

"I keep seeing my mother here," David said. "It would be hard to find anyone to fill her place."

79

Darya looked horrified. "You don't want to fill your mother's place, surely," he exclaimed. "You want to find a wife."

"I would like to find a wife who is as much like my mother as possible," David said.

Darya shook his head. "No, no—a man's wife and his mother should be totally different persons. Anything else is incestuous in concept."

David was innocent enough to look bewildered. "I should say that it was a tribute to one's mother."

"Not at all," Darya maintained. "Any mother in India would choose for her son a wife very different from herself, of equal caste and so on, but that's all."

David did not answer. He thought suddenly of Olivia to whom he had never returned. He had felt a curious and perhaps unnecessary delicacy about pursuing his friendship while his father was buying her home. Nevertheless, he had not forgotten her, as he now realized.

"A relationship between mother and son cannot be continued between husband and wife," Darya was saying with authority. They were in David's sitting room in the late afternoon of a crowded day. They had spent the morning, at Darya's wish, in art museums, had lunched at Delmonico's and afterwards had gone to a matinee. Now, they were smoking cigarettes, a new taste for Darya, and idling before they dressed for dinner. Darya was meticulous about dressing before dining with David's father, whom he admired and professed to fear.

"A man begins something entirely new when he takes a wife," he went on. "Moreover, a real woman does not wish to be also her husband's mother. If she is compelled to this unnatural position she will resent the burden and despise the man. Keep your mother in your memory, my friend, and open your eyes. It is time. It is not well for a man to live celibate when he is young. Afterwards, yes, when he thinks of becoming a sadhu, a saint, it is then becoming enough."

The fluent melodious stream of words poured over David's sensitive ear. If Darya had a fault it was this pouring golden stream of talk, the overflow of his restless and active mind, a penetrating mind, David had to acknowledge, a scintillating searchlight cast upon every person and every object and scene which presented itself. Only today he had grumbled half humorously, and yet with seriousness,

"Darya, I feel that you are showing me New York, rather than the other way around."

For surrounding every experience had been the enveloping glow of Darya's incessant comment, question, conclusion, criticism, humor, and instant understanding appraisal. His was a mind too acute for comfort, and yet in spite of this he was always at ease with himself. In these three weeks David had come not to understanding the young Indian but to the knowledge that here was the most complex person he had ever met, and one whom perhaps he could never fully understand.

He took a daring step. "You advise me to marry, and yet you did not introduce me to your own wife."

Darya opened his immense dark eyes, handsome eyes with heavy curling lashes. "I do not see the connection!"

"In the western mind there is some relevance," David said.

"In the eastern mind, none," Darya declared with dignity. "My wife is shy as most Indian women still are, and she would have been in consternation had I brought her out of her rooms to meet you, and even more embarrassed had I taken you to her. It is not our custom, as yet."

For the first time David was aware of a barrier between them. "I'm sorry if I have offended you, Darya."

"Not at all," Darya rejoined. "It is difficult for people outside to understand the relationships in our country between men and women. Yet they are very profound. Indeed, we find your celibate Christian gods difficult to believe in. Our society is based upon the pure connubial relationship between Rama and Sita. Marriage is lifted to an ideal plane because of them and therefore it is a religious duty."

"Now you are being very Indian, my dear Darya!"

81

Darya wavered between dignity and capitulation and chose the latter. He smiled his slow delightful smile.

"Tell me," he said in a coaxing voice. "According to your abominable western customs, is there no woman in your dreams?"

It was impossible to lie to Darya. He could detect the slightest deviation between thought and word. David said, "Not quite in my dreams, Darya, but hovering perhaps on the edge." And then he told Darya of Olivia, and why he had not gone back to see her. "Yet I suppose," he said, "that I have known all along that I would go back."

"So," Darya said, "why not now? Take me with you. I shall make advantage of your western customs and judge her for myself and see whether she is worthy of you."

He ignored the memorial mansion pointedly, but David did not notice the omission. He would have liked to have laughed off Darya's suggestion, but the young Indian was not easily put aside, as he had learned by now. Darya had an amiable persistence, an affectionate stubbornness, which would not be denied. And then it might be a good thing. He would see Olivia through other eyes, and he would know through his own whether her presence, hovering on the edge of his dreams, was something more than fancy.

"So be it," he replied. He had infused his voice with gaiety to which Darya did not respond. Instead his face was grave while his eyes sparkled dangerously bright.

"What is your father's idea in regard to my country?" he demanded suddenly.

Their eyes met and David drew upon his will not to turn his away first. He was astonished to see that Darya was angry.

"I shall ask my father to explain it to you," he said, still gazing quietly into Darya's eyes. "I fear I have been clumsy."

Darya rose. "It is time to dress, in any event. Therefore I will wait."

They parted for the time, and David waited until dinner was over and the coffee was served as usual in the library. Then he attacked his father with courage.

"Darya has asked to meet Miss Dessard, Father, and I have promised to introduce him. But first he wants to know about the memorial. I think if my father tells you, Darya, you will grasp it as he conceives it."

MacArd put down his cup. "The memorial to my dear wife is to be a school of applied Christianity. That is, it will train young men to be Christian in the highest and most practical sense. They will go into all the world and preach the gospel. Take your own country, as an example. I felt there the lack of a dynamic, an energy, a purpose. Your people are slack, they are listless, they allow circumstances to overcome them. A real religion, a vital faith in the true God, will inspire them to better themselves."

Darya listened to this, his eyes glittering again. "Is there more truth in your god than in ours?" he inquired with dangerous quiet.

MacArd faced him with massive power in his look. "Your temples are full of superstitious litter," he said bluntly. "Your people are confused by the legends of ancient history. A clean wind, a sweeping change, will give you fresh strength. I believe that our own prosperity proves the validity of our religion. God has been with us."

"I grant you the right to believe in your own religion," Darya said in the same intense quiet. "I have sometimes even thought that I, too, would like to be a Christian if I could become one without giving up my own religion."

"That," MacArd said decisively, "would be impossible. When a man becomes a Christian, he must forsake all other gods, and believe only in the One."

"Thus you exclude most of the world," Darya said.

"Not at all," MacArd retorted. "Any man can repent and accept the Christian faith."

"You remind me of a certain American millionaire whose name I will not speak, because you know it well, Mr. MacArd. He says he does not believe in competition but in co-operation. Therefore he proceeds to absorb into his own business the livelihood of other men, especially those in smaller corporations than his own. They co-operate by becoming his property—a trust, I believe it is strangely called."

MacArd was hurt. "I assure you I have no purpose except to

83

benefit your people. I see my own country rich and prosperous, the people well-fed and happy. I see your country poor and the people wretched. I am compelled to deduce reasons for this difference."

"Can it be because your people are free and mine are not?" Darya suggested, glints of light playing in his eyes.

"In spite of the benefits of empire," MacArd said, not comprehending, "your people continue in this poor state. Therefore they must be taught to help themselves. For this I say they need a new faith, an inspired and inspiring religion, which I did not find, young man, although I went into many temples." These last words he spoke very sternly indeed and David was alarmed.

Darya rose, a guest too courteous to quarrel with his elder and his host. "I shall be interested to see the memorial," he said. "And now will you excuse me, sir, if I say I have some letters to write? David has been giving me such a good time that I have not yet written to my brothers."

He bowed to MacArd, smiled at David and walked gracefully from the room, shutting the door soundlessly after him.

David did not speak. MacArd poured himself another cup of coffee. "A well-educated young man but still a heathen," he said drily.

David did not reply to this. Instead he said,

"I never heard you say the things you have just said, Father. I didn't know you could."

"Nor I," his father replied. He drank the coffee and put down the cup and looked at his son with humorous eyes in which there was also something of apology. "I don't know what got into me. I'm no theologian. But I guess that young Indian sitting so smug and rich, while I know the condition his country is in, just roused the American in me, and mixed up with that is my father's old-fashioned religion. Maybe it was good, after all. I know it scared me enough to keep me out of a lot of tomfoolery when I was growing up. I never could be sure he wasn't right about hellfire, and I didn't dare take the chance. I guess I still don't dare."

He leaned forward on his elbows and his voice quieted. "Son, do you know what your mother really believed? There were so many

84

things I never asked her. I always thought we'd have a lot of time together when we got old."

A humble yearning crept over his big face, he was embarrassed and tried to smile and felt his lips too stiff for it, and he waited, his thick reddish eyebrows hanging far over his sad grey eyes.

"I never asked her, either, Father," David replied. It was repulsive to see his father soft and actually quivering with inexplicable anxiety. Then, seeing his shadowed eyes, he felt sorry for him, growing old alone, and pity illumined his understanding. He had a momentary vision of what it might mean to a man to lose a woman like his mother while love was still alive between them. Out of his pity he spoke, "But I know that she believed in the things Dr. Barton talks about—in immortality, for instance."

"You think so!" his father exclaimed. "Well, that relieves my mind. I've been worrying about things, putting so much money into the memorial when maybe she—"

David did not reply and they sat in silence, neither knowing what to say, for MacArd would not face the possibility that his son agreed with the Indian. When he did speak it was to say mildly, "I shall be glad if you will go up there and see how things are getting on. I am very much engaged now."

"I wish I could be more useful to you, Father," David said when he paused.

"No one can help me," MacArd replied. "The country itself is on skids. Unless someone with common sense comes along we are headed for ruin. One of these days our creditors in Europe and even in Asia are going to get scared and insist on being paid in gold, and we haven't enough gold in the national treasury to meet our debts, that is the plain truth of it. If the Silverites win the battle and we go into bimetallism, we're done for. If only I could find some fellow, a chemist, who could work gold out of low grade ore—"

David listened without understanding. He was ashamed to confess to his father that all his years of school had not prepared him to comprehend what he meant by bimetallism. He had been an exceptional Greek scholar, and he had taken high honors in English literature and philosophy, but he had no notion of what the threat

85

in his father's words could mean, even though it might reach disastrously into his own life, and he shrank from knowing. Life was beautiful and graceful as it was, touched with sadness, to be sure, since his mother died, but beauty must contain sadness, and Shelley and Keats and Browning had so taught him.

"If I can ever be of real use to you, Father," he said, "you have only to let me know." He hesitated a moment, "I suppose I ought to go upstairs now."

"Good night," MacArd said shortly. He lifted his head and watched his son leave the room and then he sat for a long time in lonely thought.

It was the first really hot day of summer, and the two young men got out of the dusty train gratefully enough, although the ride had been so short. Darya looked about him with lively appreciation.

"These wooded hills, these empty valleys," he exclaimed. "It's a wilderness, and only an hour away from a vast city! I say, you know, David, some day it may seem to the rest of the world that you Americans haven't any right to all this emptiness. Think how people are crowded together where I come from!"

"We don't have such big families as you do," David said. He was distressed to find that his relationship with Darya was changing subtly this morning. Darya was criticizing everything he saw, always gaily, to be sure, and surrounding his criticism with an embroidery of rapid flowing talk, simile and metaphor enriching every devastating word, but he felt that inwardly Darya was sitting as a judge upon him. He was puzzled and irritated, the more because Darya never went beyond the actual bounds of courtesy as a guest. Yet he presumed upon their affectionate relationship.

"Ah," Darya exclaimed, "the old Anglo-Saxon argument, the reason given by every viceroy for not making an empire a benefit to my people, for what is the use of feeding the people when they simply increase their numbers? Starvation is inevitable, and indeed desirable, so the rulers say. It keeps the people obedient."

"You cannot deny overpopulation," David said.

"The argument of vicious and wilful ignorance," Darya declared.

86

"Have you ever observed a dying tree? When it knows that life is over, it blossoms in one frantic outburst of flower and seed, producing far more than normal, because, my friend, the law of nature, as you would call it, or Karma, as we call it with the same fateful meaning, is that though the individual dies, the species must not. Only when the species cannot reproduce, does it die. Our strength is that we can still reproduce, and so we have not perished from the face of the earth. We are still taught to respect our parents, to subdue our individual wills to the family good, else long before now would we have died as other peoples have died! 'Honor thy father and thy mother, that thy days may be long upon the land'—that is also Christian, isn't it?"

"You know I cannot argue against you, Darya," David complained. "You are much too quick for me."

"But you do not agree with me," Darya exclaimed.

"Not always," David admitted.

"Therefore you will never be convinced," Darya persisted.

"Not against my will," David replied.

"But your reason, your reason," Darya cried with passion, "is there no way of reaching your reason, you white man?"

They stood on the platform of the little railroad station, forgetting where they were. The country station master passing by looked at them astonished, a white man and a Negro, he thought, getting mad at each other. He had better break it up. He spat tobacco juice.

"Anything I can do for you folks?"

David started. "Oh no, thanks. Come along, Darya. We are making a spectacle of ourselves."

They turned their backs abruptly on the man, he spat again, and then chewed his cud, ruminating and shaking his head.

"We'll walk," David said. "It's only two miles."

They struck off up the river, mutually agreeing each in himself to give over their argument and enjoy the day. David was surprised to find how eagerly he wanted to see Olivia. He had thought of her a good deal in the night, seeing her dark handsome face clear against the curtains of his memory.

"This river makes me think of our Ganges," Darya said in his usual amiable voice. "My father goes every year and brings back jars of its sacred water for us."

"Now that I don't understand," David said. "Your father, yes, but you, Darya, no. Cambridge and the sacred Ganges—it doesn't go together."

Darya stopped. "Look at me," he demanded. "Do you see my forehead? There is an invisible line here." He drew his forefinger down from his hair to the bridge of his high and handsome nose. "On this side, the left side, the heart side, is my religion. On the other side, Cambridge, the modern world, science."

"You keep them separate?"

"Separate and inviolate."

"I can't understand that—" David began.

"Do not try to understand," Darya said. "Simply accept. Some long day hence the line may fade away. But science is far behind the intuitions of religion and until it overtakes faith, the line remains immovable."

"You are content with this?" David asked.

"I must be content," Darya declared, "for I can do nothing about it. If I were a scientist I would devote myself to removing the division, but I have no vocation for science. I am merely a man who waits."

David did not reply. There was indeed no reply possible, for as usual Darya had led him beyond himself. He realized that his own mind until now had been wholly uncreative, absorbing what he had been taught, receiving what he was given. He had no valid opinions of his own, he was far less thoughtful than Darya, though they were so nearly the same age, and he was beginning to be made uncomfortable by his very presence. It was time the visit ended. In spite of pleasant companionship, Darya's presence was becoming a reproach and a burden. He was not ready yet to ponder the large matters of the world and the universe, and perhaps not even of love. He wanted to live each day as it was given him, and he might like to remain as he was, simple-minded and not subtle. As an American,

88

he distrusted subtlety, and he was beginning, he feared, to dislike it, even in Darya. Perhaps they had passed the point of understanding each other.

They walked along in silence, the sun was growing hot and near its zenith. They had breakfasted late and heartily and Darya had declared that he would not eat again until they reached home in the evening. American food, he said, he found too heavy, it remained too long in the intestines, and sometimes he fasted for a whole day. Now he walked more quickly than David, swinging along lightly and steadily, seeming not to notice heat or dust, until the river curved and the house was before them on the hill.

"There it is," David said.

They stopped and looked up at it. "A fine place," Darya observed. "So that is to be the cradle of the teachers who are to be sent to my people. Very American!"

David was suddenly angry. "I suppose the best that any people can give to another people is its own chosen men."

"Is it to be reciprocal?" Darya demanded. "Would your people accept our men? If so, I offer myself. I will come here and preach our gospel, David, the gospel of the faith of our people. Will your father accept me, do you think?"

David turned on him. "Are you jesting?"

"Not at all," Darya said. "I am in bitter earnest. Would it not be good sense to engage a man of India to prepare your young teachers for their pupils? Would it not be well for them to know the country to which they are sent? Seriously, seriously! Would I be welcome?"

The dart pricked its target. Darya knew his man, David was just and he could not lie.

Darya had flung the demand like a javelin and he stood, fists clenched, his jaw upthrust. David stepped back. Before either could speak they heard a girl's voice.

"David MacArd! What a surprise!"

It was Olivia. She was coming up from the river, where she had been swimming. Her skirted bathing suit was wet and her long hair, dripping with river water, hung down her back. Because she was alone she had not put on bathing stockings and she wore only sandals. The sun shone on her wet arms and neck, on her wet face and eyelashes, glistening and lovely.

The two young men forgot themselves and David spoke first, "Olivia, this is Darya, my friend from India. Darya, this is Miss Dessard."

"Olivia," Darya said. "You will allow me to use the name, since David is my brother."

Olivia put out her hand. "I am glad to see you. My grandfather has told me about India many times. He visited there once. Come to the house."

They walked together, Olivia between, until the path up the hill separated them, and then she led the way, Darya followed and David was last. It was easy to see that Darya was impressed by the dark self-possessed girl, and that Olivia was enlivened by Darya. At the top of the hill David came forward and she was between them again, Darya and Olivia talking rapidly and constantly, and he had never heard her talk like this nor seen her so free. He was suddenly intensely jealous. Darya was able to make her so free, while with him she had been shy and almost silent. His heart throbbed and love crystallized with a shock. He wished that he had not brought Darya here to see her wakened like this, aware and eager and outgoing, laughing and talking as though she had always known the Indian. He walked along, helpless, and she led the way into the house. "Go into the drawing room, please," she said in her clear imperious voice, though amazingly gay. "Mother will be down, and I must go and change. We don't have tea every day as we used to, but there are wine and biscuits on the table, please help yourselves."

She ran up the stairs as lithely as a young tigress. Darya led the way into the living room and poured the wine, as much at home as if this were his house. He handed the goblet to David and then the plate of biscuits.

"My friend," he said in a low intense voice, "if you do not marry this girl, you are a fool! She is not only handsome, she is a free spirit and an intelligence. I envy you!"

David took the wine and broke a biscuit in his hand. Then he put up his shield of defense against Darya and his magnetic charm. "I have every intention of marrying her," he said, and was astonished at his own coolness as he made the spectacular decision.

That night when they reached home he continued in a daze, a mood vague and immense. He had been almost silent when Olivia came downstairs, he had not listened to the renewed and ardent talk of Darya, who devoted himself to the beautiful girl. He had talked desultorily with Mrs. Dessard, listening to her complaints of moving and storage and he had not heard anything that Darya said all the way home. The golden stream of enthusiastic words went on and on, Darya unceasing in his praise of the wonderful girl, her grace, the pride of her noble head, her long thin hands, the strength in her, the incomparable latent power.

"It will take courage to be her husband, you understand," he said ardently, "but a task how enticing! You must be strong, too, David, you must find a source of power for yourself—"

"Well," MacArd said at the dinner table, "how are the buildings getting on?"

The two young men looked at each other, stricken, and Darya began to laugh.

David flushed scarlet. "Father, we forgot to look at them."

"Forgot to look at them!" MacArd echoed, astounded.

"Yes—we got to talking with—"

"With Olivia," Darya said.

"Miss Dessard," David said under his breath.

MacArd stared at them from under heavy brows.

"Well," he said, "well, well, well!"

David did not explain, and Darya hastened to protect him.

"The setting, Mr. MacArd, is divine in itself, a place inevitably to turn the thoughts of men to the Infinity, a site for the soul—"

"That is what it is for," MacArd agreed. "I am glad you understand my idea."

Darya's instinct told him that it was time for him to leave David and continue his westward way. He had curiosity to see some of the sights of America, he wished also to see the black people of the South, and he planned to sail from California. No more was said about Olivia for he divined that David did not wish to talk about her and this reserve settled like a fog over their whole relationship.

"My friend, I must return to India," Darya said one morning. "It has been weeks since I came, how many I have forgotten, the year is passing and there is much I wish to do. My father asked me to be home again by midautumn and so I must not delay, however happy I have been."

"You must come again," David said.

"You must come to India," Darya replied. He wished to add, "Perhaps on your wedding journey," but he did not. To force a confidence was as unrewarding as pulling open a lotus flower. Neither scent nor beauty was the reward.

David smiled without answering and he stayed near Darya all day while he packed. Darya, who could be as lazy as a beautiful woman when he chose, became a man of action when he had made up his mind. He put his belongings in order, the few gifts he had chosen for his family, small but expensive, a gold bracelet set with diamonds for his wife, a diamond sunburst brooch for his mother, for his father a set of Audubon prints of American birds, so different from those in the countryside about Poona, and for his sons small strong mechanical toys. For brothers and sisters, cousins and uncles and aunts he bought watches.

By night of the next day he was ready, his bags packed, and David went with him to the train. Darya would not allow any atmosphere of farewell, "There is neither beginning nor end to our friendship," he declared. "It was before we were born, and it will never end, unless we choose to separate ourselves, which I will not do."

92

"Nor I," David said.

As cheerfully as though they were to meet the next morning Darya stepped into the train, settled himself and waved his hand from the window. They had stayed to talk until the last minute, idle talk, friendly and not profound, as though both agreed that at this late hour there must be no new revelations between them, and the train left almost immediately, and David was driven away again. His father had not come home to dinner that night, he had telephoned that he would be late, and David climbed the stairs to his own rooms. The house was now very empty, the silence oppressive. He had scarcely thought of his mother for so many weeks that he could no longer summon her presence and he had no desire to do so. The rooms were filled with the echoes of Darya's lively presence, his modulated voice, his rapid talk, and yet he did not wish Darya back.

He went into his own rooms and closed the door. He would go to see Olivia, he would simply go, on the pretext of looking at the buildings, and then he would make the opportunity to ask her to marry him. He felt an immense hunger, a hollowness of the heart and only the one name sounded its echoes, Olivia.

She was not easily found. He wandered about the roofless buildings, his eyes meanwhile searching for her and not finding her. The walls were rising above foundations and six new buildings were set in the woods about the pillared house, skilfully placed so that each seemed alone and yet part of the whole.

The famous New York architect his father had engaged was treading the raw upturned earth with dainty feet, a blue print stretched between his hands. He greeted David gaily, beckoned to him and led him to a spot where the buildings were revealed in a magnificent perspective about the central mansion.

"The approach," the architect said proudly. "I have had exactly the proper trees cut away. The effect is good, don't you think. Spiritual, and yet solid! I have kept in mind the purpose your father has in the memorial. The house is the memorial center, the

93

source let us say, the altar, so to speak. Around it the young men group themselves with their teachers. The inspiration comes from the center."

He was a finicking little man, precise in speech, his black-ribboned pince-nez dangling from his buttonhole, but he was enthusiastic and David was compelled to admit that there was an effect and the new buildings were subdued to the lofty nobility of the main house.

"Very beautiful," he said, knowing it was expected of him.

The little man was gratified. "Please tell your distinguished father," he begged. "Mr. MacArd is a man difficult to please, but so worthy of being pleased. I wish to make every effort."

David said, "I'll tell him I like it very much."

"Thank you, thank you—" the little man said.

David nodded and walked away. It was now nearly noon and he had not seen Olivia. He must find her, since she had not allowed herself to be found. He went to the house. The door as usual was open and the vista of wide rooms lay before him with no sign of Olivia. Fresh flowers were in the vases and she must be near, but he did not see her. He lifted the heavy knocker, struck it three times, and Mrs. Dessard's voice floated out from the kitchen.

"Who is it?"

He stepped inside and went toward the voice. "It is I, Mrs. Dessard. I came to see the buildings for my father, and before I go back I thought I'd—" He opened the kitchen door, "What a heavenly fragrance!"

"Grapes," Mrs. Dessard said. She stood by the stove, a tiny dignified figure, stirring a long spoon in a large pot. "Olivia is picking them and I am making jelly. It's hot work."

The weight lifted itself from his heart. "I wish I could help you," he said with sudden gaiety, "but since I can't make jelly perhaps I had better pick grapes."

Mrs. Dessard did not answer for a few seconds, then she said without looking at him, "Olivia will be glad of help. At least, I suppose she will. You can't always tell about her."

94

"I'll try, anyway," he said.

He hastened into the hall again and out the back door which stood open to the small formal garden. Olivia had made a wonder here, the box trees were clipped, the flower beds weeded, and early chrysanthemums were beginning to blossom in red and white and yellow. He followed the paths and turned to the left through a yew gateway into the kitchen garden, and there he saw Olivia among the grapevines and shielded against the sun by a wide leghorn hat. Pilate the peacock walked beside her, his tail in full display. She did not see David, or hear him, and he stood for a minute, enjoying the picture of her beside the gorgeous bird. She had on a yellow cotton frock and the full skirt flowed about her on the ground. He could see her profile, earnest above her task, the dark hair escaping to her neck and her fingers nimble among the vines. She plucked a large purple grape and put it in her mouth.

"Is it good?" he called.

Pilate screeched, she gave a start and turned her head. "How long have you stood there watching me?" she demanded.

"Only a moment, I swear," he said laughing. He came near to her and stood looking down upon her. "I wouldn't have missed the sight for a world." Her face was upturned to him, her eyes huge and reproachful. "Do you mind?"

"Yes, I do," she said. "I thought I was alone."

"It isn't wicked to eat a grape," he teased.

"I thought I was alone," she repeated.

He divined a small anger in her, and he tried to dispel it, wanting no clouds upon this cloudless day. "Shall I help you? There are far more grapes here than you can ever pick in a day."

"You have on your fine clothes," she said, giving him a quick glance, up and down.

"I don't care for clothes." He stood beside her and spread searching fingers among the vines.

"The best ones grow underneath," she directed.

"May I eat the biggest ones?" he asked.

"Only one every five minutes," she said.

He met her eyes and rejoiced to see them only mischievous.

"Is your Indian friend gone?" she asked suddenly.

"Yes," David said briefly. He did not want to talk about Darya.

"Will he come again?" she demanded.

"Not soon," he said, and then impelled by some hidden motive he went on. "It is more likely that I shall visit him in India."

"When?" she demanded.

"Not soon," he said again.

They picked the fruit in silence for a few minutes.

"You pick ten times as fast as I do," he said.

"I daresay this is the first time you have ever picked grapes," she replied.

"It is," he confessed. "I scarcely knew how they grew."

"I thought so."

"Is that despicable?" he asked.

"It depends on what else you can do," she said.

"Not much, I am afraid," he confessed and then he went on, urging the opportunity. "I am one of those men who need an inspiration before I work."

He stopped to turn his head toward her but she went on picking.

"Olivia!"

She looked up at him, very grave.

"Olivia, I came here today to see you, only you."

She did not reply or move, and he looked deep into the dark eyes under the black and finely etched brows.

"We haven't known each other very long," he faltered, "but long enough for me to know I—love you!" His breath forsook him and the last words were a whisper.

Her answer was instant and composed. "Oh David, I'm so sorry!"

He heard the words from afar off and her voice rang in his ears like the toll of a bell.

"Sorry?" he repeated, half stupidly.

"Oh, so sorry," she said remorsefully, "I didn't know, David, not until just now, a few minutes ago. I wouldn't have let you go so far if I had known. I'd have stopped you at the very beginning."

96

He could not speak a word, he could not make a sound. He stood still, looking down upon her grieving face.

"You haven't loved me very long, I'm sure of that, and so it can't be deep. You'll get over it quickly."

"It is deep!" he cried. "You don't know what you're talking about. I have never loved anybody before, I never will again."

"Oh don't say that, David!"

"Why can't you love me?" he demanded.

She let her eyelids flutter downward and saw his clenched fists. "I ought to be able to love you," she said in a small voice, "Almost any girl would. But I can't."

"I ask you why," he insisted.

She threw out her hands and let them fall in a wide and graceful gesture. "How can I tell? Maybe because you're not strong enough. I don't want to be the strong one. I want to look up to a man."

"And you can't look up to me," he said in a dreadful voice. She was looking up at him, nevertheless, her eyes dark and pleading.

"I can't," she said in sorrow. "You're just MacArd's son, aren't you? The great MacArd!"

He looked down upon her upturned face and felt bitterness acrid in his breast, dry upon his tongue. Then to his horror he felt that he must weep and he turned and walked quickly away. After such words he could not, must not weep. He hurried from the house, and down the little path to the river, and in a hidden spot he threw himself upon a bed of dying ferns. Among their curling fronds and fresh green, he buried his face and wept, it seemed to him for hours, and then weeping turned into prayer, the first real prayer of his life. "Oh God, what am I going to do? What use am I now?"

The words burst from his wounded heart, he heard them as though they were spoken by someone else, a voice other than his own, and under the awful cry, he trembled. Was there no answer? He did not hear reply. The sounds of the wood he could hear, the crackle of twigs, the flutter of leaves in the breeze, the distant call of a quail. The sun beat down upon him in the stillness and he lay

97

there with his eyes closed, the smell of the warm earth in his nostrils mingled with the scent of crushed fern. Then slowly he felt a strange quiet steal over him. He began to think.

Darya had come between him and Olivia. Had she not seen him in his strange Indian beauty, his dark brilliance, she might have spoken differently, for she would not have known that such a man existed. It was not mere charm. He could not accuse Darya of wilfully casting that net over Olivia. No, Darya had simply been himself, though inspired, perhaps, by the directness of her eyes and the fearlessness of her mind. She, too, had her charm over him, doubtless, accustomed as he was to the shy silence of Indian women in his presence.

He sat up suddenly, and wrapped his arms about his knees and stared out over the glittering river. She had said that she must be able to look up to him, and she said it because she had seen Darya. How rash he had been to propose to her so abruptly this morning, without waiting to discover her feelings! He felt himself a boy humbly young and yet wounded, wanting in wisdom, foolishly impetuous. He had gone to her and asked for her love as though it were a toy or a sweet instead of his whole life.

In the midst of the bright morning he was overwhelmed with gloom and bewilderment. Vague aches pervaded even his body, he was shot through with little lightnings of pain. He thought with anguish of his dead mother, to whom had she been alive he would have turned for comfort and laughter.

"Silly—" he could hear her tender voice always underlaid with laughter—"if she wants to look up to you, why don't you start climbing?"

He bowed his head on his knees and closed his eyes that he might hear that clear voice he remembered. It was exactly as though she had spoken to him. Perhaps she had, perhaps it was the only way she could reach him, now, through his memory of her voice and his imagination of what she would say, were she here.

All his being melted, and from the fusion a pure desire distilled and shaped itself through longing into prayer.

"O God," for now there must be God, "tell me how to begin."
He felt his heart quiver in his breast. He dared invite such leadership only if he dared to follow. He sat motionless above the cliff. The air was still and hot and the sun blazed upon him. Far off he heard the scream of a hawk whirling into the sky. He waited, his mind empty, his consciousness stayed, and suddenly he saw India, a crowded street. Dark faces turned toward him, startled and surprised, as though they had been summoned against their will.

He was frightened at their clarity and he lifted his head and saw only the river, the blue shores beyond, and the soaring hawk. What did it mean that he had seen India here except that he had asked direction and had been given answer? He had stepped over the divide between this visible world and beyond, and the way had been made plain. The prospect was too vast to comprehend and he tried to encompass it in the words of his age. He thought of dedication, consecration, mission, and the passionate words were wine to his soul. No one needed him here, but in India the human need was boundless. He did not know what he would do there but God—he spoke the name with new reverence—God would show him. This, he supposed, was what it meant to be born again. As naturally and unexpectedly as his first birth from his mother's body, rebirth had come. What had been his world ceased. He had been driven out of it first by his mother's death and now by Olivia's refusal and in his helplessness a new life was revealed. He drew his breath deeply and got to his feet.

"When did you get this notion?" MacArd said harshly.
He had seen for several days that his son was silent and absentminded and tonight at the dinner table the boy had scarcely touched his food. Then here in the library after dinner he had blurted out that he wanted to go to India as a missionary.

"It is not a notion, it is a conviction," David said.
MacArd lifted his shaggy head and caught Leila's eyes looking down upon them from her portrait above the mantelpiece. He looked away from her. "You can just get over it. I'm building Mac-

99

Ard Memorial, but not for my only son. Who's to take over after me?"

"I intend to live my own life, under divine direction," David said.

A man could not be rough with his only son. MacArd had learned that long ago when once he had whipped David for disobedience and he then had gone into convulsions of crying. Leila had flown at him, she had sobbed and declared that she would leave his house if he ever whipped their son again. Well, he had never whipped him again, nor could he now. He flung out his arms, "A fine joke on me! A fine, nice joke! I spread a net and caught my own son! I gambled on God and my son is the stakes and I've lost! Ha!"

He snorted and sighed and descended to self-pity.

"Look, son, I'm getting old. Can't you just stay with me for a few years longer?"

"I have decided, Father," David said.

MacArd got to his feet and stamped about the room, weaving his way around the vast table and between the heavy chairs of English oak.

"I guess I've wasted a lot of money building that memorial. I'd have given up the whole business if I'd thought it would give you the idea you were going to leave me. That miserable country! What would your mother say to me if I let you go? Snakes, heathen, filth—well, there's plenty of other men to go. Not my son! I'll set fire to the memorial and let India go to hell. Can't be worse than the way it is over there, anyway."

David did not reply, and MacArd after a moment stole a look at him sidewise from under his rough brows. His son was sitting quietly watching him, exactly as Leila used to do when he rampaged about something before her. The resemblance tore at his heart and he collapsed into a chair. He sank his head upon his chest.

"All right, all right," he grunted. "I don't count. I know that. I give up. But you've spoiled any pleasure I can take in the memorial. I'll finish it but I won't take any joy in it. You've ruined it for me."

"I must do what I think is right," his son said.

"Then I'll turn the memorial into a factory!" MacArd shouted.

They glared at each other, father and son, and neither moved.

Part II

V

THE sun was creeping up beyond the grey ghats and over the walls and cupolas of Poona, above the minarets and through the white colonnades and tall green palms. The streets were already astir, the bullock carts creaked and water carriers splashed the dust with small liquid spheres that rolled along like dark quicksilver.

In his bare quiet study in the mission house David sat with his teacher. This part of his work he enjoyed, the early hours of thoughtful pondering over the lacelike script of Marathi text. At first it had seemed impossible to decipher one symbol from the other but slowly he was able to read and the graceful design was beginning to be a language. He had begun by studying Sanskrit, at Darya's suggestion. The roots of Indian thought were to be found in the ancient Sanskrit texts, Darya said, but David had discovered in them amazing parallels to Christian thought. Upon the whitewashed wall, opposite the table at which he now sat, he had a text that he had carefully copied upon heavy cream-colored paper, a prayer from the earliest scriptures of Hinduism.

> From the unreal lead me to the real.
> From the darkness lead me to light.
> From death lead me to immortality.

His teacher was a tall ascetic Marathi, who was not a Christian. He sat immobile upon a low bamboo chair, wearing garments of cotton cloth, a hatlike turban on his head, his legs apart, his feet turned out and his dark hands resting exactly upon his white-clad knees. His wrinkled face was grave, his little black eyes were narrowed as he listened.

David looked up from a long passage he had been reading aloud from St. Paul's Epistle to the Romans, translated into Marathi. He smiled faintly at the dark attentive face.

"Forgive me that I read so long from the scriptures of my own religion."

The Marathi shook his head. "And why should you say this, Sahib?" he replied. "It is a religion, it is good, you do not demand that I eat your bread and drink your wine, and while I listen I can fix my mind yonder."

He nodded toward the Sanskrit prayer, framed upon the wall.

"All religions are good," he declared.

At what point, David inquired of himself, should he challenge this frequent declaration, to which he had thus far replied only with silence? Silence implied acceptance, and he could not and must not accept the easy Indian attitude toward all religions. Any religion was better than none, so far he could agree with the Marathi teacher, but he longed to explain to this kind and proud man that the fruits of western Christianity were surely better than others. He had become convinced of it during this year in India, although when he left home, last year, he would have denied it because it was what his father said.

They had remained unreconciled, although as his duty and because his mother was dead he wrote to his father twice a month and received in return a monthly letter. But in spirit they were far apart. For his father had persisted in his monstrous wrath, and he had made the place he had planned as a memorial into a factory. Instead of young men learning of God, men and women, ignorant and uncouth, crowded into the big rooms at machines and made precision instruments for the MacArd industries. At the foot of the hill along the railroad hundreds of small houses were built, and there was a railroad stop for shipping. Dr. Barton, bitterly disappointed, had ignored the whole change after two stormy hours of argument with MacArd himself. The climax had come, as he told

David, when with courage given him, he believed, from God, he had told the old tycoon the truth.

"You thought you were serving God by building a monument, Mr. MacArd. When He asked not for a monument but for your son, you grew angry. Do you think even you can be angry with God, Mr. MacArd?"

To which MacArd had replied, his eyebrows and beard bristling red, "I always make my own terms, Barton, and I'll do it with God himself—if there is a God!"

For whatever impulse toward religion had risen in his father's heart after his mother's death, David knew had died down. Stony soil, perhaps, wherein the seed could not grow! He himself refused to feel guilty, or to believe that had he obeyed his father the seed would have grown. Sooner or later the MacArd Memorial would have become something else, anyway, if not a factory then some sort of a tool for the MacArd interests.

And as he had separated himself from his father his own growth had been hastened—that, too, he knew. The powerful shadow was thousands of miles away, and he was honest enough to wonder sometimes if his call to India, which had seemed to come so simply and clearly from God that day on the hillside above the Hudson River, had been partly because even then he wanted to go far away. If so, the call was no less valid, for God worked in mysterious ways. His faith had grown deeper while it became more reasonable, and the very atmosphere of India made faith reasonable. Religion was vital in the air, and sometimes, he thought, the only vitality. His task and his challenge was to make his own religion the most vital of all.

Meanwhile, life was pleasant. The mission house was large and cool, and white-clad servants flitted through the shadows of the drawn bamboo curtains, bringing hot tea and small English sweet biscuits just at the hours when he began to feel fatigue. There was even an English society and the Governor gave parties to which he was always invited, and there was English service on Sunday in the Cathedral. His senior missionary, Robert Fordham, did not encourage his joining too often in the festivities of the English people in

Poona, but it was necessary to remain on good terms with the Governor, for sometimes favors must be asked. Missionaries must be loyal to Government, Mr. Fordham said solemnly, for only the protection of Empire made it possible for them to come and go as they wished about the countryside. Indeed, Robert Fordham often disagreed with young and rebellious Indians when they complained that India should be free, and at times he rebuked them with real severity, declaring that India was infinitely better off under the British than it had been when it was torn between the regional rulers who in the old days had oppressed the people while they destroyed each other with Oriental savagery.

It was true, David supposed, and yet something in the dark and passionate eyes of young Indians made him doubt the wisdom of the older missionary, under whose direction he was.

The morning hours passed, the sun rose high, and the compound which had looked so cool and green in the early morning, now glistened with heat.

He was aware suddenly of being hungry and he closed the book. "I must not keep you beyond your hour," he said to his teacher. "I forget how the time passes."

"For me time is nothing," the Marathi replied. "I have sat here watching you. You do not tell me what your thoughts are."

David gave his ready smile. "They are scarcely thoughts, not worth telling. I put off real thinking, perhaps because I do not know yet what I ought to think. I feel I know India less and not more as time goes on."

The Marathi laughed. "When you can think in our language, you will know us. Give yourself another year."

He rose, and David rose with him. They parted as usual, and the Marathi went away, his full white trousers swinging about him.

David put his books together and went to his room, next to his study, to prepare for the noon meal. The mission house was a large square bungalow, encircled with a deep arched veranda to keep the heat of the sun from penetrating into the rooms. A wide hall divided the house, and at one end was his study and next it his bedroom. Both rooms were big and the bare floors, the bamboo furniture and the high ceilings gave them an air of coolness.

When he had washed he went down the hall to the dining room, where Mrs. Fordham was already seated at one end of the oval dining table, ladling soup into flat English soup plates.

"Sit down, Mr. MacArd," she said with brisk good humor. "We won't wait for Mr. Fordham." She bent her head, her mouse-brown hair always disheveled, and gabbled a swift grace.

"For what we are about to receive, Lord make us truly thankful. Amen. Shall you get over to Bible Class this afternoon, Mr. Mac-Ard?"

"I think not," David replied.

"It's a bad example, you know," she said with her cheerful sharpness.

"I am sorry for that," he said.

He was accustomed to these fencing bouts with Mrs. Fordham and he carried them through with humor. As soon as Mr. Fordham came she would stop, and the meal would proceed kindly. Mr. Fordham was a large man, shrewd and tolerant from long living in a hot climate. He came in now, his heavy body bulging in a suit of wrinkled white linen, and sat down at the opposite end of the table from his wife.

"Sorry to be late as usual," he said, "the gateman found a snake in the store room. It was one of the old cobras."

"Did you kill it?" Mrs. Fordham demanded.

"I sent the gateman for a dish of milk to draw it away," Mr. Fordham said. He began drinking his soup in gulps, opening his big mouth to receive the entire spoon with each gulp.

"Oh, Robert," his wife cried. "Why will you encourage them in their superstitions?"

"It's a very old snake," Mr. Fordham said mildly. "It's been here for years, and it only wants a dish of milk each day."

"Nasty creature," Mrs. Fordham declared. She banged a small table bell with the flat of her hand and a white-clad Indian boy scurried in and removed the soup plates. Another boy brought in a dish of goat-meat curry and some boiled rice. She ladled these viands upon plates and the boys placed them before the two men.

"Well, David," Mr. Fordham said. "How's the language coming on? You should be preaching a sermon soon, you know."

David put down his fork. The time had come to tell them that he would never preach a sermon. The long quiet months alone with his books and his solitary walks about the city had been fruitful and decisive. He intended to be a missionary of a new sort. He was not content to preach in a small chapel, or to teach a few Bible classes and circle through a hundred miles of villages, admonishing half-starved people to worship a god they could not see. Instead he planned an attack upon India itself, through Indians, and those Indians would be young men, carefully chosen and highly trained, leaders of their own people. Upon them he would exert the utmost of his influence.

"I shan't be preaching sermons, Mr. Fordham," he said pleasantly.

"Not preaching?" Mrs. Fordham cried. "Why, how else will the gospel be heard?"

"Be quiet, Becky," Mr. Fordham said. "Now David, just tell us what you have in mind."

He told them in a few words, making it simple, making it plain. "I want my life to count for something. The only way it can count in a huge country like this is to search for a few people, a few hundred, if I live long enough a few thousand, and train them to teach others. I propose—"

He let the goat-meat curry grow tepid as he painted for them in simple words the picture he had been creating of his own life. A school of the highest caliber, the sternest standards, working closely with English Government schools, a college and then a university, certainly eventually a medical college and a hospital, each unit opening as quickly as possible, and the most rigid exclusion of all except the best and brightest boys and later perhaps even girls, chosen not according to caste or wealth but ability, and free scholarships for those who were poor.

"But where is God in all this?" Mrs. Fordham demanded.

David gave her his sweet and stubborn smile. "I believe that wherever man does his best, God is there."

"I don't call that Christian," Mrs. Fordham cried.

"Be quiet, Becky," Mr. Fordham said. "Where will you get the funds for all this, David? It will take millions."

"My mother left me money," David said quietly.

There could be no reply. The Fordhams had grown up in poverty, they had lived in little midwestern towns and had struggled through small midwestern colleges. They lived now on a salary too small for luxuries, and had they been at home instead of in India, Mrs. Fordham would have been the servant and Mr. Fordham the breadwinner. They were stunned by this young man with a gentle handsome face who possessed a fortune to do with as he liked. Let him serve God as he would.

"Well, it sounds very fine," Mr. Fordham said at last.

Mrs. Fordham could not speak. She was thinking of her three sons. Poor things, they had nothing. At home in Ohio they had to work on her father's farm and when they got to college they would have to work their way through to diplomas, while here in the mission compound Indian boys and girls would be having scholarships and every sort of luxury. It was not fair and God was not just.

The meal was over, and after it, as usual, David made ready for his walk outside the compound into the early twilight to breathe what coolness was there. Tonight he enjoyed it in a profound, stimulating, troubled sort of way. The streets of Poona were crowded when he stepped from the gate. They were always crowded, a solid flowing mass of men, dark faces, bare dark legs, white turbans, moving, crowding, eager, pushing, the dust rising, stirred by their feet and settling in the open shops and markets. The sun had set but the straining anxious life went on in the winding crowded streets, drivers shouting from the carts that threatened to crush the people and yet they never did, the hot hairy shoulders of bullocks pressing against human beings, and the beggars, the fakirs, the sellers of small wares, shrieking above the din. It was Friday, the day the lepers came in from the villages to beg, and they

III

were going home again, their decayed flesh, their stumps of arms and legs uncovered for all to see, while the ones most crippled rode in little pushcarts. When they saw David, a white man, they howled at him for alms, but he went his way.

He was not overwhelmed by it now as he had been at first. Now that he had made his plans and had set a routine for his life, he found it good to join this stream of life at sunset, or in the morning before sunrise when the air was cool. The Indian night was beautiful, the stars hung enormous in the sultry sky, and he turned away from the street into the Poona theater, a great, dusty, flimsy hall, lit by candles hung high in big glass bowls. Two balconies, supported by hand-hewn wooden pillars, were filled with white-turbaned men and the pit was nearly filled. Large holes, not repaired, gaped in the roof and let in the night air and starlight, but the air was still hot and the sweet rank odor of humanity was close. David hesitated, and then found a seat and sat down. Some sort of meeting was going on, students, he supposed, were making the usual outcry against Government. He watched their faces, so mobile, so intent to hear what the man said. These, he told himself, would someday be his men, his material.

A week later he was alone in the mission house for the summer. Poona was cooler than Bombay, though farther south, but even here the currents of air that prevailed usually between the two cities had died away. The heat of summer had fallen and the people waited for the monsoons, the winds which alone keep India from being a desert, uninhabitable for man. The winds begin in north India, born of the intense heat of Delhi and Agra, where, more than two thousand feet above the sea, the dry air and the hot sands draw down the rays of a sunshine fatal and intense. That heat attracts the moist winds from the surrounding sea, and for two months the winds blow toward the northwest and travel southward, circling until opposite winds blow northeast, making two monsoons, during which seed can be sown in the earth, and harvests can be reaped. If the monsoons fail, the people starve.

As yet, not a drop of moisture had fallen this year upon the glittering landscape. The streets were dust, except where the water carriers filled their jars at the rivers, and at the rivers the people gathered to slake their thirst and wash their dried bodies. Women hid in the shadows of their homes, and only the desperate women of the poor wrapped themselves in their Poona saris, nine yards long, and went down to the river's edge.

For this season the church was closed and the Fordhams had gone to the hills. David had refused to go with them.

"I want to see what it's like," he told them. "The Indians have to live through it, and I suppose I can."

Mrs. Fordham was inexplicably angry with him. "Natives are fitted for the climate and white people aren't. You had better follow the example of the British. They've been here a long time, and it's only by being sensible that we can stay here. You'll break down, you'll get ill, you'll see!"

She did not quite say that it would then be their duty to leave the pleasant hill station and come back and fetch him, but David caught the overtones.

"You have no idea how the snakes and poisonous insects abound once the rains begin," she went on.

"I have no idea," he agreed, "and that is why I shall stay and see what it's like."

They had gone at last, unwillingly, with servants and mounds of baggage and bedding, and he had seen them off and had returned to the empty house, where only the cook's son was left to care for him. He had expected to find it lonely, and instead had found it pleasantly filled with peace. Here he had pursued his solitary life, spending the hours of morning and evening in study with his tall Marathi, and in the hot hours alone, he stayed with his books. On one of these days Darya had come to see him.

"David," he said, impetuous with the purpose of his visit, "I have never received you into the inner part of my own house. Come with me today, my friend, and let me show you my children and my wife. You are such a gentle fellow that you won't frighten her. She has never seen a white man or woman, though I don't keep her in purdah, as her parents did. Still, she has the habit of shyness."

"If you wish it, I shall be happy," David said. Here was God's leading, plain! He knew that if he did not go away, if he stayed here waiting, he would be shown reason for obedience.

"Come with me now," Darya commanded him. "The day is still early. I think my house is cooler than yours."

David obeyed, his feet guided, or so he thought, and soon the two young men walked together down the blazing street. "I envy you your garments, Darya."

"Then why not wear them?" Darya asked in his lively fashion.

"I suppose I had better keep my pale skin covered," David said. "At least that is what I am told. Am I wrong?"

"I don't know," Darya replied. "How can I know? I am brown."

It was a small thing, an interchange almost childish, and yet David, sensitive to his friend, felt it a slight barrier between them. The truth, which he had not spoken, was that he could not feel at ease were he to uncover himself, to make bare his arms and legs and feet, to wear a twist of white cloth about his loins and a length of white cloth over his shoulder, and walk in sandals as Darya did. And would not the people stare to see a white man in this dress? Darya's dark skin did not look bare, but white skin would be naked indeed.

They had reached the great carved stone gate, and with a careless gesture to the watchman Darya entered, David following. Inside the gardens were beautiful and green.

"How have you managed this?" David exclaimed.

"My father employs many water carriers," Darya said with the same carelessness. "And more than that, we have a stream of water flowing through the house, a natural fountain."

Darya led the way through one gate and another and then by winding paths to a part of the house which belonged to him and his wife and children. There he opened the door into a large pillared hall, through which flowed a quiet stream, lined with green tiles. Potted palms and trees were set against the walls and low couches stood here and there.

As they entered two small naked boys climbed out of the water to run away and a young woman drew her sari over her head.

"Leilamani!" Darya called in his own Marathi tongue. "Please do not go away."

She stopped, the silken garment held across her face.

David stood waiting while Darya went to his wife and said in a manner most gentle and coaxing, "Leilamani, here is my dear friend, in whose house I stayed while I was in America. I was in his house and now I have asked him to come to mine. Is this not what I should do?"

His little naked sons came back and clung to their mother's flowing skirts, sucking their wet forefingers while they stared at the stranger their father had brought into their house.

She did not reply, and at last, very gently and as though she, too, were a child, Darya pulled at the silk across her face and drew it away. He held her hand as in a caress and he put his arm about her shoulders and coaxed her to walk with him, though she was very unwilling, until they came within ten feet or so of David, who stood waiting and smiling, and there Darya stopped, while his young wife drooped her head and let her long black lashes curl against her cheek.

"David, this is Leilamani, the mother of my children, and this, Leilamani, is David. He is my brother and you must not think he is like any other white man, but only my brother."

"Do not make her stay," David said in Marathi. It was pleasant to be able to speak that language which she could understand.

"Hear him," Darya said in delight, "he speaks as we do, Leilamani, and have you ever heard a white man speak so well like us before?"

She raised her head at this and gave him a shy lovely look and now she let the silk stuff fall and she put her hands on the shoulders of her sons, but still she was speechless.

"Another day," Darya said for her, "another day, David, she will speak to you. It is enough today that she did not run away with the children. Go now, my dove, and bid the servants bring us limes and lemons and cold boiled water and honey. The children may stay and play in the stream. It is too hot elsewhere."

She leaned and spoke to the boys then in a low voice, bidding them, as David could hear, to be obedient to their father, and she raised her hands to David in greeting and farewell and drew the silk over her head again and went away, her sandaled feet noiseless upon the polished tiles of the floor.

"Sit down on this couch," Darya commanded.

David sank on the low couch. The children, silent and graceful, slipped into the water again and played with small stones. Servants came in soon with trays of sweetmeats arranged on fresh green leaves. The sudden coolness, the soft sibilance of the water slipping over the stones created an atmosphere so new, so restful after the intense heat and the anxiety of the continued dryness, that he felt sleep creep over him as he relaxed. He had not slept well for many nights, even upon the thin straw mat which for coolness had replaced the sheet over his mattress.

"Rest," Darya said in his caressing voice. "I can see you are weary. You have grown very thin, David. Eat, my friend, and drink this fruit juice. It is sweetened with honey and that too will restore you." And while they ate and drank Darya fixed his shrewdly seeing eyes upon David and he said, "David, you do wrong to try to be a saint. Why do you not marry? Where is Olivia? Have you forgotten her? It is not necessary for a Christian to be a sadhu. In our religion, yes, the priests must be holy and they do not marry, but it is better for you to marry. You do not look well. Now you know, David, some men can be celibate, they carry life within themselves, but you, my friend, must find a source of life outside yourself. You are a transmitter, and from Olivia you would draw strength."

"I have not forgotten her," David said. The dainty morsel of sweet in his mouth, the fluff of sugared pastry, went suddenly dry. Even Darya had no right to pierce the secret of his heart.

"Have you asked her to marry you?" Darya inquired with fond and pressing interest.

"Yes," David said abruptly.

116

"And she refused you?"

"Yes."

"Ah, that was foolish of her," Darya said warmly. "She should have seen not only that you need her but that she needs you. Her only hope of peace as a woman is to marry a man who is gentle like you, David. You could teach her to be mild, and she would teach you to be strong, through love. It is the other way in my marriage, I acknowledge it. It is necessary for me to have a gentle wife, one who is obedient, who is silent when I am angry. Well, then, the foolish Olivia! But try again, David. You must not continue alone, it is the mistake Englishmen make when they allow their wives to go and live in England. The climate here is more than hot, it is fecund, our weakness and our strength. Ask her again to be your wife, David."

"It is not as easy as you think," David said. He could not explain to Darya the nature of western love between man and woman. In some ways Darya was very alien and Indian.

"I cannot speak of her," he said abruptly.

Darya pressed his hand, smiled, and shook his head. "Then we will not speak of her. Eat this cool melon, it is good for the kidneys in summer."

He ate and drank as Darya bade him do. He had not been hungry for weeks and the boiled water in the mission house was tepid and flat.

Then, grateful that Darya had not been his usual insistent self, he made talk. "Are there many houses like this in India?"

"Not many," Darya confessed, "but there are a few. You are asking why we do not renounce our riches when so many are poor. I have asked myself also and it troubles me, and yet I do not accept the renunciation. My parents are old, I am the eldest son, I have my wife and children and the family depends upon me—this, though I know that renunciation is the highest form of spiritual joy. My father says nevertheless that we who are rich perform a useful function. It is well, he says, for the people to know that there can be houses like ours, so that they too may have hope of fortune. Whether he merely comforts himself, I do not know. But you are the son of a rich man, David, and your Scriptures say, too, that it is hard for rich men to enter the kingdom of heaven. Our Scriptures say the same thing in other words."

This was the moment to tell Darya of his plans for his life and so he began, and he drew for Darya the future that he would make and how to his great school he would draw the best of India's youth and inspire them with strength and knowledge, and he would gather the finest of teachers and the strongest of faith from everywhere. What his father had not done, he would do.

Darya listened, his eyes flashing, humorous, sceptical, tender, but David talked stubbornly on.

"And shall you make all these young Indians into Christians?" Darya demanded at last.

"Not against their will," David said.

"Ah, you will charm them," Darya protested. "I know your western ways! You will surround them with comforts and you will make them believe that your running water and your clean rooms and soft beds, your great libraries and your vast rooms and healthy food are all the result of your religion and so you will make Christians out of them. And then the young doctors will all want great hospitals and electrical machines and they will not want to live in the villages and the teachers will not want to teach in village schools and the girls will want to marry men who can give them houses like yours and that is what they will think is Christianity."

"Is there any reason why a man cannot be Christian and live in a clean house lighted by electricity instead of by smoky oil?" David demanded.

"He must walk the way, my friend," Darya said. "He cannot come out of the village directly into your Christian America. He has to go back to his village that he left and make it over with his own hands, my friend."

"As you do, doubtless," David said with un-Christian malice.

"Ah, but I am not a villager," Darya retorted. "It would be false for me to pretend that I must do what I am not born to do."

"Nevertheless, I too must do what I think I am born to do," David insisted, "under God's guidance," he added.

118

"By all means," Darya agreed. "Let us not quarrel. Build your school and I will send my sons to it. But do not expect them to go into villages. They will come back here and ask me to put in electricity and I will refuse because I do not like electricity."

"Who said you must have electricity?" David demanded.

"It is the inevitable result of your Christianity," Darya said. His mood changed suddenly and he was all coaxing again. "Be happy, David. It is all I ask."

The two young men fell silent and after a while, David slept. When he woke the children were gone, but Darya was there reclining upon cushions and reading a book by the light of a small lamp of brass hung on the wall behind his shoulder.

"Do not go home," Darya said coaxingly, "stay here with me, David. My house is your house. You are too lonely."

"I have had a wonderful sleep," David said, "a restful cool sleep. But I must go back, Darya."

Darya teased him. "You are determined to be a saint, are you?"

"Not that," David replied.

It was dark, and when they came out a servant was waiting with a lantern to see that no snakes lay in the path to the gate, and when they reached the gate Darya bade the servant light the way for David to the mission house.

"Serpents come out in the summer darkness, and you must be safe," he said.

They parted and David walked behind the man and the dust rose and stung his nostrils. The night was black and stifling and the light of the lantern shone through a golden haze. At the gate he gave the man some money and the gateman lit a torch and went before him into the house, again to guard him from the creeping serpents of the night. The house was still and hot and David went upstairs alone by the light of a lamp he had lit and now carried in his hand, and his footsteps echoed upon the bare floors. He entered his room and looked about him as a habit to see whether scorpions or centipedes were anywhere near. Lizards were harmless, they clung to the walls and the ceiling and ate the mosquitoes and therefore were friendly and sometimes in the night he heard them fall with a soft plop upon the cotton roof of his mosquito net. He undressed and poured water over himself in his bathroom and then went naked to bed.

For some reason, against his controlled will, in that night he dreamed a hot and throbbing dream of Olivia. He dreamed that she had come, that she was here, and that he held her in his arms. He dreamed that when morning came she did not go away, that she stayed here, she lived here, and they were happy together. It was the first time he had dreamed of her since he came to India and when he woke in the darkness before dawn he knew that what had set him dreaming was Darya's wife. Darya loved her, and how strange that her name was Leila—Leilamani! He had been astonished to hear it spoken, and he had not wanted to tell Darya that Leila had been his mother's name. And thinking of his mother he fell into memories of his home and of his boyhood, and then of Olivia again and she came near to him and her eyes were as dark as Leilamani's eyes.

Try again, Darya had said, try again, David! He lay stretched upon the dry mat, in the blackness, listening to the almost noiseless scuff of lizards, the dry almost silent rustle of their feet. Far off somewhere now, just before the dawn, when, if ever, the Indian night was still, he heard the wiry wailing of a human voice chanting to the subdued beat of a drum. A timid woman might be afraid of India in the night but Olivia was not timid. Yes, he would try again. Darya was right. It was not good for a man to be alone in India. He rose from his bed in the night and lit the candle on his table, he pulled up a bamboo chair, and wrote the first love letter of his life.

Across the city Darya was also writing to Olivia, and Leilamani was leaning on his shoulder, her hair flowing loose down her back. She watched each curve of the English letters, admiring his skill and adoring his strong brown hand. Only a little while before that hand had caressed her yielding body with yet another skill. They had made sweet love together and when their hearts were quiet again Darya had lain thinking of David, who had no such joy, and then Leilamani had pouted and wanted to know what he was thinking about. So he told her how David, his brother, had no wife, and he told her about the proud tall girl who would not marry him, and then he had to explain that in the strange country across the black waters the young women were wilful and would marry only as they chose.

Leilamani had listened, still warm in the curve of Darya's bare arm, and she grew grave.

"It is very wicked," she said and then out of pity for the young American whom Darya loved she went on with gentle decision, "And you, beloved, should help your soul's brother."

"I?" Darya said, very sleepy.

"You should," she repeated. "You must write a letter to this Olivia and tell her she is wrong to refuse to marry. Tell her how thin he is and how he is alone in that house. Make her heart soft— you know how to do such things, Darya."

He laughed at her mildly, too happy to move, but Leilamani would not let him rest. She pushed him with her soft hands and when he would not move, she got out of bed and walked about the room, her long black hair swinging about her, and she sang so that he could not sleep, a song she made up as she went and that told him she would not come into his bed again, though he called her many times, unless he did his brotherly duty now, for tomorrow he would be here and there and she would not be able to catch him and compel, but now he was hers. So between laughing and singing and then being a little angry until she coaxed him with reasonable words, reminding him that he did often say he would do something and then forgot it or delayed until the cause was lost, at last he got up and began to write the letter. When it was done he read it aloud, translating it into their own tongue as he read.

Miss Olivia Dessard:
Dear Sister;
    You will consider it strange to receive a letter from me, but I write you for my friend-brother, David MacArd, and I think you have not forgotten him. He is here in Poona,

if you do not know it, living alone in the mission house, all other missionaries having departed to the cool hills during the hot season we are now enduring. He is a strong saintly fellow and he wishes to endure as our people are doing. Nevertheless, he is very thin and he suffers from want of wifely care. As his friend and brother, I beg you to reconsider his question and join him. In case he does not ask you again, as I have advised him to do, kindly let me know and I will beg him to take courage. I am sure that you will not find so good a husband wherever you look. I await your reply eagerly.

Your friend and brother,
Darya.

This letter Leilamani approved and when it was sealed and stamped she called for a servant and bade him to take it instantly to the postoffice and put it into the nightbox.

Then she went back into Darya's bed, where he had already placed himself, and they slept deeply.

VI

By the chance of Leilamani's insistence, Darya's letter caught a ship at the last moment, whereas David's letter was delayed until the next ship, and this made a matter of two weeks and more between the two letters as they reached Olivia's hands. She had therefore these weeks in which to laugh first at Darya's efforts, and then to grow thoughtful and then to wonder if David would write to her or not, and if he did what she would say.

When his letter did come, her heart was already prepared, and this was thanks to Leilamani, whom she did not know was alive. She took up David's letter and read it again.

"You may say to yourself, Olivia, that you have no call to the mission field. Well, dearest, do not worry about that. It is not required that a wife must also be a missionary. She will help him, she will strengthen and comfort him, she will be his companion. When I say these words, thinking of you, I grow giddy with love for you. Can such things be—for me?"

She let the pages fall into her lap and looked out of the open window beside which she sat, into the park across the street. It was a small park, she and her mother lived in an unfashionable part of New York, and on the benches old men sat drowsing in the shade of a few grimy trees. She shivered, fascinated again as she often was by their misery, their age, their loneliness, their poverty. Once they had all been young and now they were old and that was the tale of their life. It might be the tale of hers, as the years passed. Oh, she was busy enough, she had friends for the present, family friends, but she had nothing of her own except her mother, and her mother could go with her to India. David had enclosed to her a small snapshot of the mission house, it looked comfortable, set in the big compound and encircled with arched verandas. The air of romance was about it.

She rose with decision, and the letter fell from her lap to the floor. She opened the mahogany desk against the wall and began to write quickly and with resolution.

Dear David—

Well, that was the best she could do. She had never learned to use the words of easy love and she could not pretend.

I have been sitting here at the window for hours, with your letter in my hands, reading it over and over again, wondering what I really want to do, and now when I know what I have decided, wondering whether it is entirely fair to you. For I shall say yes, David. I will be your wife. I don't know if I am in love with you. If I had to decide that, it might be to say I am not, at least not yet. I don't know you as you are now. But somehow I feel that I shall love you once we are together, and I will come to India soon—"

She was not easily articulate, words did not flow from her, she had never talked to any one, for example, as easily as she had talked to Darya, but that was because he talked as he breathed, the light from his extraordinary eyes illuminating speech. She had never forgotten him and he made India easier to imagine.

She paused and sat thinking again for a long time. Then she wrote one more sentence. "At least, dear David, I am willing to try it, if you are, and having given my word, I will not take it back."

When she had written the letter, she sealed it, stamped it, and she put on her hat and jacket and walked to the corner and put the letter in the mail box.

She kept her engagement to herself for days, for she supposed that now she was engaged. The question was should she or should she not tell Mr. MacArd. David had said nothing in his letter to guide her. Perhaps she ought to wait for another letter, or perhaps she ought to write and ask him. But a wilful delicacy had made her determine not to write to David again until she had his letter and that might mean months of waiting before she knew. Moreover, she was not sure that she wanted his decision. Perhaps she should make her own. At any rate, she would not tell her mother until she knew whether she was going to tell Mr. MacArd.

The empty days of summer slipped by. Her friends had left the city and she knew that she and her mother would go nowhere. She had been born too late in her mother's life, she now realized. Her mother had reached an age where nothing mattered except the quiet of being left alone. When they had moved out of the house finally, the last of her mother's energy seemed drained away. She had made sure that the money they had received from MacArd was invested so that they could live on it and then she had ceased to think. Olivia had found an apartment they could afford and had settled their furniture into it and had hired an Irish maid to take care of them. Her mother now simply agreed to anything. The old days of battle were over, time and youth had made Olivia the victor and to her surprise she did not enjoy victory. It meant that childhood was past and whatever she did now was her own fault.

She decided, after more days of restless thought, that she should go and see Mr. MacArd herself. That much would be done, and her future would be more clear. It seemed nebulous enough sometimes, in spite of David's letter which she read over and over, for she was impatient by nature and the long silence after she had written David became unbearable. She knew that distance was the cause, she could see in imagination the ocean and that crossed then the miles upon miles of terrain of many countries and then the sea again. But the hours dragged, nevertheless, and she wanted life to begin.

One morning she woke to changed air and brilliant sunshine. A hurricane had burst over southern waters the week before and the fresh winds had blown northward against the heat and stagnation of the city. She felt every nerve quicken, her muscles were eager to

125

move, and her body urged her will. She would go downtown today and simply announce at the MacArd Building that she wished to see Mr. MacArd. Dress was suddenly important, although for days she had not cared what she wore, and she chose a grey silk skirt and jacket and a soft yellow blouse. She put on one hat after another and settled at last upon a yellow felt, broad-brimmed and soft, too. This was the day and the time, she decided, to look her feminine best, and she put on her yellow kid gloves.

Thus arrayed after her breakfast she tiptoed into her mother's room, found her asleep and tiptoed out again. Irene, the maid, was in the kitchen and she left a message that she was going for a long walk and then she was free. She walked the streets with feet made swift by health and excitement. It was a long walk, but the cool wind was a delight, her cheeks grew pink and her black eyes bright. She caught a glimpse of herself in the glass doors of the entrance to the MacArd Building, and the handsome face she saw was the last assurance she needed.

"Mr. MacArd, please," she said at the desk. "Miss Olivia Dessard."

The tired blonde at the desk glanced at her. "Have you an appointment?"

"Tell him, please, that I have a letter from his son."

She sat down on a red leather chair and waited for a very few minutes when a man came in.

"Mr. MacArd will see you, Miss Dessard. Please come with me."

She rose and followed him through corridors and rooms filled with men and women and typewriters and machines and then through corridors again until heavy mahogany double doors made a barrier. The man opened the doors and there were corridors again and offices but carpeted and quiet now, and then another heavy mahogany door confronted her. This the man opened and there, behind an enormous desk, mahogany again, she saw MacArd sitting reading a letter. He wore pince-nez and a heavy black ribbon and his suit was of black broadcloth, his stiff wing collar was whiter than any snow and his black cravat was of satin. She saw all this quickly as a frame for his grim grey face and the red-grey beard and

126

eyebrows. Underneath the brows, deep set, his small grey eyes stared at her. The pince-nez dropped the length of its ribbon.

"Well, Miss Dessard! Sit down."

The man went away and shut the door softly and she sat down in the upright red leather chair across the desk.

"Good morning, Mr. MacArd."

"Good morning, Miss. What can I do for you?"

She did not take off her yellow kid gloves but she stretched her right hand across the desk. He seemed to be surprised to see it but he shook it formally without getting up.

She smiled and leaned her elbows on the desk. "I don't wonder you are surprised to see me, Mr. MacArd, but I felt I ought to come, although I know you are busy. I have had a letter from your son."

"Indeed!" He put down a letter he was still holding in his left hand and stared at her, his eyebrows twitching.

She went on. "He has asked me to marry him, Mr. MacArd, and I have said I would. I thought you ought to know."

She waited motionless, her eyes unwavering as he stared at her. Points of light shone in the deep eyes, and suddenly MacArd laughed.

"So he's come to his senses!" he shouted. His hairy face creased in thick wrinkles.

Her eyes questioned the laughter. "You mean—?"

He banged the desk with his outspread hands. "I mean he's coming home, an't he? He'll have to come home to marry you, won't he?"

"Certainly not," she retorted, amazed. "It didn't occur to him—nor to me. He asks me to come to India."

MacArd got up and leaned on his clenched fists toward her. "What? You an't going! Why, I didn't think you'd be such a fool."

She tilted her head to look back at him. "Of course I am going!"

"Ever been there?"

"No, but I'm not afraid."

"Wait till you get there! Snakes, heat, beggars, filth, naked men strutting around pretending to be saints—"

"I thought you built MacArd Memorial to change—"

"There's no MacArd Memorial!" he roared.

He sat down abruptly and his great body seemed to crumple.

"Why, Mr. MacArd—"

"I gave it all up as foolishness," he said heavily. "I've got a precision works there now instead."

"A factory!" she gasped. "In our house—"

"Not in the house exactly—that's administration and so on. Other buildings."

"I didn't know," she said.

She looked away from him then, to the big window. Far beyond the city she saw the river swelling into the Sound. The sun shone down upon the water, metal-bright.

"I suppose I should've told you," MacArd said heavily. "Still, I'd bought the place. I daresay if David had stayed here I would have carried out the idea. But when he was set on leaving me and going to India as a goddamned missionary himself, I couldn't go on with it. My feelings changed."

"Did David know before he went?"

"Yes, but it made no difference. I guess nothing made any difference. He was set."

"I see," she said. What she saw, gazing out to the river as it rushed to the ocean, was a man different indeed from the boy she had known. He had dared to defy his father and choose his own path! She could not have believed it possible but he had done it. He took on stature before her eyes, the son of his father.

She brought her eyes back to MacArd. "So now?"

He shrugged his thick shoulders. "I keep busy, all right. I have a lot of things to interest me. Look here, this letter—" he took up the letter he had put down and fastened his pince-nez upon his nose with hideous grimaces. "You may not know anything about it, young woman, but the country is saved. That fellow Bryan is out now for good and all. He'll never be President. Know why? Cyanide, potassium cyanide! Two young Scotchmen have found the trick, and here's their letter. I'll back them to any tune. Gold in Australia, gold in South Africa, gold in the Klondike, it's all helped,

128

but this is the real savior." He thumped the flapping pages of the letter. "You remember that name—potassium cyanide! It will get the gold out of low grade ore. At last I can do it. Bryan's free silver doesn't matter any more. We have gold—all the gold we want."

"What does gold mean, Mr. MacArd?" Olivia insisted.

"It means that people are going to be able to pay their debts, it means business is going up, it means people can go to shows and spend money and have a good time! The country is solid again on gold." He was thumping the letter with every sentence.

"But what does it mean to you, Mr. MacArd?" Olivia insisted again.

The grizzled red eyebrows lowered. MacArd frowned at her. "Why, young woman, it will mean millions to me, that's what it'll mean!"

"I see." But what she saw was that suddenly she loathed this big red-haired man and she wanted to get away from him quickly.

She got up and put her gloved hand across the desk. "Good-by, Mr. MacArd. I'll be going now. I can see you are very busy."

"Good-by, Miss Dessard. And, say, I thank you for coming. I'm glad that my fool son is going to marry you, and I'll send you a wedding present. No, look here! I'll put money in the bank for you every year. A woman likes some money of her own."

"Please don't, Mr. MacArd," she begged in instant distress.

"Yes, I will, too. Now don't you say a word. I shall do it anyway. Why not? I want to do it."

She felt tears come to her eyes, to her own dismay. She could not change him. He was so big, so stubborn, so hateful and so pitiful. He would never see anything as it really was, and he could not be changed. Oh, that was the most terrible, pitiful thing, that he could never be changed! She tried to smile and then turned and hurried from the room, for of course she could never make him understand why she had to weep for him, but she had to, because she could not help it.

The monsoon winds came late, but they came at last and for days the thirsty land soaked up the falling rain. In the homes of rich

129

and poor alike the people slept night and day to the sound of the soft thunder. The terrible tension of heat and dryness had exhausted them, for even though they sat waiting for the rains they had not been able to sleep. The animals had wandered restlessly to and fro over the countryside and through the streets, looking for food and water, and men were idle because there was no use in scratching the dry surface of the fields with their shallow plows. In Poona business was at a standstill. Money was gone and all but the rich were living on borrowed cash until the rains came. Now that the winds had risen, had driven the clouds over the sea and mountains, now that the rains fell, the weary people slept through the hours without waking. As soon as there were a few days between rains, they must get out into the fields, but for the present it was no sin to sleep.

In the mission house David, too, could scarcely keep awake. His Marathi teacher did not come for a week, and alone he struggled with the books he was learning to read. On such a day the postman arrived drenched and late and handed him letters wrapped in oiled paper. One, he saw instantly, was from Olivia, and moved by excitement he gave the postman a coin. The man smiled, white teeth flashing and dark skin gleaming in the rain. He was shivering, the heat of the summer had changed to a damp coolness and his cotton garments, scanty enough, clung like wet paper to this thin frame.

"May the letter bring you good news, Sahib," he cried, and trudged away as pleased as though the good news were his own.

David went into the house, touched, as he so often was, by the warmth and humanity of an Indian. There was no distance to overcome, the least kindness overwhelmed these people, the most habitual gentleness was enough to win their adoration. They were ready to love. Yet they were not childish. It was simply that they had lived so long and in such misery that their hearts were worn bare and the nerves quivered.

He opened the envelope, eager and fearful at once. If the news were good, if Olivia were willing to marry him, what joy! And if she were not? In the weeks that he had waited for this letter he had steadfastly calmed his impatience, he had refused to be restless. He had consciously used the means of prayer to subdue his own long-ings, earnestly desiring more than anything else that the will of God be done. If she refused him he would never marry. He would devote himself to India. Living alone, studying the ancient texts, Hebrew, Greek, and Marathi, had sharpened his spiritual senses and defined the reality of God.

He looked down at the open pages and his eyes took in Olivia's letter whole. Then his heart filled. He had not believed that she would accept him, but here were her own words. She did accept him, she would come to be with him, his wife, his own. He read the letter word by word, while the rain fell hard upon the roof over his head and dripped from the eaves of the verandas in the flower beds. It was a short letter, written in her firm clear black handwriting, so plain against the dull blue of the paper. There was no sound but the fall of the rain and the beat of his blood in his ears while the tremendous certainty flooded his being. His life was changed, his difficulties were gone, his loneliness was over.

He fell upon his knees and lifted his face, he held up the letter as though to show it to all-seeing eyes. Then he tried to pray and could not because his heart was running over. India had shaped him already more than he knew. He had been worn down by loneliness and heat and the pressing misery about him. His body was thin, his nerves were taut and his heart was naked to every blow. Happiness, too sudden, had undone him, and he felt hot and uncontrollable tears under his closed eyelids.

He wanted to tell Darya later in the day when he was calm again, and he clothed himself in his English mackintosh and took a big English umbrella that belonged to Mr. Fordham and splashed his way across the city to the compound. Then he pounded on the locked gate. A sleepy watchman stirred himself at last and peered through slanting lines of rain, scratching his belly as he stood barefoot.

"My master is sleeping, Sahib," he remonstrated. "We are all asleep. I dare not wake my master."

"Will you go and see if he sleeps?" David urged.

He stood in the gateman's house and waited, and after a long time, the man came back again.

"He was sleeping, Sahib, but he turned in his bed, and so I told him that you were here and he bids you enter. But everyone else is asleep."

"I shall not stay long," David promised.

He followed the man through the drenched gardens and into the part of the house where Darya lived and there he found his friend, lying, it was true, on a cushioned couch, a silk afghan drawn over him against the sudden coolness.

Darya put out a languid hand. "David! Has something happened?"

"I had to come," David said. He stood looking down on Darya and their hands clasped. "I have a letter from Olivia. She has agreed to marry me."

Darya sprang from the couch and flung his arms about David. "My dearest friend! There is nothing I had rather hear. Now you are going to have a wife."

"I shall be married here," David said, "I want you to be my best man—you know our customs."

"I will be whatever you say," Darya cried ardently. "You are my brother and she will be my sister. Come here, we will sit side by side, and now tell me everything."

"There is only that to tell," David said, but he sat down, and Darya seized his hand again and held it between both his own in his warm Indian fashion, and while David was speechless he began to pour out his talk, the fluid eloquent silvery flow, describing Olivia as he remembered her and as she would look when she came. David listened, half entranced, half embarrassed. It was all very Indian but he was alone with Darya and since it did not matter, it was even pleasant.

Suddenly Darya paused and looked at David with mischief in his dark expressive eyes. "Dare I tell you?" he asked.

"Tell me what?" David demanded.

Darya drew up his long legs and wrapped his arms about his knees. "Will you promise not to be angry with me?"

"Why should I be angry?"

"One never knows with you western men. You get angry suddenly and oddly."

David laughed. "I feel that nothing can make me angry at the moment."

"Well, then, I had better tell you quickly. Another day you might not be so mellow. I wrote to Olivia!"

"You wrote to her?"

"Before you did, perhaps—"

"But why?"

"I told her you needed her and that she must marry you."

And making haste before the consternation of David's look, he described the midnight scene when Leilamani had compelled him to work a kindness for his brother, his friend, and so he had written a letter and she had hastened to send it.

He was somewhat dashed at the gravity of David's look. "That little Leilamani urged me in kindness, David, and it seemed to me, too, a good thing to do. Were you an Indian, David, it would be a matter of course, a tenderness, a proof of love between us. Is not your happiness my own?"

He put out his arms and embraced David by the shoulders, coaxing him with his eyes and his voice. This was Darya at his real self, his Indian self, always the deepest self and the self so near the surface that the English veneer disappeared completely. He was even speaking in Marathi, his native tongue.

"Ah, my brother, art thou angry with me? And what is it our Tukārām says?

'Can my heart unmoved be,
When before my eyes I see
Drowning men?'

So I, beholding thee drowned in thy loneliness, did put out my hand on thy behalf and wilt thou hate me for this?"

It was impossible to be angry with him, and Darya, searching David's face, caught the softening. Instantly he was lively again. He sprang up from the couch and confronted him, bending over with laughter, snapping his fingers while he laughed.

"And consider Olivia!" he cried in English. "Can you believe that anything I wrote would change her mind in the least? No, no, David, she is not like my gentle Leilamani. She will not come when you bid her come and go when you tell her to go. A noble woman, and beautiful, a wife to be proud of, but I warn you, she will always make up her own mind."

David yielded. "Darya, you conquer by incessant talk. My mind whirls like a kaleidoscope. Let's agree—you are always kind and though it is our western habit for a man to attend to his own love affair, I grant that you meant to help me."

"And perhaps I did help you," Darya declared triumphantly.

"We shall see," David said, yielding again, because argument was futile. Darya would argue with relish and endlessly, recognizing no defeat. And he wanted to be in his own rooms alone, and read Olivia's letter again. He wanted to make sure it was there where he had left it, locked in his desk.

Above all, he wanted to answer it immediately. He wanted to tell her to come at once, as quickly as she could. The words framed themselves aloud in his mind as he splashed his way through the rain and mud again to the mission house.

"Come, Olivia. Take the next boat, darling. I didn't know it, but I have been waiting for you ever since I saw you last. I can wait no longer."

The monsoons died away, the sun shone between the rains. The waiting earth sprang into instant growth and seeds that had lain in the dry soil waiting sprouted into the fresh green of fields and gardens. Time sped, the seasons telescoped, spring, summer and harvest rushed together and the surrounding beauty of the countryside beyond the city, and the mountains still beyond, brought an exaltation David had never known before. The Fordhams came back again, and with a generosity upon which they insisted, when he told them he was to be married, they moved out of the big mission house into a smaller one, long empty.

"You will be having a family and there's only the two of us, now," Mrs. Fordham said mournfully.

She helped him to furnish the house again for Olivia, but he would not allow anything beyond necessities.

"Olivia has a mind of her own," he told Mrs. Fordham. "When I go to meet her in Bombay, she will want to buy things herself, I am sure."

The Fordhams took away their modest bamboo and rattan furniture and he got along, furnishing only a few rooms from the Poona shops. Some of the Indian things were beautiful, he had not known how beautiful they were, for now Darya went with him and demanded that the best be shown him. He bought a few beautiful rugs, some inlaid silver, a low couch, and brocades so heavy with gold that insects could not destroy them. He bought also a huge English bed of teak with a hair mattress and a canopy of fine Indian muslin instead of a mosquito net, and he bought some teak chairs with woven seats. Teak was too hard for the termites to chew. Darya swept through the shops, arguing with the shop-keepers, and insisting upon Indian goods.

"Take these, David," he commanded. "If Olivia doesn't like them, she can return them. But I think she will like them."

The house was changed, Darya arranged an opulence, and this without the furniture that he conceded Olivia should buy for herself. There was only the one English bedroom, but Darya declared the English shops in Bombay were better than these in Poona, they were the best in India, in fact, nearly as good as London shops, and much better than those in Calcutta.

Alone at night David knelt at the high new bed to say his evening prayers. He knelt upon a footstool, because the rains had brought a host of insects into the house, and he did not like to be disturbed by spiders running along his legs or by a curious-minded lizard nibbling at his toes. There was also the horror of centipedes or scorpions to distract his mind from God. He felt earnest and anxious and he tried to prepare himself for the life ahead and he had two concerns. Olivia must be happy and he must take time to make her happy insofar as he was able. But, and this was the graver

135

concern, she must not divide his mind or even his heart. She must join him in the divine direction under which he lived, she must deepen the consecration. Man and wife, they must work together for God. He would, he decided, firmly continue his way of life and his habits of prayer. He would be as he was, from the very moment they met, so that she would not see him only as her bridegroom, but also as the missionary.

And he prayed, "Teach me that I may teach, O God! Take Thou this mighty love I feel for her and keep it, lest it become my greatest treasure and separate me from Thee."

His prayer went up and then he lay and dreamed of her and of how she would look when he waited on the dock in Bombay and the ship drew near, and he could see her face at last.

VII

Olivia stood at early dawn and gazed upon the shores of India. The sky was flushing pink over Bombay, the many lights were growing dim in the light of the rising sun and the sinking moon changed to a dead silver. A faint mist rose from the harbor and softened the outlines of the distant buildings. From it rose the massed outline of an old fort or castle, she could not tell which. The rosy mists, the pallid moon, the glow of new sunlight mingled to cast an atmosphere of mystery over the land.

The ship had anchored some two miles off shore, for the waters of the harbor were shallow, the captain had told her, and launches were coming to take the baggage and the passengers ashore.

She heard a man's voice call as he passed. It was a young officer. "Ready, Miss Dessard?" He was an Englishman, and he yearned vaguely over the handsome American girl who was going out to marry a missionary. In intervals of a ball one night he had tried to probe as delicately as he could the mystery of this young woman. "I can only hope you will persuade your fiancé to leave that tragic country," he had said. He was an Oxonian, a young man who hoped to better himself, one of England's innumerable younger sons who were sent to India to find fortune if not fame.

"But you don't leave India," Olivia had said rather too astutely.

"Ah, but India's our job," the young Englishman had declared. "Besides," he had added after a half moment's thought, "it's so hopeless being a missionary, you know, really it is. And only the worst Indians turn Christian."

To this Olivia had said nothing, the music had begun again and

137

she rose. She loved to dance and she knew that in Poona there would be no more of it. It had been lovely dancing on the ship, the rise and fall of the sea made one feel lighter than air. . . .

"Quite ready," she said calmly.

"Well, good-bye and good luck," the young officer said, and he put out his hand.

It was a final farewell to more than himself and Olivia had felt it so.

"Good-bye," she said, just touching his hand.

She stepped aboard the launch an hour later, her mother following, and they left the ship behind. The launch churned the water into foam and the small Indian craft rocked on the waves.

"Sit down, Mamma," she commanded, and Mrs. Dessard sat down, a quiet grey-clad figure, her withered face anxious under her white straw hat. After insisting that she could not possibly go to India, at the last agitated moment she had decided that neither could she possibly allow Olivia to come so far to marry a man she scarcely knew. She had not enjoyed a moment of the journey, and she was not cheerful even yet. She had heard that India was hot and she hated heat and was afraid of snakes. When Olivia was properly married, she would go home at once.

Olivia did not sit down. She stood at the rail and stared at the dock, coming nearer so quickly, and the glare of the sun stung her eyeballs.

She had risen at dawn, but how quickly the sun had driven away the mysterious beauty of the early morning! The island, upon which Bombay was built, rose gleaming across the water and its outlines quivered in a haze of heat. Around the launch plunging now toward the land, a brisk hot wind dashed the water into small blue waves, white-tipped.

Mrs. Dessard sat on a deck chair in silence, gazing doubtfully shoreward, and Olivia, too, was silent. A few minutes more and she would see David. The first sight was important, but she must not let it be all-important, for it was too late now for change or return. Indeed, there was nothing to which she cared to return.

Then she saw him on the dock. He stood, tall and singular, mo-

138

tionless, rigid, shining white in his linen suit and sun helmet among the vivid swarming people. She leaned over the rail, waving her green silk scarf, and he saw her and lifted his helmet.

They stood looking at each other across the moving multitude and the narrowing water, searching for what they could not yet see. Had he changed? She thought he had, he looked much taller or had she only forgotten, or was it the strange white suit? He had grown a brown beard and though it was trimmed closely to a point, it made him look very different from the young man she remembered. He was much older, his face looked dark, but that was the beard. He stood motionless now, his hands clasped in front of him while the launch edged against the dock. But the moment the gangplank was fixed he came forward and she stood waiting, and for the first time her heart began to beat suddenly and quickly. She had really committed herself and her life, not only to David but to India, a man and a country she did not know. She turned her back to the shore and leaned against the rail. It was hot, the wind had died suddenly. The green linen of her traveling dress hugged her body too close and the narrow brim of her straw hat did not shield her face against the sun. But if she moved away he might not find her in the crowd and so she waited although it was only for a few minutes, and almost too soon, before she had time to still her heart, she saw his white figure threading its way among the people who pushed on the deck, the porters, the hotel agents, the English come to meet friends.

He came up to her simply and it seemed to her not shyly, and he bent and kissed her cheek. She felt the brush of his soft beard on her face, she saw the kindling of his dark eyes. He took her hand and held it hard.

"Olivia—darling—"

"David!"

It was impossible to say more in the midst of the crowd, they stood holding hands, looking at each other but not quite fully, for Mrs. Dessard came toward them.

"David, I'm very glad to see you. It's been a fearfully long trip. Heavens, so this is India!"

She shook hands with him, and waved her hand toward the shore. "What a lot of people!"

"There are a lot of people wherever you go in India," David agreed. "One gets used to it. They are very good, actually, very friendly, that is. Where are the bags, Olivia? We'll have to get them through customs."

He motioned to a man from the Grand Hotel where he had taken rooms, the man came forward and David directed him calmly. Yes, Olivia thought watching him, David was changed. He was self-assured, almost a little too superior in manner, she thought, the old diffidence was gone, and with it something of the touching charm. He was more of a man and that, perhaps, she would like. Did she love him? It was hard to tell all in a moment, now that he was changed. Perhaps she could love him easily. It was exciting, this marrying someone she did not quite know.

"We had better get out of this sun," David said with quiet authority. "I have a carriage waiting just outside the dock. We can go to the hotel and when you are settled, Mrs. Dessard, we can discuss plans. I hope you will want to get to Poona as soon as possible, Olivia. Everybody is expecting you, and for me the waiting has seemed very long."

"You young people must decide," Mrs. Dessard said. The sun was hot indeed and she felt little rills of perspiration running down the sides of her face.

They followed David. He had given their keys to the agent and the bags, he told them, were safe enough. "Indians are not more honest than other men," he observed as they walked along, "but once you have entrusted something to an Indian, he will be honest at least until the job is done."

Olivia was a stranger, he thought she had changed and she was more beautiful and she was older. Would he have the courage the moment they were alone to kiss her as he had dreamed of doing? The kiss as he had dreamed it was to be exchanged when they met, but it had been impossible either to give or to receive in the midst of the crowd, and certainly, too, he would not give Olivia his first kiss before Mrs. Dessard. Nevertheless, he was not going to wait either until they reached Poona. Mrs. Fordham had been very stern with him about love.

"Indians are not used to our freedom between the sexes," she had declared. "It is extremely important that you are never seen alone with your fiancée. For that reason I do think the wedding should take place as quickly as possible. Meanwhile, please, no demonstrations—no fondling or—or kisses!"

The carriage was waiting and he helped Mrs. Dessard into it, and then Olivia and then he took his place, and he found her firm small hand and held it under the covering of her full green skirt. She was cool and beautiful in green, the heat did not change her lovely pallor, and her straw hat shaded her dark eyes. He felt a suffocation about his heart as they sat side by side, her slender thigh pressed delicately against him, and to restrain his love, which must not be spoken or shown, not yet, he began to talk about the streets through which they passed, the people they saw in their many costumes, Hindus, Moslems, Parsees, black Jews. But all the time he was talking for Mrs. Dessard he was passionately caressing Olivia's hand, his fingers, searching the palm, pressing its softness, and she sat motionless, not hearing what he said, gazing about and seeing nothing for all her attention, all her consciousness were fixed upon their joined hands and his searching fingers, and she did not know whether she liked it. Still, she did not draw her hand away.

He found his moment, he seized it upstairs in the hotel, when Mrs. Dessard was in her room, directing the disposal of the bags. He threw open the door into the next room.

"This is your room, Olivia, and mine is on the next floor."

Then he pushed the door though not quite shut, and behind it he took her in his arms at last and kissed her on the mouth, a kiss as long and deep as his dreams, his first true kiss.

"Olivia!" Mrs. Dessard called. "Where are you? The man wants to bring in your bags."

She tore herself away. "Here, Mamma!"

But there was time for them to exchange a look so ardent, so rich with promise, that her head swam. She was always quick to decide,

141

quick to know. Yes, she was going to fall in love. Everything was all right, and India was glorious.

Upstairs in his own room, the porter paid off, and the door locked, David fell upon his knees in wordless worship. There was no sin in loving Olivia and God would understand. He who had created them male and female, husband and wife. Yet such happiness must not absorb his heart and his mind. At first it would be hard, but he would learn to control even love, for Christ's sake. The dream had been terrifying in its sweet power, but the reality was more sweet and strong. Olivia was lovelier than he had remembered her. He sent up his wordless plea for strength, he forced his mind to dwell upon Christ, and then this occurred to him, which he had never thought of before: Christ, that member of the triple godhead, the only One of Three who had ever once been man, and so to whom he most naturally made his prayer, had died, had returned again to heaven, but never had He known the love of woman. His prayer wavered, lost its wings, and fell to earth again. No, he could not ask for help to love Olivia less. He must love God more until the greater love would rule his being. This was his task —not less love, but more.

He tried to tell her something like this in the evening of that day. She wanted to walk, she was eager to see the streets, and so they left the hotel and he led their way to the shores of Back Bay. The sun had already set but there was a bar of red across the sea horizon, and the grey tide was thundering in upon the shore. The green heights of Malabar Hill were still clear, though fading into the quick twilight. The great city clock struck the hour of seven and people were leaving the sands. Parsee priests in long white robes stood gazing toward the last light of the sun, not heeding the people about them, and Englishmen and women walked homeward along the shore, while the white children played, reluctant to let the day go.

"If I seem aloof sometimes," David told Olivia while they stood hand in hand upon the shore, their faces toward the sunset, "it isn't that my love fails. It is simply that there are tasks of consecration which demand my whole attention and my heart."

"I shan't mind," Olivia said with composure.

Across the rolling seas the evening star shone out suddenly, golden, soft, and clear.

A week later they were married. The little Poona church was filled with whispering, staring Indian Christians sitting as usual on the floor, but packed so closely together that the path to the altar was narrow indeed. Olivia walked up the aisle and if she saw the faces at her feet, or the faces at the windows, she gave no sign. Her mother walked beside her, and David waited at the altar, Darya standing beside him, and Mr. Fordham stood in his robe of service.

Olivia was very pale, she moved with dignity, and David, mindful of the Indians, did not look at her after one swift glance as she entered. She, also warned, held her head bent slightly beneath her short veil. Mrs. Fordham played the little organ softly until she heard Olivia's step upon the chancel and then she let the reedy music die away and Mr. Fordham's solemn nasal voice began the sacred words. Mrs. Dessard wept a little, her handkerchief to her lips.

"Who giveth this woman—" Mr. Fordham was intoning.

"I do," Mrs. Dessard sobbed.

Well, it was Olivia's business. The Fordhams were common people and it did not matter what they did, but David MacArd and her own daughter certainly did not have to be missionaries. Old Mr. MacArd was right. Olivia had told her angrily of that scene, but when she got back to New York she would write him a letter and tell him he was right. India was a horrid country. When she squeezed her sponge in the bath this morning a centipede ran out, and she had nearly fainted, although luckily the dangerous insect had dropped from her right shoulder to the floor without stinging her and had disappeared down the drain. She mulled rebellion in her heart until suddenly the little organ was playing again joyfully and David and Olivia moved together to walk down the aisle and she had to walk behind them. A week from now, maybe only a

143

couple of days from now, she would be on a ship and going back to a Christian country.

"Poor Mamma," Olivia said suddenly. They had been married four days.

"Why?" David inquired, not caring.

"All this," Olivia said, her hand sweeping the panorama of the hills around Poona. "I do really wish she could have seen it. Now she will never believe that India isn't what she thinks it is."

"Much of it is," David observed.

"Yes, but there's this," Olivia insisted. She was happy, utterly, wholly happy, she was in love, she had been so afraid that she could not be, but now she was in love with this strange man, her husband. When she remembered the slender boy who had once thrown himself at her feet and whom she had swiftly rejected because he had been so childish, so fond, so silly, she could not believe that he had become this calm quietly arrogant man who told her plainly when he wanted to be alone, who withdrew morning and evening for his private prayers, who was absolute in his determination to be his own master and whom therefore she could worship. She subdued herself to him, delighting in subjection. She obeyed him, astonished that she enjoyed obedience. She had been alone so long, and so long had she been wilful and her mother helpless before her that it was exciting to understand that while David did love her with beautiful passion, she was not to be his whole life. She was his beloved, that she knew, but love was not everything to this man. What was beyond she did not know and her imagination stirred. She liked even the beard, for that boy long ago had had a profile marred perhaps by the delicate chin. The delicacy in eyelid and nostril still remained, but his mouth was firm and the chin was hidden.

"Oh, I love you," she cried, suddenly ardent.

They were sitting on a veranda, from whence the mountains rolled away into the horizon, falling so steeply from the house that the tops of the trees brushed the railing.

She dropped to her knees before him, and he saw unexpected worship in her eyes. This was Olivia, astonishing him with her love, a woman who might easily never have loved him, but who by some grace of God did now love him utterly. He knew that she loved altogether or not at all, that was his Olivia, and if he trembled sometimes before her ardor, he was reassured. Had she not given herself completely, he might have found it impossible to refrain from pursuit, and in that pursuit he might have put even God aside. But now she was securely his, there need be no pursuit, and he was free. He loved her with passion but not sinfully because she did not consume him. The center of his heart was calm, and there God dwelled and not Olivia. He felt that all was right, that the balance was maintained.

"Thank God, you do love me," he said gazing down into the dark worshipping eyes.

"And why thank God?" she demanded.

"Because otherwise I might have destroyed myself. I might have lost my soul."

She did not understand what he meant, but she listened. It did not occur to her that she had a rival, or that her place had already been set. She was second and not first, she was his heart but not his soul, but she did not know the difference.

"Take me in your arms," she whispered.

He took her in his arms, safe in the soft Indian night. It was dark, the swift twilight was gone, and the dense black line of the mountains could scarcely be seen against the sky, except that at the horizon the stars stopped. Happiness flowed between the man and the woman, and for her it was enough. It was everything. But for him it was human, and though sweet, it was contentment, not more. For him the divine miracle was not here upon the earth, not even in his arms. He held her close, but his eyes searched the sky, beyond the stars. He was committed to God, he knew it now, and he felt secure.

To her surprise, Olivia liked India, or perhaps her particular bit of India. In the morning the well-trained servants brought her tea and toast. Today she lay in bed and waited for the noiseless footsteps and she feigned sleep.

145

"Memsahib!"

She heard the apologetic whisper and opened her eyes upon the fragile figure of the boy, a dark-skinned half-grown man, the son of the cook. He set the tray on the table.

"Thank you," she said sleepily.

He stole away upon bare feet and she bestirred herself indolently and alone. An hour earlier David had left the enormous bed. The coolness of the morning held the best hours for his study and prayer. She got out of bed and examined her slippers lest some homing noxious insect had sheltered there in the night. They were safe and she drew them on. The sun had risen perhaps half an hour ago but the room was already hot. She combed back her hair and braided it freshly, and going into the bathroom, she brushed her teeth from the carafe of boiled water. All water taken into the mouth must be boiled, that she had learned. Then she took off her muslin night-gown and poured water over herself from the jar of tepid water. It ran down her slender body to the tiled floor which sloped to a drain. She liked this sort of bath, it was quick and refreshing, and she dried herself on a soft towel and drew on a chemise. She had already learned to dress for comfort. Mrs. Fordham wore corsets but Olivia had put hers away into the trunk of garments that she had decided would never do for India. A chemise and a petticoat and then her muslin dress, bare feet in sandals, because her skirts were long, and while she dressed she sipped the strong Indian tea and nibbled dry toast. No butter—the butter came in tin cans from Australia and it was a soft yellow oil by the time one opened the can. She would have none of it, not even in the vegetables. But the dry toast, the dark almost bitter tea with condensed milk and lumpy sugar, were good food after a hot night. She would not eat again until noon, they had English tea at four and did not dine until dark. One needed to eat often but never much in this climate. She left the room as it was, her garments thrown where she had taken them off. There were servants enough, some paid, some unpaid except for eating the scraps from the kitchen, and she never asked how many there were. Mrs. Fordham might not approve of her, Mrs. Fordham who had to live rigorously on a missionary's salary, but

146

Olivia did not care. Old Mr. MacArd put the checks unannounced into her private account in an English bank in Bombay. She found it pleasant, after all, and David asked no questions. He let her do as she liked, and when Mrs. Fordham suggested one day that she was not a proper missionary he had agreed.

"I asked Olivia to be my wife." He had learned to be very firm with the Fordhams. "I didn't ask her to be a missionary. That is not within my power."

Still, Olivia tried at times to please the stout Christians. She was fond of Mrs. Fordham in an easy way, and she liked Mr. Fordham warmly. They were good. But it did seem a waste for them to spend so much time on poor and low caste people and why, she asked David, when there were Indians like Darya, did not he and the Fordhams make them into Christians?

Even Mr. and Mrs. Fordham had cast longing looks from afar at the proud and wealthy young Indian.

"If you could only win him for Christ," they said wistfully to David.

But Darya evaded Christ with his usual careless and half humorous grace.

"One's religion is as personal as one's marriage," he declared. "I would not dream, dear David, of persuading you to my Hindu faith, and you, my friend, are too delicately attuned to me to try to change me. Is it not so with us?"

Who could deny such charm? Olivia felt it as delicious as ever, and it must not be distrusted.

"Do leave Darya his own religion," she had then told David, to which he had made no reply.

Meanwhile she had not yet met Leilamani, nor even had more than a glimpse of Darya and the exchange of greetings and a few questions. He had seemed almost shy in her presence.

"After you are settled, and after your honeymoon," he said. "When you are quite at home here in Poona, I will invite you to my house, and you shall meet Leilamani."

He had not yet invited them and when only yesterday she had

147

wondered aloud at the delay, David had said, "Darya always does exactly as he pleases, Olivia. You'll have to wait."

His manner was remote, his voice firm and a glance showed her that he was the other David, the missionary and not the lover. But she was too happy to be wounded, content perhaps being the more exact word for her state of mind, for content was large and all embracing, and happiness was sharp and particular and must be reserved for special moments.

She finished her tea and toast and wandered out of her room. In the house the shades were drawn against the sun and the house was shadowy if not with coolness at least with its semblance. The bare floors were polished, the furniture dustless and a servant had filled the vases with fresh flowers. Olivia did not try to grow flowers but the servants found green branches and blossoms strange to her, or sometimes only huge fern leaves and small palms. She drifted across the big bare rooms for which she had never bought furniture, after all, in Bombay. She had not wanted to buy for a house she had not yet seen and so they had come straight to Poona, and she had left the house as it was. The few pieces of furniture of exquisite workmanship, some Chinese tables and cabinets, and Indian brocades thrown across their dark and shining surfaces were enough. She had not hung curtains in the heat, the jalousies were enough, too, and she did not like paintings on the walls. She was contemptuous of the English interiors, rooms as stuffy as any in London, and even less did she like the inexpensive but similar effects that Mrs. Fordham made with rattan and wicker. No cushions, not in this heat, and the insects lurking!

"The house is a bit bare though, dearie," Mrs. Fordham said.

"I like bareness," Olivia said.

She went to find David without much hope, for at this hour he might be anywhere, sitting with some thoughtful visitor, or working with the architect on his boundless plans for a vast school.

He took his own way as ruthlessly as his father did for purposes entirely different, and she knew that he planned an enormous compound, a center of education and health and religion. Some day this center would be known all over India, thanks to the MacArd millions. What, she often wondered, would David have been as the son of a poor man?

She found him in his study at the huge table he had ordered made for his plans. A young Anglo-Indian architect was with him and they were earnestly poring over the plans for another dormitory, an addition to the proposed college for men.

The Anglo-Indian saw her first. He was a slender graceful young man, his olive skin, his blue brown eyes, his straight hair dark but not black, revealing his mixed race. He was English, and his presence passionately proclaimed him the son of an English father. He had purposely forgot his mother, whose inherited features he had, for she was Indian.

"Good morning, Mrs. MacArd," he exclaimed with his slight exaggeration of Oxford accent, the little extravagance of manner which revealed his Indian blood. "I have been so hoping you would come in, you know, you have such an extrornary sense of design, such a quick eye for balance, it's always such a relief to be shown one's faults but so delightfully."

Olivia smiled and put out her hand, aware of looking charming in her soft white muslin frock. India had made her feminine, she had relaxed, her lips were no longer taut or her body tense. But that perhaps was partly marriage and the certainty at last that she could and did love the man to whom she was married. Religion, dedication, whatever one wanted to call it, had made David strong and dominant, and love had taught her the joy of submission. In her way she supposed she had longed to submit and now she could submit without loss of herself. The young Anglo-Indian's eyes were unpleasantly moist as he gazed at her and she withdrew her hand.

"Good morning, Olivia," David said. He was careful to show no marital fondness before Indians or Anglo-Indians who were always, he thought, more Indian than English. "Sit down and give us your advice, as Ramsay suggests. I'll just outline my idea first. I want a vast quadrangle here," he put his finger upon a space, "centered upon a fountain, something really beautiful. I want to tempt young men to come here."

"And when you have caught them in your net?" she asked, lean-

149

ing over him and feeling with exquisite delight her breast against his shoulder.

"Once they are here I shall assault their souls," he declared with vigor. "I shall not, for example, give them any excuse for caste."

Ramsay shook his head doubtfully and pulled at a minute black mustache. "There will be trouble. These people are all for caste, you know, Mr. MacArd. And the Marathi are a very strong people, very forceful and all that. They will be as liberal as you please and then suddenly they're frightfully superstitious. Look at the present cult of that dreadful old woman, the sect of Baba Jan! Actually, sir, there are well-educated Indian Indians among her followers. It's discouraging."

The dreadful old woman was a half-witted beggar who wandered about Poona. People said she was a hundred and fifty years old and that she could raise the dead to life again. It was true that there were young Indians, even some educated in Oxford and Cambridge, who believed or half believed in her, just as Darya, laughing but still troubled, had fetched a swami to exorcise his house when the servants were terrified because they said an evil spirit was caught in the lofty rafters.

"It's all nonsense about the Indians being spiritual, of course," Ramsay went on with the bravado, the pitiful contempt of the man who fears that in his ancestry there is concealed shame. "Indians aren't spiritual—they're merely superstitious. And lots of them don't believe in any gods at all nowadays. I know a chap, a very rich chap, too, who has had it carved above his gate, 'God is nowhere.'"

David listened in his usual intent fashion. "Perhaps it is best for the false gods to be cast out, so that the spirit of the true God may enter," he observed.

"Oh, the old yogis won't let that happen," Ramsay exclaimed with strange passion. "They pretend to be so saintly, but they are very wicked and cruel, actually."

"That depends upon the nature of the man," David replied. "There are yogis who are so kind, so winning, so good, that I fear them because they resemble Christ. They are our real enemies. The

Maratha poet-saint said—you remember Tukārām? I was reading his poems the other day;

> 'On all alike he mercy shows,
> On all an equal love bestows.'

"That's the man I fear, a saint who does not acknowledge Christ. The cruel harsh self-sufficient yogis—ah, I don't fear them! Human hearts turn to love as plants to the sun. 'Lead us from the darkness into light'—that's from the Hindu Scriptures, too, and desire is still passionate in the hearts of these people. But I want to show them the true light."

He was preaching and he knew it, but Ramsay and Olivia listened, compelled by his strong sincerity. She marveled at the attractive power in this man whom she now loved. Where had it come from except from the inner source of his own faith? She was Christian, she supposed, but not as he was. Her religion was not a force so much as an atmosphere in which she lived, and in the atmosphere there were many things, her increasing interest in life, her pleasure in her friendship with English people here, her pity for the massive poverty she saw everywhere, her delight in the hills where she and David went for brief holidays, her amused affection for the Fordhams and the other missionaries like them before whom she walked carefully because she had benefits which they could not share—poor little Miss Parker, for example, the evangelist, so snub-nosed and stubby, who must look upon the marriage of the two young MacArds as something too close to heaven for her own comfort. Oh, she, Olivia, was rich in many benefits, and so she must be humble.

"What is this scrawl?" she asked putting her finger on a corner of the blue print, but really she asked that she might lean against David's shoulder again.

"I want Ramsay to design a women's dormitory there," he said.

Ramsay broke in with his too impetuous voice. "I don't like to criticize, I'm sure, but that, I feel, is really going too fast, Mr. Mac-Ard. I cannot see the Indians willing to let their girls enter a compound where there are male students."

151

David was decisive. "If I am to cope with the new Ramkrishna revival of Hinduism, I must dare to break down old customs. The Ramkrishna people are perfectly aware of the dangers of the old Sannyasa ideas, which taught that men should be indifferent to the sorrows of the world, because all was illusion anyway. Ramkrishna believes that God takes innumerable forms and colors, appearing everywhere. It's a tempting idea in these times of rising nationalism. 'Be gods and make gods'—I've heard them say that myself. They will revive Hinduism with such slogans, and that is what I must oppose, for India would be taken out of the modern world for centuries. It's the women who cling to the superstitions and it's the women I mean to educate as the men are educated."

Ramsay sneered slightly behind his little mustache. "If you are afraid of the new gods, why not be afraid of nationalism? That's where the old religious force is really being drained off."

"I am not afraid of nationalism," David argued. "I am afraid of something much greater that nationalism might misuse—the force of the masses of these people, and people like them anywhere in the world, men and women who cannot read and write, the peasants, the ones down under, that man who in India goes out to plough his miserable field with no better plow than his ancestors had a thousand years ago, he half starved as they were, while his wife stays home, subject, as women were in ancient times, 'to the three crooked things, the quern, the mortar, and her crook-backed lord.'"

"Oh, you two," Olivia murmured. "Where will you agree?"

Ramsay laughed. "Fortunately we need not agree. It is impossible to agree about India, you know. Two Indians, even, can never get together anywhere. They argue all over the place. But I am only an English architect, and so no one minds me. I am very ill-informed about India, actually. Most of my life has been spent in England."

He said this carelessly, not looking at them but preparing to roll up the great sheets of blue prints, tapping the ends with his narrow hands, the strange dark hands, much darker than his face and so obviously Indian.

"Well, good day, sir, and madam," he said, "I'm glad you approve the fountain, Mr. MacArd, sir."

He bowed a trifle too deeply for an Englishman and went away.

"Poor fellow," Olivia said. "He tries so hard to be English."

"Foolish of him," David said. "It only makes the Indians hate him because they know he isn't English."

"Oh, let him be what he wants to be," Olivia said robustly.

She lingered, too proud to ask for his morning kiss and then he remembered.

He rose, smiled and held out his arms and she came into them. These first months of marriage were dangerously sweet, almost too precious. They were both passionate and they had found in themselves needs, desires, responses of which they had never dreamed. They were innocently sensual, believing that the blessing of God upon their union relieved them of the responsibility of self-control. Nothing was forbidden to them, since their marriage itself was sacred.

He held her in a long close embrace and bent to put his lips to hers. Their lips opened, their tongues sought each other and curled together like two coral red serpents and their bodies quivered again, in unison, though only in the night past they had met complete. Olivia drew away at last, breathless, sighing, and laid her head upon his shoulder.

At this moment they heard a cough at the door. They sprang apart, and Olivia muttered under her breath,

"How do they always seem to know?"

The interruption was innocent, the half-grown boy servant brought in a letter upon a small brass tray and David took it.

"From Darya," he said, smiling. "I think it is your invitation."

It was, and they were invited to come to the evening meal that day, entirely Indian, and Leilamani awaited Olivia, while Darya was their loving brother and friend.

Darya was at the door to greet them and Olivia saw at once that tonight he was all Indian. It was more than dress, though the rich Indian garments and the turban of brocade wound about his head

153

enhanced his always unusual beauty. The static poise of his tall figure standing in the carved doorway, the remoteness of his large dark eyes, the dignity of the noble head made him Indian and strange. He put his palms together in the graceful gesture of his people, the symbol, as he had once told her, of their recognition of the divine in every human creature, but tonight the gesture made him seem afar off. She felt shy and ill at ease, and tried not to show what she felt, and failed. For once Darya did not help her.

"Come in," he said gravely. "Welcome to my house."

He led them into a large formal room hung with brocades. On the floor soft thick rugs were spread under cushions, and he invited them to be seated, and he sat down near them and clapped his hands. Servants came in with trays of fruit juices and honeyed water and sweetmeats, and they set the trays before David and Olivia but not before Darya. He spoke to a servant in a low voice and then motioned to his guests to eat.

David obeyed, quite at ease, Olivia was surprised to see, and she followed his example. She had never tasted such food before and she found it delicious, small tartlets, hot marble-sized balls of vegetable paste, highly seasoned, honey cakes, delicate as rose petals, arranged gracefully upon fresh green leaves.

"This is all for your education, Olivia," David said after a few moments. "I have never been shown such honor before."

He glanced at Darya with mild amused eyes, to which Darya responded with a sudden burst of laughter. He removed the turban from his hand, set it on the floor beside him and took a tartlet from David's tray.

"It is quite authentic," he declared. "If you were an Indian lady, Olivia—and a modern one, for if you were old-fashioned we could not meet at all—you would be received thus."

"Ah, now Darya," David protested.

Darya acceded. "Well, let us say, my father would so receive you. I grant you that I have been spoiled. Also I am lazy. It is so much trouble to observe the old formalities. All that I can do is to try to observe the decencies. What my sons will do when they are grown I cannot tell. By that time—"

154

He looked toward the door, interrupted by the sound of children's voices, and he rose to his feet. "Ah, here they come."

The curtain was parted as he spoke and Leilamani stood there with her children, one on either side. Forever after when David thought of her, he saw her as she was at this moment, a beautiful shy woman, a tall girl as many of the Marathi were tall, her slender figure wrapped in a long Poona sari of palest yellow silk with a brocaded border of heavy gold. She had drawn the end over her soft curling black hair, and her great black eyes glowed in the golden shadows. Her small full lips she had painted scarlet, and in the middle of her forehead was the tiny circle of scarlet that was the sign of her high birth.

He rose to his feet and then Olivia rose and involuntarily she put out her hand to the beautiful Indian girl.

"Come," Darya commanded his wife, "these are our friends. This is Olivia."

Leilamani walked forward slowly, her bare feet in gold sandals, and the children clung to her as she came.

"You must shake hands with Olivia, but you need not with David," Darya commanded. His voice was imperious but his eyes were tender, and she put out a soft narrow hand to Olivia, the nails painted as scarlet as her mouth.

"Say Olivia," Darya bade her.

"O-livia," Leilamani said below her breath, accenting the first letter.

"Leilamani," Olivia replied. She pressed the pretty hand slightly and then released it.

"These are my two naughty boys," Darya said carelessly. He tumbled the curly dark heads. "This one is five and this one is four. We shall have another one, boy or girl, six months from now."

The children released their tight hold on their mother's sari. The elder leaned toward Olivia's tray and she gave him a tartlet. The small one immediately put out a minute brown palm and in it also she laid a tartlet.

"Enough," Darya said with authority. "Go away now and play."

They were obedient immediately, and walked away hand in hand, tartlets at their mouths.

Leilamani seated herself beside Darya, careful not to touch him in public, and Darya watched her with a loving and solicitous pride. "She does very well, eh? This wife of mine, Olivia, was in purdah until she married. Never did she see a strange man. When she went out with other women in the family it was always in a curtained carriage. I remember that when her father ordered an English carriage enclosed in glass, he had the glass painted so that no one could see in and no one could see out. Eh, Leilamani?"

Leilamani nodded, smiling, and did not speak.

Darya coaxed her. "Now Leilamani, you must speak some English. I have been teaching her, Olivia. I have told her that she must learn to speak English as fast as you learn Marathi. That is fair, isn't it?"

"I'm not sure that it is," Olivia said, smiling at Leilamani. "I think English is easier."

"Now, now," Darya cried.

It was all banter and small talk, and David sat listening and taking no part but enjoying it and understanding very well that Darya was gently and patiently helping his wife to forget her shyness and show them her delicately gay self. Slowly she did what he wished, first by gentle movements, then by eating a favorite sweetmeat, then by smiling and then by a soft laugh, until when Darya grew too bold, she gave him a little push with both hands against his cheek.

Olivia was enchanted. She had never seen such a woman as Leilamani, a creature so young, so childish, and yet so profoundly feminine, so sophisticated in her femaleness. Leilamani was all woman and unconscious of any other possible being. She patted her little round abdomen and then touched Olivia's flat waist with tentative fingers.

"Yes?" she asked softly.

"No," Olivia said, shaking her head.

"Soon?" Leilamani asked with pretty hopefulness.

"Perhaps," Olivia said, very uncomfortable.

Darya burst into laughter again. "You mustn't mind, Olivia! Like all Indian women who have not been spoiled by western life, Leilamani feels her first pride is in being able to have children. It is a proof of her quality as a woman. Indian women had rather be dead than be barren. Is that too hard for you to understand?"

"I think it is," Olivia said.

She was aware now that Leilamani was watching her with enormous and reflective eyes. She was fearlessly examining Olivia's face and hair and figure. She put out her hand and felt the stuff of her thin blue silk dress, then she took Olivia's hand in her left one and stroked it gently with her right one. She smiled frankly and sweetly at Olivia, coaxing her to friendliness.

It was an enchanting sight and the two men looked on enjoying it.

"She is telling you that she is going to love you as her sister," Darya said. "You must not be shy, Olivia. We believe that love is the best gift of all and never to be withheld when it exists. I can tell you that Leilamani does not often give it so freely. She is a proud little thing, this wife of mine!"

"Tell her I am happy that I came and I hope she will let me come often," Olivia said. It was too little to say, when Leilamani poured over her this warmth of affection and trust, but she was confused. She was aware of strange feelings within her, a melting of inner hardness that she did not know she had, a softening of her heart, a new perception of woman, something that Leilamani was which she was not and which she was not sure she wanted to be, and yet which attracted her strongly. Leilamani was a mixture of witchery and wisdom, youth and age, simplicity and complexity, emotion and shrewd common sense. She felt crude and bigboned and harsh, she wanted to go away and she wanted to stay and gaze at Leilamani. She was repelled by her and yet she longed to embrace her. She was jealous of her beauty and delighted by it. It was an overwhelming, inexplicable exciting hour and when it ended and they came away, she was exhausted. She was not at all sure that she was going to like India entire or even that she could bear it always.

157

That night in his bed when he was drowsing off to sleep in the darkness and the whining of the mosquitoes was dying away in his ears, David was astonished to hear the patter of Olivia's bare feet on the floor. He woke up at once for never had she dared to walk at night in the dark or without her shoes.

"Olivia, is that you?" He sat up and felt for the matches and the candle always inside the net.

"Yes, don't light the candle."

"Why not? What's wrong?"

"I don't know. Oh, David, love me!"

"But darling, I do love you!"

"Oh, but more, more, more!"

She was half sobbing and he did not know what to make of it. He lifted the net and pulled her inside. "Come in, dearest. Why are you crying? Are you ill?"

To none of his questions did she reply. Here was an Olivia he had never seen before, melted in weeping and clinging to him, passionate and demanding and insistent.

"Oh love me—love me—" she was crying, and at last he abandoned himself to her, passion rising and then rising again to climax and finally to exhaustion. Never, never had he allowed himself to be absorbed like this, never had he been compelled beyond his own control.

When it was over and she was asleep he could not sleep. For the first time since their marriage he had a sense of sin. What he had done, what she had compelled him to do, was not good. He had never seen this demand in her before but it was not right for him. He lay deeply troubled and after a time he rose and went into the bathing room and washed his body clean from head to foot. Then he put on clean garments and went into his study and closed the door. He lit the lamp and tried to read some scriptures but the words were empty, and would be empty until he had acknowledged his sin. He had been overcome. She had tempted him, yes, but he would not use that excuse as old as Adam. His soul was his own, and he had not kept it undefiled.

158

He turned the lamp low and got down on his knees by his desk and bowed his head and sent up his prayer in shame and contrition.

"God, forgive me—"

After a long while he felt comfort pervade him slowly, like light rising over a mountain, but his prayer was not finished. He lifted his head and prayed again, "God, give me strength."

And while he prayed, Olivia slept.

VIII

The weather turned and grew cool, as cool as Poona weather ever was, but Olivia was languid. Her days were spent in a routine, pleasant enough but unchanging, and she marvelled that she did not mind. She was getting very lazy, she told herself, and it was an effort to return the dinners to which she and David had been invited, most important of which was a dinner due the Governor and his wife. She made the effort, because David insisted that he must be friendly with Government or he could not do his work. It was difficult, nationalism was rising, Government was irritable and irritated. Americans were suspected of being sympathetic with the nationalist movement and ultimately with independence for India. History was against them.

"I am very glad to find that you are sound, Mr. MacArd," the Governor said somewhat patronizingly at the dinner table.

Olivia, at the opposite end of the oval table, listened for David's reply.

"I am against revolution, Your Excellency," David replied calmly. "That is not to say I am against change. I am doing my best to educate young Indians who will wish eventually to rule their own country, doubtless, but it will be within the scheme of evolutionary order and not in my time or yours, probably."

"Oh, well, as to that," the Governor said tolerantly, "we shall of course give them a gradual independence as they are fit for it. Certainly they are not fit for it now, with four fifths of the people illiterate and ignorant."

Olivia spoke too quickly. "Your Excellency, I've wondered so much why they are like this after hundreds of years of enlightened rule under the British Empire."

She dared not look at David. Instead she fastened her eyes brightly and defiantly upon the Governor's dignified square face. His voice sharpened, "Oh, come now, Mrs. MacArd, don't you go saying such things. It will take more than a few hundred years to change India completely. Consider her condition when we came in, and how long it took us merely to establish order. A hundred years passed before we could begin really to govern. As it is, we are still not responsible for the entire country. There are the Native Princes. We are not tyrants, you know. We don't force things down Indian throats."

A general movement swayed the guests into conversation, as though by common impulse they moved to cover Olivia's question. Nothing more must be said, and Olivia's brief emergence was drowned. She yielded, as she yielded in everything nowadays. She sat quietly smiling, eating with good appetite for she was always hungry, to her own surprise, and yet food gave her no energy.

The evening passed, and when the guests were gone she waited for David to reprove her for the question, but he did not. He was aloof, but he was always aloof now, and she supposed it was because he was so busy. The buildings were going up rapidly, and he was already receiving students. Ramsay was with him every day and on some days all day long, and she saw very little of her husband.

The servants put out the lights, and they went to their rooms. She clung to his arm as they walked down the hall.

"Are you tired?" David asked.

"A little," she confessed. Tomorrow she would tell him that she was always tired and perhaps something was wrong with her. But she did not want to tell him tonight, she was too tired for explanation. He stood aside for her to enter their room and she swept past him, holding up her long silken skirts with both hands.

In the doorway she paused, "Did I look pretty tonight?" she asked.

He hesitated and she saw his eyes grow wary. "Very pretty," he said calmly.

Why don't you kiss me? That was what she had been about to say. When she saw the withdrawal in his eyes she leaned and kissed his cheek.

"Good night, David."

"Good night, Olivia. But why now, my dear?"

"I think I shall sleep in the guest room tonight. I am tired."

He waited a second, two seconds, before he replied. "A good idea, perhaps. You look a little pale."

She turned and left him then and for the first time since their marriage she went to bed alone.

He did not care, then! That was what she began to think. He did not call to her and tell her to come back. He did not love her, actually, as she loved him. She began to cry softly and it occurred to her that these days she was crying too easily.

The next afternoon, beset by this strange new loneliness, she thought of one friend after another whom she might go to see. Not Mrs. Fordham, certainly, who was always voluble with disapproving advice because Olivia never went to prayer meeting and seldom to church, and not little Miss Parker who made her sad, and none of the formal English ladies, because they did not like Americans. Who then but Leilamani? At the thought of Leilamani she felt her heart relax, and she called her carriage and without telling anyone, for David was nowhere to be seen, she bade the driver go across the city to Darya's house.

There she found Darya not at home and the gatekeeper very hesitant about allowing her to enter his master's gate. He conferred long with the driver in Marathi, of which Olivia could only gather enough to understand that Leilamani never received English ladies.

"But I am not English," Olivia said and then found that when she spoke Marathi it was enough. No English ladies spoke Marathi, and the gatekeeper admitted her at once, and she bade a servant inside the gate to tell his mistress that she was there.

She stood waiting in the beautiful garden, where birds cunningly tied to branches of trees sang as sweetly as though they were free and a pet gazelle, brought perhaps from the foothills of the Himalayas, came dancing to her to sniff at her hand for cakes. She touched its wet dark nose and it sprang back, staring at her innocently and fearfully.

The servant came back and invited her to come in and when she had entered three doors, she saw Leilamani herself walking toward her, hands outstretched to grasp her hands and hold them.

"Sister, you have come alone," Leilamani said. "Now we can talk, I am so glad you have come."

"Speak very slowly, please," Olivia said. "My Marathi is still very bad."

"It is good," Leilamani exclaimed, "and I still do not know any English. I am too stupid. He tries to teach me but it makes me laugh and then—" she broke into rippling laughter and shook her head. "Come in, come, sister."

Still clinging to Olivia's hand, she led her into the room where the children played and each child must come forward and greet Olivia with his hands together and she kissed each one on the cheek while Leilamani watched, and then she obeyed Leilamani's inviting gesture and sank down on the cushions.

It was pleasant here and she felt relaxed and at ease. The afternoon sun shone in the open door and the little boys played quietly at the far end of the long room. Tall brass vases held fragrant lilies and the air was faintly perfumed and very still.

"It is so quiet," Olivia said. "How is it your house is always quiet even with children?"

"It is not quiet when he is here or our relatives come," Leilamani said. "It is only that I am quiet, because I like to be so. Others talk but I listen. Sleep, sister—you look weary."

Olivia smiled and leaning against the cushions, she closed her eyes. "I mustn't sleep," she murmured. "I'll just rest a few minutes."

But she could not rest and opening her eyes, she found that Leilamani was watching her with an intense gaze. She caught it and moved away, turning her head to look at a hanging on the wall and then to speak to the children. Servants brought in the usual fruit juices and sweetmeats, she ate and drank concealing her inordinate hunger and thirst, she thought, and then Leilamani's watching eyes were not to be avoided. She met them fully and suddenly Leilamani broke into laughter and clapped her hands.

"You, too, sister!" she cried. She leaned over and patted Olivia's waist with both hands. Olivia stared at her, not comprehending.

"Yes, I know it is so," Leilamani said half singing. She patted her own swelling abdomen. "Feel me, sister—another boy! Yes, feel how high he is, just like the other two, and so it is a boy. I will tell you in a few months whether yours also is a boy—"

A hot blush rushed over Olivia's whole body. She understood. Yes, perhaps—and if it was so, that was why she was so languid, so hungry, so careless of what happened in the house.

"I did not know it myself," she faltered.

"Ah, it is good for me to be the first to tell you," Leilamani said joyfully. "I am the bearer of good news. It is certain that I am right. I shall tell him, my sons' father. He will be very happy and he will tell his brother in your house and we will all be happy."

She sat up listening. "Ah, is that he? I hear him. I will tell him now!"

"No, no, please," Olivia begged. "I must tell my own husband first. I must go home now."

She did not question Leilamani's certainty. Instinctively she felt it true, it explained all that she had not understood.

"Go then," Leilamani said, excited, "go, and come back soon. I shall pray to Sita that it is a son."

When she reached home David was waiting for her, a letter in his hand. She stopped in the door at sight of his grave face.

"I have been to see Leilamani—"

"So the gateman told me. I have received a letter from the Governor, Olivia. He is displeased at what you asked him last night and he takes great pains to explain—"

She burst into wild inexplicable tears. "Don't scold me, David—not now! I am going to have a baby."

She threw herself on his breast and felt his arms close about her and the letter dropped to the floor.

164

He had come with her to the hills for a week, that they might be alone together. A week entire from his life he gave her as a gift, because she was with child. It was true, the British doctor in Poona confirmed it to him. Then he had added advice.

"She's a bit nervy, though, Mr. MacArd. Get her away for a short holiday."

Up from the shallow valley in the hills they heard at evening the thin wailing song which was the song of India, the human music of the villages.

> Till my heart, O Beloved,
> As I am tilling this land.
> And make me Thine,
> As I am making this land my own,
> Till my heart, O Beloved!

Somewhere in the swiftly fading dusk a man worked late upon his land and he sang while he worked. They heard his voice, and David felt the quick grip of his wife's hand.

"What are you feeling, Olivia?"

They were sitting in the enclosed veranda of the hill house, safe against the night insects, and the cool high air was refreshing. Though he had decided upon this week alone with her, he could not leave his thoughts behind in Poona, nor his spreading plans, nor, above all, his doubts. His life, he sometimes thought, was a series of strong steps forward, and then long pauses of doubt. Thus, was it wise to set up these great buildings, to erect vast edifices for the future? Was he building in God-driven faith, or was he simply the son of MacArd, compelled by his inherited perspectives to create hugh shapes of brick and stone? And yet India herself compelled large thinking, immense plans. Millions waited and he could not consider in terms of one and one and one and one—

"That music makes me fearfully lonely," Olivia said suddenly.

"Why?"

"Even here with you I am lonely, a sort of world loneliness I cannot define."

"Perhaps it is only that you can't see the face of the man who sings," he suggested.

"Perhaps."

They fell silent, it was too much effort, she thought, to explain herself to him. For if she did, or could, his mind would not stay upon what she said. The voice of the lonely man had sent him far off. He was dreaming his vast dreams and though he loved her and she was sure of that, she knew now that she was not his only love. She must share him with millions of people, with these singers in the night, whose faces he did not see, though they were continually with him, the stuff of his thoughts and dreams. She had lost him for herself alone. These few days in the hills had shown her clearly enough that she could never possess him because he was already possessed and her hold upon him, whatever it was, could grow only if she became a part of all that he loved. That is, she, too, must give herself to India. Even the child could not make David wholly her own.

For a wild solitary moment she was desperately homesick for her own country, for home, even for her mother, and certainly for the streets of New York. What was she doing here in this lonely countryside, lifted upon these tiger-haunted hills above the valleys of India? She gripped his hand, clinging to it for all she had. There was no response, though no repulse. He let his hand be held.

And if she had been able to love David when he was the young boy who had thrown himself at her feet, begging her to love him, the boy who had seemed spoiled and childish, not a man worth loving for a strong girl like her, but if she had foreseen this man he now was and could have loved the boy in patience, would he then have loved her only and with his whole heart? Ah, but had she loved him, and let him so love her, he would never have grown into this man whom she adored because he did not bend to her. She had what she wanted, a strong self-contained man, intent upon his work, and perhaps such a man could never love only a woman, not even her, not at least when her rival was India.

"The air is getting damp," she said.

"Shall we go in?" he asked.

"Yes, I am tired."

They walked together into the big central room, a lamp was turned low and the light was dim. He put his arm about her and she leaned upon him.

"David, I am glad we are going to have the baby."

"Tell me why." He was suddenly tender. "I know, my darling, I feel it's God's blessing, but tell me why."

She could not tell him the truth as suddenly it appeared to her. If she had a baby, if there were children whom she must tend, then she would not be free to give herself to India. She would not have time, she must put their children first as her duty.

"I want four children, at least," she said, her face against his breast. "And while you do your work, I will take care of them. I won't make demands of you, David. I will let you be free to do your work."

"My perfect wife," he murmured.

She felt his hand smoothing her hair, and she closed her eyes and pressed herself to him fiercely. Oh, she would live her life around him, her love would be his atmosphere, and though he might not know the air he breathed, he would never know, either, that his God was not hers, or that she needed no other god than love.

At the end of the week they went back to Poona and the mission house. She dismissed the Marathi teacher. Let the communication with India cease. She would be only David's wife.

She sent word to Leilamani that she was not well and could not visit her, and when Darya came up on their return from the hills, she was distant with him and he did not reproach her because Leilamani had told him, and he knew that pregnant women were wilful and changeable.

"It tires me," she told David when she found that he was displeased that she had sent away her teacher.

It was to be her weapon, this easy fatigue in a climate unnaturally hot, and he did not protest. How could a man protest? The woman carried the burden of the child as well as herself. She needed double energy, twice the amount of sleep, and her appetite had failed. He would not harass her, he would be more considerate of her, more tender toward her, remembering the immensity of the task that was only hers. He kissed her gently, and forgave her for the quick retort she made.

"I'm not made of glass, David! Don't kiss me as if I were something breakable."

She flung this at him and he was startled by the anger in her dark eyes. Then he laughed.

"You temptress," he muttered and taking a step toward her he pulled her into his arms and kissed her hard and long.

"That better?"

"Yes—but again—" she whispered.

In the midst of their long embrace, standing in the middle of the floor, their bodies pressed together, the door opened and the ayah looked in, saw them and shut the door, horror upon her astonished face. They turned their heads, they saw the look, and he drew away from her.

"Oh, that ayah!" Olivia cried under her breath.

"After all, Olivia, it's the middle of the afternoon and I ought to be at work."

"You haven't really kissed me for days, not since we came back from Poona."

He laughed, embarrassed. "Ah, we're married, my love. We're together, aren't we? And I must be off, now."

"Oh well—"

He saw her pouting look, he caught her face in his two hands and tipping her chin upward, kissed her heartily, but without passion, smiled down into her rebellious eyes and went quickly away.

And she stood there alone in the middle of the room, and made a symbol out of what had happened. It was India that had interrupted them and would always disturb them and separate him from her. What could one woman do against that stealthy and eternal figure?

This was the year the monsoons failed. At first the anxious people had told each other that the sacred winds were only late. Sometimes they delayed for a week or even a month. Delay was grave enough, for delayed monsoons meant a meager rainy season, and so much the less water for the fields and the year's needs.

Week passed after week and hope gave way at last to certainty. The warm currents of air had swept aside, they had curved to other regions. The north had abundant rain and even the east had short but heavy rains. On the west of India, beyond the high central plateaus, no rains fell, and David foresaw inevitable famine and the people yielded themselves to hopelessness. Yes, there would be a famine. There was no possibility of avoiding it now. Food supplies, already at the lowest ebb, were hoarded still further and the poor prepared to die.

In the midst of this distress Olivia was delivered of her child. She had refused to go to Bombay and the English hospital for her confinement, and the local British doctor had tended her, and a pleasant Eurasian nurse had come in to stay for a month.

The child was a boy. He was born late in the afternoon while the dry heat shimmered over the city of his birth. The air was so dry, the doctor grumbled, that he could not sweat. He was grateful that his patient was young and strong. He disliked delivering white women and he always advised them to go to Bombay, but this one was stubborn against all advice. Had there been complications he would not have felt responsibility. But there were none. The mother was strong and controlled. She had asked that her husband be summoned and when it was found that he had gone into the native city, she had accepted the situation and had set herself to her task. He did not believe in using the fashionable modern anaesthetics in childbirth and he had let her proceed, watching her constantly and encouraging her.

"Brave doing, Mrs. MacArd," he murmured. "You'll have a good baby."

A few hours later, when it was over she lay gasping for a moment and then she drew a deep breath.

"Is it a good baby?" she asked.

"A fine son," the doctor replied. "I congratulate you."

The plump little nurse, eternally smiling, held up the tiny new-born boy, wrapped in a square of blue flannel, and Olivia looked at her son for a long instant. Then she laughed.

"Why, he's the image of his old grandfather!" she said cheerfully. "He'll have red hair and red eyebrows and a bad temper."

They laughed with her, and the doctor twisted his dyed mustache. A pity the husband wasn't here, he thought. Such courage was rare. White women usually went soft in this climate. He went away feeling proud of himself, and was very stern with the nurse lest she bungle the case, after all. One could never trust these half-Indians as one trusted a real British nurse.

When David came in at nightfall, every light was lit in the house and servants waited with gleaming eyes and hushed voices.

"Sahib—"

"Sahib—your son—"

"Sahib—"

They chattered together, each trying to be the bearer of the royal news, and then the nurse heard them and came out with the blue bundle in her arms, and David, as dazed as though he had not known for months that this must happen, stared down into the round firm face of his son.

"Mrs. MacArd says he looks like your father, sir," the nurse chirped.

"So he does," David exclaimed. He was not at all sure that he liked the idea. Nevertheless, the resemblance was plain. The boy looked back at his father with astonishing calm.

"I don't believe he likes me," David said.

The nurse laughed. "He cawn't see you, sir. They never do at this age."

"That's a relief."

He felt suddenly gay in spite of a most depressing day. In the native city the streets were already lined with refugees from the country. He had gone to see for himself what was happening, and he had listened to their stories of empty granaries and cracked fields. Their cattle were dead skeletons and their wells were dried. Only in the city were there still stores of food and to the city they had come to beg. He had made up his mind as he walked homeward that he would appeal to the local Governor for help tomorrow, but he knew that the remote and pessimistic Englishman would probably only shrug his shoulders and refer him to the Governor-general in Bombay. Well, then to Bombay he would go if he must. Meanwhile, ironically, his school was as full as ever. The sons of the rich were his pupils.

All this was now forgot. He smiled down at his son, and then passed to enter the room where Olivia lay.

"She's sleeping, sir," the nurse exclaimed.

But he went in nevertheless and tiptoed to the bed, beside which a candle burned. Through the misty white of the mosquito net he saw Olivia lying straight and still. She had been tidied, he supposed, by the nurse, for her dark hair was carefully brushed and braided into two long black braids over her shoulders and her hands were folded on her breast. The sheet was drawn up tightly and doubled back under her arms, and the lace-edged ruffles of her white linen nightgown framed her unconscious face. She was breathing deeply and softly, and he noticed now as he never had before how long her dark lashes were as they lay upon her white cheeks.

Standing there, seeing her without being seen, he felt a rush of new and unutterable love for her. How beautiful she was, how faithful, and how strong! Another woman would have complained that she was left so much alone, even alone at the hour of birth, but she never complained and would not now. He had not treasured her enough, he thought with remorse, and from now on he would show his love more plainly while they shared the child. But he longed to show her now how he loved her, and lifting the net he crept inside and sat upon the edge of the bed and put his hand gently over her hands.

She opened her eyes slowly, as though she came back from some far place, and then she saw it was he.

"Darling David," she murmured, still asleep.

He leaned to whisper to her. "I saw him, dearest. I saw our lovely son!"

A smile flickered at her lips. "All MacArd!"

"Isn't it funny? But perhaps he is like you inside."

171

"I want him to be like you."

"We'll wait and see."

"Oh, but I'm sleepy—" Her voice trailed away in sleep and her eyelids trembled downward.

"Sleep, dearest," he said. "I shouldn't have waked you."

The eyelids quivered upward at that, and she gave him a look of heavenly happiness and slept again.

He stole away, closing the door noiselessly behind him, and went to his study to be alone that he might give thanks to God.

IX

"Famine is chronic in India, Mr. MacArd," the Governor-general said in Bombay.

He was a tall handsome Englishman, a man of pride and dignity, a righteous man.

"Does it have to be so?" David demanded.

"It always has been," the Governor-general replied. "We have reduced the incidence, we have built railroads, irrigation works, even reservoirs and tanks to catch the Himalayan waters. We are feeding millions of people, we are giving employment to millions more so that they can afford to buy imported food, and yet in spite of that I estimate that Bombay presidency alone will lose fifteen percent of its population in the next three months. In some provinces it may be as high as twenty-five percent. Statistics can never be accurate in India."

David listened with proper respect. The Governor-general was always courteous to him, first perhaps as the son of the great American financier, but now also, as the years passed, he was courteous to him in his own right. He had been scrupulous in his relations with Government and he was building up a school of such caliber that his graduates would be going into the Indian civil service. MacArd men must be well trained and loyal, for in these days loyalty alone was beyond price.

"My father would say that India needs more railroads," he suggested. "I understand that there is food in the north. It is a matter of distribution."

The Governor-general was irritated at this and tried not to show it. "Ah, there is no such easy way to solution! The real problem is overpopulation. Indians are obsessed with fears for their fertility. The native newspapers are filled with advertisements for remedies for sterility, yet to my knowledge I have never seen an infertile Indian, man or woman. No, Mr. MacArd, all the resources of the Empire can never catch up with the increase in population among this people. Some are doomed to starve."

David pondered reply. He knew well enough what Darya would say for he had dared once to quote this judgment of Government and Darya had leaped to passionate resentment.

"Ah, how that sickens me, David! It has been made the excuse of every delay by Government. And did we not propagate too rapidly to please these Englishmen, India would have ceased to exist. Consider our life span—twenty-seven years! Is this our fault? Consider our death rate—half our children die before they are a year old! Can we afford not to have many children? We are helpless before the worst climate in the world and an indifferent government."

These words could not be repeated here. David was prudent, he had occasional favors to ask and it would not do to anger this good Englishman. Besides, Darya might be wrong. He was often wrong.

He rose. "Well, Your Excellency, I suppose we shall just have to weather through this famine. It doesn't touch me personally, my school is fuller than usual."

"Ah, I suppose the families want to get their sons into a safe place where sickness can't reach them. That is the worst of famines, I think. Starvation breeds disease. We are preparing for epidemics, of course."

"I am sure you are. I'll say good-bye, Your Excellency."

"Good-bye, Mr. MacArd. I am sure you know I appreciate very much all that you are doing for India."

"Thank you."

The two men shook hands, and the Governor-general allowed his approval to express itself in a warm smile. This tall grave young American was no common missionary. He had given up a world of wealth and pleasure to become a missionary schoolmaster, a very

174

Christian act. "Except ye leave all and follow me—" and so on. One did not often see it.

Outside the palace gates where the tall Sikh guards stood in scarlet uniforms, David got into his hired carriage and was driven back to the hotel. He was sad and troubled, and the dusty dry air that hung over the city seemed a miasma of ill omen. He wished that he had not brought Olivia and the child to Bombay with him, but in Poona it had seemed a good thing to do. She needed a change and there had seemed to be no good reason against it. So they had come with an entourage of the ayah and a manservant to hold an umbrella over the child whom the ayah carried, and the few days in Bombay had done Olivia good.

This evening when he entered their rooms she was in gay spirits, dressed for dinner in a soft white muslin frock and her cheeks were even a little pink. The rooms were quiet.

"Ted is asleep?" he inquired.

She made a little face at him. "Theodore is asleep."

They had named the baby Theodore, Gift of God, and she would not hear to a contraction.

"Wait until he gets into college on the football team," he teased.

"I shall always call him Theodore," she said decisively.

She put up her face for his kiss, but he warned her off. "Wait, dearest, until I have washed. We must always wash when we come in from the streets. Never forget, Olivia—promise me?"

"But I do," she protested.

"That's right."

He soaped hands and face thoroughly at the china basin in the bathing room and then came back rubbing his face with a towel. She stood at the mirror, fastening a necklace about her neck.

"Pretty?" she inquired of his image in the mirror.

"Very pretty," he replied. "What are they?"

"Crystals," she said. "I got them today in the native city."

He dropped the towel. "The native city, Olivia?"

"Yes, the clerk said the shops there were wonderful and they are."

He checked the protest upon his lips. She should not have gone. He ought to have warned her. She was still new in India and she did not know the dangers of famine time. Then he decided not to frighten her. Epidemics came afterwards, and it was early in the season.

"Don't go any more, Olivia," he bade her, nevertheless. "It is better to stay away from crowds in famine time."

"Very well, David. Certainly I will do as you say."

"That's right."

He went to her then and gave her his usual kiss, and was glad that he had not frightened her. Her dark eyes were bright, and he saw as he had never seen before that she was more beautiful now than she had ever been.

"The crystals are very becoming," he said. "Let's go down to dinner."

The plague crept into the great city of Bombay, unseen by the white men, for in the native quarters people hid the deaths of their own people. The city seemed as beautiful as ever, for the white men had learned long ago to look beyond the dying and the hungry whom they could not save. They looked to the mountain and the palm groves, to the many ships in the splendid harbor, to the great shops where the rich of every nation and people came and went. They looked to the past and to the future for they did not want to see the present. Hundreds of years before when a few English traders pushed into the harbor, Bombay had been a handful of islands with the sea racing between them, a small port, a cluster of houses and fishermen drying their half-decaying fish, but Englishmen had clung to it because the sands had silted into the harbor of Tapti, Surat had declined, and only the great natural harbor of Bombay remained. And during the hundreds of years between the day when the few Englishmen had come ashore and the day when the Governor-general sat in his palace on Malabar Point, the town grew into a place of mansions and towers, colleges and temples, a city of magnificence.

Yet India possessed it, in spite of the English, and in that year when the monsoons failed and famine fell, plague crept into the streets where no white men lived, and servants in the vast hotel who slept at night in the plague-ridden hovels of the native city came in by day to serve the white men, and they told no white men of the night.

When they had returned to Poona, Olivia one morning felt a headache, an intolerable pain and dizziness. She woke out of sleep and was surprised by an amazing weakness. David had already left his bed, and she tried to get up to go and see whether the baby was awake in the next room. She could not lift the curtain of the mosquito netting and she fell back upon the pillows.

In his study upon his knees, David was suddenly aware of an urgent command within himself, wordless and yet too strong for refusal. He rose, compelled and unwilling, and found himself walking along the wide hall, still cool from the night, and into the room where an hour before he had left his wife sleeping. She was not sleeping now. Through the mist of the white netting she lay upon the pillows, her dark eyes wide and listless.

"Olivia," he cried. "What is the matter?"

"I don't know," she whispered. "I'm suddenly—weak. My head—it hurts terribly."

He dashed aside the net and reached for her hands. They were hot and limp.

"I'll get the doctor immediately—lie still, dearest."

She tried to smile, it was quite plain that she could do nothing but lie still. The lids drooped over her eyes and her face was white. He strode down the hall again to his study, jerked the bell rope for a servant and scribbled a note for the British doctor resident in the English hospital. "Take this chit," he commanded the servant already waiting. "Take it to the hospital and fetch the doctor now."

The man slipped out of the room like a swift shadow and was gone, and in less than an hour the doctor was there. David sat at Olivia's side, waiting. She could not drink her tea, nor could she lift her head to swallow even water.

"Let me alone," she begged in a gasping whisper.

So he sat there, holding her lifeless burning hand and when the doctor came in David beckoned, his lips pressed together. The tall lean Englishman in his fresh white linen suit came to the bedside and made his examination. Olivia did not speak. When he asked her a question, she nodded, very slightly, the effort immense. Yes, the pain was unbearable, very hard to breathe because of this weakness, the giddiness severe so that she could not see his face.

The doctor straightened at last and drew the sheet over her, and she was too indifferent to care what he thought. He motioned to David to come into the hall.

"Have you been recently in Bombay?" he asked in his gravest voice.

"Last week," David said.

"Was she in the native city?" the doctor demanded.

"Once," David said.

"I fear it is bubonic plague. I heard only yesterday that it has broken out in Bombay—hundreds dying every day."

David could not speak. Plague, the dreadful companion of famine, almost certain death, to reach for his beloved!

"What shall I do?" he cried.

"There is nothing to do, alas," the doctor said. "We can only wait. I will send an English nurse. We shall know within forty-eight hours."

Within forty-eight hours, while David neither slept nor ate, the chills of death descended. In Olivia's slender body the inguinal buboes swelled. The doctor, feeling her soft groins, knew the fearful signs.

"You must prepare yourself," he told David sternly.

David stood waiting by the bedside, where Olivia lay unconscious.

"She will not live through tomorrow," the doctor said. "Nothing can save her."

"I shall pray all night," David said with dry lips.

"Do so, by all means," the doctor said. He was too kind to tell the Christian that prayer might comfort the soul of the living but he did not believe that it could save the one doomed to die. He gave a few directions to the faithful middle-aged English nurse. The younger nurses would not take a case of plague but good Mrs. Fortescue went where she was sent.

178

"Oh, it's sad, her being so young, and the little baby," she was moaning.

"The child may escape," the doctor replied. "Nature is careful of the newly born." He turned to David again. "Mr. MacArd, you must live now for the child. Go away and rest—or pray."

David hesitated, and obeyed. He left the room and went down the hall to his study, and when he had closed the door, he fell on his knees to pray not with words but with all the agony his heart could hold that his beloved might live.

In the little compound church the Fordhams gathered the few Indian Christians, and he heard the wailing of their prayers through the hot December day and all through the night. . . .

Sometime near dawn the nurse touched his shoulder.

"She's gone, Mr. MacArd."

He lifted his head. While he prayed that she might live, Olivia had died! He rose to his feet, his mind dazed, his heartbeats shattering his body.

"There's nothing more you can do now," the nurse said. "Try to think of your little boy."

But he could only think of Olivia. He gasped a few words, staring down at the nurse.

"I must see her again—"

"No, no—think of the boy, sir—"

She held his arm, and before he could reply, they heard the sound of sad singing. Someone had already run across the compound and told the Christians that death had come and they lifted their voices in the Christian hymn, "Nearer, my God, to Thee."

It was foreign music to them, the tune was uncertain, and suddenly it was drowned in a wild wailing throughout the compound. Every servant and every neighbor was crying aloud until the instinctive human sorrow of India, always brimming and ready to run over, broke into the old music of the centuries.

"Ram—Ram is true—"

The cry of desperate faith in the presence of death rang like a

179

shriek through the dawn, the old heathen words welled up out of the heart of India and David heard them and did not lift his head.

The plague swept through Poona and one out of every ten of Poona's people died. Among them were Darya's two sons, and when they were dead Leilamani and her baby daughter followed them, and Darya was left alone in the beautiful house built over the fountain of living water.

But David had his son.

Part III

X

THE sun was sinking into the Red Sea in a fury of dying color. Heat smouldered along the horizon, it inflamed the half clouded sky and as the sun touched the water the hot light ran across the smooth sullen water like liquid metal.

"I haven't seen such a sunset since I left India," he said.

"It is terrifying," the girl said thoughtfully.

She was slim and white clad, English, her fair hair drawn back from the pale oval of her face. He was tall and slender of shoulder, his hair was a bright auburn, and his eyes were grey and deepset. Both of them, Ted MacArd and Agnes Linlay, were going home. They had met in ship fashion, attracted to each other because they had come from India and were going back again. Her father was Governor-general in an eastern province, and had his father been an ordinary missionary she might not have allowed herself to continue the casual friendship begun soon after she came aboard. Everybody in India knew David MacArd, the famous missionary, who was Ted's father. Besides, he was the grandson of the great MacArd, the American financier. Nevertheless, though he was pleasant, equally at ease with the dancing set as with the missionaries who clung to him, she did not know how far she wanted the friendship to go; neither, she felt, did he. He did not pursue her and yet when she appeared on deck after tea he was there as though he had been waiting for her. Yet she was not sure that he had been.

"How do you think of India?" he asked rather abruptly.

She lifted her accurate brown eyebrows. "Meaning?"

"Is it home or isn't it?"

She gave honest thought to the answer. "I don't know. I want to see my parents again, of course, and in a way where they are is home. I am not sure that I really want to see India, and yet bits of memories fly into my mind, and did, all the time I was away. You know, early morning when the air is still cool and I hear the bulbul singing in the garden, or evening and the dusty sunset, and the ayah folding my clean clothes."

"And the wailing music in the night," he added.

"I wonder why there is always music in the night," she agreed.

"So many people—"

"I know."

They were silent, gazing into the flaming sky from which the sun had suddenly disappeared. The fiery stream faded from the oily sea and the curves of the ship's wake caught long lines of crimson afterglow.

"Perhaps we are never quite at home anywhere," she said. "When we're in India, we talk of going home somewhere else, England for me, America for you. When we're there—at least when I was in England, I was always thinking of India."

"So was I when I was in America."

Back of the sunset was the country he had left, his own and peculiarly dear because he had been so much an exile. Once during the ten years he had been there he had gone back to spend a vacation with his father in India, and twice his father had come to visit him. He had had a good time at school, first at prep and then at college, although he could still remember how he had cried secretly when he left Poona, at twelve. But he had soon forgotten that, and his old grandfather had been fond of him and had bought him anything he wanted. He had spent his vacations with his grandfather in the old Fifth Avenue house, now so out of fashion and yet so comfortable. He had not been lonely, because he had brought friends home with him, and besides, he had always felt the life of the house and the family and been proud of it. When his father came back there were the three generations of MacArds together, although the two women who had been the links between them were dead. He had studied their portraits often, both women beautiful and aristocratic, his grandmother gentle and his mother proud.

"Though your mother changed," his father had said once when they stood together before Olivia's portrait. "She was a proud young girl but after our marriage the pride disappeared, for some reason, and she was often very humble and sweet."

"Did she change or you, Father?" Ted had asked.

"I don't know," his father replied. "India doesn't leave a man unchanged, certainly."

That summer, only two years ago, his grandfather had excited himself, feeble as his massive frame had become. There had been a reconciliation of some sort between his father and his grandfather and he was glad for it. Then he had been half afraid to tell his grandfather that he, too, wanted to go back to India. But his grandfather had not protested.

"I don't know what you see in that damned country, but do as you please." That was what he had said in his grumbling way and then he had said in a voice suddenly strong, "The second time it doesn't hurt. Children don't pay for their keep and I've learned to manage alone."

Nevertheless it had been a happy summer. His grandfather had even talked of opening the long closed Maine house but in the end they had simply stayed together in town, and he enjoyed being with his father. The two older men had talked and he had listened, as usual. He was not a great talker except in that superficial chatter of his own generation. Perhaps that was India again. He held a world of memories within himself which other young men knew nothing about, and which he could not explain to them for they had nothing wherewith to understand, memories of the close black nights in his childhood when he woke to see the tiny oil lamp at his ayah's bed burning in a flicker scarcely larger than a lit match and yet which made him feel safe, memories of the endless slow moving stream of white-garbed people in the streets outside the mission compound, or of the students at his father's school, stopping to fondle him and practice their English upon him. He could still remember the smell of clean brown skin when they wrapped him in their arms, a smell as fresh as new cut grass on the lawns because being Hindu they ate no meat and he could remember, too, how dark were their eyes, and how the whites were tinged with blue. He remembered above all the endless kindness toward him. He had not missed his mother's love, no, nor his busy father, so often absent, because there had been many people everywhere to love him and caress him and hold him in their arms. That was his first memory now when he thought of India, the boundless outgoing love, not because of what he was but simply because he was a child and perhaps because he was motherless. Women in the streets, old grandmotherly women, and younger mother women going to the well to fetch water, jars on their heads as they walked, and sister girls all knew him and paused to speak to him, to give him a bit of fruit or an Indian sweet, and he accepted all and he ate foods which would have frightened his father had he known, but there was much Ted never told his father or anyone and that he shared alone with India. He understood early that his India and his father's India were two different countries, and for him there was only one, his own.

He had never known any girl well until now he was beginning to know Agnes. In his childhood he had no girl playmates. Mrs. Fordham, it was true, had given birth to a belated girl child to her astonishment and even embarrassment, but Ruthie, as they called her, was three years younger than he, a round-faced, round-eyed child with whom he would have been ashamed to play. When he visited his father, she had already been sent back to some church school in Ohio, and Mrs. Fordham was as briskly childless as ever. And it always seemed too much trouble to explain to any of the girls in America why he was going to India and, since they did not know and probably could not understand, they had remained far from him even while he carried on the gay conversations that were suitable. But this remoteness had made him shy of falling in love, and now he did not want to be more than friends even with Agnes. Some day, of course, he must marry and have children. His grandfather had been plain about that.

"You are the only scion of the family, Ted," his grandfather had said the night before he left. The old man was lying in his bed, very

186

straight and thin and only his big bones made him still look big. He was easily tired and he went to bed early, but he liked Ted to come in and talk, and he had gone on, "Your father never married again though I wish he had, but I couldn't say anything because a second marriage would have been impossible for me too. We Mac-Ard men are faithful to our women."

He had champed his jaws under his big snow-white beard which he never bothered to cut nowadays and he had turned his eyes away from Ted to the portrait on the chimney-piece opposite his bed. He could not see it very clearly any more but memory lit the dim outlines of the beloved face.

"Marry a good woman," he commanded in a loud voice, "marry and have a lot of children. She always wanted many children and we had one. Your mother ought to have had a dozen children, she had as lithe and strong a frame as could be found, but India killed her."

He closed his eyes, overcome by the fitful sleep which fell upon him now at any moment, and Ted waited. In a moment his grandfather had suddenly opened his eyes. "What the devil are you going to India for?" he demanded.

"I don't know yet," Ted had said. "I want to go and I may not stay."

But he knew that he would stay. He had found no place for himself in America—pleasant, oh yes, that indeed, and everybody waiting to be his friend. He had missed the war by his youth, spending those years cloistered in boys' schools, and now, college over, he had come out into a world he did not know, glittering, laughing, corrupt, and reaching for him. The heir to the MacArd millions could scarcely escape the reaching hands and he had retired quickly to the old house where his grandfather lived, emerging shyly to accept invitations, moving with a gay poise that puzzled the mothers and the daughters to whom he was so eligible a young male.

Even his father had not urged him to come back to India. "Don't feel you must come back to India," David had written. "There is always a place for you here, of course, and there are times when I sorely hope you will come at least for a few years, that we may learn to know each other again. But I did not follow my father, and you must not follow me."

It was not his father, it was India. He was going back to something he knew, an old world, a gentle world, often poor and starving and always kind. Nobody and nothing in America needed him, so he had felt. But perhaps his India did.

He knew already that his was not the India that Agnes knew.

He had found after only a few days at sea that they must not discuss Gandhi or Indian nationalism or any of the matters of which his Uncle Darya had written him. While he was a little boy he had seldom seen Darya, and when he did come to the mission house, he remembered hearing his father and Darya talking together and then almost quarreling. It had seemed to him that it was quarreling, and once, much troubled, he had asked his father, "Is Uncle Darya a bad man?"

His father had replied quickly and firmly. "He is a very good man, and I think he is going to be also a great man."

"Then why aren't you friends?"

His father had tried to explain. "Ted, these are strange times in which we live, and nobody can understand them. Many things are wrong and good people are trying to make them right. I believe that my way of doing it is best, but your Uncle Darya has quite a different way and he thinks his is best."

"But can't you be friends?" So he had insisted.

"I hope so," his father had said soberly.

A few months ago, quite unexpectedly, Darya had begun to write to him. "Dear Ted: Your father has written me that you are coming back to India. With his permission I am writing to you. I think you should know the India to which you are returning, for it is not the country you left."

From then on Darya's letters had come almost regularly, and he had explained to Ted the changes he would see. Of course, Darya told him, there was the old India of the villages, almost untouched. It would take years of independence to improve the villages, and perhaps there would even have to be another world war before India could be free, but the weapons of independence were being forged, and Gandhi was drawing the villages into the struggle as no one else could. They would have to have the help of the peasants, since most of India lived in villages, and only Gandhi could get their help.

None of this was real to Ted, it fitted in nowhere with his memories, but he was curious about it and he had spoken to Agnes of his curiosity. To his surprise, though of course he should have expected it, he told himself afterwards, she had grown suddenly cool toward him. They were dancing that evening, and he felt the coolness pervade her physically. She drew away from him in the middle of the first dance.

"Do you mind if we sit down?" she asked.

They had sat down and watched the dancing and after a moment she turned her lovely pale face toward him.

"I can't forget what you said after dinner about that wretched little Gandhi! I wonder if you know how wicked he is really and how he is disturbing the peace of India. When I think of my father and all the sacrifices he has made for the Empire, and how kind he is to every Indian, much kinder and more pitying than he is to any of his English staff, it seems to me the grossest ingratitude in these new Indians to be so disloyal to Government."

He had replied in peaceable fashion. "I can quite understand how you feel. Now shall we dance again?"

She forgave him, and he was careful not to talk about Gandhi or his Uncle Darya again, and in her reserved way she resumed the threatened friendship. And he liked her, in spite of this, because she was simple and direct with the mannerliness of the well-bred English girl. He liked her because she had no coquetry and yet she was so feminine that he wanted to be with her because he had never been friends with a girl before. There was something delicious about her, or perhaps simply about being with a girl. He felt an enticing difference in her, not only physically, but in her way of speaking and thinking. They looked at the same scene and she saw it with other eyes than his. He never knew just what she was feeling, and so there was always surprise. Every morning she was new to him and he waited eagerly until they met, and they had come to watch the sunset together, as they did now.

189

"There," she said, "the sun has whirled below the sea. Soon it will be dawn in England."

"What do you see when you think of dawn in England?"

"The amber light, stealing over the Cotswold hills. I've watched it often from the windows of my grandmother's house. The light comes up like a river running into the valleys. What do you see in America?"

"The towers of the tall buildings in New York, catching the light first, but it is silver, isn't it? Amber makes me think of evening."

"Perhaps," she agreed.

The twilight descended swiftly and the rays of the almost full moon cast a pale glow over the darkening water. The first gong for dinner rang in a series of musical tones and she turned reluctantly from the rail.

"Will you be dancing tonight?" he urged.

"Yes—will you?" she replied.

"Yes. Shall we meet at the usual place?"

"Yes."

Their eyes clung for an instant, they nodded briefly and she left him.

He lingered, reluctant to leave the peaceful sea and the quieting sky. Life ahead was as familiar as his childhood, and yet it would be new. He was not a child but a man, young, of course, but a man. As a man he must meet his father and establish his own independence. It had not been worthwhile to insist upon it with his grandfather, they were not to live in the same house and he had yielded to the old gentleman's whims and demands with a mild amusement. It must be different with his father. He was going to India as a teacher in his father's school and he could not allow his father to dominate him, even by his powerful persuasive courteous presence. He loved his father but he knew that they were different men.

The second bell rang and he went down the stairs to his cabin. The ship was not crowded, he had the small room to himself as he prepared to put on his evening clothes, the formal black trousers, the short white jacket, black tie and wide black cummerbund of the tropics, a garb becoming to a tall and slender young man with grey eyes and auburn hair. He looked like his grandfather, except that the darkness of his mother had tempered the fiery red of the elder's hair and beard. His own face was smooth-shaven, but his beard was stubborn and he shaved again tonight.

Nevertheless he was ready too early for the final bell, for he had learned to dress quickly in the years at school, and his skill at sports had taught him a compact co-ordination of movement with no waste of action. With the few minutes left him he did what was habitual to him. He pulled a small book from his pocket and opened the pages at a marker. It was a New Testament and he was reading the Gospel according to St. John. His father had never compelled him toward the Christian religion, but when he had left India, a little boy, his father had asked him to read the New Testament every day, and he had made the promise and kept it, inconvenient as it often was. The words of grace had crept into his mind without effort, and while in earlier years they had often been meaningless, now, when his young manhood had sharpened every nerve and feeling, they impressed upon him meanings at once poetic and profound.

"Many believed," St. John had written, "but Jesus did not commit himself to them, because he knew all, and he needed not that any should testify, for he knew what was in man."

As usual the seemingly simple, deeply significant words stirred his imagination. He closed the book thoughtfully and put it back into his hip pocket, but the words haunted him as he went downstairs to the dining salon. He was seated at the captain's table because he was young MacArd, that was inescapable, but he had learned not to mind, and he took his share in the table talk, smiling, provocative, observing, and seeking, in his way, too, to know what was in man.

Meanwhile David MacArd was in Bombay to attend the Durbar for the Prince of Wales and then two days after, to meet the ship that was bringing his son back to him. It was a doubtful time for a Durbar. India was seething with new discontent and Darya had

191

made one of his rare visits to Poona months earlier to protest to David the assertion of Empire and to beg him to advise the Viceroy against it.

Their paths had parted five years ago. Darya had chosen to follow Gandhi, subduing his own powerful personality to the firm little leader whom David did not approve.

The visit had not brought the two nearer. David had seen at once that Darya had become a single force, gathering all his soul and mind into one thrusting purpose, that of independence for India. He had left his father's house and had given his inheritance to his brothers. Stripped by death of Leilamani, their sons and baby daughter, Darya had for the first years wandered from village to village, a sadhu except that he had no religion, a beggar except that he needed nothing. Thus he had come to know his own people and the bitterness of their life. But he had no talent for common folk, though they were his own. He was an aristocrat, a man of learning and wealth, and they were afraid of him. This he could not bear, that a peasant, starved and nearly naked, should fall to the ground before him and take the dust from his feet, and worse, when he raised the man up and forbade him to grovel, that the man would not believe him, and would run away from him in fear. There was no way in which Darya could make the poor and the ignorant trust him and without trust they would not follow him. Angry at himself and peasants alike, he had left the villages then, to seek Gandhi and in that wry and humorous man he had recognized the necessary leader. With an unselfishness which Gandhi seemed not to notice, Darya subdued himself. He bent his far more subtle mind and complex spirit before the practical little man who was neither aristocrat nor peasant and yet could understand both.

"David," Darya had said, "you must use your influence with the Viceroy to prevent this visit from the Prince of Wales. It is not the time for a show of Empire. I tell you, the nationalists will not stand for it. They are still furious because we were compelled into the world war without our wish or will, and our dire poverty made still worse. I tell you, there will be mass riots everywhere and the life of the Prince will be in danger. I warn you, Congress will boycott the whole Durbar. We will declare *hartal* in Bombay when he lands there."

It was autumn, the heat was subsiding slightly, and the college grounds were filled with swarming students. David had been aware of unrest but he had ignored it. The years of mastery over young men and women had taught him order and command. He saw no order in the unruly shouting mobs that swarmed about Gandhi, and he did not respect Gandhi as commander. He repressed the Gandhian movement in his schools and admired the steadfast calm of Government, while he disliked its use of force. The bombing of Pathan villages, even though the people had been warned to leave, troubled his Christian conscience and he had remonstrated with the Viceroy himself about shooting into mobs. Yet the whole of India was disturbed and this wretched Gandhi had begun it all with his passive resistance, the non-cooperative movement which a year before Congress had adopted as its policy. He was sorely torn, for he could not as a Christian approve the military rule in the Punjab, where thousands of innocent people had been killed by British soldiers, and he shrank to the very soul from the Amritsar massacre, where the dead and dying were left where they fell after that attack by General Dyer and his men. Even the wounded had not been cared for. "That is not my business," the General had declared.

"You know that I agree with the Viceroy that India is not ready for independence," David had replied sharply to Darya. They sat together that day in his study, two middle-aged men, different indeed from the two young men who had once felt as brothers. They had been drawn close for a little while after the tragedy. Yes, he and Darya had clung together weeping that day when he heard of Leilamani's death after he had lost his own Olivia, and he had hurried to Darya's house. He felt guilty even now because he still had his son and Darya had no one.

"You know, too, that I went to the Viceroy myself after Amritsar," David went on irritably. He took off his spectacles and smoothed his greying beard. "The Viceroy did not like my interference. I am only an American."

"You are the son of MacArd," Darya had said grimly.

193

"I am also a missionary," David had retorted, "and we are all suspect."

"Who can suspect you?" Darya had flung back. "You are conservative, successful, rich—Christian, an upholder of the powers that be. No one could suspect you of sympathy for us."

David had been deeply wounded. For a moment he could not answer. Then he had said, very controlled, "You are angry, Darya, and so you do me an injustice. I have not said that I do not sympathize, but I say you cannot accomplish anything by revolution. You must first show yourselves fit for self-government."

Darya had leaped to his feet, a tall thin flaming figure burnt black by the sun, his darkness enhanced by his white cotton garments and the little white cotton Gandhi cap on his head. In a voice tremendous with wrath he had shouted at David, "How can my people be made fit, as you call it? Starved, despoiled, robbed, beaten! All these years the English have lived here as our masters but they have never known us, they have not tried to understand our minds or hearts. They have ruled by force and by force alone, trusting to their vast military and police organization. They have never tried to win our love or loyalty, though we were ready to love them—yes, even I, in the years at Cambridge, I loved England. In spite of India, there was that to love, and they could have won by love but they trusted to their guns. Now they resent what they call our disloyalty! Yes, yes, you are right, they act in self-defense, but why do they fear us? It is because they have made us hate them. It is too late, David! What has begun cannot be stopped. You will see years of strife and we shall win!"

He had left the mission house with a proud step, and David had sat long in troubled thought. If the law and order of the British Empire were destroyed there would be chaos. The university here in the compound, his life work, the climax of the network of schools he had built up throughout Marathi-speaking India, the fine hospital, they could not function in a lawless country. Time, time was necessary, and when the young men and women pouring from these halls were enough in number to leaven the whole country, independence would be the logical end to a peaceful evolution. But

Darya, misguided by Gandhi's fervor, was forcing an era out of its time. He had sighed, doubted, and then, suddenly resolute, he had taken a sheet of paper and written a brief note to the Viceroy, advising against the Durbar. There had been no answer. The Durbar went on as planned.

He viewed the spectacle on this morning of the seventeenth of November. It was barely dawn and the moon, not quite full, was low over the horizon. Strong searchlights from the shore played through the pinkish light of the approaching sun and fell upon the ship *Renown,* and upon the launches which were taking officials, both English and Indian, to welcome the Prince of Wales. They had left the shore in the early light to the roar of saluting cannon, first the Vice Admiral and then the Viceroy, wearing only the Star of India as decoration upon his grey morning suit. With them were the highest among the ruling princes of India, three maharajahs and two nawabs who were to travel with the Prince in his royal tour and on shore later in the day these were to be joined by three more, the Raja Sir Hari Singh of Kashmir, the Maharaj Kumar of Bikaner, and Nawazada Haji Hamidullah Khan of Bhopal, according to the program.

The splendor of the scene could not be denied. The sun rose clear and glorious, and a brisk wind whipped up small waves in the harbor. The *Renown* lay too far out for him to see what was going on on the decks, but he saw her flying standard. Every ship in the harbor was decked with fluttering flags and only fleets of Indian fishing boats went their usual way. The heat already shimmering above the water lent a quality of mirage over the whole scene, a shining, quivering mist of light. It was soon too hot to stand longer, and he made his way to the enormous amphitheater which had been prepared for the assembly of the day. A long vista of red carpet led to the entrance where a reception pavilion had been erected, roofed with golden minarets and domes. Upon the central dome there blazed the royal coat of arms.

He presented his card of entrance, was admitted, and saw before him an immense space bounded by flag decorated towers, and in the space, rising thirty tiers high, thousands of persons were already

195

seated. Most of them by far were Indians, the official and the rich, their bright many-colored garments shining in the sun, their turbans sparkling with jewels. The sober black garments of the Europeans were here and there, but only the blue and scarlet and gold imperial uniforms of the English officers could match the Indian splendor.

He took his seat, one of the severely garbed, and with the crowd he waited in the hot sun. An hour before noon the roar of welcoming cannon told them that the imperial entourage had come ashore. They waited not much longer. He rose with the crowd and saw the young Prince of Wales walking beside the Viceroy in a stately procession toward the pavilion where the flags were flying. There seated on a gilded dais, he received the ruling princes of India, the men of his own Indian staff, and finally the members of the city council.

It was a spectacle, and in spite of Darya's warnings, David told himself, it was a success. Yet he could not be easy until it was over, for among the gorgeous robes and turbans he saw too the spartan Gandhi cap, the homespun white cotton that marked the rebels. Outside upon the streets, however, the people had gathered in suffocating crowds and he heard their shouts of greeting to the British Prince.

"Yuvraj ki jai! Yuvraj ki jai!"

Nevertheless, he was glad that the royal tour of the city was not to include the Byculla quarter, where the rowdies and the riff-raff lived, and where if riots were to break, would be their focus. The *hartal,* which Darya had threatened, might even now be a failure. The markets were closed, it was true, he had noticed that this morning with foreboding, for when *hartal* was declared, it imposed upon people a religious necessity for a period of mourning within one's home. So far the people had not heeded the command of the rebels. They could not resist the royal display.

And he, too, was compelled to admit and willingly did admire not only the carefully planned pageant of Empire, but the grace and sincerity of those who took part in it, and most especially the grace of the young Prince himself. That slight dignified figure now came forward at the appointed time and standing he read the King's address with extraordinary composure and clarity. It was impossible not to believe in his goodness and not to be touched by his youth. With the same natural pleasantness, he received the welcome of the city, which Sir David Sassoon presented, and in reply spoke so simply and with such earnestness and honesty, that David wished Darya were present and could hear. "I want to know you," the young Prince said, gazing upon the vast audience of India, "I want to know you and I want you to know me."

The beauty of order, the strength of control, the power of law, all were here, and surely they would prevail, David told himself.

The great assembly was over and music burst into the air. The royal company prepared to descend from the dais, and the crowd rose.

Suddenly at this very moment David heard his name called in a whisper. He turned his head and saw Darya standing among a group of Indians just behind him.

"Even I," Darya said, under cover of the music. Then with his invincible smile, he said, leaning forward to be heard, "Look at me, David—you will not see me for a long time."

"Ah, Darya," David said anxiously, "what are you planning now?"

From whence had Darya come? He must have taken advantage of the crowds and made his way in. Among the vivid silks of the courts of the native princes he was dangerously conspicuous in the whiteness of his cotton garments, his little Gandhi cap stark among the gorgeous turbans of scarlet and blue and gold.

"In a moment I shall be arrested," Darya whispered and his look was proud. He stood with his head high, his arms folded. It was not a moment. Almost instantly two British guards stepped forward and clapped their hands on his shoulders.

"This way, please, sir," they said with respect, but command.

Darya turned his head this way and that, he met the eyes of those who gazed at him, he smiled again at David and then walked with dignity down the carpeted aisle between the two tall British guards. For a moment the royal company paused, though without confusion, and then as Darya disappeared, the band struck into new music, and the imperial show went on.

Ted saw his father first, tall, gaunt, bearded, his eyes shadowed by the oval brim of his sun helmet. He stood near the gang plank ready to be the first to descend from the ship, and while he waited this last instant his father caught sight of him and raised his hand. Ted lifted his hat high and waved it, and then stood smiling, but only in the instant for almost immediately the gang plank was fixed, the quick dark hands of the dock sailors fastening the ropes with skill, and he leaped down the few feet of board and clasped his father's hand.

"Dad, this is wonderful—"

"I'm glad to see you, son."

His father was sunburned almost as dark as the Indians themselves, or perhaps heat-burned. His grey beard cut close to his cheeks was a startling contrast to the brown skin and tragic dark eyes. It was not a smiling face, but Ted had never remembered ready smiles upon his father's face. It was kind and it wore a controlled patience, a stillness almost terrifying. It was a stern face, as he remembered, in repose or prayer.

"We'd better not stand in this sun," David said. His son looked so young, so tender, that he felt immediately anxious, the old sickening anxiety of the boy's childhood in this devilish climate. Twenty-two was too young to begin life here, but it was either here or get rooted in America, and Ted had chosen India.

"I shall have to get hardened to it again," Ted said with gaiety. There was gaiety in all he said and did, a sparkling youthful, springing quality. Tall as he looked, he was not as tall as his father or his grandfather, and the peculiar brightness of his white skin, his grey eyes and the auburn hair enhanced his natural spirit with an electric lightness. He was more slender than father or grandfather had ever been, inheriting from Olivia his narrow wiry build and movements too quick for absolute grace. Mercurial, David thought regretfully, perhaps too fine-drawn, too taut, too sensitive for India! Though Ted did not look like Olivia, she had bequeathed something to him of her inner self.

"I have taken rooms at the hotel," David said. "We can leave the luggage with the porter." They got into a carriage and sat down side by side in the shelter of the hood, and the horses ambled slowly down the street.

"Do you plan to go straight home to Poona tomorrow?" Ted asked.

"Unless you have some reason for delay," David replied.

Ted hesitated, then decided against mentioning Agnes. Did he speak her name it might be too much, his father might think the friendship deeper than it was. She would not be at the hotel, her parents were staying at Government House, and he had not asked to see her there. They had told each other good-bye this morning after breakfast.

"We shall meet again," he had said with his quick nervous hand clasp.

"Of course," she said.

"And may I write?" he asked.

"I hope you will," she had replied.

He looked deeply for a moment into her charming blue eyes, the sweet steadfast eyes of good and highborn young English women, and impressed upon his memory the gentle oval of her face, the serious mouth and firm chin, the fresh and lovely complexion, the slender elegant figure in white linen, the low beautiful English voice. Something trembled in him for a moment, words rose to his lips, and he restrained them. It was too soon, he did not know what he wanted to make of his life, he could not speak of sharing it in any degree with her until he knew for himself what it was to be.

"I shall write after I get home," he said. "And you, too, write me. Tell me what the first hours are."

"I fancy we shall be feeling somewhat the same," she replied.

So they had parted, she had left him quietly before he met his father, and he had caught a glimpse of her with a tall sallow Englishman and a thin sallow graceful woman in a green frock, her parents, he supposed, come to meet her, and to take part in the Durbar, but she did not introduce him. So he could not speak of her now, and certainly he did not want to call upon her in Government House. It would be far too significant, especially with the Durbar going on.

"I'd like to get straight home," he told his father.

They rode in silence for a few minutes, and he gazed about the scene, so familiar and yet so new, the swarming crowds, the dark, amiable, tense, proud Indian faces, the turbans of every shape and color, the women in their brilliant saris, far more of them on the streets now than there used to be, a few Englishwomen, too, and some Eurasian girls, very beautiful in English garb, and the ever present beggars, wretched, deformed, emaciated, their high voices, pleading for mercy, threading all the noise of the everyday life, and no one paying them any heed.

"I wonder that something isn't done to get the beggars fed and off the streets," he said abruptly.

"I suppose it is still as it was in the time of Christ," David said. "The poor we must have always with us."

His father spoke, or so Ted thought, almost with indifference, as if India had worn down even pity, or mercy, and certainly the hope of change for such as these. He understood, and rebelled. However long he lived here, he would not allow himself to become indifferent. He would keep his heart alive.

So they did not stay in Bombay. He had no desire to see the Durbar, and they left on the earliest train. He was very quiet, sitting by the dusty window and watching the familiar landscape slip by. This was more than coming home. It was beginning his own life at last.

XI

"Here we are," his father said.

The train journey had been long and hot, the dust grey and fine seeping in through closed windows, creeping up out of the shaking floors of the cars, sifting from the cracks of the wooden walls and ceilings. The green grass, the hanging vines, the spreading trees, and the big brick buildings made the compound heaven by contrast.

"How much you have done!" Ted exclaimed.

"I have finished the plans I made before you were born," his father said gravely. "The chemistry building yonder was the last unit. The dormitories are all built and occupied. Over the whole presidency there is a network of lower schools, headed by our graduates, and these feed into the university." He nodded toward a low beautiful building at the south end of the compound, a graceful compromise with Indian architecture. "That is the girls' home-industry college. I have named it The Olivia MacArd Memorial, in memory of your mother."

A bell rang at this moment and a stream of girls in soft-hued saris poured out of the doors, laughing and chattering as they came. When they saw the two men, they pulled the flying scarf-like ends of the saris over their heads. They all knew that the Head's son was coming to teach, and they stole quick looks at the tall fair young man who did not look at all like his father, and turned their faces away before he could see them, curious, half fascinated because in a way he belonged to them and they to him. He would, they supposed, succeed his father some day as India's great Christian educator. Yet there was a hint of hostility in their looks. Gandhi and

Dr. MacArd were not friends, and the students were all secret followers of Gandhi, or nearly all, but because of Dr. MacArd there had been no open attempt to join the nonviolent resistance movement. The fair young man might or might not follow in his father's path. They hurried on, young and hungry for their night meal.

"Was my mother interested in all this?" Ted asked.

His father hesitated as always when he asked a direct question about his mother. Then he said, overcoming silence with effort, "Your mother died so young, she had not time to fulfill herself. We were married and the next year you were born. She had the task of adjusting to India and to marriage. I tell myself that she would have been interested, had she lived. She was full of energy, vitality, spirit —many gifts."

"And beauty besides," Ted mused.

"Yes," his father said abruptly. He turned toward the house. "We must go in and get washed for dinner."

On the wide veranda the servants had gathered to greet the son of the house come home. They held garlands of flowers, and one by one now they came forward smiling, humble, tender, as they looped the garlands over his neck. Then they stooped to take the dust from his feet and escorted him into the house like a prince.

His father was patient with all this, but abstracted, and in the hall he picked two notes from the table. "The Fordhams," he said, and opening it he read aloud.

"Welcome home, dear Ted. We'll leave you to yourselves this first evening. We look forward to tomorrow—"

The sealed pink note addressed to Ted was from Miss Parker. He opened it and read her underscored lines, remembering Auntie May, as she had made him call her all the time he was a little boy. He had been fond of her but distantly, because even then he had known that she loved him because of his father, and he had divined even in childhood that she had her dreams, the brightest one that some day David MacArd would ask her to be his second wife. The years had faded this dream, his father had never thought of such replacement, and Ted knew it and had learned to pity the aging lonely woman.

"Dear Ted, my special welcome to you. It is almost like a son coming home—my own son, I mean, but I just cannot put it into words. I have so many memories of you, and now you are a young man and come back to be your noble father's strength and help. With fondest love from Auntie May."

His father did not ask about the pink note, there was no need. They went upstairs together into the rooms he knew so well, where he had grown up lonely and yet never alone, loved and adored by the dark people and spoiled, as he knew very well now, by every one of them, guarded and shielded even from the stern father, and yet he had loved his father best, always.

"I shall be down in about half an hour," his father said, almost formally.

He knew his father felt strange with him, that he was searching for the new relationship, father and son, yes, but man and man, teacher and superior, comrades in Christ. Ted's heart softened suddenly, its old trick. He was always too easily touched and moved.

"By the way," his father paused. "I have had your room changed. The old one was small, I thought. I have put you in the front room, it used to be the guest room, you remember."

"Thanks," Ted said. But he was startled. His old room had been small, but it was next to his father's room. Now perhaps the older man did not want to be so near to the young one.

"I shall miss you," his father was saying with a shy smile, half hidden in the grey beard. "But you must have room to grow."

"Thank you, Dad," he said.

And then he was glad that he was not in the small room after all. This front room was wide and pleasant, just now almost cool, the shadows from the veranda dimming the sunshine. There were no flowers, there had never been flowers in this house that he could remember, only green things, ferns, palms, that the servants arranged.

A punkah above his head began to sway slowly and a strange loneliness, a homesickness of the spirit crept over him like a mist from the past, when this world was the only one he knew. It had crept over him often in America, even while he knew that was his own land and he an American. There it was India that he missed.

Here, standing in the midst of the familiar past, he felt a pang of longing for his grandfather's house, the clean avenue, the taxicabs, the well-dressed people, his own people, the cool brisk air. Perhaps if he were in New York at this moment there would even be snow, it was only two weeks until Thanksgiving! He had not spoken to his father while they were driving homeward in the old bullock cart, the bullock bandy, from the train an hour ago, he had not spoken of the streets he remembered so well. They were unchanged in all these years, the straining dark faces, too eager, too tired with heat and hunger, the thin dark bodies, that life of the streets all open to the passerby, the unpainted houses, the unfurnished rooms of the common people, the narrow streets crowded with vehicles and bullocks and people, the priests and beggars, and pressed against the walls the vendors of spice and grain, crosslegged in the dust, and women carrying water from the wells, the jars on their heads, and dyers stretching bright green and orange and yellow lengths of cloth in everyone's way and the twang of a weaver's loom somewhere behind a thin wall. In the streets all India swarmed about him again, and though he stood in this oasis of quiet, it was there, it was there.

He reached into his hip pocket and brought out the small Testament. Its leather covers were wet with his sweat and he opened it and read.

"For God sent not His Son into the world to condemn the world but that the world through him might be saved."

It was extraordinary, he was not superstitious, but there it was. India was not to be condemned, it was simply to be saved. His fear lifted suddenly, he was even light-hearted. He had come here to work, and there was work to do. The vast old house on Fifth Avenue was thousands of miles away, and years would pass before he entered it again.

"Where is Uncle Darya?" Ted asked.

They sat at the English mahogany dining table, he and his father alone as they had always sat during the meals of his childhood, but now his place was set at one end of the oval instead of at his father's right hand where when he was small his father could lean toward him and cut his meat. His father, he supposed, had given such orders. The servant, in snow-white cotton garb, was passing chicken curry and rice, tinted bright yellow with saffron.

"Darya would have been here to greet you," his father replied, "except he has gone and got himself arrested. He is in jail."

"In jail!" Ted exclaimed.

"Darya has committed himself to that fellow Gandhi." His father's voice was calm, but Ted knew his elder well enough to see the signs of concern, if not of agitation in his look, in his lips pressed together in his beard.

"But jail!" Ted remonstrated.

"Darya wanted to go to jail. I cannot understand what is going on in India nowadays. There is a perfect madness to get into prison, a passion for martyrdom, a perversity of patriotism. The Viceroy is deeply troubled, because he believes firmly in India's right to eventual independence. It is simply a matter of when the people can be made ready. But Darya has become almost as fanatical as Gandhi himself. He even protested the Durbar."

"I never thought Uncle Darya a fanatic," Ted said. "He was a little sad—or so I remember him."

"He became a different man after he lost his family. I have had you but he has no one nearer than his brothers and their children. He is a very personal sort of man, as Indians are, affectionate and so on. It was difficult for him to adjust. An ordinary Indian would simply have married again, but Darya seems really to have loved his wife. Did you know her name was Leilamani? Your grandmother's name was Leila."

"I know. And so now what will happen?"

The servant was passing spinach cooked until it was grey, and peas black with pepper. He had forgotten about the execrable vegetables, cooked always as Indians ate them. But his father took them as habit and helped himself to both.

"Sooner or later Gandhi will have to be put down," his father was saying with sudden vigor. "Government cannot tolerate this sort of thing. Nonviolence sounds mild enough, but it can cause the greatest annoyance and real disruption, the people lying on railroad tracks, for example, with complete disregard for their lives, and of course they can't be run over or the country would be in an uproar. I shan't be surprised if we hear of riots in a day or two about the Prince himself."

"Have you ever seen this man Gandhi?" Ted inquired.

"Only at a distance," his father replied. "An insignificant ugly little man. I am surprised that Darya finds anything in him."

"I'd rather like to talk with Gandhi," Ted persisted.

"I advise you to stay away from him and all his works," his father said rather stiffly.

They ate in silence for a few minutes. At some point, Ted was thinking, he would say to his father that now he was a man, young it was true, but his own master nevertheless, and he must decide for himself what he would do, whom he would see.

"At least you wouldn't mind my going to visit Uncle Darya in prison?"

David hesitated. "I suppose not, though he won't be there long. Government simply wants to make an example. The Viceroy has talked at length with me about the strategy."

"Rather a pity that they had the Durbar at this moment, don't you think? A sort of display of power?"

His father corrected him. "A display of strength, not power, and strength is essential."

Now or never, Ted thought, and from the very beginning he must have courage to disagree with his father.

"I wonder, even so, if it is wise," he said pleasantly. "The people here have such a profound recklessness of themselves. They have so little to lose, I suppose, a mud hut, two lengths of cotton cloth, a handful of pulse or wheat. They don't mind death, it comes so soon anyway—twenty-seven years is the life span, isn't it? And I suppose for most of them prison is a good deal better than everyday life for at least they get fed."

"I agree that they have too little," his father replied. "And it has been the whole purpose of my life to create better leadership for them, so that conditions can be improved. I think I am making the greatest possible contribution toward their independence in providing educated Indian leaders, Christian if possible. The sooner, then, can independence become a reality. England would welcome responsible Indian leaders but not a fanatic who insists upon wearing a dhoti and spends half his time spinning on a primitive wheel, so that the people won't buy good English cloth."

"I know too little to agree or disagree," Ted said honestly. "But I shall go to see Uncle Darya."

His father did not answer. The plates were removed and the servant brought on what Miss Parker, Ted remembered, used to call a shape. It was a trembling block of blancmange, surrounded by a circle of thick yellow custard. He helped himself to the accustomed dish and ate it without too much difficulty.

"Go to the villages," Darya said.

The guard had allowed the tall red-haired young American a special favor. He need not talk with the prisoner through the barricade. Instead the wooden gate was unlocked and Ted had come into the bare room opening upon a grey dusty patch of ground. Here he had found Darya alone, writing at a table made of two boards supported on posts driven into the earthen floor. He had looked up startled and for a full second he did not recognize his visitor. Then he saw who it was and he sprang to his feet and threw his arms about him.

"Ted, my friend, my son—"

"Uncle Darya, I had to come as soon as I knew you were here."

"Your father did not object?"

"No."

So they had begun their talk. Ted sat down cross-legged on the earth, refusing the stool Darya tried to give him, and one question was enough, "Uncle Darya, how came you here?"

"You must know," Darya began, and he took up the story of his life from the moment when he saw his little younger son die and after him the older son, and then Leilamani had died and the baby girl and at last Darya was left alone.

"I said I would become a sadhu," Darya declared. His great eyes darkened, his mobile face grew tragic. "I divided my property between my brothers, I put on common clothes and sandals, I set forth by foot to travel everywhere through the villages, not begging as true sadhus must do, for I knew myself still richer than the people in the villages, and I fed myself and even gave to them when they starved. Oh Ted, if you would know India, go to the villages!"

Ted did not speak. Across his clasped knees he listened, watching the handsome weary face of his father's friend.

"North and south I went," Darya was saying, "east and west I traveled, alone and always on foot, and I slept at night with the peasants, I ate with them, I listened to their talk, staying sometimes for days and weeks in a single place until I knew the people as my own. I buried my sorrow in their sorrows, I forgot the death in my house because they died by the thousands and the hundreds of thousands. I saw my India, a wretched starving suffering people, living upon a rich soil never their own, oppressed by greedy landlords and driven by debt and taxation. The whole country moves to and fro with the restlessness of the misery of the people and I forgot all that I had ever been. I am become another man, a single flame burns here—"

He knotted his hands on his breast, "And then I found Gandhiji."

His hands dropped. "Mind you, I am not a blind worshiper of this man. No, indeed, I can see him as he is, but still I will follow him because he is not working for himself. Ted, I tell you, renunciation is the test. If a man renounces all that he has for the sake of others, then that man can be trusted. Without renunciation, trust none."

The heat in the small room was like a weight of lead. The high wall kept away the hope of any wind, and the dusty patch of earth outside the door where not a weed could grow, reflected an intenser sun. There was no shield.

"What will you do here?" Ted asked in actual distress. "It will grow hotter until the monsoons come and that is many months away."

"I look at the clouds," Darya said. "Morning and evening the clouds float across my bit of sky and I stand in that patch of dust and gaze at them, and I imagine them as they go. They come from the north, the Himalayas, and of the snow-covered mountains I dream, and of the valleys between. Did you know? Those valleys are full of flowers, fed by the melting snow."

His voice, so harsh and impassioned a moment before, was suddenly tender, rich, a wonderful flexible voice, slow and soft, swift and powerful, responding to every mood and thought. Ted heard it, but he must not allow the beautiful voice to catch his emotions, no, nor the beautiful face and the spirit of this man, the enchantment of renunciation, the enchantment of righteousness. It was there, he could feel it, the sweetness of yielding one's whole self. He had been tempted even by the teachings of Jesus. There was a delight of surrender which he tasted but which he had resisted, fearing the distances to which it might lead him. He searched Darya's face and found in it no bitterness, no anger and no sorrow, only content and joy and exaltation.

"Uncle Darya, what is your hope?"

"To see my people free," Darya said, "to see them able to help themselves, to see them owning their own land, choosing their own government, living in decency and self-respect and mutual co-operation." He lifted his face to the square of sultry white sky, where the light was metal hot. "And one day, I shall see them so. I shall see flesh on their bones, and the children will not wail with hunger any more, because they will be fed and not one will be hungry."

"By the grace of God?"

Darya's face changed, he opened his eyes and stared at the young white man. "No! By the grace of man! That is what you Christians always say. God, God! How dare you speak his name? Look into your own holy books— 'Not every one that crieth Lord, Lord—' can you not remember?"

The gentle voice was a roar and Ted was silenced. It was true— and how had he mentioned the name in the presence of such renunciation? He had no right to speak the name of God.

"Uncle Darya, I must go." He got to his feet and held out his hand. "You have shaken me, I confess it, not by what you have said, but by what you have done. You are right. I am not worthy to speak the name of God. I ask you to forgive me."

Darya grasped his hand in both his own. "No, no, I let myself be angry and that is not good. You are not guilty, you are like a child. I must keep my anger for those who are guilty. Come again, my son—come and give me joy."

"I will come, Uncle Darya, though not often, alas, because Poona is too far from here. But my father says the Viceroy will not allow you to be in jail very long. It is only a symbol, my father says."

"A symbol of power," Darya cried, "and I will resist it. If I am released, I shall make them arrest me again and again and again, until they see that it is no use. I, too, have power, and no one can take it away from me. Ted, you will see Gandhiji himself in jail before long, remember my words, I tell you it will be so."

"I hope you are wrong."

"Have you seen him?"

"No."

"When you see him you will understand why we must follow him. He is the only one who gives us a road to walk upon. And who are we?" Darya spread out his beautiful dark hands. "Men without guns!"

"Uncle Darya, I must go."

"Go, then, but come back."

He went home wondering that Darya had joined his life with Gandhi's. For if he had understood his Uncle Darya aright in all the years of childhood, it was to know that the beautiful and intelligent man loved life, he enjoyed physical pleasure, he was fastidious and thoughtful. And all this rich humanity was yielded up now to the ugly spare little man who did not care what he ate except that it must not be better than a peasant's food, who chose a length of white cotton homespun as his garment, a little dark ascetic who lived by choice in a mud hut and walked barefoot. Renunciation, honesty, purity, whatever one chose to call it, whatever the charm, there it was, and Darya was not a man to be easily won. He knew the best as well as the worst even of England, he could wear an Englishman's morning coat, striped trousers and silk top hat not only with enjoyment but with exceeding grace. He belonged by birth in a palace, his father's mansion. Now he had chosen jail, now he had chosen poverty, and the renunciation was precious to him, not for God's sake but for man's.

Something trembled in Ted's heart, a flickering flame, a marveling light, but he turned from it. He did not wish at this moment to examine his soul. He was young, his life was pleasant, the future hung bright over the horizon. For Agnes Linlay was constantly in his mind. He must hear her voice and see her in her own surroundings and know for himself what was between them, and what could be, before he examined his soul.

And by day the other country where his grandfather lived receded from his living thought and feeling. The old habits of childhood returned, they rose out of the shadows where they had waited during the years that he had spent in America and again the old half-Indian ways of the mission house became his ways, the hot nights, the shadowy days behind the dropped bamboo curtains and under the slowly waving punkahs, the foods peppered to sting the palate, the cooled melons, the flowering vines in the garden, the dark white-clad servants hastening to meet his possible need. And even in the schoolrooms, the eager, the too eager faces of the young Indian men, the half shy and always charming faces of the girls, their slender hands hovering ready to draw their saris over their heads, a gesture modest and enticing, coquettish and severe. There was much more here than Gandhi's India.

And every week or two Agnes wrote in answer to his almost daily letters, the letters he sent in his need for companionship, for though he loved and revered his father, there was no possibility of companionship with a man who was now altogether missionary, and more than that, a missionary prince, a man upon whom the Viceroy called for advice when Church must come to the aid of Government. And Mr. and Mrs. Fordham were old and ridiculous and touching. Of all their children, only Ruthie was coming back. They talked a great deal about her and even showed him her picture, a roundfaced, simple pretty girl, whose small lips were too full for prettiness in the pleasant common face.

Besides these, there was only poor old Miss Parker in the compound, and her he avoided and knew himself cruel. He could not help it. She had grown moldy and unhealthy, and even religion had not kept her flesh sweet. She did not dry and wither, instead she grew stale and in the heat an odor, sour and rank, betrayed her presence in any room. It was hard, he supposed in his fastidious youth, for the old to keep clean, anyway in tropic heat.

In his loneliness he read and reread the letters from Agnes, always with vague disappointment at the end. She came no closer for the interchange. Though he poured his thoughts and feelings into his own letters, his increasing warmth brought only her kindly cool regard, her mild gaiety. Twice he had asked to see her, and twice she had put him off. The first time when he visited Darya he had wanted to continue eastward to her, but she put him off because she had planned a holiday with her parents into Kashmir, where her father liked to hunt, and again when he asked, she replied that everyone was too busy with plans for the visit of the Prince of Wales, who was to arrive on Christmas Eve.

Riots were expected, she wrote him, for there were rumors that nationalists were sending in malcontents from the jute mills, paying them each six annas a day to stir up the people against the Prince. But Government was rounding them up before the royal visit, and more than three thousand rebels were in jail. As for *hartal*—

"Actually complete *hartal* will be helpful," she wrote, "for the people will stay at home. Otherwise many might be crushed to death in the crowds on the streets."

Her letters rose to enthusiasm when the Prince of Wales arrived, and Ted read them thoughtfully, remembering Darya lonely in his prison cell. "It has all been a great success," she wrote in January. "Most satisfying to us, of course, was the vast entertainment on the second day after Christmas, given entirely by the Indians. It was in the open, on the *maidan*, and thousands came to see him. How they cheered when the Prince drove slowly around—and it was so very comforting to us. Then he mounted the magnificent dais, and sat down, although he rose as soon as the program began, to receive the sacred offerings—silver coconuts, sweet rice, flowers—all on silver platters. He was finally garlanded and could sit again. Then three great processions came slowly toward him, the first one of priests in their saffron robes, chanting Sanskrit hymns to the most beautiful music, soft and yet wild and sad. Then came thirteen bullock carts, each with a spectacle, a tableau of Indian life, the figures so motionless and poised one could have sworn them of bronze instead of flesh and blood. Then there was the Thibetan dance procession. Of course there was everything else—Manipur dancers, very pretty and so young in their stiff golden skirts and dark bodices, and finally a tremendous historical pageant of the Mogul era. Oh, but the best was when it was all over and the crowd surged forward toward the Prince simply to show their love! And even on the twenty-ninth when he left, the cheering crowds gathered along the river to see him off, although the *Pansy* was moored by Outram Ghat and his departure was supposed to be private. They were all middle class and working people, too. A great triumph for the British Empire! My father is delighted and so are we all."

Ted put this letter down. She had never been so warm, so excited, but none of this emotion was for him. It was time indeed to go and see her face to face.

XII

He reached Calcutta on a day already growing hot and went at once to the hotel after the dusty journey. His bearer had fetched his bags and bedding and now hastened ahead to prepare his bath and tea. In the lobby he lingered at the desk, hoping for a letter from Agnes. There was a chit, an invitation not for immediate luncheon, but for tea this afternoon and tennis, a cool little note, not unfriendly perhaps but wary, or did he so imagine? The pale grey paper was thick, and it was embossed with the crest of Government House. But Government House, he reminded himself, was home for her. He must not expect her to be as she had been on the ship, simple and single and free to be herself. She was the Governor's daughter, and an English woman in India. He stood fingering the note, remembering with a sudden blush the frankness of his letters. He had all but made love to her, for love was very easy. He was still lonely, the nights were hot and long and he dreamed of companionship.

Well, then, he would sleep and rest and read, perhaps even study his language lessons, for he was determined to master not only the literate Marathi but Hindustani and vernacular Gujerati, and after that if possible the other chief languages of India so that wherever he went he could speak to people. Poona, he was beginning to feel, was not to be his final home, but the future was not clear until he had seen Agnes. He mounted the marble steps then and went to his room. There his bearer had already let down the mosquito net, had drawn the shutters and the punkah was in motion.

"English bath, sahib," the faithful one said, grinning white teeth in a dark face, meaning that here was a vast porcelain tub and cumbrous plumbing and running hot and cold water.

"That is good," Ted replied. "Now bring me some food, and then you go and sleep, too. I shall sleep all morning."

"Yes, Sahib."

The man drifted away, closing the door silently. The room was suddenly quiet, the thick walls shut away the sounds of the street and there was only the faint squeak of the punkah, moving to and fro.

The gardens at Government House were a display of imperial splendor. The heat had not been allowed to scorch the flowers, English larkspur mingled with the luscious Indian blooms and roses, and orchids grew in the shadow of huge lath houses. Lawns spread in acres of green and in the center the dignified mansion rose like an immense English country house. The hired carriage rolled along the driveway and stopped at the entrance steps, his bearer leaped nimbly down from beside the driver and Ted got out.

"You may come back in two hours, or wait," he directed.

"I wait, Sahib," the bearer said with dignity. He was handsome in fresh white garments, and he was aware that he did honor to his master, even here.

"Very well," Ted said.

He mounted the steps and at the open door behind the mosquito screens a servant, a Sikh, tall and bearded, splendid in a blue and gold livery, waited for him.

"Miss Linlay," Ted said.

"Expecting you, Sahib," the Sikh said suavely and ushered him into the reception room to the left of the huge square entrance hall.

There he waited, but only a moment for almost at once she came, looking cool and beautiful in her white linen tennis frock, as he saw immediately, her fair hair drawn back into a large knot on her neck, and her face pale, though touched with a faint sudden blush. At her throat she had fastened a yellow rose.

"Agnes!" He took both her hands and looked down into her smiling face, and how blue her eyes were, he thought, more blue even than he remembered and her lips even more sweet. He was overcome with a sudden impulse to bend and kiss those lips, an impulse so strong that he could resist it only by the utmost will. But he knew that she could be deeply and delicately offended, and he would not risk it.

She stood looking at him, smiling, warding him off nevertheless and he imagined that she was changed, less free, at least, than she had been on the ship. But he was prepared for that.

"You had my note quite safely, I see, arriving so exactly," she said, "and it is still too hot for tennis, I fear. Perhaps it is as cool here as anywhere."

She sat down on a rather high chair of teak, cool and polished, and he drew a small gold chair near to her, and sitting down he gazed at her frankly and with delight, determined not to allow her to withdraw from him.

"I have come a long way to see you, and I have waited a long time. I wanted to come last autumn, when I went to the United Provinces to see an old friend. But you wouldn't let me, and again—"

She fended him off. "And who is the old friend?"

"An Indian friend of my father's, I call him Uncle. He is Darya Sapru."

"Ah, that name I know," she observed. "My father says he could have had a knighthood last year if he had not joined himself with Gandhi."

"Really? But I don't think he would have accepted a knighthood."

He saw the slightest hardening of the lovely clear blue eyes, and he hastened away from the subject. "Anyway, my father and Darya have been lifelong friends, although now they are rather apart, because my father does not feel Gandhi is right."

He stopped abruptly, smitten with guilt.

She said, "I am glad to know your father feels that."

"Yes, and I mustn't take shelter behind my father," he said resolutely. "I don't know if Gandhi is right or wrong. There is so much

216

I don't know now. The old India was nicely clear, or so I seem to remember it, maybe because I was only a child, and now everything seems complex. I had to listen to Darya, of course. Seeing him in jail was very confusing."

"Why?" she asked. "He made a demonstration during the Durbar in Bombay."

"It is you I want to talk about," Ted said. "Not the Prince, and not Darya, and certainly not Gandhi or politics, nor even India. Only you—"

He took her narrow white hand as it lay on her knee, and he held it only long enough to discern response. There was none and he put it down again.

She got up almost at once. "Let's go out to the courts. After all, they are shaded, and the darkness falls so quickly after the sun sets. My father will soon be home."

She gave him a quick glance, her eyes upon his shoes.

"I am quite ready," he said, smilingly submitting himself to her survey. "White linen suit, white shoes."

"Very handsome," she retorted, thawing nicely into an answering smile.

They sauntered across the green lawns and approached the courts. There were already people playing, ladies sat under the green striped umbrellas and liveried Indian servants were offering tea, sandwiches and cold drinks. Agnes introduced him casually as they came near.

"Lady Fenley, this is Ted MacArd, from Poona. Sir Angus, Ted MacArd, and Lady Mary Fenley, Ted MacArd. Frederick Payne, Mr. MacArd, and Bart Lankester, and Mr. and Mrs. Oscar Wayne—"

He shook hands, smiled, repeated names, and she disposed of them all by offering to play him at singles immediately upon a still vacant court. He tested some racquets, chose one rather heavy, they tossed for the serve and she won.

He suspected that she played well, but he did not imagine her superlative, as indeed she was. She seemed scarcely to move about the court, and yet his balls were returned with swift accuracy and in the least convenient spots. She used no tricks, no cuts or pretenses, a straight game, but devastating and hard. He was put to it to match her, and he lost the first three games with scarcely a point. Then he rallied himself, forgot who she was and that he was very nearly if not altogether in love with her, and concentrating upon her as an adversary, he won two sets out of three by a bare margin. Defeated, she came to the net and they shook hands formally. Her fair skin was rose red and the straight short strands of hair about her forehead were wet.

"You play too well," he said.

"Impossible," she said, "since you beat me."

"I had to work hard," he retorted.

"Why not?" she asked.

They sauntered side by side to the umbrellas again, and she took hot tea. "Don't drink that cold stuff," she suggested, disapproving when he chose lemonade. "It's dangerous when you're hot."

"Not for an American," he replied, determined for a reason he could not understand not to yield to her. "We're used to cold and hot together."

"There's my father," she said, nodding toward the green.

He saw the tall Englishman walking slowly across the lawns toward them.

"He looks tired," she said. "Things are so difficult again, since the Durbar."

Everyone rose as the Governor approached and she introduced Ted formally. "Father, this is Mr. MacArd. I told you we were shipmates. He is from America, you remember."

"Ah, yes."

The Governor shook hands with him limply. "I think I've met your father. Of course I know of your grandfather."

"Thank you, Your Excellency," Ted said clearly.

He sat down again when the Governor was seated, he chatted with Lady Fenley, he glanced at Agnes once or twice, rather restlessly, until he perceived that this was to be his visit. There was not to be a stroll alone under the great banyan tree at the far end of the lawns, nor did she seize the opportunity he made by suggesting that they look at the rose gardens. In sudden anger he got up after a half hour or so.

"I must be leaving now," he said, refraining from her name.

"Must you?" she murmured.

"I shan't leave Calcutta until the day after tomorrow," he went on. Actually he had no plans whatever, but he said not tomorrow, because it gave him a day longer. Yet he warned her that it might be only a day. A day would be enough to see whether she wanted to see him again. She did not speak. She gave him her hand, he pressed it and released it, he bowed to the assembly under the green striped umbrellas and went away. The sun was setting ferociously over the great temple of Kali as he got into his carriage and they went down the road toward the city and then along the Chowringhi, that most famous street of the East, and so to his hotel. He was still angry and his lips were tense and white.

Sleep was impossible. It was the inner heat that kept him awake, not the thick black heat of the outer night. He tossed and turned and sat up and threw the pillows on the floor. Then he got up and lit the table lamp and drew out sheets of the hotel paper, slightly mildewed at the edges already, though it was fresh yesterday, he supposed, and he began to write down all the angry thoughts he had been speaking to her in the darkness while he could not sleep.

"Why did you let me come to see you?" he demanded. "Why not simply tell me that we were friends on the ship and no more? Why accept my letters? Why let me all but tell you that I love you and want to marry you? Very well, I tell you now. I do love you, and I want you for my wife. There are distances between us, all India, perhaps, but I love you. If you can love me, there will be nothing to separate us, not India and not the seas between your country and mine. You will tell me I am impatient, you were always saying on the ship that I was impatient. Yes, I am—I am like my grandfather and he is the most impatient man I have ever seen, and my father is the most stubborn man I have ever seen, and I am both of those. So I shall come to you tomorrow afternoon at

219

four o'clock for your answer. Nothing shall prevent me from coming."

The first signs of the thunderous dawn were streaking the sky with crimson when he had emptied himself of words and of anger, and he sealed the letter. Then he went to the door where his bearer slept on the threshold outside. He touched him with his foot and the man leaped awake.

"Take this to Government House," Ted ordered. "Stay there with it until a reply is put into your hand, then bring it to me at once. I shall be here in this room."

The bearer got up in silence. He wrapped himself twice in the length of cotton which was his garment. He straightened his turban and taking the letter he went away.

Upon the silver tray, with the tea and toast and the ripe yellow mangoes, Agnes saw the letter and recognized it, but she did not take it at once. She sat up in bed and the ayah piled the pillows behind her and handed her the brush and comb. She brushed out the long fair braid and twisted it around her head. Then she dipped her hands into the bowl of cool water the ayah brought to the bedside, she took up the linen towel that lay in the water and squeezing it half dry she wiped her face and neck.

"Now," she said, "I will have my *chota hari.*"

"The man waits for an answer, my rose, my darling," the old ayah said in a tender, singing voice.

"I will read the letter when I have had my tea," she said. "Then I will ring the bell for you to return."

"I will return instantly," the ayah said.

She went out silently and Agnes put down the cup and took up the letter. She expected it. It was not likely that Ted would simply go away nor really did she wish him to do that. Her father and mother had asked many questions about the American, they were reluctant, as she had seen, that she should let him come, and yet they loved her sincerely and knew that she must be allowed to do what she wished to do.

"The Americans are so odd," her mother had murmured. "One

220

never knows where they are. I mean, some of them actually encourage Gandhi, you know, darling, and that is so embarrassing for your father. I mean, if the white people don't stick together, you know, and all that—"

Her mother seldom finished a sentence, it trailed in the air, not quite a question, something more than a suggestion. It was true that the times were dangerous. Agnes did not like to believe that the danger had anything to do with her life, and yet of course it did. India always had everything to do with her life because she was her father's daughter. If she had not been, it would not have mattered so much whom she married. She could have allowed herself to fall into love with Ted as pleasantly as though he were an Englishman. It was, of course, of immense help that he was a MacArd, old David MacArd's grandson, and even David MacArd's son. For David MacArd was famous, too, in his own way, though her father said it was a pity he had let himself choose to be a missionary, a great disappointment it must have been to his powerful father, who naturally would have hoped that his only son could have looked after his vast financial interests, so vital and far reaching into almost every country. The Viceroy had said, however, that the graduates of MacArd University in Poona were among the most loyal of the younger Indians, and for that David MacArd must certainly be thanked.

She read Ted's letter thoughtfully, and when she had finished it she read it again, very slowly. Then she lay back on her pillows, allowing her tea and toast to grow cool, as cool as anything could be, but it was odd how one craved something very hot, too, by way of contrast instead of the eternal tepid. Perhaps that was why she found this American so fascinating, he was positive. Most young Englishmen grew tepid, after a few years in India, it was the only way to endure the climate, perhaps, but one could almost guess what they would say when they opened their mouths to talk, especially to her. In a way she wished she could have stayed in England, and yet she did not like it there. It was a small place, and everything was set in a pattern that could not be broken. After living in India and being the Governor's daughter, the pattern was petty. The trouble was that there was a pattern here, too, super-imposed upon the undercurrents and the restlessness of India itself. One could never be sure of the foundations. Nothing was more powerful and more eternal than the British Empire, and it was simply a matter of time until the followers of Gandhi were put down, and men like her father would do it kindly and with justice, but one could not forget nevertheless that there were so few white men and so many of the others. Even here in Government House itself, there were only the handful of English surrounded by In-dians, loyal of course, loving their masters in a way, and yet only someone who had grown up in India could understand the rum-blings and the tremblings of the foundation. Her parents underneath were rooted in England, but she was rooted here. The things she had seen that they had never seen, the things she heard and under-stood because she knew a language that they did not! Ah, children heard and saw. That was why she felt so safe with Ted. He had been a child here, too, a white child in a dark country.

She got up and went to her little rosewood English desk and wrote, "Dear Ted, I shall expect you at four. Agnes."

The great oval drawing room was shadowy at the far end but he saw her rise from a gold satin-covered couch and come toward him, a figure in filmy white.

"This is always the coolest room," she explained. "And we seldom use it except for big parties. We'll not be disturbed."

"I am glad of that," he said gravely. "For what I have to say is not to be interrupted."

"Oh, Ted," she cried too softly, "must you say it yet? We're still so young—"

"I know," he said, "but we aren't as young as our years, Agnes. We talked about that on the ship, do you remember? We said that India makes people grow up fast."

She turned rather abruptly and sat down on the gold couch again and he sat beside her. The pillows, stuffed with down, were unex-pectedly soft, and the thick satin felt almost cool to his touch.

"More than that," he went on, not putting out his hand to hers.

222

"We shall be forced, I think, in still another way. Agnes, your father stands for one kind of life. It is the same side my father is on. But I may choose the opposite side. I want to know that you'll go with me."

"What do you mean by that?" she asked. Her eyes were steadily upon his and her voice was calm.

"You know what I mean," he retorted.

"I want to hear you say what you mean," she insisted.

"Then I dread to say it, and yet I must say it. I must tell you, first of all and above all, that in spite of the Prince's visit, there is a terrible struggle coming. Darya is on one side with Gandhi, and your father and mine are on the other side. I don't know where I am, Agnes. I shall need time to know where I am. What I must know is—will you go with me wherever I go?"

"How odd to put it like that," she exclaimed.

"Odd?"

"One would think you were planning something dreadful."

"Perhaps it would be dreadful for you."

"I can't imagine anything very dreadful happening to you," she said, beginning to smile.

She meant, what is there dreadful that could happen to a tall and handsome young man, the son of the MacArds?

"Aren't you being dramatic?" she asked.

"What if I am?" he demanded.

"I might want to laugh," she suggested.

He gave a large impetuous sigh. "We are fencing. I am making the thrusts and you are fending me off. Let's speak plainly. Agnes, do you love me?"

She bent her fair and graceful head. "I don't know."

"Perhaps you do love me," he urged. "At least if you don't know?"

"There is so much more than just love," she said.

"Just love!" he repeated with reproach.

"One doesn't just decide by feeling."

"I do!"

"A woman then."

223

"An Englishwoman perhaps," he said with quick bitterness.

She accepted this. "An Englishwoman, especially here in India. To be English here carries more than the usual weight, especially now."

"Why especially now, if it is you and me?"

"I can imagine that if you should be friends with Gandhi, for example," she said thoughtfully, "it would make an immense difference if I were your wife. It would separate me entirely from the world where I belong, from my parents, certainly. I must consider that."

"And may it not separate you from me, if you do consider it?" he demanded.

"Ah, yes, perhaps," she agreed, "but then I am not quite in love with you. There is still time to stop myself."

His heart leaped at the possibilities of her not being quite in love with him, which must mean nevertheless that she was on the way to being in love with him, not with the heat and urge and demand of his own nature, for she was as cool as a flower and that was one of her lovely qualities. He had absorbed some of the heat of India, but she had grown up more cool, more still, by contrast.

"Then you are a little in love with me!" he exclaimed.

"I know that I could love you," she said honestly. "I do want to love you, Ted, if I can be sure—"

"Sure of me?"

"Sure that being your wife would not destroy what I am."

They looked at each other, a long half yearning look, she reluctant and he arresting his heart. "Is it because I am a missionary?"

She hesitated, searching for her own feelings, restraining the impulse to throw herself into his arms and give herself up to loving him, which she could so easily do.

"If it were only that," she said, "I would not hesitate, because you are still yourself, Ted, though you choose to be a missionary. There are all sorts of missionaries, and some are repulsive, I grant you— ignorant and pushing and all that. But your father is a great gentleman and you are his son. No, no, it's not that."

"Then what, my darling?" He was tender with her, being grateful to her because it was plain that she wanted honesty.

She said unexpectedly. "I suppose the easiest way to put it is this —if you were English, I shouldn't hesitate. But you're American."

Now he was taken aback. "What has that to do with it? You do amaze me, Agnes. I shouldn't have thought you guilty of prejudice!"

"It's not prejudice, Ted. It's simply that being American you can't easily understand the English point of view. You don't see our responsibility here. You might be angry with me, even if I were your wife, if you saw me standing by my father, for example, when you might think him very wrong. If there is ever a crisis, Ted, I should have to stand by my own people. I think they are right."

"I see."

He did see. She could never marry him simply for himself, by herself. She was like all other English of her class, she assumed their burden, she recognized their cause. He had to confess a certain nobility here, however mistaken he felt it might be.

"I wish I could take you in my arms, darling. Will you let me do that?"

She shook her head. "Please not, Ted. It's too soon. Please! I shouldn't like to make a decision against you, and I think I would if I were . . . swept off my feet."

"Very well, then." He rose, but he allowed himself to take her narrow hand, and she did not withdraw it. "Shall we go on as we are for the present, darling? Or do you want to stop that, too?"

"No, I don't want to stop, Ted. It's just that I don't want to go further—not until everything is more clear."

"Everything being—?" he inquired.

"You and me—and India," she replied.

XIII

So he traveled home again to Poona, but not by the way he had come. He did not take a swift transcontinental train, he did not leap from city to city. Instead he remembered what Darya had said in jail. "Go to the villages," Darya had said.

He took a train westward for a few hundred miles and then getting off he wound his way uncomfortably through a network of villages accompanied only by his indignant bearer, to whom such conduct in a sahib was dangerous and absurd. Midway through the United Provinces the bearer left him, and Ted continued his way alone and for the first time in his life no one stood between him and India, not even an Indian.

He knew now why Darya had not tried to persuade him, and why he had simply said, "Go to the villages." For the villages spoke to him, in their mute misery, the scores he saw with his own eyes and the tens of thousands he did not see. They clung to the hillsides of north India, they rose out of the central plateaus, and on the low-lying southern plains, they were mounds scooped by human hands from the dust and the mud of the Indian earth, hollowed into hovels for the barest shelter from torrential rains and bitter burning sun, and from the chill of frost and cold winds upon the hills. Generations had lived in them, without memory of more or hope for better. He looked into the faces of a starved people, the faces of the too many born, because too many must die, for Nature herself urged birth because she foresaw death too soon. Starvation was the culprit, not swift or instant, not alone the starvation of flood or overwhelming famine, but the slow starvation of those who never have had enough to eat and never will. It was an India as far from the mission house as it was from the palace and his father was as guilty as the governor.

He returned weeks overdue to Poona, and his heart was a burning fire in his breast, and he had made up his mind, independent even of love.

His father welcomed him in his spare half-silent fashion, without reproach. "I have distributed your classes among the assistants. Now you will want to gather them back again."

"Yes, Father," Ted replied.

He knew it would not be for long, but of this he would not speak now. After a few minutes he excused himself to his father and went to his own room. He had not written to Agnes during the weeks of travel, nor did he expect letters from her and there were none among the letters on his desk. The long solitary journey, crowded with men, women and children among whom he moved, had cut him off from everyone he knew and even Agnes was far from him. Alone he had gone and now alone he set himself to discover what he was, where he had arrived, and whither must he go. Like Saul of Tarsus, he had been converted by the roadside.

In the stillness of the mission house he came and went and did his daily work, while the months passed into summer. He read his scriptures constantly, over and over again the cries of St. John, and then the spare sweet words of Jesus. He read, too, the psalms of the Marathi saints and again and again this one:

> How can I know the right,
> I, helpless one!
> Of pride of knowledge, lo, O God,
> I now have none.

In June the heat reached its height and the city waited from hour to hour for news of the breaking of the monsoons, first upon the eastern shore of the country where the plateaus sloped most easily to the sea. It was during this most tense and breathless month when even the punkahs scarcely stirred the burning air, that he quarreled at last with his father. Out of the controlled calm of their

227

days, their quarrel rose as suddenly as a typhoon rises out of a quiet tropic sea.

The cause was a young Sikh, Jehar Singh, whose father, a man of great wealth and ambition, had sent him to MacArd University, where he might receive the most advanced western education in India. Sirdar Singh did not wish his son to be trained in the English tradition and therefore he had not sent him to England. He foresaw, while taking no part in the nonviolent revolution of Gandhi, that empire in the old English sense was finished, and whether Gandhi was successful or not, empire would be compelled to its end because of the enormous pressure of Russian communism. He feared and abhorred all that he heard in these days from Russia, and casting his mind shrewdly about the world, he fixed upon the United States as the one power and nation likely to be able to face the New Russia when the day of crisis came, as he feared it would. Therefore, he decided, he would have Jehar, his only and beloved son, taught by Americans, who could be trusted to cling to the principles of individual property of which he owned so vast a share. He was uneasy, it is true, because MacArd University was a missionary institution, but he had been reassured by Dr. MacArd, the president, so obviously a gentleman and a man of culture and wealth, though a Christian. Moreover, he was the son of one of America's great capitalists, and by his father's bounty he had built up a magnificent compound, replete with luxury and American ways. Were Jehar trained here, it was not likely that he would graduate with any ancient notion of renunciation or poverty, such as the emaciated Gandhi was putting forth as a net to catch the idealistic young. Sirdar Singh was vastly pleased with what he saw at MacArd, and especially with Dr. MacArd, with whom he talked, stressing with him that his son was the heir to one of India's great fortunes, as well as the only scion of a very famous, powerful and old family. The president had accepted the responsibility and had welcomed the tall dreamy poetic-looking youth who appeared at the beginning of the next semester.

Young Jehar had been at MacArd for the required four years and now was among those to graduate with first honors. What

228

then was Sirdar Singh's horror when he arrived in magnificence this June to be present when his son received his honors, to discover that the young man wished to be a Christian! He heard this in the evening after the important day, Jehar having been reticent until the graduation was over. Then when his father talked with him ardently concerning marriage, business, foreign travel, and all those important matters always upon a father's mind when he thinks of his son, Jehar lifted his handsome head and said,

"My father, to me none of these things is important. I intend to become a sadhu."

Even then Sirdar Singh did not grasp the full horror of what his son said. A sadhu was a Hindu saint. To be a Hindu saint meant renunciation and poverty, dreadful enough for a rich man's ears to hear. But the next words his son spoke were even more awful. Jehar said,

"I do not mean a Hindu sadhu, my father. I mean a Christian sadhu."

"What is a Christian sadhu?" Sirdar Singh demanded. He was a tall strong man, as Sikhs are, but in late years he had given up restraints and had grown exceedingly fat, so that his figure was now immense.

"I shall travel on foot over India," Jehar said, "teaching and preaching as Jesus did, but I shall remain an Indian. As an Indian I will portray an Indian Christ, such as He might have been had He been born among us."

"Where did you get this mad idea?" Sirdar Singh asked in great terror. "I am sure you did not get it from Dr. MacArd."

"I got it from no one," Jehar replied. "It came to me when I was reading the Christian scriptures."

Though it was now past midnight and the whole compound was quiet, Sirdar Singh could fix upon only one idea.

"Let us go to Dr. MacArd," he gasped. "I must have help from him."

So it was that the quiet of the mission house was broken and all the household set stirring by tremendous beating on the gate by the Sirdar's bearers at midnight, reinforced by the Sirdar's own bellowing. The gateman opened the gate and at once ran to call his master.

"Sahib, Sahib," he shouted at David's door. "The Sirdar is here in distress. There is something wrong with his son."

These were the cries that Ted heard also from his own room, his door open because of the heat. He got up from his bed and put on his silk dressing robe and went down the hall to his father's room. There the light was already shining and he knocked and went in and found his father dressing himself, in haste but still with suitable formality.

Meanwhile the Sikhs, father and son, were waiting downstairs.

"Shall I come, Father?" Ted asked.

David threw a glance toward him. "Yes, but get into your clothes."

"Yes, Father."

A few minutes later when Ted went downstairs, he found the drawing room door shut and all the servants and bearers waiting outside on the verandas. He opened the door and went in. The Sirdar was sitting on the long couch and on a chair near him was Jehar, listening to what his father said, but with no air of repentance, although with full respect.

Ted knew the young man, having taught him English literature, and he remembered him especially because Jehar had revealed a poetic talent and a quick perception of the quality of beauty.

The Sirdar stopped abruptly in what was obviously a verbal torrent as the door opened.

"My son," David said. "He has been Jehar's teacher and I have asked him to be present."

The Sirdar gave an upheaving sigh. "Is he a Christian?" he demanded.

"Naturally, he is," David replied.

The Sirdar turned to Jehar. "You see this, here is a young man who is even a Christian but he does not talk of being a sadhu! No, he is a comfort to his father. He teaches in his father's university. He obeys his father, and his father trusts him."

230

Jehar turned his head to look at Ted, and gave him a shy smile. "Are you a Christian?" he asked.

So absolute was the honesty in this question that Ted felt humble. "I wish to be," he said, "and I hope that I am."

Sirdar Singh listened to this, sighed loudly, and turned to the other father. He began once more to plead. "I did put my son into your hands, Dr. MacArd. I wished that he be taught how the Americans do everything. The Americans are strong and rich and very powerful and they will become more powerful. They will be the only ones who can fight against Russia when that day comes as already we can see it must come. We have had one world war and there will be still another. Everybody is saying it. After the next world war the English will be weak but the Americans will be strong. I wish to stand with the Americans at that time. So I sent my son to you. Surely I did not expect him to become a Christian. This was not my wish."

The Sirdar's English was excellent but he was beginning to lose the idiom.

"I suppose, Sirdar," David said calmly, "that if you send your son to a mission university you must take the risk of his becoming Christian. But you cannot expect me to agree that being a Christian is so dreadful a fate as you seem to imagine. A good number of our students are Christian before they graduate, and although we do not make the attempt deliberately, we hope that the atmosphere of MacArd is such that they will wish to become Christian. There is no compulsion, however. We believe in freedom."

"I also believe in freedom," the Sirdar said eagerly. "I have always given my son much freedom, except he is compelled to remember he is my son and he cannot act in such ways as my son should not act. Therefore he cannot renounce all his inherited wealth which he will have from me, and become a sadhu."

David could not repress his surprise. "A sadhu?"

"Well, he wishes to become a Christian sadhu," the Sirdar cried more agitated.

"But this is impossible," David replied. "A sadhu is a Hindu, not a Christian.

231

"A sadhu is a saint," Jehar said. "I shall be a Christian sadhu."

"I have never heard of such a person," David said.

"Now you will hear of me," Jehar said gently.

"You see!" the Sirdar exclaimed.

He spread out his large fat hands. "What will you do, Dr. Mac-Ard? This boy is very stubborn. I know that. He has always been stubborn from birth. And his mother is dead. She cannot help me."

Ah, Ted thought, now what will my father do? He was suddenly deeply excited by what was happening. The young Indian was extraordinary, his face, always so delicately handsome, took on in the lamplight an unearthly beauty. He sat with motionless grace, his hands lightly clasped in his lap, his white garments flowing about him.

"Will you do as the sadhus do?" Ted asked. "Jehar, will you wander about from village to village?"

"As Jesus did," Jehar answered, and his dark eyes were quiet with peace.

"You see, you see!" the Sirdar wailed.

"Sirdar Singh," David spoke with decision. "Leave this to me, please. It is clear that Jehar does not understand what he is saying. He has confused two religions, Hinduism and Christianity. They are not to be confused. I suppose you have no objection if he wishes merely to be a Christian?"

"Certainly not," the Sirdar said in his ardent eager fashion. "Let him be a Christian if he likes, but as you are, sir, Dr. MacArd. Let him be a reasonable man, though Christian, it is all I ask. Let him remain my son, which he cannot be if he is a sadhu."

"Then leave him to me," David said. "It is very late, you are tired, and Jehar has been excited by the day. Tomorrow I will talk with him myself, and I will explain to him what it means to be a Christian. Certainly he cannot be a sadhu. The Christian church would not recognize him."

"Thank you, sir, thank you, Dr. MacArd," the Sirdar cried warmly. He clasped his hands on his bosom. "If you knew! But my only hope is in you. I know now this son never listens to his old father. I have done everything for him, how much money it has cost me to send him here for four years, and he ends by talking of sadhus! You see how my money would be wasted. Really, there is some responsibility for you, my dear sir."

"I accept it," David said firmly. "Now go back to the guest rooms, Sirdar. Jehar, do not trouble your father any more tonight. Come to me in my study tomorrow morning at nine o'clock."

Jehar rose. "Thank you, sir," he said. "I will come because of my father."

He put out his right arm to his father, who clung to it and hoisted himself thus from the sofa and they went away after their farewells for the night, the father still leaning upon the son.

In the drawing room David turned to put out the lamp when Ted spoke.

"Wait a minute, Father."

His father stayed his hand and glanced at him. "What is it?"

"I must say something."

"Well?"

"I hope you will not try to change Jehar."

"What do you mean?" his father demanded.

Ted spoke firmly. "Jehar has an immense idea—one that might revive the whole spirit of Christ in India!"

"I don't see what you are driving at—"

"Father, an Indian Christ!"

"That's blasphemous—or would be if it were not absurd."

"Not blasphemous, and not absurd!"

He gazed at his father with clear eyes, his heart beginning to flame. "I wish I could have thought of it, only I am not Indian. I wish I were! To see the spirit of Christ incarnate again in an Indian—"

"Ted, I will not listen."

"But, Father—"

"It is very late and I am exceedingly tired."

"Very well, Father, but I warn you that tomorrow I shall see Jehar, too."

"I must beg you not to do so. I have an obligation to Sirdar

Singh. It is very distressing for a father to know that an only son—"

"Are you going to try to keep Jehar from being a Christian?"

"Of course not. Could I do that when I myself have devoted my life to Christian education? I shall try simply to make him understand what it means to be a Christian in the place where God has put him, in the household of Sirdar Singh, and what great influence he can wield there, as a Christian. It would be folly to give it all up."

"But Father—"

"Not one word more, if you please."

His father put out the light and walked upstairs, and Ted stayed alone in the darkness. For a long moment he stood, thinking of Jehar's face, and then suddenly, involuntarily, he lifted his eyes to pierce the enveloping night. He prayed, though without words, his whole soul reaching outward and upward for guidance and for light. From where does guidance come for the human soul, and where is the source of light? Where, oh, where had the light come from that fell upon the soul of Jehar?

The darkness did not change, he went upstairs to his room and read scriptures, he prayed as he had never prayed before because his prayer was simple, asking for nothing except for light. Still no light broke and at last he went to bed again. . . . He rose before dawn, as soon as the sultry darkness of the sky brightened delicately in the east with the golden edge of a cloud. He washed in cool water and went out to the small chapel, where sometimes the Christian students prayed. There as he thought he might, he found Jehar. The young Indian stood silent before the altar, his head uplifted, his eyes open.

Ted spoke, "Jehar!"

Jehar turned and saw him and smiled. "Teacher," he replied.

"I thought I might find you here," Ted said. "It is good. Let us talk together of what has happened. How is that you did not tell me?"

"I do not know you well," Jehar said without diffidence. "I did not think you needed to know about me."

Ted was hurt. "How have I behaved that any pupil of mine

234

should think I needed not to know him? Come and sit here on this bench."

Jehar came down the aisle, very graceful in his fresh white cotton garments, and he sat down and waited, the smile still on his lips. His large dark eyes were clear, he showed no sign of sleeplessness or weariness or fear. Peace was in him.

"You are not going home with your father today?" Ted asked.

"I am going home," Jehar said, "I shall go home with him and I shall live there for a while until he understands my heart."

"And if he does not understand?"

Jehar's face was calm and his bearing full of dignity. "Then I must leave my home."

"You are very young, Jehar."

"I am not too young to know what I must do. If I had not seen what I must do, I should also be preparing for my life's work, either to take the management of my father's estates, or to be a barrister, or some such thing. Now I know what my work is."

"You cannot really beg for your food as sadhus do. Surely it is not suitable, Jehar. After all, people know who you are."

"I need not to beg. God will give me what is necessary."

"To me it sounds dangerous and strange."

"That is because you come from the West, sir." Jehar's voice was courteous but positive. "To us of India there is nothing strange in wishing to become a sadhu. There are many sadhus, as you know. People do not wonder. It is so, and that is all. But I shall be a Christian sadhu and that is all."

"What church will you join?"

"None, for if I join one then the others will not allow me to belong to them. I have inquired of this of my teacher, Mr. Fordham, who explains Christianity to us every week twice, as you know. From him I understand that church is good for many people but also I see it is not good for me, because I wish to belong everywhere, to everyone, only first to Christ and only to Christ."

"Does he know you wish to become a sadhu?" Ted asked.

"I have not told him," Jehar replied.

235

"And what makes you think that you know best how to follow Christ?"

"I do not know, except for myself," Jehar said. He laughed unexpectedly, a pleasant boyish laughter. "I am not so stupid as that, surely, so that I think I can decide for others. It is only for myself that I know."

"So you will take a bowl, a blanket—"

"I will take my bowl, my blanket, and I shall wear my saffron robe, so that men know I am a sadhu, but I shall preach only Christ."

"Jehar, you make me afraid. It is so absolute."

"Why are you afraid? I simply do what many have done, except I am of Christ. Siva and Ram I do not condemn, Kali I will not worship, nor Ganesh, for I cannot see them good or beautiful. But Christ I see is beautiful because he committed no crime and he harmed no one, and he spoke of God."

"This one thing I will say," Ted replied, after a moment, "you are renouncing the life of a man before you know what it is. I have seen Indians renounce life, Jehar. I saw Darya himself in prison."

All India knew the name of Darya, and Jehar lifted his head in interest. "Did you see him indeed?"

"Yes, and he, too, has renounced everything except it is for his country, or so he believes. But he is not a young man as you are. He has known marriage and fatherhood, and only after these were taken from him did he accept renunciation."

"I have no need to wait," Jehar said confidently. "I have had a vision. Perhaps Darya had no vision until God had taken from him his wife and his children."

"What vision had you?" Ted asked. It was impossible to be less than gentle with Jehar.

"I saw Christ plain," Jehar replied. "It was not a vision of the spirit, you understand. There are such visions also, but I saw him with these very eyes."

He touched his eyes with his two forefingers.

"I have read the books," he went on. "I knew the Bhagavad Gita by heart before my mother died. She taught me that to be a saint

236

is the best that man can know, but I did not think I could be a saint, and so I was unhappy. When I first came to this university how unhappy I was, and I did not like to hear of the new religion. It seemed not so good to me as our own more ancient faith. Once I even tore to pieces the Bible Mr. Fordham said we must use in the class room. I was so unhappy to read it. I did not wish to be compelled by him. And then suddenly I saw Christ, there in my lonely room."

Ted sighed. "I hope you have not changed your whole life because of this—vision, as you say it is."

"I have changed my life," Jehar replied.

What more could be said? Jehar was simple and pure and quiet and he could not be changed. The sun tipped the edge of the horizon red gold, and coolness faded quickly from the air. The day had begun. The two young men rose and walked together across the lawn and parted with a handclasp and no spoken word.

Thus harmlessly begun, the day developed into a strange storm, not between Sirdar Singh and Jehar but between Ted and his father, who had never quarreled before. He had half expected to be called into the conference between his father and Jehar. At seven o'clock the first light meal of the day was served, the chota hari which was eaten wherever they happened to be. His father was already in his study. Ted accepted the tray on one of the small veranda tables and ate there, seated in a wicker armchair. Jehar passed him and lifted his hands in greeting, palm to palm, and went on into the hall and the study. The door to his father's study closed and Ted waited, finishing his tea and toast and ripe mango and then he sat, still expecting to hear his father's voice.

The call did not come. After more than an hour the door opened again, and Jehar came out, looking pale and almost weary. Again he passed with the silent greeting and without speech he descended the steps and went away. Then Ted got up and went to the study. His father sat at the desk reading some papers, his face stern.

"Father?"

His father looked up. "Yes, Ted?"

"How did it go?"

"You mean the conference? I am convinced that Jehar is out of his mind. He talked of visions."

Courage, Ted thought, courage to speak, to take Jehar's side, to declare that visions are possible.

"There is plenty of evidence for visions in the Scriptures, Father."

His father stared at him. "Surely you are not going to justify Jehar?"

"Only to say that there is scriptural justification for visions."

"Ignorant men wrote the Scriptures, as you very well know," his father retorted. "They put into concrete form the feelings of their hearts. I do not expect that sort of thing from the graduates of my university."

"I wonder if Jehar has not decided upon a rather brilliant act, nevertheless?"

"What do you mean?" his father demanded.

"I mean, we have tried our way of preaching Christianity for some hundreds of years, churches and hospitals and universities, all this you have here, but it doesn't make Christians."

"It does make Christians," his father said harshly. "There is a statistical gain every year in Indian church membership."

"No real gain," Ted said doggedly. "The villages are as they have been for all these hundreds of years. I saw no sign of Christianity there, Father. The same old poverty, the same old misery, the same greed of the zamindars and the landowners, the same ruthlessness of the rich over the poor, the evil over the good—"

"These things have always been and always will be," his father said.

"Then of what good is Christianity?" Ted cried passionately.

He met his father's astonished eyes, he saw his father's concern, and he leaped to deny his father's faith.

"Jehar is right," he cried. "I wish I had the guts to be like him! I wish I could give up all and follow Christ!"

There was a look of real terror in his father's eyes and this at last he could not face. He turned and strode away.

What had he said? He had said that he wished he could give up

238

all and follow Christ. But what did that mean? He stopped in the big empty drawing room. As clearly as Jehar had said he saw the face of Christ, he saw the face before his eyes. It was the face of a peasant, a nameless face, a face he had seen in one of the scores of villages through which he had passed, had seen and had forgotten, but it had hidden itself in the folds of his brain, a face twisted with pain and labor and starvation, a hopeless face except for the deathless burning eager eyes, and the eyes demanded of him, "Is there no hope for me?"

He stared at this face, and while the eyes made their demand upon him, he heard the door to his father's study suddenly close.

Alone in his study David fell to his knees. He had turned the key in the lock, ashamed, or perhaps only shy, lest he be discovered in prayer at this hour. But he was driven to prayer, for now he was afraid for his beloved and only son. All the year since Ted first came back to him he had waited for the time when he could speak freely to Ted, when he could tell his son his problems and the fearful weight of his task, and he had not spoken. He had been confused with memories. When he looked at Ted, he saw his own father, as he might have been when young, and yet Ted was like Olivia, he had Olivia's ways, her quick feelings. And thus confused and accustomed to loneliness, he had not spoken to his son even of his fears and burdens.

And now Jehar!

If the Indian people were touched enough with unreality so that they could follow a fanatic, their ignorance was still appalling and he had begun to see that all he did would not be soon enough to save the country, because Gandhi had lighted such a flame.

And now Jehar!

With Empire his work, too, would collapse. The millions of ignorant peasants in the villages could not soon enough be taught or their poverty relieved to save the day for Empire. The task should have been begun three hundred years ago, if Empire was to hold. He knew now that his own student body was rotten with disloyalty. He tried not to know it, but the secret meetings, the private slogans, the Gandhi caps and the homespun cloth were conspicuous. If Gandhi won, then the Christianity upon which he had built his life was only shifting sand. And Ted had today defied him, as yesterday Jehar had defied his own father. Oh, the cruelty of sons to their fathers!

There on his knees while his thoughts prevented his prayers, he suddenly remembered his own youth. So had he defied his father, and his whole life had been a defiance and still was. That aged man lying bedridden now in the old mansion, he had deserted, too, in his own fashion. The tears rushed to his eyes.

"God, let me go back to my father and explain to him—"

It was not at all the prayer he had planned to make.

"Have I been wrong, O God? Should I have obeyed my earthly father instead of Thee? Am I punished now in my own son? Give me wisdom that I may know what to do."

He knelt there for a long time, waiting, but no answer came, and he got up from his knees. It had been long since he had been aware of any answer to his prayers. Somehow without knowing it he had lost the sense of the presence of God, even while he spent his whole life in that service. Loneliness descended upon him again, the awful loneliness of the spirit. When Olivia died he had known loneliness and in a sense he had never learned to live without her. But the loneliness then was not absolute, as this was. He had not given himself to Olivia as he had to God Involuntarily he groaned aloud the cry that once Christ had made, "My God, my God, why hast *Thou* forsaken *me?*"

But why, but why?

Ted strode from the drawing room down the hall to his own room and closed the door silently and then stood motionless. His heart was beating with joy! Wave after wave of joy, astounding joy, whose source he did not know except that it came from outside himself, infused his being. It filled him like an atmosphere, cooling and invigorating. He laughed aloud, he felt the hair prickle on his head and his fingers tingled. He wanted to run and leap and dance. Yet why except that there alone in the drawing room when he had seen his vision, he had reached a decision so clear that it was absurd not to have known before that it was inevitable. He must leave Poona and go and live in a village. How simple a resolution, but he had been struggling toward it all these months since he had seen Darya, and only Jehar's directness and childlike purity had led him to the end.

"Why should I follow my father's footsteps? I must leave him so that I can live alone with India and myself. There was that little village in the north that I liked so well. That is where I shall live."

He stood enraptured with the thought. Hindu saints, like ancient Christians, were acquainted with the state of ecstasy, and this, he supposed, was what they meant. When a decision was right, because it was the will of God, or perhaps only because it fulfilled the soul's deepest unspoken desire, then such ecstasy was the confirmation, a powerful happiness, an accord which was complete.

He sat down quiescent, wondering and grateful, and after a time the joy subsided and peace remained. He made plans, he thought of the village, Vhai, and of all that he could do there—yes, and receive. He would go there humbly to learn as well as to teach.

XIV

"I cannot understand you," David said.

"I don't expect you to, Father," Ted replied.

They sat at dinner together that night in the orderly house. His father looked exhausted. The heat had risen unbearably during the day and the monsoons were due at any hour now, and would probably begin before midnight. Meanwhile the air was fetid. Neither of them could eat and they made no pretense. The languid servant removed their plates and brought in coffee.

"Does this decision mean that you have given up the thought of marriage?" David asked.

"No, not if Agnes will come to the village with me," Ted said.

"I hope you will not be so inconsiderate as to ask her," his father replied severely.

Ted laughed. In spite of the heat he had continued singularly lighthearted all day. He had busied himself with packing a few of his things, a change of garments, some books, a cooking kit, an army cot and a mosquito net. When he got to Vhai, he would build one of the mud-walled houses with a thatched roof. There was no reason for delay now that the school year was over.

"Does it seem laughable to you?" his father asked drily. Humor between the generations was perhaps impossible. He remembered the jokes which his father used to tell and laugh at loudly which even in his youth had seemed to him childish and certainly not funny.

"Not at all," Ted said gaily, "but I suppose Poona was rather remote when my mother came to marry you."

"It was not the same," his father retorted. But he did not explain how it was. Instead his mind busied itself suddenly with an inspiration. Why should not he write to Agnes Linlay and beseech her good sense for his foolish son? Let it be a secret between them, let him convey to her delicately how happy he would be if ever she became his daughter-in-law. He could praise his son honestly in several ways, and then hint that though he was extremely young and could benefit the more from a sensible wife, yet he felt he could promise that she need never regret her choice, if now Ted could be kept from an unwise decision to go and live in an Indian village, an act which must somehow be prevented by his family and his friends. There were proper ways for a white man to live in India and she above all young women perhaps must know this and could help to save Ted from folly.

"I shall just drift off in a day or two, Father," Ted was saying cheerfully.

"I am surprised that you have let Jehar so influence you," David said.

"It is not Jehar alone," Ted said. "It is even partly Darya. Most of all it is my own wish just to strip off everything that you and Grandfather have given me, though I am grateful to you both and must always be, and yet I want to be only myself at least for a while —not a MacArd, perhaps."

David did not reply. He was haunted by this morning's memories of his own youth and he could not speak without seeming to echo his own father twenty-five years ago. He must rely on Agnes Linlay.

Their meal was interrupted by a commotion on the veranda and the announcement that Fordham Sahib and Memsahib were waiting.

"Ask them to come in," David told the manservant. They came in not two but three, and the third was a young girl, a girl with a face as fresh as a pansy, and indeed very like a pansy, the large soft brown eyes and thick soft brown eyebrows, full red mouth and pointed chin combining the effects of that simple flower. She was

243

extremely pretty and childlike, and Mrs. Fordham introduced her with bursting pride.

"Our daughter Ruthie, Dr. MacArd, and this is young Mr. MacArd, Ruthie. Do forgive us, but we couldn't wait."

"She's come, has she?" David said, essaying a smile. He had forgotten and so, he supposed, had Ted, that Ruthie was to arrive.

"Oh yes, and very lucky it is just before the monsoons, so difficult to travel in those pouring rains, but they're very near."

"I went up to Bombay to fetch her," Mr. Fordham said, staring at Ruthie with eyes shining behind his small steel spectacles. "Ain't she pretty?" he added with mischief.

"Papa!" Ruthie cried in a sweet, loud, young voice.

"Papa is just the same as he always was, dearie," Mrs. Fordham said fondly.

"He's awful," Ruthie said to everybody. She opened her red lips and laughed, her teeth sparkling white. She was quite at ease, her rather plump young body relaxed and even indolent, and she wore a pink short-sleeved dress, for which Mrs. Fordham now felt it necessary to apologize.

"Ruthie, your sleeves are a mite short, aren't they? For a missionary, dearie? We have to set an example."

"Are they?" Ruthie said innocently.

They all gazed at Ruthie's smooth and pretty arms, and Ted stared at her frankly. It was astonishing to remember her even as vaguely as he was able to do and then see her as she was now. That round-faced, round-eyed troublesome small girl who had tagged him mercilessly as soon as she could walk, and whom he had avoided as completely as he could, had become this fresh and natural flower, a little stupid perhaps, but of a gentle and sweet disposition, as anyone could see. His grandfather had said once, "Marry a good disposition, Ted. Your grandmother had a sweet nature and it is the most important gift for a woman to have. I've known men ruined by their wives' dispositions."

When the guests were seated Ted asked his father, "Shall I tell the Fordhams?"

"With one explanation," David replied. "That is, I do not approve."

"What is it now?" Mrs. Fordham was as usual lively with curiosity.

"I am going to live in a village," Ted said.

"For good?" Mrs. Fordham exclaimed.

"I hope so," Ted said.

"Mama means is it forever," Ruthie said, laughing.

"I don't know."

"But how queer," Mrs. Fordham exclaimed. "To leave your father, and this lovely house and everything—what for?"

"I daresay the end of the summer will see him back," Mr. Fordham said.

"I don't know," Ted said again.

"A lot of young men think they are going to do something new," Mr. Fordham said. "I remember when I was young, I had such ideas. But a village can be very uncomfortable."

He broke off and they all looked at him. "I don't know what the authorities will think of it just now," he went on, answering their looks. "They may take it to be a bit on the revolutionary side, you know."

"I shall explain matters to the Viceroy myself," David said.

"In that case—" Mr. Fordham stopped.

"I think it would be fun," Ruthie said. "I've always liked country Indians. They appreciate you and they're not proud the way the educated ones are. There was an Indian girl in school at home, she was the daughter of a native Prince, one of the very smallest ones, but she wouldn't speak to me. She looked down on missionaries."

Nobody answered this until Mrs. Fordham said piously, "I hope you forgave her, dear."

"I let her go her way and I went mine," Ruthie said.

"You should have prayed for her," Mrs. Fordham said.

"I didn't bother," Ruthie replied.

Ted laughed. He suddenly liked Ruthie, without admiring her in the least. She had grown up lazy, he supposed, as so many missionary children did, waited on by ayahs as he himself had been.

245

The thought occurred to him that he might even now be thinking of a village as an escape, a place of no demands, and, as Ruthie said, of gratitude and appreciation. Gratitude was a habit-forming drug, he had seen white men who needed more and more of it to keep them self-satisfied until they became ridiculous and pompous with false righteousness.

"We must go home," Mr. Fordham said. "The gentlemen want to finish their dinner."

"Hark," Ruthie exclaimed. Her eyes widened, listening, and they all listened. Far off they heard the howl of rising wind, it came nearer with a rush, and then they heard the splashes of rain from the purpling sky. The monsoon had come.

"Run for it," Mr. Fordham shouted. They ran out of the open door, and Ted stood watching them. Mr. Fordham sprinted ahead, Mrs. Fordham lifted her skirt over her head, letting her white petticoat flutter in the wind, but Ruthie did not hurry at all. She walked slowly, her face lifted to catch the full force of the rain, and she spread her plump little hands palms upward. The wind snatched the curly strands of her hair and pulled at the knot at her neck until it fell upon her shoulders and the rain whipped her cheeks. She was not afraid, and that, too, Ted liked.

"I admire Ted," Agnes Linlay wrote in her upright large hand-writing, after a suitable number of weeks had passed. "At the same time I quite see how impossible it is to accomplish anything by what he is doing. Believe me, Dr. MacArd, I feel honored by your confidence in me, but Ted and I did not come to an understanding. I might almost say it was quite the contrary, and that we parted upon disagreement. I have been brought up as an English girl is brought up in India, and I suppose I cannot help my own feelings of proper responsibility. I fear we can only wait for Ted to come to his senses, and meanwhile there is no obligation of any sort between us. If he writes to me, as he says he wishes to do, I shall express my own point of view."

A dignified young woman, David thought, exactly what he would like to have had for a daughter-in-law, and exactly what Ted needed for a wife. He wrote a careful reply to her, in his own rather fine tight handwriting, expressing the hope, as he put it, that some day they might meet and talk about Ted, and meanwhile he would appreciate anything she could do to keep her point of view before his son. For his own part, he deeply valued what the British Empire was doing to bring the people of India into a position where they could be independent and take their place in the family of modern nations and he deplored the ingratitude of young intellectuals and their leaders, among whom, he was sorry to say, were Indians whom he considered his old friends.

He did not tell her that he was feeling lonely since his son had left. For Ted was gone. He had stayed only a day or two after the monsoon broke and in pouring rains he had set out to the northeast for the village of Vhai. There, his first letter had reported, he found the whole countryside a lake, reflecting the clouds when the sun burst through for an hour or two at a time. But Vhai itself was on a low hill, a small flattened mountain, and the earthen streets were not too muddy. He had a found a little house and had set up his housekeeping, although so far he had not been able to do anything except let the villagers stare at him, which they were able to do because they did not need to work while the rains fell. He was glad he had learned their language, for he exchanged jokes with them, and nothing seemed to them more of a joke, though they liked it, than that he declared that he had come to learn of them. The whole village was only a cluster of earth-walled houses and in this handful of minute homes every sort of small industry went on, spinning and weaving, pottery making and carpentry and grinding meal. The people were on the verge of starvation, of course, but cheerful now that the rains were generous. There was even a little temple to Ganesh in the village, the little fat elephant-headed god of whom the people were fond because he was innocent and tried to do his best.

Ted was happy. He was free, the ecstatic gaiety held, and he lived from day to day. The rains would cease in due time, and the lake grow dry and become fields of rice and mustard and beans. He would not visit Poona soon, he wrote his father. He was learning very much, and the people were no longer afraid of him.

He did not write to Agnes for many months, not until the winds blew cool from the foothills of the Himalayas, and not until his life was established in the mud house, and the routine of his days was clear. In the early morning he rose and taught two hours of school for anyone in Vhai who wanted to read and write. Then his pupils went to work and he set up a small dispensary under the overhang of his thatched roof, and there the sick came to him from an ever widening area, and he healed some, persuaded some he could not heal to go to the nearest hospital and agonized over those who went home to die. The afternoon was spent in arbitrating petty quarrels, with which Vhai was seething, and thus in patient talk and shy advice the day passed and night fell. It was a simple routine, accomplishing much less than he dreamed of for the future, but it was established, and so he could write to Agnes at last.

"You and I had no chance really to know these people when we were growing up. I wish I could share with you the stories that happen every day here in Vhai, the extraordinary, the sad, the sweet stories of this everyday village life. It is so much more exciting than the life we lived behind our compound walls. Here in the village street, and in the scraps of gardens behind each house, walled with earth for a tiny privacy, I see human life and see it whole. My darling"—and these were his only words of love—"does it offend you that they have put up an image of Jesus now in the temple? But he looks like Jehar, who is a Christian sadhu. Perhaps Jesus did look like that. He stands beside Ganesh, but they have made him tall."

Two words in the letter moved her to write to him immediately. "Ted, I cannot let you call me your darling. I do not know how to tell you and so I will just tell you. I have promised to marry your father."

No news came to Vhai, no gossip from the outer world, and his father's letters had given him no warning. He understood that deep reserve, or perhaps even delicacy, which made it necessary for Agnes to be the one to speak first. Had he lived in the mission house he might have seen the strange disparate friendship growing between her and the man who was his own father. But he had seen nothing.

He had lived his joyous life in the village, the joy isolating him for a time, at least, even from the need of love, so that he had not written her sooner. He had to imagine from her letter and his father's, which now came promptly, and thus he discovered that it was he who had brought them together. They had written letters about him, and then in September his father had gone to Calcutta to see her, distressed indeed because of his own new feelings. His father made it plain that he was distressed.

"I never thought to put another woman in your mother's place, but I have been driven by loneliness since you left, and in my loneliness a friendship has developed with Miss Linlay." This was his father's scanty explanation.

Ted did not leave the village for the wedding, and the wedding journey which was to have been to China and Japan was instead to New York. The speechless old man, father and grandfather, was dying.

David and his young wife reached New York on a fine bright day, when the city was its brightest beauty. A wind blew from the sea, and the sky was brilliantly clear. He was happy as he had never dreamed of being happy again, the fair-haired English girl at his side was wife and daughter both, he had somehow won her for himself, and pride and complacency filled his heart. He loved her not as he had loved Olivia, but with tender fondness and infrequent passion. Fortunately she too was cool. He had been troubled, before the wedding, lest the long years of celibacy might make him diffident with her, but it was not so. She had delicacy and good breeding, a taste at once understanding and compliant, and there had been no confusion between them. When the marriage was consummated finally, his last loneliness disappeared and with it his slight enduring sense of guilt toward his son. Though she said that she knew now she could never have married a man so young as Ted, though she affirmed her love for him, David had felt guilt until the final act which made her all his own.

To his old home he took his English wife, and she settled into

249

the rooms which had been his mother's and he was proud to see how well she liked them and how much at home she was.

"It might be an old London house," she said, wandering here and there, looking at everything. The French taffeta and the satins which his mother had chosen a lifetime ago had scarcely faded and were not worn.

"These stuffs are very fine," Agnes said. "I love the old materials."

He embraced her tenderly, and because she was as shy as he, he pressed her the more warmly to his breast. There was no need here for withdrawal. Olivia demanded but this woman would never make demands and so he need not fear her. His life had fallen into pleasant places. God was good.

"Go to your father now, dear," she said reasonably. "I will wait."

His father did not know him. He stood beside the massive bed and stared down at a large skeleton, elongated and immovable. The grey eyes were open and saw nothing, the whole effort was for life drawn in with each shallow breath and almost lost when each breath went out.

The nurse stood by, large and placid. "He can't last long, poor man," she sighed. "Any day, any hour now. I'm glad you got here, Dr. MacArd."

"Has he asked for me?"

"He don't ask for anybody, Dr. MacArd. He's too busy drawing his breath."

"Call me if I am needed. I shall not leave the house."

"Yes, sir."

He tiptoed out again and went back to the sunlit rooms where Agnes waited.

"I don't want you to see him as he is now, dear," he said. She lay on the chaise longue where his mother used to lie, the satin cover drawn up and a book in her hand. She put down the book and he took her hand.

"It can't last but a few hours, at most a day or so. Then when he is at peace—"

"Thank you, dear," she said. "It's very thoughtful of you."

On the fourth day when he went as usual he heard his father's

250

voice, still strangely strong. He entered and saw that the nurse was at the bedside, pressing the old man's shoulders.

"Lie down, do, Mr. MacArd. You'll hurt yourself."

"What's this?" David inquired.

"He come to, all of a sudden," the nurse exclaimed.

From his pillow MacArd stared at his son, his dry lips open. The nurse had cut off the famous beard, and the jutting chin and thick pale mouth were plain.

"Where's Olivia?" he demanded.

He was glad he had not let Agnes come into the room with him. "Father, Olivia died more than twenty years ago."

"Olivia dead, too?"

"Long ago, Father."

"Leila," old MacArd muttered, "Leila, Leila, Leila—"

"Hush," the nurse said, "now you are beginning to fret again."

The snow-white bushy eyebrows lifted with old fury.

"Shut up," the old man bawled. "Shut up, woman!"

The effort was too much. Upon the wave of wrath he stiffened with sudden amazement, thrust up his naked chin and died.

"I'd rather like to live here," Agnes said. The old Victorian house, though surrounded now by skyscrapers and business offices, made her think of London.

"Then we will some day," David said. "I have my work to think of still."

"Of course," she said quickly. "I was only imagining. We'll be happy in India, though I'll never be a proper missionary's wife, David. You know that?"

He stopped himself from saying that he had told Olivia long ago that he did not expect her, either, to be a missionary's wife.

"Only be happy," he said instead. He was relieved that she seemed inclined to be happy in spite of the disconcerting discovery that an American physician had made, that she would be unable to have a child. He had been fearful that he might at this age have young children, a possibility which alarmed him and made him somewhat ashamed. His dignity might be threatened perhaps, certainly in

India, if his sexual reawakening were made so manifest. Then she had felt that there should be an examination while they were in a city where the physicians were excellent, and so after the funeral of his father, that notable funeral in St. James Cathedral, where the church had been filled with white-haired men and women in broadcloth and satins, had come this news that there could be no children. Whatever heirs there were to be for the MacArd fortunes, must come from Ted. He did not mind; indeed he was glad. Doubtless Ted would marry. Young men in India inevitably married. A woman would bring Ted out of that village and make him sensible again.

XV

In the village, Ted was expecting his first visitor from outside.
Darya was freed from jail again, and he was coming to Vhai. While
he was in jail he had heard of the lively young white man, American, for what Englishman could do such a thing, who had left his
home and gone to Vhai to live like an Indian, though he was a
Christian. His father was even a rich man.

"What is the rich father's name?" Darya had inquired, guessing
who it was.

"MacArd, Sahib—"

"Ah," Darya said, "it was I who told that young man to go to the
village."

"And he obeyed you," the new fellow prisoner said, admiring him.

"Ah," Darya said, "I have known that young man from the hour
he was born."

So, freed, he went immediately to the village of Vhai and found
Ted, his fair skin blackened with the sun and his blue eyes like
lamps in the darkness. The village was all astir and agitated with
Darya's coming, whose name was almost as great as Gandhi's own,
and Ted's glory rose.

"Now," Darya said, gazing at the tall young man grown exces-
sively thin on village fare, "you are a true Indian. You might have
come from Kashmir, you know, with those blue eyes. Aha, even a
dhoti, and very skillfully worn!"

"Thanks," Ted grinned. "It's cooler."

The crowd stood to listen and to admire.

"And this is your house," Darya went on, gazing at the neat

253

earthen house, now enlarged to two rooms and a small veranda, made of rough wooden posts and covered with thatch. "How do you support yourself?"

"Still on the old bounty, I fear," Ted said.

"Expensive poverty, eh?" Darya said, half teasing. "The sadhu tradition is good, but you do not travel, eh?"

"I have not yet learned here all that I want to know," Ted said. He made a sweeping gesture with his hands to include the crowd, and they fell back a few feet and grinned with modesty and shyness.

"The best of teachers," Darya declared courteously.

They went into the little house then and sat down on mats on the earthen floor and they talked. Darya's tongue was eager to wag after the many months in jail, and Ted was eager to listen to someone his superior, to receive instead of to give. The villagers were kind and good and they taught him much but their words were the words of children, while Darya's language flowed in Hindustani or Marathi or Gujerati or English, or French or German, whatever language he chose, a dazzling array of tongues, all fluent and acute together.

"Gandhi is in Yarvada prison," he began. "He is not well, and I hear there may have to be an operation. If so, he will be freed. Until I can talk with him, I must not plan the next strategy. To resist without violence demands the utmost in wisdom, in attack, in endurance. Violence is simple and easy, it is the sword of the stupid and dull-witted, and it always leaves chaos. To carry on a positive revolution without violence—ah, that is a challenge to intelligence!" Darya spoke with relish, a lively enjoyment upon his lean and vivid face. Prison had sharpened and refined both mind and body and had charged his spirit with compulsive energy.

"Is Gandhi the absolute leader?" Ted asked.

"Spiritually, yes," Darya replied, "and until we know the feelings of his spirit none of us acts. The situation grows more complex every day. The hope of freedom sounds simple, does it not? But hope is a releasing force, and what it releases is not always simple. You would think it is enough to dream of India being free, but no, there are other more petty freedoms also desired. The Muslims cannot only be free Indians, they wish also to be free Muslims, and so it is with the Hindus, and now even with the Sikhs. And it is not enough for these lesser freedoms, but labor is divided, some pulling to the left with Russia and some to the right. Labor wishes to be free of capital. Meanwhile eighty-seven percent of capital in India is British, and Indian capital also wishes to be free of British capital, and above all, there is that for which I will fight with my whole life, and is the freedom of these land people, the peasants, who are ruled by the landlords and the money lenders, and now, alas, these two are becoming one great evil, for the land is falling into those grasping hands, and landowners do not even come near the land. They live in the cities and send out their agents to take the land away from the peasants who cannot pay their rents and debts."

It was true. Moneylender and landlord were becoming one and because of this the peasant was being pushed off the earth. "Dangerous rumors are creeping over the border from Russia," Darya went on, "sweet promises to seize the land by force from the landlords and give it again to the people. While Gandhi insists on nonviolence, the people are muttering of force. I have asked Gandhiji what he will do if the peasants break into violence."

Ted had no answer. He was still learning of the deep restlessness in the heart of India and he had never seen Gandhi.

Through the next few days they talked as they could, but Darya must stop often to greet visitors, for when it was known that he was there, men walked for many miles to look at him, to hear his voice and touch his hands, and to ask him, "When shall be we free, punditji, and will the land then be given to us again?"

Darya made always the same steady answer. "Our only hope is in Gandhiji."

At night Ted could speak in English without fear of offending those who could not understand, for he would not speak during the day in a language foreign to the villagers, a delicacy with which Darya was impatient. For, as Ted soon saw, with all his passion and concern for the peasants, Darya was not one of them. He could be impatient with them and speak to them with unconscious arrogance, whereas Ted, the American, did honestly feel no difference between a peasant and any other man. He wondered at Darya's lack and did not know how to speak of it, for understanding is a gift and Darya did not have it with each man as he was. This was the sin and the fault in the intellectual Indian, and if the revolution failed, Ted thought, it would be because of it. For none was quicker to observe this arrogance than a peasant himself, and after a few days the villagers drew away from Darya and Ted felt them come nearer to him, though he was a foreigner, than they were to Darya. They were courteous and kind, but they withdrew, and Darya did not seem to notice.

After Darya had gone away, on foot, his imperious head held high and his mind full of plans for the people's freedom and his heart full of indignation on their behalf, though he was a rich man who had given up all he had for their sake, yet the villagers waited until he was gone before they came crowding into Ted's little house again, asking their questions about Gandhi and how far freedom was away. They respected Darya and knew him a leader, but they knew, too, that though he would give up his life for them, he could not eat with them or sleep under their thatched roofs.

The day after Darya was gone, Ted received a letter brought as usual by a carrier on foot. The envelope was square, the paper was cheap and pink, and it was stamped with the name Fordham. The writing was not that of Mr. Fordham, and certainly he would not get a pink letter from Mrs. Fordham. He opened the letter and found inside two double sheets covered with a childish handwriting in purple ink. The name at the end of these lines was Ruthie and now he was embarrassed as well as surprised. She said frankly that she wrote without the knowledge of her parents, and because she was lonely. She had no companions of her own age, she was nineteen, and her parents would not let her meet any of the young Englishmen in business or Government, lest there be talk among the Christians.

It was plain indeed that she wanted simply to write to a young man and she had chosen him not knowing why she did, an urge of the blood which he must not encourage, although it was touching.

He had not written to Agnes except for one letter wishing her happiness, but her presence in the mission house would make it impossible for him to be there again. His father had written, however, that he planned to build a house for himself and Agnes in a separate compound when they returned to Poona, releasing the mission house for others. Agnes wanted to live where other English families had homes, he said, and he could see no objection, since he had never accepted funds from the mission and was to that measure independent. The time might even come, his father went on, when he would give up his active presidency of the university and become a liaison between Church and Government. The Viceroy very much wished him to undertake this larger mission, and Agnes would enjoy the travel. Ted could not read that name without pain, but his father used it firmly and with ease, taking for granted that his son would know how to behave and to feel toward his father's wife.

"How I envy you," Ruthie wrote now in large round letters. "I would like to live in a village, too. I love Indian food and the little Indian children. I could bathe the babies and teach the mothers about them. I read quite a lot of books on child care. It is such a pity that one must think of the conventions."

Thus began an artless and on his side a half-amused friendship. She sent him her picture, a snapshot taken in the brightest sunshine. Her round arms were bare and her hair was a mass of short curls. She had cut her hair, she told him, because it was so hot, although her mother was angry. But she could not always listen to her mother.

"Mother keeps wanting to see your letters, for of course she found out, nobody else writes to me except a girl from school in Ohio, but I won't let her see them. There is no reason why she shouldn't see them but I must have something all my own."

She was teaching in the lower school, she told him, Bible and English, but she did not enjoy teaching older children. It was really the babies she loved.

"And aren't you coming to Poona even for Christmas?" she asked.

"Not even for Christmas," he wrote back. "Vhai is home to me now."

Yes, Vhai was home, the home of his spirit. He knew that his father believed that one day he would come back to Poona but he would never go back to Poona or to the mission. He could not teach or preach Christ there in that comfortable house, far removed from these millions who were the true India, and why only India? These were the people of the world, the world was full of them, and until they were saved, until their sickness was made health, until their starved bodies were fed, their ignorance enlightened, Christ was not preached. And all this must be done without robbing them of their honesty and their loving kindness, for never were people so truly loving as these who had nothing to give but their love. So he could never go back to Poona or Bombay or New York, never to Calcutta or London or Paris. His place was here.

He began to find a certain simple comfort in Ruthie's letters, as months went on again, and because he had to fill the pages somehow when he wrote back to her, and he liked to write because she made no demands and she enjoyed whatever he told her, he conjured up small incidents and minute observations. Darya had told him of the companionship of insects and small animals while he was in jail, he had described the secret life in the crannies of the prison walls. So thinking of something that might interest Ruthie's youthful mind, Ted now began to observe for himself the presence of other lives in his own two-room earthwalled house. The sun drying the earth had made cracks and from the cracks there came stealing slender lizards, some blue tailed. They moved swiftly, but sometimes they clung motionless for hours to a certain spot upon the wall or ceiling and when a fly or moth came near, out flicked a bright thread of a tongue to lap the unwary insect into a narrow gullet. Centipedes and scorpions provided on a little scale the same terrors that tigers did in the nearby jungle, but the real hazard and excitement of everyday life were thieving monkeys. Some were red-bottomed or blue-bottomed, for spectacle, but the common hordes were small and brown and incessantly noisy. These lives that shared his household and village life were not strange to a girl brought up in a compound in India, and so further to amuse her he created personalities for his most frequent insect and animal guests, none of which he killed unless it made a threat. Old Mossback, the father of the lizards, was his nightly companion, a grey and grisly little reptile, innocent of any guile except toward foraging for food. And he made a wilful pet of a tiny female monkey thrown by its mother to the ground and therefore wounded with a broken leg. She clung to his trousers like a child and wailed if he put her from him, and he named her, for no reason, Louise.

Thus he described the simple round of his days, and how in the short twilight of each day the villagers gathered around his door and he read to them from the Bhagavad Gita or the Koran, the Christian or the Hebrew sacred books, or he told them stories of other countries across the black waters, as they called the seas. Sometimes he told them tales from their own history books which none of them could read. After he had spoken, they commented or questioned or they drew out of the recesses of memory stories that they themselves knew, experiences and wonders, and after all had spoken who wished, he wove the evening's talk together in some way to lead toward God, who was One, however worshiped and by whom, and then he prayed the prayers they understood and craved, the prayers for food and health and safety.

"Even at night," he wrote, "the village is not quiet. Sometimes I hear voices from the jungle animals, sometimes a child cries because of illness, but when we part at dark we are full of peace."

Such letters went between them, until one day when he had been in Vhai for more than a year, and knew that years might pass before he left it, he had a letter from her which he had guessed might come, had dreaded and half expected, and had put off thinking about because he did not know what to think. It came and as soon as he opened it he knew what it was.

"Let me come to the village," Ruthie wrote. "Let me come and be your wife. I don't ask anything, you needn't even love me. But I love you."

What makes a marriage? He did not know. The demands of his young body were strong but subdued by prayer and fatigue. There were times when he was sleepless and then he got up and lit his lamp and read, although this meant that he would hear footfalls in the night, kindly neighbors come to see if he were ill, or perhaps because they were ill themselves or also sleepless.

India is not a place for long hours of sleep, even in the dense blackness of night. The undying heat, the restlessness of insects and beasts, the frail children crying in their dreams, or wailing because they are hungry, such sounds habitually broke Ted's rest, unless he was exhausted by the day's work, which he tried to be. Yet his deepest sleep would be on the edge of waking and when his own restlessness was added, he could not sleep, indeed. Yet did he wake, he could not be alone.

In Vhai he was everybody's concern, and upon him they all depended. What they would think if he married he did not know. No one had suggested marriage, they thought of him as part sadhu, part Sahib, although he repudiated both offices.

He could not imagine any white woman living in Vhai except Ruthie and he did not love her. He had a queer half-amused fondness for her, but he could not even imagine loving her, and he did not want to love any woman. Love would completely disturb the life he chose to live. Jehar came to his mind, of whom he had heard nothing, and he wondered if Jehar had married or would marry— not while he was sadhu, certainly, but had the primary need of a man's life overcome the saint in him? Or had he made the compromise that fakirs made, impregnating women under the pretense of being gods? But Jehar was nowhere near and there was none to whom he could go for advice or comparison.

Meanwhile the letter waited. He found he could not reply with whole-hearted repulsion to the thought of Ruthie's cheerful childish presence in his house, nor could he make the excuse that she could not bear the life here. She could bear it as well and perhaps much better than he did. Her plump little frame was probably immune by now to most of the germs of India, as well as to the heat. He sought relief in prayer and scripture reading, but the pages opened perversely to verses encouraging the natural life of man. So Solomon sang to a woman and he read,

Come, my beloved, let us go forth into the field,
Let us lodge in the villages.

And even in the Sanharacharya he read,

> For only where the one is twain
> And where the two are one again
> Will truth no more be sought in vain.

He searched for guidance and found it finally not in one voice or answer, but in the slow and growing conviction of his own heart. He had chosen where he would build his house and Ruthie was the only woman who wanted to live in it, and he had never lived in the house with any woman who was his own. His grandmother had died long before he was born, his mother had died before he could remember and to his father's house he could return no more. He wrote the shortest of letters in reply.

"If you will accept me as I am, Ruthie, then let us be married."

"Ted and I might as well be married right away," Ruthie said to her mother.

They were living in the mission house again where the young woman had been born and had grown up. David MacArd had not yet returned, and privately Mrs. Fordham considered that he had deserted the ranks of the missionaries, although Mr. Fordham, who was less spiritual than she was, had pointed out the advantage of the new Mrs. MacArd being the daughter of a British Government official.

They had been amazed at little old Miss Parker, however. She had suddenly screamed at them both.

"Worshipers of Mammon! That's what you are! David MacArd never was a missionary and you know he wasn't! His own glory, that's all he ever wanted. A humble and a contrite heart, Oh God—"

She suddenly began to sob in loud hoarse snorts, to the consternation of the good Fordhams.

"She's crazy," Mrs. Fordham gasped.

"I'm afraid so," Mr. Fordham agreed.

But he was kind to the sobbing crazed little soul, and a few days later he took her to Bombay himself and put her on a steamer for home. Somewhere in a quiet small asylum in New Hampshire Miss Parker lived out her life, refusing to speak anything but Marathi to her attendants, and even the Fordhams had forgotten her.

"I don't think you ought to be married before Ted's father comes back," Mrs. Fordham now said to Ruthie.

She was conscious of conflict within her heart as she gazed at her pretty daughter whom she did not in the least understand. Ruthie was not at all like herself when she had been young in a small Ohio town. She feared Ruthie was neither religious nor conscientious, and yet Indians loved the girl with adoration, and she could not understand why.

Ruthie did not care to improve anybody. She was gentle and mild, she was kind because it was the easiest way, not with intention of performing good works. She was careless and she did not mind dust and dirt, she was reckless enough to eat all Indian food however spiced and peppered. She had no sense of shame, and while she understood the slightest nuance of caste and never offended anyone, she mingled with Brahmans and untouchables alike though never at the same time. Children clung to her and she treated them with easy love and let them do what they willed, because she did not want to bother. She was at home anywhere, and Mrs. Fordham knew that the ladies in purdah counted all the days between Ruthie's visits because she gossiped with everyone and told everything and did not know the meaning of the word secret. She carried back to her parents unspeakable tales of life behind high walls where she was a beloved visitor and however horrible the tales she told them all in the clear level childish voice with which she asked for a second serving of sliced mango. She feared no insect or beast and went without a hat in the midday sun if she felt inclined, although her routine was that of an Indian, for she rose early, and she spent the four middle hours of the day asleep, refusing the punkah because it was tedious for the punkah boy to pull the rope. She was not a good teacher in the lower school because she let the girls laugh and talk and she had no conscience about their not learning anything. When a girl fell ill in the foreign dormitories and it was too far for their families to come, that girl always cried for Ruthie, who came and sat beside her and held her hand and told her she need not take the medicines unless she wished, speaking in whatever language the girl best understood. With all this Ruthie did not say her prayers at night, and in many ways Mrs. Fordham felt she could not really be called a missionary. So far as Mrs. Fordham knew, Ruthie never even told anyone about Jesus, and when she pointed out to her daughter the opportunity she was missing, Ruthie said she felt she did not know enough herself.

"But you could learn, Ruthie," Mrs. Fordham often remonstrated.

"I suppose I could," Ruthie always said agreeably.

"I don't believe Dr. MacArd will want Ted to marry me," Ruthie said now without rancor.

She did not intend to tell anybody that she had first suggested the idea of marriage to that tall and adorable young man with whom she had fallen in love the moment she saw him. There were many things she told to no one, in spite of all she did tell.

"Then we certainly ought to wait," Mrs. Fordham said in some alarm.

"Why?" Ruthie said in innocence. "We had better get it over with before he comes."

Mr. Fordham, when the question was put to him, agreed with his daughter, not in order to escape MacArd wrath, but because he was indignant that his daughter might be considered not good enough for anybody.

"We are plain Christian people," he said, "and we are good enough even for the MacArds."

Thus it was settled. Ruthie wrote to Ted that she would just as lief get married now, if he were willing, and then they could have a Christmas together in Vhai. The wedding would be small, she said, and she would just as lief not have many white people come to it, and she would ask only her best Indian friends. If he wanted to wait until his father came home, she would wait, but she would just as lief not.

This letter Ted received at the end of a day of unusual exhaustion

263

after his clinic, and doubts beset him. He was probably doing the wrong thing, but the affair had gone too far now to stop. He divined that even in this a subtle India had influenced him, so that marriage seemed not so much a matter of romantic love for two individuals as a convenience in his life. It would be very convenient as well as pleasant to have a sweet-tempered girl busy about his house and managing the details of housekeeping for his comfort. A girl from America, or England, or even from the levels of white society in India, would never live in Vhai, even for love. After all, Ruthie was unique.

These thoughts occupied several hours of the breathless night, when the burning darkness sat on his chest like a hot and furry beast. He slept at last, convinced that Ruthie was his fate.

A pleasant fate, he decided, in the midst of the marriage ceremony, when she stood up beside him in a short white linen dress. She had cut her hair very short and it curled in flat ends close to her head. He looked down on this feathery mass of gold, and saw upon her sunbrowned cheek a soft fruity down. Her lips were red and her brown eyes serious. Mr. Fordham was performing the rites and the university chapel was crowded with staring, lively Indians. None of the English were there, and only a few white missionaries of other sects in Poona. He knew them all from childhood but of their children not many had grown up and come back.

"Do you, Theodore, take this woman—" Mr. Fordham's voice trembled slightly. He questioned now the wisdom of his performing the ceremony in Dr. MacArd's absence. but Ruthie had persisted and as usual he had yielded.

"I do," Ted said almost gaily.

"Do you, Ruth, take this man—" he spoke each word clearly and almost sternly for Ruthie's ears and she replied with unconcern, "Yes, indeed I do, Father."

It was over, they walked down the aisle to the wedding march which Mrs. Fordham forced out of the wheezy baby organ, and there was no nonsense about rice. Rice was much too precious to throw about and the Indians would not have understood it. They did not have a reception or any food because castes were too complicating. Ruthie went back to the mission house and put on a thin brown cotton frock for traveling, she bade her parents good-bye, pursing her full soft lips to kiss them heartily on each cheek and to hug her ayah, and then she turned to Ted, who was waiting.

"I'm ready, Ted, let's go."

They got into a tonga, the driver suggested to his horse that he begin his duty, and thus they left the mission house. Mr. and Mrs. Fordham stood side by side on the porch and watched them out of the gate. When the gate shut they turned to each other.

"Well?" Mr. Fordham asked.

"I don't know," she said, hesitating. "I never saw a couple just like them."

"I guess there isn't a couple just like them," he replied. "But I believe they will suit each other. Anyway, they know India and what they have to cope with."

"What they have to cope with," Mrs. Fordham said with some spirit, "is each other."

Mr. Fordham avoided this and looked at his watch. "It's time for me to get out to the west chapel. I have to preach there this afternoon, wedding or no wedding, and I am taking a load of tracts."

"Ruthie, I want to say something to you."

It was the middle of the afternoon of their wedding day and the train was rocking along in the hot dust.

"Do," Ruthie replied. She opened her eyes and yawned. "I'm ashamed that I went to sleep, but I usually do sleep in the afternoon."

They had lunched on the train, a poor imitation of a wretched English meal. After it they had returned to their own compartment and she had placed herself compactly upon one of the wooden benches, her cloth handbag under her head for a pillow, and had slept for two hours. He was amazed, and when she woke he remarked that had he known she wished to sleep he would have told his servant, Baj, now their servant, to open the bedding for her so that she might have been comfortable. To this she had made no reply but he saw her cheeks flush a very pretty dark pink, and he knew the time had come to say what he had to say.

"We haven't had much time for talk," he went on. "But there is plenty of time ahead, and so we needn't hurry things."

He had done much thinking in the days before his marriage and he had prayed more than usual for wisdom and self-control and the fruit of prayer was that he had made up his mind he would not take Ruthie in a hasty carnal fashion. They must be friends before they became lovers. Only thus could he respect himself and her, but mostly himself, because it was necessary for him, and he feared that she was so soft, so yielding, so childish, that she would do whatever he said, without knowing his deepest necessity, which was not of the flesh, but the spirit.

"Tell me what you mean," she said. "You needn't be afraid of me. I'm not a bit shy. Heavens, I guess I couldn't grow up in India and see all I've seen and hear all I've heard and still be the least shy."

He felt relieved by her frankness.

"I will say what I have in mind," he replied, "and yet I want you to understand at the same time why I have made the decision."

"Decision?" she repeated, her pansy eyes opening wide at him.

"I am a normal man, I suppose," he said with plenty of his own shyness now. "It would be easy enough for me just to—"

"I know," she said, "go on, please."

"I would like to—to wait until it means something more to us than just the flesh," he said. "I can put it in a verse of the Scripture, perhaps. 'That good thing which was committed unto thee, keep by the Holy Spirit which dwelleth in us.' I think our marriage is going to be a good thing, Ruthie, but I want to keep it in the Holy Spirit, and spirit must come first."

She pondered. "Hasn't it come in you?"

"Not yet," he replied. This was very hard. "I feel the flesh but not the spirit."

"I feel the flesh, too," she said rather sadly. "And I wouldn't like to wait too long, because, honestly, I want a baby, Ted, just as soon as possible. I would like to have a lot of children."

266

He stared at her. He had not thought of a baby, but of course she had. His motherless life had not taught him to think of children, and so he had thought only of himself, and his soul.

But she was not thinking of herself, she simply wanted a baby, and that, after all, was the purpose of marriage. The people of Vhai were right. They married their sons and daughters to each other so that there might be children born, but he had been making of marriage a complexity entirely his own, of spirit and sinful flesh.

He laughed suddenly. Ruthie was right and he was wrong and there was no reason why she should not have children as soon as she wanted them. Why should he prudishly deny her children because he wanted to test the quality of his soul?

"What is making you laugh?" she inquired.

The heat of the train had forced little rills of sweat down the sides of her cheeks and her curls were damp about her forehead. The shaking car had scattered dust from its cracks and this mingled with her sweat to make delicate lines of mud.

"I wonder if my face is as dirty as yours," he said gaily. "Come here and let me wipe it off."

So she came to his side where he sat, and he blessed the solitude of English trains which locked them alone in a compartment together until they reached the next station, three hours away.

"It's not dirt," she protested, "just earth blown off the fields."

He pulled out his handkerchief and wiped the stains away, tenderness mounting in him. Her brown eyes were lovely, deep and soft, the lashes thick and dark, and her face was really like a pansy, just as he had thought when he first saw her. His heart began to beat hard and his breath quickened. This was not love, of course, but love would come. He could not possibly feel all this without its ending in love. She had small richly convoluted ears set close to her head, and a pretty neck. He glanced down and saw the rise of her breasts, where her frock opened, then hastily looked upward and caught the full pleading look of her eyes.

She said in her honest fashion, "You haven't kissed me—did you mean not to do that, too?"

"I don't know," he muttered helplessly, "I don't know just what I do mean."

He looked at her lips now, parted and fresh, her small teeth white between, and suddenly he bent his head.

Part IV

XVI

"Livy, I'm scared to tell your father," Ruth said.

She looked at the dark and beautiful girl who was their eldest child. They should have sent Livy home to school in Ohio long ago, but they had let her stay on even after the three boys went, who were younger. She had begged to stay because she said she had no friends in America.

"You'll soon make friends," her father had said.

"But here I have them already," Livy had replied too quickly.

They should have sent her anyway, Ruth thought, gazing at Livy with quiet troubled eyes. Ten was the oldest you ought to keep them and Livy was sixteen. They had sent her to an English boarding school last year, and she was back in Vhai again for her long vacation. She had changed too much in the year, or maybe they had not noticed before how much she had grown. Girls grew up fast in this hot climate. Livy was a woman, slender but full-breasted, and her face had lost its childish curves. She looked like the picture of Ted's mother.

"I'm not frightened of Father," Livy said. She spoke with a soft English accent which she had learned from her schoolmates, and which she chose to speak.

She was a quiet girl, self-repressed, torn by rebellion against the deep caste feelings of English girls. She believed passionately in her mother's literal acceptance of all Indians as human beings. Her father accepted too, but Livy was shrewd and intelligent and years ago she had observed that her father and mother were two different people. Her father believed as a Christian that Indians should be treated exactly as white people and he was careful to do this, but here was the difference, he was too careful, while her mother was entirely careless because she could not help treating everybody the same and Livy knew that of the two her mother was the more powerful. Her father could never belong wholly to Vhai, but her mother could and she did belong here as much as the banyan tree with its hundred roots.

She had counted upon her mother's understanding now and it must not fail. For in her heart she was terrified at what had happened to her. She had fallen in love with Jatin. It was inexplicable, she did not know how it had happened, for she had known Jatin for years, at least three, and she had not thought of loving him. He came from Poona, and he had been graduated with highest honors from the medical college of MacArd University and so her father had invited him to come to Vhai and set up a rural clinic and a small hospital. She had heard her father praise him and declare that he was someone to depend upon, someone who could take over the whole of Vhai's village improvement work and the widening effect it had in the whole province, and perhaps on India too, since independence. The new Indian government was talking of pilot centers of village education and public health and local government, such as her father had built up in Vhai. The village was beautiful now, and she never tired of hearing how different it had once been. But it had not occurred to her that she could fall in love here. She loved it with her whole heart, but still that had nothing to do with falling in love with Jatin.

Nevertheless, it had happened. When she came back from school only a month ago, she had fallen in love with Jatin at first sight, but of course it was not first sight, for she had seen him hundreds of times. But this time it had been different, only not different really, for when she got home she had to go and see everybody she knew and so she had run over to the clinic one bright morning to speak to the two Indian nurses, and to Jatin, too, of course, and she had stood in the doorway looking about and he was the only one in the little entrance hall where he was slipping into his white coat, and he looked at her as though he saw an angel. That was the way she felt. No one had ever looked at her like that before, and she had felt hot all over.

"Livy, how beautiful you have grown." That was what he said. Then he had come straight to her and had taken her hands and looked down into her face, so tenderly and kindly that her heart crumbled.

"I'm just the same," she had stammered.

"You are not," he had said, "you are grown up, so lovely."

He dropped her hands and stood looking at her and then the nurses came in and the moment was over. But of course they had seen each other almost at once and alone. She could not keep away from him, and she pretended that she wanted to help in the clinic and she did want to help, but because he was there. And after a few days of that, it was natural to stay late to wash up, because he always stayed late. And then it was only two weeks and a day until they were alone every day, or nearly every day, because he was very fearful about gossip and so sometimes he sent her away as soon as they kissed. Yesterday he had been troubled because he was sure that the sweeper saw them.

"I don't care," she had retorted. "Of course we have to be married, Jatin. That's what people do when they are in love."

He had been very troubled at this, his handsome eyes immediately sad. "I think it is not possible for us, my Livy."

"It is, it is," she had insisted. "My father and mother are not like other white people."

"Ah," he said in his quiet way, "they are not, indeed, but will they be willing for marriage between us? I think not."

"Then I shan't believe they are Christian," she cried.

"Don't speak so, Livy," he had begged her in his gentlest voice. "You know they are Christian. But—"

"What?" she demanded.

"It is very difficult to reach the ultimate of one's religion."

She did not understand what he meant and so she had simply repeated herself. "If they are willing, Jatin, then will you let us be married?"

"My darling, we will hope."

"I'll make them," she had declared confidently.

Now she sat with her mother over the mending basket, a task she detested, but which could not be done by a servant because Indian women did not know how to sew well enough. Saris needed no sewing, and the children wore no clothes when they were small, beyond a shawl wrapped about them if the night was cold. Still, this morning she had welcomed being alone with her mother, for her mother must know first and then talk with her father. There was a strategy to be followed.

She said, "Father ought to be willing for me to marry Jatin. He's always saying that Jatin is wonderful."

"So he is," Ruth replied. "But that's different."

She sat gazing at her daughter, her pansy brown eyes dark with anxiety. The monsoons had come early this year, and though she was grateful as everybody was, still there was melancholy in the long ceaseless rains. They must expect another week of it before clouds parted to show the darkly purple summer skies. Meanwhile she sewed, and this was her relaxation. Livy had flung down the pillowcase she was mending and was walking around, her under-lip pouting.

"Sit down, Livy, do, and don't pout at me. Here, you can turn this hem. Sara grows faster than I can keep her dresses let out. I'll finish the pillow slip."

Livy sat down, again fitted her thimble to her middle finger. She was a tall girl and she moved with an indolent yet active grace she had learned from Indian girls who were her closest friends, not only the girls in the village, but the daughters, too, of the men whom her father had gathered around him. Long ago, as she knew, he had come here alone, determined to live as the villagers lived, and then her mother came as his wife, and the next year she herself was born in one of the two little rooms which were the first part of the house. The house was still earthen and its roof thatched, but ten rooms had been added and under the thatch was stretched heavy blue cotton homespun cloth for ceilings, so that lizards and insects and snakes could not drop out of the thatch to the floor and bite their bare feet, although as children they had felt no fear. They were used to searching their slippers and shoes in the mornings, instinctively they looked before they stepped, and Vhai was their home. Around the low and sprawling house her mother had planted grass and flowers, so that it no longer looked the house it had been when she came to it as a bride.

Vhai itself was changed. When her father first came here to live, as a young man, so bitterly against her grandfather's will, as she knew, the village of Vhai was as barren as a desert, as all villages were. But her father and mother, while they shared the life of the people, had improved it in small ways, and then in big ones. Her father had even engaged an artesian well digger to come all the way from Bombay and put in more than twenty wells. Other villages had seen the benefit of the irrigated fields and they had dug wells, so that the whole region of Vhai had become beautiful and productive. It was a low region, over-sheltered by the distant Himalayas, and in the season of monsoons the land became a lake. But her father had taught the people how to dig ditches and lay village-made pottery tile, so that around Vhai, at least, floods no longer rotted the earth. Far beyond Vhai he did not go, declaring that people would hear of Vhai and come and see for themselves. This they had, but not as much as he felt they should, which made him gloomy at times. But Jatin had said, "How can half-starved people walk hundreds of miles to see something which they will never have the strength to do? First they must eat and grow strong enough to work for themselves. Alas, they have no food, so they must first be given food, and there you have the worst problem."

Jatin was clever and strong and handsome and she loved him because he could say things like that even to her father. Only why was he so timid now? They could be married and live in Vhai forever, because she loved Vhai almost as much as he did.

Ah, but she could never explain Vhai to the English and American girls at school. "Do you live in a nasty village?" That was how they put it.

"A village, but not nasty," she always said.

Yet she did not try to explain more than that for they could not understand. How could they? When they thought of India it was

275

of great houses encircled with verandas, set in vast compounds, of uniformed Indian servants and dinner parties where the guests were always white people. None of them spoke any Indian language, except perhaps a servant dialect, half pidgin, which they had picked up from their ayahs. How could they understand the depth of love she had for Vhai, this village full of people, all of whom loved her, because she was not only herself, but also the daughter of her parents? And she could never explain to them how she loved this house, reaching far enough to make rooms for herself and her brothers and her sister, but whose floor was brushed every morning with cow dung. That she could never explain, because the girls would give little screams of horror and they would never believe her if she told them how cool and smooth the earthen floors felt under bare feet, the earthen floors beaten as hard as marble and then brushed with the water from a pail in which had been flung a handful of cow dung, and the two mixed until the mixture was complete and clean. When the floor was dry, it was like old mahogany, polished as satin. But how could the English girls believe it was so?

She learned to live two entirely separate lives, one the life with the English girls where, because she was a MacArd, they did not treat her as they might a common missionary's daughter, those persons who were only a little better indeed than Anglo-Indians, and the other when she came home to Vhai. Oh, the deep and solid comfort of coming home to Vhai, where she could walk with no more on her feet than sandals, where often after her morning bath, she simply put on a cotton sari with a little short-sleeved blouse, pleating and knotting the long ends as skilfully about her narrow waist as though she were an Indian girl! And indeed she was much an Indian, for it is not only blood that makes the human being but the air breathed, the water drunk, the food eaten, the sounds heard, the language spoken and those with whom communication is made most deeply, and for her these were all Indian. She was closer to her mother than to her father because her mother, too, was much of an Indian woman, though her blood was American white. That was not quite the same as English white.

276

Yet, now, her mother could not understand her love for Jatin. She had thought she would, because she had been so sure that the India she and her mother loved were the same. They loved the little things in Vhai, the way the monkeys fought in the trees even when their quarrelsome chatter woke them in the mornings, the hum of the grindstone, the tinkle of silver bracelets and anklets as the women came and went with their water jars on their heads, the clatter and rattle of spinning wheels, for everybody these days tried to spin at least an hour a day because Gandhiji was the Mahatma, the leader of all the souls of India.

"And I don't want you to think that I approve, either," her mother was saying. "For I don't, Livy. I can't go so far as to think it right that a white American girl should marry an Indian. Jatin isn't even an Anglo-Indian."

"You act as though he were an Untouchable," Livy said with anger.

Her mother refused this insinuation. "Livy, I won't have you say that, after all your father has done for Untouchables. Why, when Gandhiji took an untouchable girl into his household to be an adopted daughter to him, your father said that it was the final proof of his sincerity and he has believed in him ever since. And have I ever shown in this house that I cared about caste?"

Livy said, "Jatin and I want to be married."

Ruth sighed. Oh, the terrible stubbornness of Livy! She was all MacArd and had been since the day she was born, and, thank God, the others were not. Sara was like her, and the boys were more Fordham, too, than MacArd, but Livy had not a drop of Fordham in her. She was glad now that they had sent the boys home early! They were safely in a church school in mid-Ohio, and so she should have done with Livy, except that the child would not go, and year by year they had let her keep on growing up here in India until now this had happened.

"Don't make me have to tell your father, Livy," she pleaded. She had never been able to discipline the children, and she used their love for her shamelessly for her own protection when she feared Ted's reproach.

277

"I won't," Livy said. "Jatin and I will tell him ourselves."

"Oh, dear," her mother groaned. "It will kill him. He loves you more than all the others put together, I do believe."

"What else can we do?" Livy asked.

She had finished the hem and she folded the small dress carefully and put away the thimble and needle.

"I don't know," her mother sighed. "I couldn't have believed such a thing could happen. Much as I love India—"

Livy took the sentence away from her. "Much as you love India, you could never have loved an Indian."

"Not in that way," her mother amended. "You don't understand."

"You are right, and I don't understand." Livy got up and began walking about the room again with her peculiar smooth grace. "Jatin is a wonderful doctor, you and Father have said so. He gave up a fine practice with his father in Bombay and came here because he believes in what Father is doing. And Bapu Darya says he will be one of the great men in India. So I don't understand. And I counted on you, Mother."

"Oh, dear," Ruth sighed. She shook her head and bit off the thread from the pillowcase. How could one explain anything to Livy when she already knew everything one was going to say?

There was no need to speak. Livy went out of the room and probably to meet Jatin somewhere. She supposed that in a way she had failed her child, but indeed she could not face what it would mean. She was still a white woman and she could not see her daughter dragged down into the mass of the dark people. Jatin himself could not prevent it and Livy could not lift Jatin up. She, in spite of her love for him, and he, in spite of his love for her, could not keep from sinking. She wished it were not true, it was hard enough to be a Christian among the Indians, who were literal-minded, but it was true and not all the saints could make it different.

She sighed again and let her mind subside gently until at last she was not thinking at all, simply sewing, and breathing to the rhythm of the stitches.

278

Livy walked down to the banyan tree where the shadows were deepest, her eyes instinctively watchful for snakes, although she was not afraid. The rain had abated in the last half hour until now there were only drifts of mist. She had put on her heaviest cotton sari and drawn the end over her head and Jatin, waiting for her, thought how exactly like an Indian girl she looked as she came toward their usual meeting place. That was something they must face, too, that this meeting place had been discovered and so they must abandon it. But where could they meet? In the clinic they saw each other now always in the presence of others. If her parents approved their marriage, of course they need not hide their meetings, but he had not succeeded in overcoming his natural and secret despondency. He was an Indian, however high he rose in his profession, and only because her father was so sincere a Christian could he find the conviction of human equality for which his pride hungered more than ever he had hungered for food. To Mr. Mac-Ard he owed everything, and he felt guilty of ingratitude, because now he had fallen in love with Livy. Yet how could he help it when he discovered that she could love him? He had taken it as play, as nonsense, the young girl home from boarding school, and he was already twenty-six years old, a graduate doctor at the Vhai hospital. But he had begun to dream nevertheless, and when her eyes met his with increased meaning and wonder, how could he keep from loving her?

"How dark it is," she said, coming into the shadow where he stood. "It must be later than I thought."

"We must not stay long," he agreed.

His painful sensitivity, aware at once that something was amiss, kept him from going to meet her, or from touching her when she stood beside him.

"Did you speak to your mother?" he asked.

"Yes. She is not willing," Livy said.

"Even she!" he whispered.

"She does not dare to tell my father." They spoke in Vhai dialect, her childhood language, which he had learned in the years that he had been here.

"What shall we do?" Instinctively he gave her the leadership.

"We shall have to go to my father and tell him," she said.

"Both of us?"

"Do you not wish to be with me?"

"Of course—but suppose he sends me away."

"Then I will go with you."

She saw the shadow of despair on his too intelligent face. "Ah, Livy—" he was speaking English now, which he spoke perfectly, although he had never left India. All MacArd graduates spoke English perfectly. "Nothing is so easy as you think it is."

"Why should we wait?" she demanded with a wilful stoicism in her voice and look. "Perhaps he will be kinder than we think. He has always been kind to us."

"Separately," he reminded her.

"Oh, Jatin," she said in quick young anger, "why will you be so easily defeated? Come with me!"

She seized his hand and led him out of the shadows with her.

Ted was alone in his study. It was a small quiet room, the last in the chain of rooms opening into the common court which was also back garden, walled with earth. One side of the room was windowless and against it he had hung, years ago, the portrait of his mother, which his grandfather had willed to him, instead of to his father. Years ago he had been reconciled to thinking of Agnes as his father's wife. He had never regretted his own marriage to Ruth. She had helped him to plunge deep into India, so deep that he had had no furloughs in the seventeen years since their marriage. Neither he nor Ruth had wanted to break the continuity of the days and the years.

And where would he go if he did go to America again? Such shallow roots as schooldays had given him were withered away and his grandfather was long dead. Let him be honest with himself. The thought of his father and Agnes living in the old Fifth Avenue house made return impossible to that only home he had known in his own country. It was one thing to be reconciled to his father's marriage, it was another to enter into the house which now belonged to Agnes. It was absurd to think of her as a stepmother, and certainly her influence must pervade the house since it was she who had made his father decide not to return to India. Explain it as he would, his father had never been able to explain that withdrawal.

"I have finished with India," his father had written after his grandfather's death. "Younger men must carry on my work. I had dreamed once that you, my son, would have taken up my mantle, but since that was not to be, the springs have dried in me. I should have been lonely, indeed, were it not for Agnes, my sweet young wife. She has a right to live the life which suits her so happily here in New York."

He had blushed when he read the fatuous phrase, "my sweet young wife," and even now as he thought of it a dry heat spread under his skin. He supposed, unwillingly, he was to blame for that marriage. If he had stayed on at MacArd as his father had wished him to do, perhaps he would have married Agnes and all these years would never have been. Had he not done what Darya had bade him do, had he not come to Vhai and lived among the lowly people of the earth, how different his life would be now!

Yet he had followed the light that shone for him, and if he needed comfort, Darya gave it to him. They did not meet often, for Darya was absorbed in his office in the new government, but once he had come to Vhai. That had been a great day. The villagers had gathered for miles around and fifty thousand people sat on the dry fields and listened to Darya tell them what the new India would be. He had stood above them like an aging king, his lean figure still tall and straight, his white hair flying, his thin face still unlined, and the wind had carried his powerful voice over the multitude.

"Here in Vhai you have lighted a lamp for the nation. What you have done, every other village in India can do. I love you, people of Vhai, and first of all I love you because the man who has lit the lamp for you, as you will light it for others, is the man who is like my own son."

That day was his reward, and thinking of it now, as he thought of it so often, Ted straightened himself and lifted his head. Yes, he had his reward. When independence was declared, many white men left India and no Indian spoke against their going. But he, Ted MacArd, had been invited and urged to stay, not only by the new Prime Minister and by Darya, but by Vhai itself. The people would not let him go. Ah, he had his rewards! Jehar, travelling to and fro over India, came sometimes to this quiet room, and then at early morning or as now at twilight, the Christian sadhu taught him that faith comes from many sources. It was Jehar who had explained to him the spiritual ties between all the greatest of the leaders of men and to the same God, whatever His name. Thus Moses and the Hebrew prophets, thus David and Paul, were brothers to Tukārām, the Sudra grainseller, who sixteen centuries later had lived in Dehu, a village some eighteen miles northwest of Poona itself. Tukārām had gone through his own Gethsemane, and famine, white over the land, and the dying voice of his young wife crying for food while he had no food, had driven him into the complete service of God.

This evening, for his devotions, Ted had been reading again the story of Tukārām, so strangely like the life of St. Francis of Assisi. He read of the birds that perched on Tukārām's shoulders in the temple, knowing him to be "a friend of the world." As Pharisees and Sadducees had persecuted Jesus, so the Brahmans had persecuted Tukārām. They would have none of him because of his lowly birth and because he could not believe, as they did, that Nirvana was the highest state of the human soul. He did not wish, he said, "to be a dewdrop in the silent sea," and he shared in the lives of men, and thus he sang:

> "The mother knows her child—his secret heart,
> His joy or woe.
> Who holds the blind man's heart alone can tell
> Where he desires to go."

As always when he was moved by the Hindu poet-saints, Ted returned again to the Christian New Testament, sometimes frightened, as he himself knew, lest the seat of his heart be shaken by those who had never known Christ, and he read again, "Except ye become as little children—"

Then he heard footsteps, a double rhythm, the soft sandalled footsteps of a girl and then the slower steps of a man. At the curtain they paused, and he heard his daughter's voice, "Bapu, may we come in?"

Livy spoke in the Vhai version of Hindustani, but he answered in English, "Come in, my dear."

She was indeed his dear daughter, his best-loved child, and he looked up from the sacred books on the table before him to see Jatin Das with her. His heart chilled and he put down his Testament. Nothing is secret in a village, and he had heard whispers, half hesitating and reluctant murmurs, that Livy had been seen alone with Jatin. He had not heeded talk. Livy was an American, and though she had grown up in Vhai until she went to the boarding school in Simla, he could not believe that she would forget her origin. Jatin, too, belonged to no ordinary Hindu family. He had been reared in Bombay, where the English were proud and he would not reach for what must remain beyond him.

"Come in, Livy," he said in his usual kindly manner. "And you, too, Jatin. Seat yourselves, please. Has the rain stopped?"

"Yes, but there are mists," Livy said.

She sat down quietly and folded her hands in the manner, he suddenly perceived, of the Indian girls among whom she had lived. He saw, too, that she wore a sari as she often did, but now it seemed to him that he had seen her in no other garb since she came home from school.

"What will you do when you go to America to college and cannot wear a sari?" he asked lightly.

"Father," Livy said. "I do not wish to go to America."

Now he was really disturbed. "Of course you must go, Livy. Your grandfather would be very angry if you did not go. And your great-grandfather put money in trust expressly for you, before you were born."

Livy looked at Jatin from the corners of her long, dark eyes, asking him to speak for her.

283

"Sir," Jatin said and cleared his throat. "Sir, we are in great distress. She and I—we have fallen into the wish to marry one another."

"We have fallen in love," Livy said distinctly.

"Yes, it is so," Jatin said, and taking courage now that the difficult word was spoken, his words came in a rush, liquid and fluent, overwhelming his diffidence. "It cannot be helped, Mr. MacArd, sir. It is the logical sequence, the inevitable outcome of the teachings of our childhoods. You have taught us to love one another, she has learned at your feet, sir, to regard all human beings as equal, alike children of God. And I, sir, taught in MacArd Memorial school in Poona, there took courage to cease to be a Hindu as my own father was, and I was converted by the great Jehar and nourished by Daryaji toward independence. I do not fear to love her. I glory in our courage. We are the fruit of all that has gone in the past, we are the flower of our ancestry, the proof of our faith!"

His fervid eyes, his glowing words, the impetuous grace of his outstretched hands, the long fingers bending backward, the thumbs apart and tense, the white palms contrasted against the dark skin, all were too Indian, and in one of the rare moments of revulsion which Ted considered his secret sin, he was now revolted and sick. What—his Livy, his darling daughter? None of his other children had her beauty or her grace, or her brilliant comprehending mind. She alone was all MacArd, and was she to give up everything for this alien man? For a moment his soul swam in darkness. No, and forever no! He had given his life to India in Vhai, but Livy he would not give. It was not to be asked of him. This was a cup which even the saints had not to drink, and Jesus, the celibate, who had never a child, could make no such demand.

"No!" The word burst from him. "I cannot allow it."

Jatin's hands dropped. He turned to Livy and they exchanged a long look, his despairing, hers hardening to anger.

"Livy," her father demanded. "Have you told your mother?"

"Yes," Livy said, "and she said she did not dare to tell you. But I dare."

He got to his feet. "Where is your mother?"

284

"In the sewing room," Livy said.

He went away, the door curtain swinging behind him, and Livy stretched out her arms to Jatin.

"I shall never give you up," she cried under her breath, "Jatin, faith, hope, and love, but the greatest of these is love—"

He turned away his head. "Not our love."

"Yes, our love," she insisted. She went to him, she put her arms about him and held his head against her breast.

Under his cheek, he felt the quickening beat of her heart.

XVII

"You see for yourself that it is impossible," Ted insisted.

"Oh, yes, I see," Ruth agreed indistinctly. She had not stopped her sewing, though she knew as soon as he came in that Livy had told him. Well, he had to know.

She lifted her eyes from the seam. "What are you going to do about it?"

"What are we going to do about it," he corrected her. Without waiting for her reply, he went on, inconsistently, "I shall buy steamship tickets for the first boat that sails from Bombay. We are all going to America. I shall put Livy in a girls' college."

"Livy isn't really a girl any more," Ruth said. "She's grown a woman, the way they do here, so fast."

"She's a girl in years and in mind," he said. "When she gets to America, she will take her place among other girls."

He got up from the bamboo chair where he had flung himself, walked up and down the room and sat down again, waiting for Ruth to agree with him. But she sat silently sewing, as he had seen her do hundreds of times through the years of their marriage. She found a spiritual calm in sewing, he supposed. A good wife, he knew, and he had learned to love her without ever being in love with her.

Yet what was love? One could not plant a palm tree in the courtyard with another person without in a sense feeling a sort of love, and he and Ruth had done everything together, building the house and rearing the children, teaching and preaching and carrying on the clinic, isolated by what they were, two white people in

286

a world of darkness. They had believed in the goodness of what they did, they were sure of their faith, and absorbed in their purpose, he did not stop to ask if he loved Ruth as once he had dreamed of loving a woman. All men dream, he told himself, and the reality was best, for reality alone was unselfish in love. Exhausted often in the parched climate, fatigued often beyond endurance by the desperate demands of the people, he and Ruth clung to one another, and each maintained the other in steadfastness. And this, too, was love, a love which bore visible fruit in hundreds of human lives.

Oh, she could sit silent like this forever while she sewed!

"Well," he said impatiently, "have you any other plan?"

"No," she said slowly, "I don't know that I have. It's just that I hate to leave Vhai. I guess you're right, Ted. We had better take her away from India."

"Will you tell her or shall I?"

"You had better do it," she said, and did not lift her head.

So he told Livy the next evening, his heart soft and hard together. He sat on the veranda, in the swiftly passing twilight, watching her toss a ball with Sara, the only one of his children who was still a child. Sara was like his great-grandfather, a fiery, bone-thin child who passionately loved her elder sister. He kept his eyes on Livy, graceful in her soft rose-pink sari, moving here and there with gliding steps to catch the rag ball Sara threw wilfully here and there.

"Livy!" he called through the dusk.

"Coming," she replied.

She seemed in good mood, her soft oval face was cheerful and she came at once. India was her climate, the heat did not depress her, she looked fresh and cool, though the night was humid.

"Sit down, daughter," he said.

She sank on the bamboo couch near him and Sara, deserted, cried in a high childish voice that wound itself into the singing rhythm of Indian speech, "It will soon be dark, come and play, Livy."

"This is for you, too," the father said.

She came and squeezed herself between them. "What have I done?" she demanded.

"Nothing," the father said.

"It is I who have done something," Livy said smoothly. "It is I who have been naughty and now Father is going to punish me."

"Livy is not naughty," Sara insisted. "Never she is naughty."

"Sometimes I am," Livy said. Her dark eyes hardened and glowed, and she turned them sidewise upon her father, but he refused the challenge.

"It can scarcely be called a punishment to go to America, and that is what we shall do. I have written for the tickets and the gateman has posted the letter already. Perhaps we must go even in a very few days."

Sara clung to Livy's waist and tightened her arms. To go to America was at once a dream and a dread. She had asked hundreds of questions about America and sometimes she lay awake in the night to think about that beautiful and even imaginary place, but now that her father said so coolly, "I have written for the tickets," Vhai was immediately too dear to leave, even though in America snakes did not crawl in the garden, nor scorpions hide in the shoes at night.

"Isn't that good news, Sara?" her father asked.

"Perhaps the children there won't like me," Sara said.

"It is not good news, Father," Livy said. Entire awareness was implicit in her voice and her furious dark eyes were fixed upon his face.

"It isn't good news, Father," Sara echoed, clinging to Livy's waist. "If Livy doesn't think so, I don't think so."

"Nevertheless, we are going," the father said, "and we shall stay for a year, except Livy, who will stay four whole years, because she is going to college. She will go to college and learn to be an American girl, and grow into an American woman. And maybe she will marry an American man and stay in America."

"Oh no, no," Sara cried, "for then how can she live with us in Vhai?"

"Perhaps then she will not want to live in Vhai," the father said.

288

"America is a wonderful country, there are wide roads and cars and great trains, even airplanes flying everywhere. Livy will have pretty clothes, and she will learn to sing and play the piano, and in the summer she may go to England and to France."

"Let me get up, please, Sara," Livy said. She tugged at the arms about her waist.

Ted did not stop her or ask her where she was going. He had dealt the blow and he must let her take it as she could.

"Come and sit on my lap, Sara," he said, ignoring Livy. "I will tell you more about America."

The little girl loosened her clutch upon her sister's waist, and diverted by the invitation, she went to her father. In the darkness, lit only by the glow falling through the open doors and windows as servants went about lighting the lamps in the house, he told her about America, the endless mountains and the long rivers, the great cities and the house where her grandfather lived, and before that her great-grandfather, whom she had never seen, who now was dead.

"America is your country, you know," he told her. "India is not your real country, and Vhai is not your own place, not really, you know."

"I didn't know," Sara said in wonder, "I always thought it was."

He fell silent when she said this, smitten like Peter of old, by conviction of betrayal at night, while his heart reproached him and he heard the wailing music of Vhai winding up from the streets now hidden by darkness.

In the dark Livy was walking with swift and reckless steps, heedless of the snakes and the night insects, the folds of her sari gathered in her hand and over her head the scarf which hid her bent profile. At this hour Jatin would be in his room next to the clinic, the little lean-to which her father had built for him when he came to be the resident doctor for the Vhai hospital. She had never been in his rooms except the day they were finished, before he moved in, when with her parents they had inspected the place for his coming. There were four rooms, enough for his family when he married, for, of course, he would marry, her father said, and four rooms would be spacious here in Vhai. And four rooms would be spacious for her, too, she could have made a home there with Jatin, she had dreamed of it, she had even talked of it, though he would never listen.

"It will never happen—never can it be so," Jatin had said again and again.

"Jatin, you are always discouraged," she had cried. "You must be bold, you must insist! If I want something very much I always insist."

To this Jatin had replied only with dark sad looks. His eyes, tragic in their shape and color, large and liquid, the lashes long and thick, carried in their shadows the memory of unknown sorrows, a deep racial grief which he had inherited and now possessed as his own nature. He was always sure that the worst would happen, he would not lift a hand against fate for he could not believe in happiness and he accepted disappointment before it fell.

Oh, tonight, she told herself, he must be made to understand, tonight he must be made to see clearly that a man seizes his own, he holds it fast, and she was his. Her feet scarcely touched the grass as she ran, winged with fear as well as love, fear of death and fear of life. What if a snake bit her, and what if Jatin did not have the courage? He loved her, that she knew, for he was deep-hearted and passionate, yet even love might not make him strong enough. He gave up too easily, small wishes and great longings alike he surrendered quickly if he were opposed. Tonight she would insist, yes, she was the one to insist.

She ran up the three steps of the small veranda outside the four rooms. The light burned within, the mellow light of his oil lamp, and she knocked at the open door. He sat in his study and she could not see him, but the light fell in a bar upon the floor of the little entrance hall. He heard the knock and came out at once, barefoot, wearing a sleeveless singlet and dhoti, expecting no one at this hour, unless a call from the hospital.

"Livy," he cried softly in a voice of horror. "Why are you here?"

"Let me in, Jatin," she said. The screen door was hooked and she shook it slightly.

He unhooked it and she slipped inside.

"I must put out the light," he whispered. His face was anxious. "They will see you—perhaps someone has already seen you."

"For that I don't care," she said in her natural voice. "Don't whisper, Jatin—what does it matter who knows, now that my parents know?"

Yet he was uneasy and he stood, hesitating.

"Very well, then," she said. "We will just sit here in the hall in the shadow. I will not stay, Jatin, since you are so afraid. But I had to tell you. Father has sent for steamship tickets. We are going to America and he will not allow me to come back. A year, Jatin—they will stay a year, but I must stay four! And how could I come back to Vhai if he will not let me? So you must demand me in marriage, Jatin—or we must be married secretly if they will not let us marry openly."

"How is it possible for us to be married secretly?" he asked, his voice agitated by his distress. "We would have to go to the American Consulate in Poona, and there your father and your grandfather are well known. The Consul would tell them before he gave us the permission. There is no way. We must give each other up."

She bit her lips and turned away her face. "I knew you would say that. I knew you would not have the courage. I don't know why I love you."

"Nor I," he said humbly.

In misery they sat side by side on a stiff little rattan settle, the bar of light falling like a curtain between them and the open door. They faced the door and he stared into the shadowy night, piercing the darkness to search for hidden figures, for eavesdroppers and prowlers. Nothing was hidden in Vhai, nothing was secret. Of course the people knew, but never before had she come to his rooms. Yet his easily roused blood quickened and grew warm. She was sitting close to him, her slender thigh pressed against his leg, bare under the cotton dhoti. She was silent, a graceful droop-

291

ing shape beside him, and he reached for her hand and took it between his and stroked it gently in long soft movements, palm against his palm, his fingers stroking between hers. She drooped toward him, and he put his arm about her waist. Love could be denied, yes, but sometimes it was uncontrollable. Here in the night, with everything forbidden them, love itself was uncontrollable. Nobody had seen her come and none need see her go. The night was growing late. He could put out the light and the house would be dark. No servant slept in the house, and if a message came from the hospital, he would have to go to the door, but there was also the back door, the one that led from his bathing room, where the gardener carried the water in and out, and she could slip away from there. The gods of Vhai would protect her from serpents and insects, and she could flee across the lawn again.

He rose and hooked the door and then he went into the other room and put out the lamp and in the darkness he came back to her and sat down again. Stroking her hands he stroked up her arms and about her neck, down her cheeks and into her little ears. Then, still in the same desperate silence, he opened the tiny buttons of her short-sleeved vest and he stroked her bare skin, her shoulders, her back, and then at last her breasts. When his hand smoothed the rounded curve of her breasts, she gave a great sigh.

"What now," he whispered, "what now, Livy?"

She trembled, she put her arms about his neck and leaned her head upon his shoulder, and did not speak a word. He took her silence for reply and he lifted her in his strong dark arms and carried her into the house.

Once he halted at the threshold of his sleeping room. She was murmuring against his breast. "What do you say, Livy?"

"I said I want it to happen—whatever will happen, I want it."

"But we must keep it secret."

"I want it!"

This once, he was thinking, he was promising himself, only the once and it was not likely that anyone need know. It was very seldom that anything happened the first time, a virgin carries her own protection, and some risk love must take, only the once, and then, of course, they must part.

He had known it from the first, he had never had any hope, none at all. But hopeless love was the worst, the most terrible, the most enduring, and this would be the end.

Yet whose fault but hers that it was not the end? For it was she who went silent-footed through the darkness again and yet again, the mischievous gods protecting her bare feet from serpents and noxious creatures and there was no end to their love.

She was frightened at her own wickedness but she did not cease it. Here was she, the child of Christian parents, she who knew the Commandments and knew too the meaning of goodness and purity and righteousness, those great swelling words which shone like suns above her and in whose light she had supposed she walked, and yet she came and went by night like any magdalen. She did not for one moment confuse the God of her father and her grandfather, and only less intimately her mother's God, with those local gods she had seen in the temple, not only here in Vhai, but in the great temples of Poona, Ganesh the elephant-headed and Kali, the evil one who lured human creatures to worship wilfulness and crime. She was no longer a child and she knew what the women in the temples did, and how the priests played god to their virginity. She had been repelled from the dark confusion of such worship, she had been glad of the clear simplicity of her own faith, borrowed from her parents, and yet here she was, no better than any temple virgin and with no excuse for sin.

Night after night she went to Jatin, and now, he too, lost his fear in desperation. Let the villagers whisper and cross their eyes and pretend not to see. His love grew monstrous, possessing him like a disease, inflamed by the certainty that any day would decide the hour that Livy must leave him forever. He did not doubt the end, but he seized each day as it came, and waited for each night.

Eleven days and eleven nights thus passed and her father did not suspect, for had he imagined what happened in the night when he slept behind his mosquito net, could it be imagined that he would not speak? He would snatch Livy away and take her at least as far as Poona, and that would be the end, too.

And Jatin did not know how Livy behaved during the day, how quiet she was, how obedient, how sweet-voiced and yielding to her father's least wish, and how candidly her gaze met her mother's doubting eyes.

She played with Sara, she mended and sewed and helped her mother pack the trunks for the journey, she served her father's guests with little cakes, with slices of melon and with sweetmeats and the guests, looking at her, kept their peace. Some knew and some did not, but soon all would know, and Livy felt their knowing, she saw it in their dark speaking eyes, she heard it in their words, for they greeted her intimately, as one of them, or they greeted her with hostility, but now not only as the daughter of her father. She bore their greetings, however they came, for she could not have drawn herself out of the net into which she had thrown herself, and she knew as well as Jatin did, that there was no hope. There was no hope in him, she knew that now, and so she must accept him as he was and snatch what she could in the shortening hours.

At night she went early to her room, the little room at the end of the house, and she let the ayah wait upon her and see her undressed and bathed and upon her bed. Sometimes she was sure that the ayah knew the pretense, but she did not prove it. Unspoken, the ayah was not responsible, but were the words spoken, she would be compelled to tell Livy's parents, and so she would not know. So far the secret was clear between them, and neither wanted it more clear. Sometimes actually she went to sleep, and once or twice she slept through until dawn and then it was too late. But seven out of the eleven nights she woke, or she did not sleep, and then she slipped across the grassy paths, feeling beneath her feet the dreadful chance of the night-roaming cobra, but none came near, and then she tapped softly at the door, the back door of Jatin's house, and instantly he let her in, knowing desperately that he destroyed himself by what he did. And yet he received her, he took her into his arms and there was no delay or dallying. They came together quickly and deeply and they clung to one another briefly, their words strangling with love. Then she went away again.

XVIII

Meanwhile Ted strove to put his domain in order so that when he returned to Vhai there might be no loss. He was grateful for the task which kept him busy day and night, so that he need not face himself in the mirror of his own soul. He could not now decide right from wrong. He must have time to consider, to ponder and to meditate. More here was concerned than that Livy had fallen in love with the nearest young man, who happened to be Jatin. This fact, an experience common, he supposed, to every father, had strange deep roots inside himself. Why did his flesh and his mind rise up against the knowledge that Livy wanted to marry Jatin? He could not answer his own question but he was so disturbed by it that he found himself repelled by the very sight of Livy moving about the house in graceful silence, even while his heart yearned over her. When he had time, on the ship and in America, he would look into the hidden mirror and face himself. Not now, however, not on this soil could it be done. He had to get away but first he must get Livy away so that he could be free from the nagging necessity to know where she was every moment of the day. Only when the ayah came out of her room at night and he knew her safely in bed, could he rest and even then it was no rest, for there was Ruth, his wife, watching him thoughtfully and asking no questions. Oh, she had them, he knew, but she would not ask them now, and he could not risk them. They were pent up in her and he dared not release them, nor did he wish to know what she thought, if she were thinking, as perhaps she was not, for she had an Indian trick of simply allowing a matter to rest inside her mind

296

until in silent growth it took on shape of its own, and then she was voluble and persistent. Let that come on the ship, or in America, when he had Livy safely away.

And he did not know, how could he, that every Indian in the compound watched over Livy and that they shielded her from him by complete silence. When he was gone, they would talk endlessly, but now it was the child they protected, the little Livy who had grown up among them and who was part of them while he was not and never could be. He belonged to the white men, but she had come, a solitary little figure, toward them. Whenever she came to Jatin, she came to them. They longed to stretch out their arms and draw her into themselves, but they waited in silence, to see whether he would take her away. Not a hint did they give of the secret, and part of the shield and the covering was their obedience to Ted, their quick willingness to help him prepare everything for the departure.

Nevertheless Jehar, the Christian sadhu, walking southward, was met by rumor, a seemingly unspoken communication which spread from mouth to ear, village to village, until it was brought to his ears. He heard and hastened to Vhai, knowing what must be going on in the earth-walled house. He arrived there one evening when the sun was setting over green fields. The monsoons were ended, the fields had not yet dried to dust, and the sun fell behind the horizon in clear color as he stood before the gate door of the house.

Ted looked through the open window of his study, aware that someone had passed, and seeing the familiar and well-loved figure he rose and went to the door himself.

"Jehar!" Ted exclaimed. "There is no one whom I had rather see at this moment."

He put out his hand and clasped Jehar's large smooth hand, and drew him into the house and thence into the study. There he closed the door and the two stood gazing at each other. Jehar was taller, a mighty figure, his height emphasized by the small, closely wound turban on his head and by the sweeping folds of his saffron robe.

"Sit down," Ted said. "Are you hungry or thirsty?"

"Neither," Jehar replied. His voice was deep and peaceful, his

297

great eyes, intensely dark, were mild and affectionate, and his black beard and brows made his olive skin pale but not colorless. His feet were bare. Barefoot he had walked over much of the world, even in the snows of Tibet. He had been to Europe and to England, and at last to America, but everywhere he was the same.

Ted sat down near him and putting his hands on his knees, he continued to look at his old friend. "I had no idea that you were near Vhai."

"I was not," Jehar replied. "I have been preaching among the Sikhs. While I was there, word came to me that you were planning to return soon to your own country, and so I came to inquire if it is true and if it is, when you will come back to us."

"It is true," Ted said. He hesitated and then suddenly the need to confide his trouble overcame him. There was no one to whom he could speak so freely as he could to Jehar, no one who would understand so well why he felt that Livy must not marry Jatin, even though Jatin was good. So he told Jehar exactly what had happened and why he was taking Livy away quickly.

Jehar listened, nodding his head now and again. "I can see," he said, "I understand. I could not have understood, perhaps, had I not seen your home. Ted, my brother, I have never told you that I saw your father in New York."

"My father told me," Ted replied with some diffidence. His father had written him almost angrily that Jehar had behaved in New York exactly as though he were in India, and while he had made an impression, it was not as a Christian, but as a swami, a fakir, someone strange and even false. "He has not been asked to speak in any of the important pulpits," his father wrote. "There is something distasteful to the true Christian in this parading of Indian robes, bare feet, and so on. It was distressing to us all."

"Perhaps he did not tell you that he felt it his duty to rebuke me," Jehar said with a smile. "I accepted his rebuke for I knew that he must make it, but I went on as I was. I was not a swami, I told him, for that name means 'Lord,' and I am no lord. I am only a sadhu, that is, a religious man, and being an Indian I may use that name even though I see God through Jesus Christ."

"Did my father understand?" Ted asked.

"I do not know how nearly his heart and mind are one," Jehar replied. He sat thoughtful for a little while, and Ted, accustomed to such silences, waited.

When Jehar spoke, it was not to mention Livy's name. "You will remember," he said, "that verse from the Mahabharata which Gandhiji likes so well to quote."

He paused, drew in his breath, closed his eyes and then began to chant with a deep pulsing rhythm,

"The individual may be sacrificed for the family;
The family may be sacrificed for the sake of the village;
The village may be sacrificed for the sake of the province;
The province may be sacrificed for the sake of the
    country;
For the sake of conscience, however, sacrifice all."

He opened his eyes and looked earnestly at Ted, his dark and penetrating gaze seeming to cast an actual physical warmth upon Ted's flesh, or so Ted imagined.

"What does your conscience say?" Jehar inquired.

"I do not know," Ted replied. "I have only acted as I felt I must."

Jehar listened to this, his gaze still affectionately upon his friend. "You have been busy, but when all is done, then you will have time to listen. Each conscience is different from every other, and mine must not speak for yours. What is the conscience? It is the most highly developed part of the human being, the core of the spirit, the most sensitive, the most tender. It is shaped by the mores of a given society, it is developed toward wisdom by individual experience, it is maintained by the strength of the will. Your conscience is different from mine—as mine is different from every other. For me it has been right to live the life of a sadhu in the old Hindu sense, while preaching only Christ. As I told your father, love and home and wealth are wrong for me, while right for others, and I have my rewards. Here in Vhai you have done a great thing, and you have made a renunciation far beyond that of most men of your kind, and you have your rewards as I have mine.

Your father cannot understand this, any more than he can understand me. No matter—you have your reward, as I have mine. But now—"

He shook his head, and Ted recognized the old light of ecstasy in the fathomless Indian eyes.

"But now," Jehar went on, "a new opportunity has come to you. It is not for me to counsel you. The opportunity comes to you from God as all things come to us from God. What does it mean? You may ask yourself, is what you have done not enough? If you feel it is enough, if your conscience says it is enough, then it is enough and you will have your reward. But, if in the quiet of the ship upon the sea, your conscience tells you that what you have done is not enough, that God offers to you the opportunity for more, then listen to your conscience. The ladder to Heaven is made of steps. With each step we think we have reached the goal. But there is another step, and the final one before the gates of God is the one when all of self is given."

Ted fought the old magic of the dark eyes and the powerful gentle voice. He tried to laugh.

"Jehar, you will never make an Indian of me! I am hopelessly American, though I trust I am as good a Christian as you are."

Jehar smiled. "Why should I wish to make you what you are not born? It is because you are an American that I delight to call you my brother, and I have seen for myself how much you have renounced in order to be a Christian in India. What I have given up is nothing in comparison to the riches, the pleasures, the honors you might have had in your own country. But you have chosen to live your life here in an Indian village, in an earth-walled house covered with thatch. I am humble before you. You have even brought up your children here, and I have had no children. I do not know what it is to have a child demanded in sacrifice. But what I see, in my humility, is that you have lived so fully the life of a Christian in my country that you are now given the final invitation to accept an Indian for your own son, and his children as your grandchildren. It is possible now for you to take the step of complete brotherhood, in flesh as in the spirit. God has made this

300

possible for you that your life may complete the whole meaning of Christ."

The very air was trembling with intensity. Jehar's grave voice quivered, he lifted his magnificent head, he closed his eyes, and went into silent prayer.

And Ted, too, was compelled to silence. He could not pray, but he sat immobile, not thinking, not feeling. With his whole will he resisted the magnetism of Jehar. He refused to be compelled.

It was over in a moment. Jehar opened his eyes and gave his natural vivid smile. He rose. "I am glad that you told me yourself. Others will tell me and I shall tell them that I know all, and that whatever you do is according to your conscience. And now, Ted, dear brother, I shall go on my way."

"Stay with us tonight, Jehar." He made the invitation, but he did not urge it. He felt suddenly very weary and for some reason depressed. Usually Jehar lifted up his spirit but tonight Jehar could not reach his heart.

"I cannot, Ted," Jehar replied. "I am expected tomorrow morning some thirty miles south of Vhai and I shall walk through the night."

They clasped hands again and Jehar put his left hand over their clasped hands.

"Come back," he said. "At least come back to India."

"Of course," Ted said.

Jehar said no more. He stepped back, and looking into Ted's eyes, held his upraised hands together, palm to palm, in the old Indian greeting and farewell. "I see God in you," the gesture said.

Ted bowed his head and stood watching half-wistfully the tall figure walking barefoot toward the south.

And after Jehar had gone, he remembered. Why had Jehar said India and not Vhai?

On the last day, Ted called Jatin to him.

"Jatin," he said. "I leave you in charge of the compound. You will keep the medical work going and I have sent for a young man from Poona for the schools. Jehar will pass by now and again and hold the church together. You will not miss me too much."

"We shall miss you," Jatin said.

He stood before Ted wearing his hospital gown, tall and steadfast, his arms folded.

"Sit down," Ted said.

Jatin sat down. Whatever his duty was he would not tell of the seven nights. They would be hidden in his memory, deep as jewels in a cave beneath the sea. Life would flow over them, but no one would know.

"I wish to thank you," Ted said. "You have been very faithful to me. Livy is young and you might have stirred her emotions to the point of no control. Instead you have been kind and strong. You have made her feel that her childish preference for you is to be forgotten. I am grateful for this, and yet I feel I should make some sort of apology, for I discern in the whole matter a fault in myself. I say that Livy is too young, and indeed she is, but if I am honest with myself as I wish to be, I know that I—that there is more than this reason for parting you." So much Jehar had worked in him.

"Please go no further, Mr. MacArd," Jatin said. "I understand. It is natural for parents to feel that their children should marry within their own kind. Indeed, it may be this is right. At any rate, it is not my wish to insist against you. It is karma between your daughter and me. We were fated to love one another, we are fated by our birth never to marry. I know this and I accept it."

"I must say more," Ted insisted. "I am a Christian, Jatin, and it may be that as a Christian I should not have such feelings. I thought I had yielded my life to my God, and yet, perhaps, I have not."

Jatin smiled. "I would not wish to accept Livy as a sacrifice to your religion."

Ted could not smile. "It is not Livy, it is I myself. I should perhaps be willing to carry the meaning of love to its ultimate. The very essence of Christian love leads us to the ultimate. I feel a failure in myself. I am not ready to face the ultimate nor to accept it."

302

He was surprised by the warmth in Jatin's face. "Dear sir," Jatin said impulsively. "Please do not feel you are at fault. The love of which you speak is not only Christian, it is human, and it cannot be forced. Livy is able to feel it, but then she has been born a generation after you. I feel it, though I am not a Christian, but then I have been born a generation after my father. I shall not marry Livy. Sir, I promise you that—it is not within my fate. Livy knows this also. But some day when Livy is married to a man of her own kind, if her child wishes to do what we have wished, then she will allow it. Time and the generations work together with fate, sir, and this is true. This is what I believe."

"You make me feel small," Ted said, and he was much troubled.

"Then I do wrong," Jatin replied.

He rose to his feet. "Let us speak no more and think no more of this matter. What has been cannot be changed, and what is to be had been decided upon."

That night Livy came to him for the last time and that night he did not take her to his bed. Instead they talked long, in whispers, clinging to one another and at last he spoke his fear.

"If there should be a child, Livy?"

"Oh, I hope there is a child!" she cried.

"No, Livy, I hope there is not. But if there is, you must not keep him."

"I will keep him, Jatin."

"No, I forbid it. I cannot live in peace if you are burdened with a child and I cannot share the burden with you."

"But what should I do?"

"Give him away to someone else. He would be dark, like me. The darkness of our people stains the blood, Livy. Give him to the dark people in your country."

"But our child would not be a Negro, Jatin," she cried, shocked at his command.

"Hush—" he put his hand on her mouth. "Let him grow up belonging to them, since he could not belong to us. But perhaps he will never be born and that would be best, for you must be free of me, and I must be free of you, and our burden must not be laid

303

upon a child. This is our fate and so it must be. Yet all that there can be we have had."

He held her at the last, knowing that only minutes remained, and then he let her go. She clung to him but he pushed her gently from him toward the door.

"Now is the end," he whispered. "It is over, and we have had everything and it shall not be taken from us. Good-bye, Livy, good-bye!"

He locked the door and stood, hearing her lean against it and sob. He wept then, but he did not yield and at last he heard her go away.

XIX

The ship pulled away from the dock and Ted watched the receding shores of Bombay. The last light of sunset was falling from the west upon the green heights of Malabar Hill. A tall clock tower caught the final ray and shone out the hour, and upon the street nearest the shore the colors of the garments that people wore flashed into sudden brightness, amid which the robes of Parsee priests were shining white.

He had a sense of leave-taking that was foreboding in its finality. Would he never see these shores again? Was he leaving India as his father had done, without knowing it? Was something changed in him, some virtue gone? He did not know.

He felt a touch upon his arm and turning his head he saw Ruth at his side. Again, as so often, he saw her apart from himself, a sturdy apple-cheeked woman, neat always and now unfamiliar in a blue serge tailored suit.

"Where is Livy?" he asked involuntarily.

"Downstairs unpacking," she said. She slipped her hand into the crook of his elbow.

"Well, we have got her safely away from India," he said. The strip of water between ship and shore was widening. Twenty feet, twenty-five and soon fifty, and then the miles would mount.

"I suppose so," Ruth said.

He would not inquire what her doubt might be. He felt tired and dislocated, and perhaps he had lived in Vhai too long. For years he had poured himself out, and now he felt empty and weak. It occurred to him that he had not eaten much in the past weeks, worried and pressed as he had been by his distress about Livy and the hurried leavetaking. It would be good to sink back into the comfortable life in the old mansion, where his father and Agnes were expecting them. He needed rest.

The dinner gong rang through the corridors of the ship and upon the decks.

"I believe I am hungry," he said.

"Then let's go down to the dining saloon now," Ruth said. But they lingered a moment. The sun was slipping behind the horizon of Bombay and the shadow of night stole swiftly over the city and the sea.

"I hope Livy will not wear her saris," Ted said suddenly.

"I told her not to wear them any more," Ruth replied quietly.

"Did she mind?"

"No, she said she had already decided that she would not."

So often, he thought, his conversations with his wife were commonplace, the merest question and answer, and yet he knew again that she had thoughts which she did not speak, and so there were overtones to her words. He seldom inquired what these were, and he did not do so now. A sudden breeze had arisen damp and chill.

"Come," he said. "There is nothing more here. Let us go below."

Livy, on the high upper deck, continued to gaze alone into the night. The lights of the ship fell upon the smooth and oily water of the bay and upon the long lines of the prow of the ship. But Livy did not see the near waters, nor even the sparkling lights of Bombay in the receding distance. Her mind's eye drove its straight beam northward upon Vhai, and she saw Jatin in his little house alone. She knew that he would be busy as he always was, reading his books, eating his plain evening meal, and then reading again. In an hour from now he would be at the hospital making his last rounds of the sick as they lay upon their pallets on the floor, or on low wooden beds, rope-bottomed, just as they would have lain had they been in their own homes. Her father had always insisted that everything was to be Indian, he would not have anything in Vhai that was like the beautiful colleges and the hospital at MacArd in Poona, and yet she was no longer deceived. She had thought, oh, she had truly believed, that her father had meant what he said when he taught them to behave courteously toward the people of Vhai and of all India, and she had believed that he meant what he said when he bade them learn the language of Vhai, and when he encouraged her to wear a sari as easily as she did a frock, until a sari now seemed more natural to her and certainly more comfortable than a buttoned frock, for to tuck the pleated material into the folds at her waist so that it hung a graceful skirt and then to throw the other end about her shoulders was much easier than getting into sleeves and belts and buttons down the back. He had encouraged them to play with the children of Vhai and to look upon them as brothers and sisters, telling them that God was their Father in Heaven, and they were one great family. She had believed he meant all that and now she knew he did not. For if he had truly believed what he preached, then he would have been willing and even glad for her to marry Jatin, for that was the whole acceptance, wasn't it, and if one could not accept the ultimate, then there was no real acceptance. Perhaps there was no truth in God, either.

She shivered, unutterably sad as her mind fixed itself upon Jatin. It was not his fault, surely, for he had never been deceived by her father, and that had been their first great argument.

"Jatin, I tell you, my father will be happy. He likes you, and he will welcome you as his son."

This she had insisted upon, and Jatin had only smiled his dark sad smile.

"Then you don't believe in my father!" She had accused him thus.

"I do believe in him," Jatin had replied. "Yet I know his soul reaches beyond the rest of him. His faith is far up yonder—" he pointed to the zenith. "But his flesh is more prudent than his soul and it remains upon the earth. And his mind is uncertain between the two. He believes in his ideals, and he considers them necessary, but he says that it will take time to fulfil them, much time. What he does not know, is that if one does not immediately practice ideals, they are lost. They die unless they come quickly to reality."

So much that Jatin had said she had not understood when he

307

spoke because his presence agitated her. She had not often been able to fix her mind upon his words because her eyes were fastened upon his lips. Remembering those lips, her heart hung in her bosom, a weight of hot and leaden pain. She would never see his face again, of that she was now sure. Her father could not have kept them apart, she thought rebelliously, but Jatin himself had sent her away. If Jatin had been in the least willing to defy her father, it could have been done, but he was not willing, not through fear, but through his belief that to part was their fate, the world being what it was.

"You must go back to your own country," he had told her, "and after you have finished school, then you must marry a good man."

"I will not," she had cried passionately, the tears streaming down her cheeks.

"But I say you must," he had insisted in his grave voice. "And Livy, one more command I give you. Do not tell him about me. This is for your own protection, for if your father, who is so good a man, cannot bear the thought of our love, then that one who is to be your husband cannot bear it, either. He will draw away from you because once you loved me."

"I shall love you forever," she had declared, "and I shall never marry."

To this he had not replied. He had simply stroked her cheeks with his delicate powerful palms. In the hottest weather his palms were cool and dry, and yet they were never cold. There was healing in his hands. She would never see anyone like him, never meet a man who could compare to him, but because the smooth skin that covered his handsome body was dark, they must never be man and wife, a coating so thin though dark, that it could be pierced by a pin and underneath the flesh was as pale as her own and the blood as red. Yet it was the paper thin darkness of the skin that forced them on their separate ways, on opposite sides of the world.

She did not agree, nevertheless, with all that he had decreed. There was still her hope in the child. The child, if there was a child, she would not put away as he had commanded her to do. If there was to be a child then she would go back to India somehow and insist that Jatin marry her and recognize his own son. She would not be as her father was. What she believed in she would do. Love one another, the Scriptures said, and so she had loved all that was India. She had loved Vhai and the people of Vhai and she had loved the children and the women, and her ayah's flesh was real to her as her own mother's. Then, finally, she had loved Jatin.

She clung to the rail and closed her eyes in profound entreaty. "Oh God, if You are there, then please, please give me what I want most! Give me a baby, so that I can go back to Jatin!"

The intensity of her prayer was so great that instantly she felt sure her prayer had been heard. A soft night wind blew over her. A moment before there was no wind, and now suddenly there came the wind, a sign and promise! She opened her eyes in an ecstasy of hope, and felt the ship rise and fall beneath her feet. They were beyond the bay and out upon the sea, but she would come back, for God had heard her and He had given her the sign. She toyed with the idea, just for a moment, of telling her mother that there would be a child and then she decided against it. No, not yet—she might be wrong about God. It would be days before she could know.

She shivered, suddenly cold with the chill of the sea wind. She must not lose Jatin in the dark. Vhai was there and it would always be there. Though she was being carried far away, she would come back—if she was right about God.

Yet she was young and while she waited, there were hours when she almost forgot. The ship's company was gay, young men and women pressed her into their games, and when they persuaded her, she sang for them the Indian songs she knew, the sweet twisting melodies of Vhai, her voice lifted high and never dropping low, but winding in and out like a brook in a valley between the mountains.

They were charmed by her and she could not but respond, for it was pleasant to be told that she was pretty, that she had a lovely voice which should be trained, that she was a natural dancer, and had she ever thought of Hollywood? She was shy, she answered their pressing coaxing compliments in a shy little voice, her brown lashes on her cheeks and now lifted in unconscious enjoyment. No, she had not thought of Hollywood, she did not believe her father would like it, and certainly her grandfather would not. Yes, they were going straight to New York where they would stay in the house that had belonged to her great-grandfather, and yes, he was David Hardworth MacArd, and yes, she supposed he was *the* Mac-Ard, though her grandfather's name was David, too. She was so young that it pleased her to observe the slight pause that followed the speaking of this famous name, and when she got up to go away, it was with dignity added to her grace. She was the great-granddaughter of *the* MacArd.

Yet her heart was faithful and night and morning she said her prayers and thought of Jatin, and many times during the day his face came before her. She would glance at her little gold wrist watch which her father had given her last Christmas and then she would ask herself where he was now, and wherever it was, she would see him, at work or alone. She was still not parted from him, nor could be, so long as there was the possibility of their child.

The days passed, the ship was in midocean and one morning the certainty was there. The answer was clear, there was to be no child. Nature announced it, she saw the rose-red stain and knew that love had borne no fruit. She had risen early that morning, and the wind was white upon the water and the sun shining over the horizon. She had waked uncontrollably gay, for she was too young for constant sadness, and now suddenly she knew and the day stopped abruptly at dawn. She went back to bed and drew the covers about her and cried silently into the blankets so that Sara might not hear from the other berth. But Sara heard, that sharp child, and she went and called their mother, upon pretense of visiting the bathroom, and Ruth came wrapped in her pink cotton dressing gown and so suddenly that Livy had no time to wipe her cheeks dry or to insist that she was not crying.

"It is just that I don't feel well," she murmured, trying not to turn her face toward her mother. But Ruth's strong hand seized her daughter's dimpled chin and pressed it toward her.

"You don't feel well? Where?"

"It's just the old curse—"

"Oh—" Ruth's hand relaxed. "But why cry? It's nothing."

"People do cry for nothing, sometimes," Livy said.

"Not you," Ruth retorted.

She looked down into her daughter's face and saw the eyes closed, the lips quivering. The girl was pale, she had gone through more than they knew, maybe. She remembered that as a child she, too, had always cried when they left India. And now there was Jatin, besides, and she did not know how far that had gone, but anyway Livy was safe. Love had not gone too far except perhaps in the heart, and that would heal.

"Cover yourself up real warm," she said briskly. "I'll have your breakfast brought in."

She bent and kissed her daughter's forehead, and was glad enough not to know what she had not been told. No use knowing, since nothing could be helped and whatever had been was ended.